WHIRLIGIG

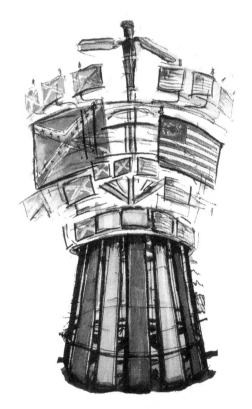

BOOK 1 OF SHIRE'S UNION

WHIRLIGIG

KEEPING THE PROMISE

RICHARD BUXTON

OCOEE PUBLISHING

First published 2017 by Ocoee Publishing
www.richardbuxton.net

ISBN 978-0-9957693-0-4 Paperback
         978-0-9957693-1-1 eBook

This is a work of fiction. Names, characters, places and incidents
are either a product of the author's imagination or are used
fictitiously. Any resemblance to actual people living or dead,
events or locales is entirely coincidental.

British Library Cataloguing in Publication Data
A CIP catalogue record for this book is available from
the British Library

Cover design and typesetting by Head & Heart

For my father,

Tom Buxton

Richard lives with his family in the South Downs, Sussex, England. He completed an MA in Creative Writing at Chichester University in 2014. He has an abiding relationship with America, having studied at Syracuse University, New York State, in the late eighties. His short stories have won the Exeter Story Prize, the Bedford International Writing Competition and the Nivalis Short Story Award.

Whirligig is his first novel and the opening book of the Shire's Union trilogy. Current projects include the second book in the series, *The Copper Road*, as well as a collection of short stories.

To learn more about Richard's writing visit www.richardbuxton.net.

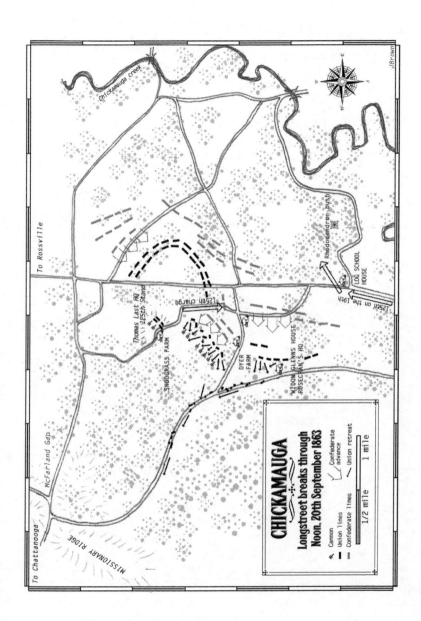

Chickamauga Creek

To Rossville

Rhododendron bush

LOG SCHOOL HOUSE

125th on the 19th

Thomas Last HQ of 125th Stand

125th charge

SNODGRASS FARM

DYER FARM

WIDOW GLENN'S HOUSE
ROSECRAN'S HQ

McFarland Gap

MISSIONARY RIDGE

To Chattanooga

J.Brown

CHICKAMAUGA
Longstreet breaks through
Noon, 20th September 1863

Cannon
Union lines
Confederate lines

Confederate advance
Union retreat

1/2 mile   1 mile

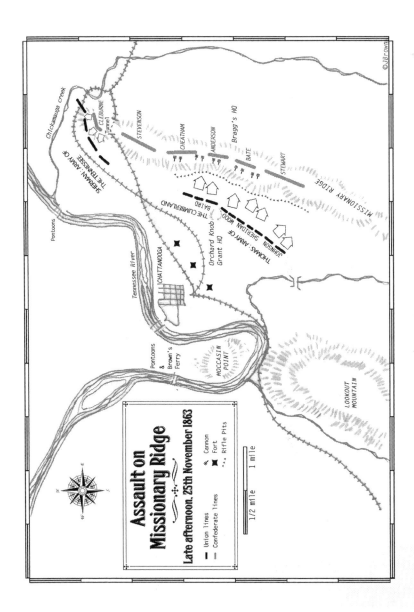

Assault on Missionary Ridge

Late afternoon, 25th November 1863

— Union lines
‒ ‒ Confederate lines

✖ Cannon
⬙ Fort
∴ Rifle Pits

1/2 mile | 1 mile

MISSIONARY RIDGE

Bragg's HQ
STEVENSON
CHEATHAM
ANDERSON
BATE
STEWART
CLEBURNE
Tunnel

JOHNSON
SHERIDAN
WOOD
BAIRD

THOMAS' ARMY OF THE CUMBERLAND

Orchard Knob
Grant HQ

SHERMAN'S ARMY OF THE TENNESSEE

Chickamauga Creek

Pontoons

Tennessee River

CHATTANOOGA

Pontoons & Brown's Ferry

MOCCASIN POINT

LOOKOUT MOUNTAIN

©J.B.OWN

Prologue

You had to be as tall as a musket to be trusted with one. That was Father's rule. The boy followed his brother through the scruffy woods and felt the injustice of it. He'd have to wait at least two years to get his own gun. 'Three shots,' he called ahead. 'You only get three shots.'

'That's what I said, ain't it?' Will called back. 'Quit whining.' Ahead, his brother carried the gun in both hands, weaving it between the low branches and saplings that crowded in on the path. A still mist hung amongst the higher leaves that were just on the turn, the first damp hints of yellow and orange about their edges. The two dogs brought up the rear, wise enough to keep behind the gun.

Injustice, the boy believed, was the correct word to describe how he was feeling. He mustn't call it fairness; Father had no time for fairness. He'd say, 'Show me a man asking for a fair break and I'll show you a weak man, most likely a Yankee.' Injustice was somehow a different thing, though the boy wasn't sure exactly how.

They reached Low Bald, a clear circle of wet grass. The mist was so thick he could barely see to the other side. Ordinarily they'd have made for High Bald, but that was another hour of climbing. They didn't want to wait that long to fire the gun.

Earlier, he'd watched Father stand the Springfield musket alongside Will and say there wasn't a worn cent's thickness either way, then hand Will the gun along with a dozen cartridges and some percussion caps. 'Get a good way into the hills,' Father had said, 'so that Mother won't hear.'

Before they'd left, Will had told him to go get something to shoot at. A plain white plate out of the kitchen would have done, but it was busy in there. The parlor was better: there'd been no one to see him slip the piece of china under his coat.

When, as she did so often in the years ahead, Mother would wonder aloud why she had a plate missing from her wedding set, his gut would pull tight and he'd never utter a word.

Up on Low Bald his brother took the plate from him and wedged it in the crook of a tree. The glazed, pink rose at the center made a good target. They walked twenty paces back around the edge of the woods so they could fire across clear ground. The dogs slinked past and sat behind them. He had nothing to do but watch his brother.

Will bit open a cartridge, spat out the paper, and tipped the powder and ball into the barrel. Then he took the ramrod and reached high to slide it in and force the ball home. Placing the percussion cap onto the nipple was a struggle: the gun was awkward to hold in one hand.

The boy only wanted to help. 'You want me to put it on?'

His brother twisted away. 'I can do it.' He pulled back the hammer, lifted the gun and aimed at the plate.

The snap of the first shot died in the mist. Though it hit nothing, they smiled at each other. The novelty of firing alone, without Father, was enough. When the third shot followed the first two into the woods, not even hitting the tree, Will frowned. 'Go set it higher.'

'It's my turn.'

'It's too low. I wanna try it higher.'

'Then go set it yerself.'

Will just loaded and fired again.

'That's four. I get four turns now.'

'Not until I hit it.'

'You couldn't hit that plate if it was on the ground right next to yer.'

'Shut up, Mommy's Boy. You can't even reach to ram in the ball.'

'I can too.'

One of the dogs started whining.

Will fired again.

He'd use all the cartridges if he carried on. The boy picked up an acorn and flicked it at his brother's feet. 'C'mon. I got the plate for us.'

'Go move it higher.'

'I ain't no slave.' He collected a whole handful of acorns and threw them one at a time, harder and harder. The dogs began to bark.

'Quit it!'

'Let me shoot.'

Will ignored him and reloaded. But this time, when he came to squeeze the trigger, the gun didn't fire. He tried once more. There was nothing but a flat click. He cursed and forced back the hammer again.

This was all wrong. The boy wasn't allowed his own gun and now he wouldn't even get a turn. He pelted a bigger acorn at his brother and caught him under the chin.

'Start runnin', runt.'

He wouldn't run. Why should he? It was his turn. Will strode over and pushed the stock at his face. He grabbed hold.

A month from now, his parents will still be asking how the gun came to fire. To placate them, to shut them up, he'll say maybe the dogs jumped up at Will. It's enough to get the dogs shot.

He didn't hear the blast, just felt the wet sting of blood, warm as summer rain, spray his cheeks and lips. The gun's weight was unbalanced and he let it drop. When he opened his eyes, Will was on the ground. There was a last animation of sinew and jaw.

Later that day, after he's run screaming up the steps and into the hall, after Mother has shaken him to make him talk, after he's led them to Low Bald and they've carried Will down from the hills, his Father will lock the door to the hunting room, turn and ask, 'How was it, when your brother was in charge of the gun, he came to be shot in the face?'

PART I

Ridgmont, Bedfordshire, England – October 1862

The church rested in the dell like a coin in a beggar's palm. It would be a long hour until dawn. Shire, breathing deeply on the cold air, looked down from the slope onto a dreamlike scene. The small Norman church, the untidy congregation of graves and old sleeping trees, were all thrown into bold relief by a quarter-crescent moon. It looked like a sketch, the features outlined in heavy charcoal.

This whole venture was unreal, he thought: ghosting through the trees and fields on a chill autumn night, intent on passing by the dead to steal into the church. He was not used to such undertakings. At home he'd lain awake for hours thinking what to do, finally persuaded to this errand by some new, insistent voice. He moved off the ridge and half-sidestepped down the steep slope towards the church. What if he were caught and taken for a common poacher? They might transport him to Australia. Although, given that he carried no snares or game, they could only prove trespass. And in the last resort, would he confess his tale and risk the truth of it?

He knew this estate as well as anyone. This was his parish church, and he'd played and worked on this land all his life. The gamekeepers rarely patrolled the grounds at night; there was no one here but himself. He fancied he could hear his own heartbeat. The slope ended next to the wide path which led to the church gate. His steps crunched on the loose stone so he moved to one side. Even so, his boots squeaked on the frosted grass as he crept up to the low wall beside the lychgate.

A greater fear than capture took hold. As a boy, he would scarce have dared to enter the churchyard in the light of day, even with all his friends. His child's mind used to imagine the dead beneath his feet, picture the ivy-covered tombs, leaning this way and that, succumbing to age and gravity to spill their untidy bones. Before he was ten, a bigger boy had dared them all to creep closer and peer into such a tomb. The braver boys had gone ahead. Shire had stayed with the timid set and watched from behind this very wall.

Beneath his fear, his conscience circled between self-chastisement and self-justification. He'd always felt comfort in rules – laws; he got that from Father. It had never occurred to him to question them, let alone break them. And to enter the church at this hour, steal from it if he had to, was more than an earthly transgression: it was a sacrilege, and all in the sight of God. But then surely he was here to find proof of a greater wrong. If he couldn't attain it, he would be home before dawn and this night would soon be nothing more than a fool's memory. If he found it, the means wouldn't matter.

He peered over the wall. The tombs and gravestones, with their starlit names, seemed to rise up out of their moon-shadows. He jammed his cold hands under his arms, looked behind, his breath steaming. This was no child's game. It was two years since he'd come of age and there were stronger emotions in this world than fear. Spurning the lychgate, he slipped over the wall and around to the squat, square tower at the western end. Crossing that boundary fed his determination, that small kernel of stubbornness Father said came from his mother. The descending partial moon was uncannily bright, drawing the yellow from the sandstone church. He reached the large arched doors at the base of the tower.

He paused again, collecting his courage to cross the next threshold. His gaze was drawn towards the far corner of the churchyard. He knew the exact spot, his eyes finding the fresh mound as yet without a stone, the flowers wilted silhouettes above the grave. The soul it housed had an interest in his errand. He stood, unblinking, a shiver in his gut. The vicar, unlike any gamekeeper, was here this night. He was in that grave. No doubt wearing the same disapproving expression he used to point at a young boy to make him sit still in church.

At the funeral, Shire had been nervous of his duty. Harland

was heavy, the wood slippery in the rain. But they all followed Father's lead, setting the casket carefully beside the grave and then using the wet ropes to lower it down. Harland Rees had been vicar to the Ridgmont Estate for more than twenty-five years, so there'd been a respectful gathering. Shire had gone to stand behind the duke and his family with the other parishioners. He'd watched Grace. She was alone despite the crowd. Her lips didn't move as prayers were said over her father, laid to rest alongside the graves of her mother and her infant boy.

A barn owl, luminous as an angel, shot across his reverie. He liked to believe himself more rational than superstitious, but alone, standing at the church doors, looking out on the old and new graves, he felt a preternatural chill. He took a thoughtless step backwards, right hand groping for the iron ring on the door. Forgetting the single step, he fell, hitting his back and head hard on the thick oak. The thump resounded down the nave inside. He scrambled to his feet, his hands rushing to turn the cold ring and heave open the door.

Once shut inside, he took a moment for the pain and the panic to ease. It was Grace he should be worried about, her welfare. But his heart had always lived somewhere else.

Coming in from the cold night, there was an illusion of warmth in the church. His breathing slowed. The Harvest Festival was a few weeks past, but the hint of overripe fruits lingered above the resident scents of musty books and polished wood. Passing into the nave, he found a new, unearthly setting. The moonlight was filtered by the stained glass, translated into a bible of colors and cast across wood and stone, ethereal petals fit for a spirit marriage. God was here. God was watching. If he dared to step forward, if he joined the scene, would he dissolve into nothing more than light and memory?

A gargoyle lived above the altar. It had frightened him as a boy. Listening to Harland intone Revelations, his eyes used to drift upwards to the stretched mouth and pointed stone tongue. He dared not look on it now, for fear that in this otherworldly light it would turn to stare down and berate him, for coming here not to worship but to trespass. It became as frightening to stay as it was to go forward. He ran down the aisle, beneath the gargoyle and beyond the pulpit.

To the right was Harland's private room, mercifully unlocked. Inside, it was dark but for one small, high window, dotted with a handful of stars. He reached up and drew across the velvet curtains. He would need his candle and didn't want to show a light outside, no matter how small the chance that it would be seen. Once lit, the flame twitched shadows about the stone room. There was a lamp on Harland's desk so he lit that in turn, gaining a more even and friendly light. He sat down and opened a drawer. Inside was a locket, blue eggshell on a delicate silver chain. Grace had worn it at the funeral. She must have put it here since. He opened the clasp and found two locks of hair, one deep brown, the other fairer and softer.

After the burial, the three of them had walked to the vicarage: Grace, himself and Father. Whereas the parish had paid its respects to Harland, no others followed to the house to show respect for Grace. They held none. The parlor was cold, ashes in the grate. Father had set to clearing it.

'They think I brought on his death, don't they?' said Grace.

Father stood up, gently lifted her chin. 'No, Grace,' he said, 'God alone calls us. And we must all endure until he does.' He took the basket outside to fetch wood.

As she put her mourning veil aside, Shire poured her a glass of sherry. 'Here.'

Her arms tight to her side as if cold or sick, Grace took the glass in both hands. She was hardly older than Shire, but today looked like she might have ten years on him. Her tired, brown hair was tied back carelessly with a black ribbon. At first she sipped, but then on some impulse emptied the glass. She set it down, smoothed her dress with her hands and sat rocking on the edge of her chair. He could find no words to fit the moment.

She lifted her dry, dark eyes to him. 'What now, Shire? What's left to do?'

'You must look to yourself,' he said. 'Find the strength and will only for that.'

'What good is my will? What good has it ever been? When they buried my mother they said it was God's will. That wretched church has them all.'

'The church holds them until a glorious day.' His own words sounded hollow.

Grace ignored his gentle correction. 'What good was my will to keep my child alive?' Her voice was a breaking whisper. 'I didn't even will his life.'

Those were her exact words. He remembered them clearly.

Shire had been party to the rumors concerning the identity of the father. He was on the list of candidates, due to their friendship. But he'd never felt that way about Grace. Even before the child and the shame, there was always some sad untouchable essence about her. Perhaps it was just that she was a vicar's daughter. Finding no other to share the blame, in the end the parish had settled all of its disdain on her.

'I followed the will of my father, who I loved. And now he's gone too.' She poured herself more sherry. Then, to his shock, she began to laugh.

'Do you know, today I should be celebrating? On this day, indeed!' It was as if she was just aware of it. 'This day, three years since, I was asked *my will*. In that church, 'though there was only one answer my father would take. He would see me shamed before the parish, but not before his God.'

In that 'wretched' church, Shire closed the locket and sadly returned it to the drawer, remembering Grace's revelation of her secret marriage. It didn't include the groom's name, but more than enough for him to make a confident guess. Anger and injustice stirred in him once more. And in that mix, he couldn't deny, nestled a tiny parcel of hope. He'd no doubt as to the truth, but in the days that followed the funeral, he'd returned again and again to the issue of proof. Without it, he could do nothing. So here he was.

There was a Bible in the drawer too, probably Harland's own, but nothing else. In the bottom drawer were the several large black-bound books he'd expected to find. He put them on the desk. Harland was a fastidious man, and Shire was gambling his errand on it. As he'd hoped, all God's works were recorded, weddings as well as births and deaths. He found the book containing 1859 and hurried through it, the deaths more prevalent in winter, the marriages in spring and summer. Holding his breath, he looked for the date three years to the day before Harland's funeral. There was an entry. It simply said, 'October 25th 1859 – Marriage – Before God.'

So it was true, but proof only of a service. No names. He had failed. All the same, he took the letter-knife from the table and cut the page from the record. He folded it and placed it in his pocket. He put the books back, but found himself pacing the room, reluctant to start for home. The graves would be waiting for him outside. But there was nothing else here, nowhere else to look. He sat again and took out Harland's Bible. It opened on a page holding a piece of paper; notes for a sermon Harland was never to deliver. Shire recognized the passage from John: 'Beloved, let us love one another, for love is from God; and everyone who loves is born of God and knows God.' Perhaps Harland should have dwelt more on love before forcing Grace into a life without it.

He looked inside the front cover for Harland's name, but found something else: an envelope stuck there and sealed in dripped wax. To think was to waver. He picked up the letter-knife again and sliced through the seal. It was a certificate, a full, witnessed certificate of marriage. Grace Rees, spinster, and above her, the name he'd expected to see. So he was right.

Satisfied, he read the names of the witnesses: Edwin Matlock, the estate manager, and to his utter disbelief, Abel Stanton, his own father.

Comrie, Tennessee – October 1862

The red-brick kitchen stood squarely on its own, clear of the house. Without knocking, Clara opened the door and looked inside. The chatter cut off and she was met with an array of black faces, each slave momentarily frozen mid-chore. One leant on a floured rolling pin, one was knuckle-deep in dough, a third held a soup-ladle half-way to her mouth. It was comical, but Clara couldn't spare a smile. There was too much on her mind.

'Have you seen Hany?' she asked.

'You lost her again, Miss Clara?' said Mitilde, setting to work on the dough once more. 'Why, that girl has a talent for being nowhere at all, 'specially when she's wanted.'

'Perhaps she's in her cabin?' Clara looked over the herb garden to the clutter of slave huts nestled under the slope that climbed sharply up behind Comrie. Children raced in circles and an older girl was pegging out some washing, but she couldn't see Hany.

'You didn't oughta have to run after the girl. We'll find her.'

Clara moved back to the house. It was only wedding business. *Everything* was wedding business. Emmeline had re-pinned the wedding dress and wanted her to try it on again. She'd had to put that dress on every day this week. She walked through the house, her steps loud in the stone hallway and out through the open double-doors.

The portico, facing west as it did, was all in shade this early in the day. She much preferred the chill mountain air of October to the high heat of the summer just gone. Whenever she had time on her hands, the portico was her favorite place. This view was so often her only company. She looked down the wide flight of stone steps to the empty circle of river shingle. Ten days from now it would host her wedding carriage. The drive fell away to the right and then switched back several times as it fell across the steep meadow to the trees. And the forest simply proceeded down and away, riding the ever smaller waves of the Appalachians, which spent themselves on the gentler shore of Eastern Tennessee. Every overlapping ridge was nothing but color: dark reds to bright yellow, oaks, hemlocks, cherries and walnuts, all trumpeting the season. Clara took a breath of cool, blue air. Whatever her other doubts, she was content to be marrying in the fall.

Two years since her first autumn here, she thought. Ridgmont and England could be someone else's life, someone else's memory. And still her marriage lay ahead of her. That hadn't been the plan. But then they hadn't counted on the war. She thought of Shire of course, he always came to mind when she thought of home. What would he tell her to do? He'd never been much use in matters of the heart.

Down to her right, on the flat grass terrace that extended above the drive, was William's headstone. She admitted to herself that she'd come to resent it. For the wedding it would be the first thing their guests would see as they reached the top of the zig-zag drive; hardly a friendly welcome. And Taylor, what did it say to him as a child and even now, every time he came and went from his home? It was a reminder at best, at worst a punishment. She'd never dared to ask Taylor about it. She had intended to marry him in her first spring at Comrie, early summer at the latest. Maybe she should have, but then the war had begun and cast doubt over so many things. She remembered asking Hany about the grave once, standing right here in the portico that first spring. That was another day when she'd had to send someone to find the girl.

The winter of 1860 had been a cold one for Polk County, so Clara was told, but today was the third warm April day in a row and all the late snow had gone. It would be so good to get out into the hills at last – to explore. From the edge of the steps she scanned the tree line below. There was no sign of Taylor. Waiting didn't come easily;

it never had. There was sweet air rising from the forest. A thin mist lingered in the spring coves, so that her view was patched both white and green under a blue sky. How much longer was Taylor going to be? Not that she didn't have plenty to occupy her mind. News had arrived a few days ago that the war had finally begun back in Charleston, in the very harbor where she'd first set foot in America. Her maid, Ellie, who'd come from England with her, had asked to return home, fearing that the war would spread. Clara had let her go; no one should stay where they're not happy. Ellie had left yesterday, so this morning Clara dressed herself in her riding clothes.

There was a letter from home. Father had been ill, it said, and wasn't fit to travel for the wedding. Of course Mother would stay with him. What hurt almost as much was that the letter was by proxy from Matlock. He'd written, *The Duke suggests that you and your fiancé take your own counsel, but that proceeding with the wedding seems advisable.* That man made everything sound like a business transaction. He'd signed it *per procurationem* below the Ducal crest. But why get angry at Matlock? It was her parents' decision.

She sat down in one of the rocking chairs. Rushes woven tight across their backs and seats, they were permanently at ease. The wooden arms were cool on her hands and wrists. She'd pinned her hair up for riding and the breeze was chill on her neck. It was always peaceful at the front of the house; not so at the back, where the slaves worked in the kitchens, the gardens and the stables. *Servants*, she corrected herself. She mustn't get used to calling them slaves as Taylor and his mother did. And what were they so busy about? There was only Emmeline and herself enduring the long days between visitors. All of Comrie had a feeling of unnecessary scale: though there were many horses, there was a surplus of stalls; the smokehouse hung meat enough for a small army; even here on the porch she sat on one of a half-dozen rocking chairs. Who were they for? Comrie felt miscalculated.

She rocked gently and watched Mitilde help Emmeline towards William's large headstone that perched not a foot from the sharp cut of the slope. A slope steep enough to enjoy rolling down, she thought. Emmeline, soon to be her mother-in-law, wore a winter dress and a thick shawl despite the sunshine. She carried an open basket full of the earliest spring flowers that looked as frail as she did. Mitilde had her sleeves pushed high up her strong, dark arms. Her bulk squeezed out a grunt as she knelt to lay and smooth a blanket. Before leaving, she helped Emmeline to sit and begin arranging the flowers about the stone.

'Miss Clara.'

Clara stood up, stilled the chair and faced little Hany, who looked her usual bright self: short hair, parted in the middle and held back behind the ears on either side. Wide, kind eyes, cast down just now, out of proportion to a neat nose and a small mouth struggling to stay closed. She'd be a good choice. Her hands were held in front of the white apron that covered her grey dress. Simple. Pretty.

'Hello, Hany.' She even liked the name. 'I have something to tell you.'

'Mitilde,' Emmeline called at the grave, 'I'll need some more spring violets.'

Clara was distracted. 'Tell me, Hany. Is it a special day?'

Hany followed Clara's gaze towards the grave. 'Miss Emmeline, you mean? Why no. It's the first day the grass has been dry enough for her to sit out and tend to the grave. From here on she'll do that most days when the weather allows. Done it ever since the boy died. She's been chafing, what with the winter hanging on.'

For a moment Clara pictured her own sister's grave in the churchyard at Ridgmont. She remembered her mother had taken her to visit more than once. She'd always asked Clara to lay the flowers. She'd found little comfort in it.

Hany lowered her voice and leant closer. 'Crazed place for a grave ain't it, miss?'

It certainly was.

'It ain't right. They should a jus' picked him out a shady tree up the hill like normal folk would.'

'Why didn't they?'

'I didn' oughta tell. But it's 'cus his father was touched, tha's why. You know the boy ain't buried right neither? No, mam. Master Robert wanted the stone right on the edge, but him to lie facing toward the view. So the headstone is where his feet is. And I heard they buried him on a slant too, so he was half upright and could look west. Touched, his father was. Poor boy. I didn' oughta tell.'

Hany moved still closer and took Clara's hands. A presumption, thought Clara, but she enjoyed the intimacy. The girl's fingertips were as hard as a book cover.

Hany whispered, 'Why, I sometimes think by now he'll be just a heap a bones at the low end of the casket. Won't be lookin' nowhere. Not that he had a face to see with when poor Master Taylor took them to him in the woods. Gun went off plain in his face, I was told. Miss Emmeline, his own mother, weren't allowed to look on him. Sometimes I think that's half her trouble. Why, she's not so old to need Mitilde to help her along. I didn' oughta tell. I got mysel' all upset.' She clutched Clara's hands.

'It's alright. I need to know these things. Master Robert, Taylor's father, he's not buried here.'

'That's right, miss, he ain't. Though it was him who built Comrie thirty years back. Right after they got rid of all the Injuns hereabouts. Why he'd want to plant it in the middle of nowhere, he only knew. Touched, he was. Only after Will died, he hardly came at all. Always someplace else. Stayed in Charleston or New Orleans. He died there.' She whispered again. 'We – meanin' us slaves – heard tell he wanted to be buried here, next to his boy, but Miss Emmeline wouldn't have it. One grave out front was enough for her. Buried him instead in some fancy tomb down in Louisiana. She ain't never been to see it. I didn' oughta tell.' She made to leave.

'Wait, Hany, I've not told you my news.' She squeezed Hany's hands. 'You're to become my maid, now dear Ellie's gone home.'

Hany looked shocked. 'Why, thank you, Miss Clara,' she said, 'but I's more use in the kitchen. I don't know how to be no maid.

You should pick one of the older girls.'

It was as if she had sent her to work in the fields rather than given her a position of trust. 'That won't do, Hany. I thought you'd be happy. There's little to the work and you can learn.'

Hany remained sullen and said nothing, but Mitilde, returning with the violets, had evidently heard Clara's raised voice from below. Lifting her skirt, she climbed the steps, rocking her weight from side to side, talking all the way up.

'Why we's gotta live in this here house on the side of a hill I never know. Flat land is what God intended for houses for sure. Then we might not need all these here steps. They needs a clean. I'll get some girls up once you're away riding.' At the top she laid a weary hand on a column. 'Lady Clara, is this girl causing you trouble? She has a face like a whipped dog.'

'Well, yes. Hany doesn't want to become my maid. And you know I prefer to be called *Miss*.' Being addressed as 'Lady' served no purpose here. Her English nobility was nothing more than a novelty.

'Why, it ain't her place to have 'pinions. You ought to be thanking Miss Clara. Back you go, girl.'

'But you know I –'

'No buts. You can 'tend to her this evening like you been told to. Quick now!' Mitilde shooed her backwards into the house and then returned to fuss with Clara's hair and riding dress. 'Ain't my place, Miss Clara, but why'd you choose that girl?'

Was Mitilde going to question her choice as well?

'She's quick enough in the kitchen and I'll have to ask for a field hand to come in to replace her. She don't know nothin' 'bout dressin'. I've girls better an' older that will be 'fended she's jumped ahead.'

'I'm sorry,' said Clara, thinking that her hair and dress were fine and turning to look for Taylor again. 'I thought someone younger might suit. I thought she'd be pleased.'

'I ain't sayin' it's a fuss. It's proper you have a black maid.

Weren't seemly to have a white one. None of us knew what to say to the girl. But it ain't Hany's place to be happy or not 'bout it.'

'She is unhappy then. Why?'

'Oh, 'aint nothing. I done spoke to her before, when you told me you might pick her. It's not that she doesn't want to 'tend you. She does. Only the kitchen slaves take turns every week going into town to get what don't take to the ground here. She's partial to her monthly turn is all and sad to lose it. Her mother and her little sister live there.'

'Well, that's easily remedied. Tell her she can keep her turn. I can manage a day without her.'

'Well, alright then.'

Clara noted a smile escaped before Mitilde resumed her harried air and took the steps back down to Emmeline. 'Course, the others'll complain that she's still getting kitchen perks as well as waitin' on you, but I'll soothe 'em all right, don't you worry.'

The flowers all placed, Mitilde helped Emmeline up and to the side of the house, foregoing the steps. Clara was left alone to wait. She felt as if she'd been waiting for Taylor all winter. Of course it was right and proper that he'd moved out for the duration of their engagement. Often he was further away: business took him to Charleston or the Gulf Coast for weeks at a stretch, leaving her to abide with his mother at Comrie. She looked north over the fields cut into the hillside to provide for the house. Comrie wasn't a cotton plantation, there were none to speak of in Eastern Tennessee. Comrie's wealth came from other enterprises, which she was hoping to learn more about if Taylor ever got here and they could start their ride to Ducktown.

Across the flower garden, in the shade of a fine beech tree, was a wooden seat for two. It hung on stiff, ageing chains. There was a similar swing – better kept – in the Italian garden at Ridgmont. She used to play on it with Shire when they were little. She felt a childish urge to try this one; there was no one to watch, but as she took her first step, Taylor rode out of the trees at the low end of the meadow, his horse walking quickly left and right up the drive.

She slipped behind a column to watch. He rode with a casual grace, holding the reins in one hand. Clay was his favorite, a Tennessee Walking Horse. There was nothing like them at home – at Ridgmont. The horse's head and pink muzzle bobbed up and down, powering its hurried walk. It was amusing, but she knew better than to make light of it. It didn't do to prick a southern man's pride. The black gelding had a light mane and tail. Whether by design or by accident it complemented Taylor's long, blond hair, escaping from under his hat. He was outrageously beautiful. She felt the familiar physical rush.

When he'd dismounted and climbed the steps, she stepped out to surprise him. With an easy smile, his strong hands on her waist, he lifted her to a tiptoe kiss. Soon, disregarding the drive, she was easing her horse down the meadow. Before they escaped into the trees she stole a glance back up the hill. The columns of Comrie towered over them stark and white, like a latter-day Parthenon, kept company by the sad, grey headstone.

Ridgmont School – October 1862

Shire endured the morning teaching at school. Tired as he was, it was unlikely he would have slept if he'd feigned illness and stayed home. He was sharp with the children, not his usual self, and set them board after board of arithmetic. They seemed to sense his mood and kept quiet, low to their slates, scratching away, their clack-clacking not allowing him to think clearly. He'd never had cause to pit himself against Father – never once. But a tumor of anger had taken hold, and he was disinclined to reason with it.

He thought on Matlock, the other witness to the wedding. No one ever had a kind word to say about him. Their paths seldom crossed these days, why would they, Matlock running the duke's estate? But from his younger life, when he was allowed to play at the Abbey with Clara, Shire remembered a stony-faced man pacing the halls and gardens. Matlock always carried an air of displeasure, indignant that Shire should be there at all. If they saw him in time they used to run away or hide.

Shire would wait until he was home to confront Father; Abel and Owen Stanton, schoolmaster and scholar, always in accord. Father was the only person in the world that didn't call him Shire. But in the end his patience wasn't up to it. As soon as the children were dismissed and outside, he marched into his father's empty classroom. He found him setting the room straight, ready for the next day. Father turned to him, silently questioning his bullish entrance. Shire tossed the marriage certificate onto the desk.

His father put on his glasses and unfolded it, then slumped into his chair. 'How did you come by this?' he asked, not looking up.

'You let Clara leave to wed a man who's already married!'

'They will not wed.'

Shire leant over the table. 'You can't know that.'

Father's grey eyes looked heavy. He closed them and rubbed the bridge of his nose. 'There's much you don't know. Much I don't know in all likelihood. What was I to do? Harland told me Grace was with child and that Taylor was the father. There was to be a wedding before dawn the next day. We spoke hard on it, but he wouldn't be swayed. He believed it the best way to protect Grace. I did this as his friend...'

'Why not go to the duke?'

'He was away, in India. And he's not the easiest of men. You should know that. It would have gone badly for Grace. Taylor was to return to America and there was little time. It was only in promising not to tell the duke that Harland could get Taylor to marry – with help from Matlock.' Father held his hands open. 'This was all before I knew a jot. And we didn't know that Clara and Taylor would get engaged. Their courting might have led nowhere. I wanted to tell you, but I gave him my word.'

'And the times when I was down to be the father?' said Shire, his chin jutting upwards. 'You left that on me.'

'Or do what? Pipe up and say I knew who it was, by the by? It moved on.'

'Not from Grace it didn't.'

'Aye, that's been hard on her. It'll be more so without her father. The marriage was supposed to protect her. Do you not see that?' He tapped the certificate with a finger. 'This was to ensure an income for her and the child.'

Was Father really going to defend his part in this? 'And what of Clara?' Shire came closer to the nub of it. 'How do you square that? When they did get engaged and you let her away to America to marry into bigamy.' There, he'd said it.

A girl squealed from outside. They both listened for a moment but nothing followed; just the children dallying. But his father used it as an excuse and hurried from the room. A few moments later Shire heard his booming voice from outside, berating the children, telling them hurry on home.

He turned to look out of the tall classroom windows where low, grey clouds raced above the trees, and recalled when he and Clara had been no older than those children outside. Clara's sister, a dozen years older, had died in childbirth late in the spring. He'd spent all summer with her in the woods, watching her run and hide from the sadness. Shire's mother, who was dress maid to the duchess, died in the early autumn of the same year. Clara was as kind as she could be, of course she was, but he remembered a certain relief in her: that now she had someone who understood.

There was a great oak, out in the estate grounds where each tree was given its own space. One heavy bough rested on the earth and was an easy climb. 'We should make a promise,' Clara had said. He could still see her young face and her long dark hair, surrounded by the autumn leaves. 'To each other, that if ever one of us needs help, the other promises to come, like a mother or a sister would.'

And they had. A solemn promise made high in a tree. It had been used many times after that. Sometimes for trivial things, almost as a joke, but also when each of them was lonely in their turn. Perhaps it had always meant more to him, wrapped and gifted as it was, so soon after his mother's death. Now, standing here, he was honest enough with himself to know that, to him at least, the promise had come to mean something more.

He heard Father come back into the classroom, hopeful, no doubt, that the interruption would have taken the steam from their argument. For a moment Shire felt the edges of his anger fray, but then remembered cocksure Taylor, here all that long summer. He spun around. 'There must be more. How could Harland let the engagement pass? And how could Taylor plan to marry Clara?'

'I only know what Harland told me, and he became tighter in time. I think Matlock has some interest in Clara and Taylor marrying. I don't know what, but I expect money's at the root of it. The man cares about nothing else.'

A sudden drift of rain peppered the windows.

'Maybe Taylor believes it's possible for the wedding to be

annulled or for a divorce if Matlock's fed his mind on it. And the couple were in love, no denying that, my boy. Then the war started. A year and a half and there's been no news of a wedding. He knows he can't marry again. Why else would he wait?'

Shire sat and held his head.

'So there we were,' said Father, 'in beds of our own making, no one daring to do anything and all trusting to events. I think the worry of it brought on Harland's illness, although lately Matlock had told him the match wasn't going well.'

Shire looked up.

'Aye, but don't you put any faith in what that man says,' continued his father. 'He'd tell two tales if it suited his ends.'

There was a timid tap on the open door. Little Lucy Collier had left her coat. Father snapped at her to be quick. She took it from the hook and ran out.

'Matlock knew Harland had much to lose if he spoke up. There was no longer a child to show a likeness, and little other than this piece of paper as proof. Where was it? At the church?'

Shire said nothing.

'I see. I'd thought you had your own tryst. I'm not so deaf yet that I can't hear my own front door. So you have the proof. Though I don't see you're in any better position to help Grace than I was.'

Shire looked down. May Grace forgive him; it wasn't her he was thinking to help.

Comrie, Tennessee – October 1862

Clara imagined what it would be like to have one confidante, one true friend she could open her soul to. Maybe then she could find the heart of her unease. She sat making corsages with Emmeline in one of the guest bedrooms that they'd commandeered for wedding preparations. Her wedding dress stood on its mannequin in the corner, looking sad and deflated without the crinoline underskirt.

Emmeline was a confidante of sorts, a surrogate mother perhaps, but Taylor was her only living child. Clara could hardly be honest with her about her misgivings. Comrie was so remote. Young women hereabouts were mostly from tenant families, likely to have husbands in Taylor's regiment. Other than that, she had nothing in common with them.

She cut out another small circle of silk. Mitilde had dyed it yesterday to an autumnal orange using some extract of birch bark. Emmeline hadn't said a word since breakfast. She had her own thoughts and memories, Clara supposed. Her mother-in-law wanted twenty corsages made up. How could they possibly need that many? Three silk roses per corsage, five circles per rose. This would take all morning.

She filled the silence with memories of that ride to Ducktown in her first spring here; it had changed everything. Perhaps she'd been too young, too besotted, to see things as clearly as she should have.

Leaving Comrie, she'd followed Taylor into the laurels and the oaks. They rode down the path to a creek, which tumbled south towards the Ocoee River, the horses picking their way with the ground still slippery. The woods were celebrating the recent warmth with a rush of green. Early butterflies, Tiger Swallowtails, Taylor said, danced above the grass in the few clearings. Miss Stuart would have had something to say about this: a duke's daughter and her fiancé going out to ride unaccompanied. Her former governess had feigned illness soon after they'd arrived in Charleston, as she'd ever done at times of her own choosing. Clara had come on ahead to Comrie. It was no surprise at all when the letter arrived telling her that Miss Stuart was sailing home; so much for a chaperone. Clara had invested little affection there over the years. She'd never wanted a retinue to accompany her to America. Her parents hadn't thought to send a replacement. She'd believed she could look after herself. This new freedom came with Taylor; it came because she'd chosen to come here.

Through the trees she could hear the rush of the Ocoee and they reached it where a wider road, the Copper Road, borrowed its course. They had come this far in the autumn, but no further. The rapids roared in the narrow valley; the river unburdening the Appalachians of the winter snow. They set their mounts walking up the road and deeper into the hills. Clara leant from her horse to prompt a kiss. The water became quieter as it took a bend in the river, but a new sound found its way to them off the wooded slopes. A fiddle played out a doleful tune from somewhere up ahead, as if at a wake. When they rounded the corner there was a wagon, heavily laden and pulled by six mules. Only, there was little pulling going on, the wagon being stuck fast in a sump of mud, born of melt-water spilling across the road. The fiddler, a white man with his shirt rolled to his elbows, faced the mules as if playing just for them. The unhappy beasts were slumped in their traces, muzzles down close to the ground. A second man, draped in a long coat and wearing a slouch hat, stood to the side with a flat look, drawing on a pipe. As Clara and Taylor came up, the fiddler finished his mournful tune and walked over to take a pull on his partner's pipe. He raised the fiddle to his neck.

Clara called out, 'Sir, would you like some help? Or are you punishing these poor beasts with so sad a tune?'

The man turned and lowered his fiddle. 'Why, no, mam,

Mr Ridgmont,' he nodded, his hat being on the wagon seat. 'I 'pologize, I didn't hear you comin'.'

He didn't look the least bit embarrassed.

'You see, I'm settin' the music to their mood. These lazy miscreants,' he pointed with his bow to implicate the mules, 'know it's a long way down to town and we're only partway through the day, so their spirits ain't high. Once they think I'm understandin' how they feel, I can lift them up a little. It takes three tunes, always three. One to empathize, one to entertain and a third to get them movin'. And if you'll excuse me, mam, they're waitin' on the entertainment.' He turned to his moribund audience and played an altogether more pleasing piece. A waltz, that rose and fell as he weaved through the mud amongst them, serenading each pair as if they were sweethearts.

'Trouble is,' he said, tapping the end of his bow gently between the ears of the lead mule, 'that I do believe I've spoiled 'em. They've come to expect three tunes and won't ever move until the third one. Sometimes, if the lead mule is a mite bored, I've seen him cut over to the mud just to get stuck an' take in a melody.'

While he was talking, his partner took station behind the wagon, ready to lend his weight when the fiddler struck up again. And this time he played a lively reel, fit for a harvest dance. Clara clapped in time. From the first bar the mules all lifted their heads, pricked their ears and set their chests hard to their collars, and with a sound like a litter of piglets sucking on the teat, the wagon pulled clear of the mud. The fiddler danced on ahead while his partner hurried aboard and took the reins. Taylor laughed along with Clara. The wagon creaked off down the road.

'That was Mr George Barnes,' said Taylor. 'Quite a boy, ain't he?'

'Is this one of your teams?' asked Clara.

'No, we use niggers as drivers. These men are independent with their own wagon and get paid by the load. Copper down from the mines and supplies back up.'

As they went on, the hills closed in ever more tightly to the river. They rode through a gorge, the water so loud that they couldn't talk. Later, Taylor picked out a flat rock on the edge of the river. There was spiced crayfish with bread and butter from the Comrie kitchen, and a French Muscato that Taylor cooled in the river until his hand was wraith white.

After the meal Taylor laid on his back, his hands behind his head and his golden hair spread on the rock like a halo. 'The news in town is that Governor Harris has ordered the mobilization of the State.'

Clara didn't want more news.

'It's not clear how things'll fall out, but I plan to raise a regiment. Some counties to the north may vote to stay in the Union, and in Cleveland they've raised a new Union flag in the town square, but I reckon Polk County is all for secession.'

'Another vote?'

'It looks so. A straight yes or no – are we in or out of the Union? There's more. Lincoln has asked for volunteers to invade the South. Old fool. That'll swing Tennessee against him for sure. I should head up to Nashville, get in the thick of it. Why, you could be marrying a colonel next month.'

'A colonel?' In England a colonel's commission was hard to come by, even for the wealthy.

'Comrie will equip the regiment. That should count for something. Besides, who else around here is fit to do it?'

Other unwelcome thoughts intruded: Ellie's departure, the fighting in Charleston, her parents unable to travel for the wedding. And now her fiancé was set to become a colonel. She'd never planned to marry a soldier.

The sun was high when they came to the ferry. It didn't cross the Ocoee but a tributary called Greasy Creek. Wherever the name came from, Clara could see it was at odds with the main river, the water barely moving. A rope was stretched tight across to the far side where a flatboat was moored up. There was a small shack beyond. Next to Clara a bell as big as a bonnet was hanging from a post. Its copper was weathered green and a short length of metal hung next to it. Clara leant from her saddle and picked up the rod. Over the creek a dog started barking and a man stumbled from the shack. He held his hand up to acknowledge them and made for the flatboat. Clara chose to strike the bell anyway, shying the horses. It produced a stilted, unrewarding note.

She followed Taylor and encouraged her horse to the water's edge, next to a small pontoon, and let it drink. Taylor stood in his stirrups and reached into his pocket for a coin.

'You don't own the ferry?' asked Clara.

'No,' said Taylor, 'but not from want of trying. McGhee,' he nodded towards the man pulling on the rope, 'he won't sell. Any other tolls on the road we're free of as shareholders in the turnpike company.' He lowered his voice as the ferry drew closer. 'But this old goat was here before the Cherokee were cleared out, got his claim staked nice and legal. He'd charge St Francis himself if he pitched up.'

McGhee raised a worn hat between pulls on the rope. 'Well, good morning to you, Mr Ridgmont. And to your lady friend.'

The man went barefoot, though his feet were much the color boots might have been. His braces held up torn and patched trousers. When he came level with the pontoon, they rode the horses onto the raft. He reversed the pull on the rope, leaning back to get them moving. Clara felt her horse tense beneath her. It was a curious sensation, floating on a horse.

'If you'll pardon my sayin', you're a mite behind. I took over Mr Raht and his friends a good hour ago. They'll be waitin' on you at the Halfway.'

'It ain't a day to rush,' said Taylor, sharing a glance with Clara.

'It's a fine one. It is that. But you know Mr Raht. That man's always in a hurry. He asked me if you'd gone by.'

Clara looked over the edge. A large, whiskered fish was

skulking amongst the sunken branches and above the brown silt. Did she imagine it or was McGhee slowing down as they crossed? When they reached the pontoon, Taylor passed down his coin. They rounded the barking dog and hurried on up the road.

'McGhee is finely suited to that work,' said Taylor. 'The man draws a real pleasure from being in people's way.'

Close by the Halfway House, the land was fenced off from the road. The field behind was cleared and well ordered, but as yet no shoots rose from the tilled earth. The inn itself had been mentioned many times during the long winter at Comrie. So much so that Clara had prepared in her mind what she thought might be a fair image. Her own construction turned out to be altogether grander. Instead, the reality comprised no more than a long, single-story, wooden house with a smoking chimneystack at one end. Outside, three fine horses were tied to the rail. Beyond the house was a second field of scrub grass in which rested two wagon teams, one of mules, one of oxen.

Taylor showed her inside. There was the warm smell of some sweet stew, the way they liked it here. They were hailed from a table close to the open fire.

'We were beginning to think McGhee had refused you passage.' A soft Germanic accent – if such a thing existed. That must be Raht.

Clara smiled as two men and a boy stood. George Trenholm embraced her, handsome as always, his grey hair smartly set. Such warm eyes. It surprised her how happy she was to see him again. It seemed a long time since she'd stayed at his grand home in Charleston. His youngest boy, Frank, was with him, both too old and too young for an embrace. He nodded, she smiled.

'My dear Clara,' said Trenholm. 'I'm guessing it's not you who's the laggard.' He was elegantly dressed for a long ride. When had she ever seen him inelegant? 'May I introduce Captain Julius Raht. Will you eat? If Julius has not finished all they have?'

'I didn't want to waste the time,' said Raht.

Clara could see from the detritus on the table that Raht had wasted very little. 'We ate on the way.' Clara had expected Raht to be older. He was stocky. His dark hair had a pronounced widow's peak. She guessed at mid-thirties.

After bringing himself to attention, Raht kissed Clara's hand. She forced herself not to pull her hand away as his jowls brushed her fingers.

'A captain. Are you a military man, Mr Raht?'

He laughed.

'Heaven forbid,' said Taylor. 'I don't think we're expecting to see Mr Raht in uniform anytime soon. The superintendents of the mines in Ducktown are all called captains.'

'Nevertheless, I enjoy the title.' Raht smiled.

Taylor could have told her this before; then she need not have looked a fool. 'I understand there are several copper mines at Ducktown, Mr Raht.'

'Julius, please.'

'Julius. Which mine are you in charge of?'

It was Trenholm who laughed this time. 'Forgive us,' he said. 'We should make him a general. He runs all of the mines. The whole show.'

Coming back out into the sunlight, they put on their hats. Frank's was oversized, perhaps an old one of his father's. A line of oxen trudged by, helping another heavy wagon roll out of the hills. Looking for Taylor, Clara saw he was having a quiet word with the proprietor, who smiled and glanced over at her, before nodding some private affirmation.

Trenholm helped her to mount. 'Come along, Taylor,' he called, as he might have addressed his son, 'Julius wants to get busy at the mines. You won't mind if I borrow your fiancée for a while as you don't seem to be attending to her.'

They started up the road again, ever deeper into the hills. Taylor paired up with Raht in front, while Frank quietly trailed behind.

'I brought you something.' Trenholm patted his saddlebag. 'The *London Times*. Not a common gift for a young lady, but I know you have an enquiring mind. They're easier to come by in Charleston.'

Clara was delighted.

'I'm afraid they're rather dated. Your father's been speaking in the Lords. I've marked the passage.'

'Thank you. And I'm pleased to hear my father is well enough to address the House. I wish he'd take time to address me. He's not able to travel to my wedding.'

'I'm sure that's hard for you. But if you will marry so far from home.'

Clara wasn't inclined to make light of it.

Trenholm continued. 'You know he has asked me to watch over you when I can.'

'Along with his other investments?'

Trenholm merely smiled and Clara looked ahead. Taylor and Raht presented such different shapes from behind. Her fiancé was tall and on the taller horse, already a military bearing about him, while Raht was heavier in the saddle, his horse more labored as the road gently climbed. They were riding in silence. 'I'd have thought they'd have business to discuss,' Clara said.

'I think their minds are tending in different directions from the same subject, namely the war.'

'Taylor tells me he plans to start encouraging recruits.'

'Indeed, though perhaps it's a little soon with Tennessee yet to secede. I don't doubt that she will. He's keen to start playing soldier.'

'You wish he wouldn't?'

'It's still strange for me to see him without his father. My own sons and sons-in-law are all signing up.' He leant closer and whispered. 'Except Frank here, he's not quite done yet,' then continued, 'I could hardly wish otherwise for Taylor. The chances are the war will stay in the East and be over before we know it.'

Clara didn't doubt that Taylor would make a fine soldier. It just wasn't what she'd wanted. 'And Mr Raht? Where does his mind tend?'

'Oh, he has a sadder duty, to cut back production on the mines – lay men off. It's hard on him. He's more akin to me, only twenty years younger. Always looking to build, to expand. Why, we're almost Yankees. The money backing the mines comes from the North. They're not keen to keep investing in a state that's looking to secede.'

A raspy scream made them both look up. A hawk above the trees was being mobbed by a pair of crows. Trenholm shaded his eyes. 'Red Tail.'

They worked their horses up a rise in the road. 'Julius has it all set up so neatly. As well as overseeing all the mines, he operates the Turnpike company that keeps the road, has his own teams of copper haulers, and manages nearly everyone else's. Then there are his stores to sell the miners what they can't do without. He can even deduct what's owed him from the miners' pay. The mine-owners take all the risk and Julius gets paid every which way. A man after my own heart. Now he has to slow it all down. Poor Julius.'

Clara imagined it would be harder on the miners than on Raht.

'But it does give Taylor a chance to get men interested in joining an army that doesn't yet exist. Better than no work at all. I have an interest in both their errands. The South is going to need copper and armies.'

Later, Taylor and Trenholm swapped places. Clara was content to listen to her fiancé's commentary. When the road afforded them a view, he pointed out places: Big Frog Mountain, Slick Rock Creek, Wolf Creek, Licklog Ridge, Boyd Gap, Brush Creek Spur. He told her about the last Cherokee village up on Little Frog Mountain. It was as new a world as she could have wished for. Her Taylor was bound tight into these rivers and hills.

As they neared Ducktown the river ran faster still and began to pull up and away. The light dimmed and the air was stripped of its sweetness.

'Sulfur,' said Taylor. 'We're close to the mines.'

Clara wrinkled her nose at the memory. She picked up a circle of orange silk in the tweezers and held it a few inches above the candle flame. The edges puckered and curled in the heat until it was a reasonable imitation of a petal. With the petals sewed on top of each other and dried fall leaves pasted behind them, they would make a pretty enough corsage. But it was slow work.

She could think of precious few occasions they had ridden out together in the year and a half since that trip to Ducktown. Taylor was away with the army for months at a time. And he wrote to his mother far more than to her.

For the inner petals Clara needed to hold the silk closer to the flame, risk its destruction to transform it into something new. It was strangely hypnotic.

She could understand that Taylor wouldn't want to get right back on a horse on his brief furloughs at home. But riding together meant something to her, or at least it used to: some expression of freedom, just the two of them alone. She'd first met Taylor when he had come to England with his father to renew old family ties. Riding was bound up with their courtship. They had hunted together. She smiled at the thought. He'd been so incongruous, his blond hair trailing behind him as he'd galloped through the Bedfordshire countryside.

He was a skillful horseman. The hunt had lost its shape, the hounds dispersed. She knew the ground well. Her home, the great, pale abbey, was away behind them. She raced around the lake, through the spaced chestnuts, oaks and poplars. In the near distance was the square tower of the estate church. Taylor pulled up alongside her in the red jacket he'd borrowed, the buttons all undone.

'Is this as much as you English ladies can do? Why, I know girls back home who could keep this pace with a mule.'

Clara doubted the jibe's veracity but rose to it nevertheless, racing over the low rise to their front. Taylor and his gelding fell off her pace. She galloped towards a large spinney. A lane ran along this side, but there was a gate where a second lane set off into the trees. She aimed straight for it, Taylor whooping behind her.

She'd made this jump many times. She gave her mare the slightest check, found her balance and sprung cleanly over and into the shadowy lane. The recent rains made for a muddy landing. If that had been the only problem, the mare might have coped, but just yards away stood a large working horse before a cart. The mare slipped then caught herself so suddenly on her second stride that Clara was pitched forward and into the mud. Taylor's horse followed and for a moment feared she'd be trampled. Taylor had to fight his spooked gelding. Clara heard him curse as he careered off down the lane.

She had any number of reasons to laugh: exhilaration from the fall, heady relief at finding herself unhurt, and the fact that she was presently lying in cold mud. But most of all, at the novel experience of having the enormous, blinkered face of a working horse descend to her, upside-down, as some form of polite, ponderous enquiry.

'The adage *look before you leap* seems in order,' she heard.

'And where would be the fun in that, Shire Stanton?' She rubbed the proffered nose, rather liking its warm, snorting breath. 'If we all had to stop to look where we were to land, we'd have a slow and boring old life.'

'Perhaps,' said Shire, 'but probably a longer one.'

He offered Clara his hand. She took it but made no effort to rise. Shire looked different from this perspective. But then she'd not seen him in a while. Maybe it was the shade of the woods that made his eyes look darker. 'What would my father say?

'Tom's here. And he's come nearer to a kiss than I have.'

She giggled her last and pulled on Shire's arm, but in rising lost her balance and fell into him. He gently righted her as Taylor returned on the gelding. Jumping from the horse he threw his reins at Shire, who let them drop.

'Take my horse, damn it.'

'If you'll be good enough to steady the lady, sir, I'll be happy to.'

Clara transferred her weight to Taylor, who gripped her arm tightly. 'Perhaps farmhands should stick to tending horses rather than ladies.'

'Begging your pardon, sir, but both are agreeable to me.' Shire gathered and soothed the gelding.

The bravado, gentle as it was, was unusual for Shire.

'This is my cousin Taylor from Tennessee,' Clara said, as Taylor helped her to remount. 'Shire only helps on the estate when it suits him. His father's the schoolmaster. Shire's a teacher too.'

Taylor climbed onto his own horse and snatched the reins back from Shire. 'Schoolboy or farm hand,' he said, 'he should know his place.'

'That would be right here, sir!' Shire said.

Taylor cantered off past the cart and down the lane.

'Clara!' Emmeline cried.

It was over in a second, the silk circle nothing but flakes of ash floating down to the table.

'My dear, whatever were you thinking of?'

Images of the lane through the spinney and of the Copper Road blurred and faded. 'I'm sorry,' Clara said. 'I must be tired.'

She stood to wipe the table. The memory of the hunt echoed inside her, a residue of unhappiness that two people she cared for had been at odds. But there was nothing to be done then or now. It was right that Shire should always be there, in England, that he should always be part of Ridgmont.

Ridgmont – October 1862

The yard of the Ridgmont Estate farm was surrounded by a tumble of yellow brick sheds and wooden barns. It was quiet as Shire strode in. Old George Bantams was in the bunkhouse, tending the fire. With no teaching today, Shire had got away early before Father was up. He handed George his breakfast dish and made straight for the stable block. There was a stubborn deposit of resentment towards Father that he couldn't shift. Or perhaps he didn't want to.

The horses, his friends, were all waiting. Seventeen or eighteen hands at the withers they looked down on him. As was his habit, he greeted them by reaching up to ears, muzzles, manes or rumps; whatever came to hand. Deeper, Diamond, Bay, Duke, Betty, Dinah, Harry and last, Old Tom, his special charge.

'Well, old boy, I might talk your ears off today.'

He'd walked here quickly through the sandy woods, trying to calm his anger. It was Grace who was suffering. He should be thinking of what he could do for her, not entertaining wild designs of how to help Clara. Memories of Taylor arrived in bursts, neatly wrapped parcels of hatred, set hard like most feelings conceived in youth. But the smell of the horses, the leather tack and the hay were a comfort. His mood eased. Old Tom lowered his head. Shire put his chin on the giant nose and looked into the rheumy eyes. He'd always been Old Tom to Shire, though he supposed there must have been a day when he was simply Tom. 'Just for once, it'd be good if you could answer.'

'Talking to the horses again, are we?' It was Aaron. 'Better than talking to yourself I suppose.'

Shire considered sharing his problems; Aaron usually gave sound advice. It was Aaron who had taken him under his wing when he'd started to help out on the farm; taught him how to work the great animals at their own steady pace. He'd christened him Shire, which had stuck. Shire liked it. 'Is Ocks here?' he asked.

'Just. You're early.'

To avoid the temptation to tell all, Shire went to find the foreman. Ocks was his usual gruff but efficient self. Shire knew better than to trouble the ex-army sergeant with any pleasantries; they were never returned. Once he understood the workload for the day, Shire calculated the corn rations for each horse, mixed it with chaff and tipped it into the mangers. The farmhands showed in ones and twos, most scratching about the yard until breakfast. Shire helped Aaron take the horses from the thick stone standings and together they began to harness them. The work came easier than when he was a boy, though the tack was still heavy; the bridles, collars and breeching all made of thick, strong leather with chain and brass fittings. It was a good escape from teaching. Old Tom obligingly lowered his head to receive the collar. Shire put it on upside-down before turning it to attach the harness. Tom wore the weight tiredly, but he had a few seasons in him yet.

The horses readied, Shire and Aaron were able to join the crew in the bunkhouse. Shire's breakfast dish lay by the fireplace. He had learnt to do as the others did: bring a small pie dish with a cooked piece of bacon and a fried egg covered with a thick slice of bread. Wrap this in a clean rag and put it by the fire first thing. He sat down next to Aaron and opened his shut-knife.

The conversation was owned by the older men and Shire only spoke if spoken to. They were a fellowship and he enjoyed being part of it – or nearly part of it. As the schoolmaster's son he had some standing. But when working on the farm he did his best to lose it – to fit in. Yet there was only so far he could get. He was educated, they were not. He spoke well, they spoke with the local drawl. Most of all, he chose to be here, while they *had* to be here. On occasion, he was addressed as 'Master Stanton,' or suffered a tugged forelock in his direction. But he liked to think he was a chameleon of sorts, whether working with farmhands or riding with dukes' daughters. The farm was a second home.

Unattended thoughts fell back to Clara and Taylor. He recalled the same scene three years ago. Ocks had been starting to give instructions for the day's work, when two men rode into the yard and asked for a farrier.

'Aaron, you're needed,' Ocks had said. 'Young American master from the abbey with a loose shoe.'

Shire had followed Aaron outside. All of the farmhands spilled out as well, curious to look on this American, the rumored match for the duke's daughter. Shire's own curiosity had been more than satisfied a few days ago when Clara had fallen from her horse. He moved away to stand next to Old Tom, adjusting the harness while listening in. Taylor and his companion dismounted. A brace of pheasants hung on each saddle.

'Good morning, master,' said Aaron. 'What can I do for you?'

'Take a look over her front shoes. She's favoring her right leg.'

'Right oh.' Aaron began cleaning the dirt from the hoof. 'Up early for some hunting?'

'Such as it is,' said Taylor. 'Your game's a little on the small side. These birds were a slow target.'

The onlookers smiled and nudged each other, entertained by the American accent. Shire caught Taylor watching him.

'But I'll admit these British muskets fire well enough.'

'Glad to hear it, sir,' said Aaron. 'You carry a pistol too. We don't see those so often. Not much use for that on a hunt.'

'Habit of mine. Don't like to be without it,' said Taylor, distracted, but then he sharpened. 'Would you like to see it?' He pulled it from its holster and offered it to Aaron, who dropped the horse's hoof and took the gun with genuine interest. The audience, except for Shire, edged closer.

'Back home, you're never sure when it might come in useful. Indians and the like.'

Shire doubted that there were many Indians still east of the Mississippi, but the eyes of the farmhands collectively widened.

'An' anyhow, it's sometimes needed to finish off the bigger game. Deer – or a bear. Musket's too slow if one of those is runnin' at you.' He recovered the pistol from Aaron and sauntered over to Shire. 'Useful on the farm too, for culling out the older beasts. Young Shire, isn't it? I don't believe I thanked you for your help the other day.'

Taylor could only be older by two or three years, and the tone wasn't lost on Shire. But in this setting, in this place, he couldn't find the wit he'd shown off to Clara. Not even a chameleon can be two things at once.

'It was no bother, sir. We were glad to help,' he answered quietly, checking Old Tom's girth.

'We...? Oh, you mean your partner here.' Taylor patted Old Tom on the neck. 'Why as I recall, he was more the problem than the solution. Damn near jumped into him myself.' He laughed and invited the crowd to laugh with him. They obliged.

Taylor turned back to Old Tom. 'But this is the kinda fella I mean. Why he must have twenty-five years on him. Better to have a youngster in these traces.'

Shire spoke up, 'Old Tom's the strongest horse here.' He'd sounded like a ten-year-old.

'It's true enough,' laughed Aaron. 'And what he's lost in brawn he makes up for in brain. When he's past it, we'll give him a few years in the field for his service.'

'Why, what for?' said Taylor. 'No time for such sentiment in the New World. We have to move on. And the pistol helps.' He held up the gun, placing the muzzle a few inches below Old Tom's ear. 'I'd be doing you a favor.'

The crowd laughed again. Shire felt sick inside but could see he was being toyed with. He wouldn't rise to it. The laughing lessened as Taylor cocked the hammer.

'No!' cried Shire, lunging for the gun.

And it stopped altogether as Taylor pulled the trigger. Old Tom's only reaction was a twitch of the head. Taylor pulled the gun away from Shire's reach. 'Whoa. Easy, young Shire. I'm only foolin'. I wouldn't kill your best friend.'

The laughter returned and, despite his best efforts, tears escaped down Shire's face, plain for all to see as he wiped them away.

'Only one chamber loaded,' Taylor said, just to Shire, 'so the odds were with him. It don't do to get too attached to things you can't keep.'

'What's the point of bringing your breakfast if you're not going to eat?' Aaron said.

Shire stared down at the congealed egg. The tale of the American pretending to shoot Old Tom, and of Shire's tears, had been retold all that summer. 'I'm getting tired of these breakfasts,' he said, offering it to Aaron.

Aaron took it, but kept his eyes on Shire. 'Looks to me as if you're stuck somewhere behind yourself. Whatever it is, it doesn't do to spend too long thinking. I usually find, if I'm looking for the next thing to do, I already know what it is.'

Aaron was in the habit of saying this. And more often than not, he was exactly right.

Comrie – October 1862

Putting the letter on the sideboard, Emmeline said, 'Cousin Lenora fears that were she to come to the wedding, she'd return to a house burnt down to the roots.' She reached for Clara's hand. 'I'm sorry.'

It was hardly a blow, thought Clara, just a continuation of the declines and apologies they'd been getting for weeks. She didn't need Emmeline's sympathy, but indulged her. 'Will there be no one from Virginia then?'

'It's understandable. Virginia has it worst. They can't come away. The Yankees raid and burn even into the south of the state. And they'd likely have to take a roundabout route on the trains to get here. Why, I'm surprised the letter found us.'

'Mr Trenholm will still come from Charleston?'

'George has wedding duties, to you as well as Taylor. He has a soft spot for you, I believe. He will come.'

'It's men we're short of,' said Clara, 'with so many away at the war.'

'I'll write to Mr Raht, ask him if some of the mine captains at Ducktown would like to attend.'

Clara had come to know many of the mine captains since that first visit to Ducktown. Raht would often have one in tow on his visits to Comrie. She doubted that any of them could dance beyond a reel with a whiskey jug. She imagined them in their Sunday suits, reeking of the sulfur. She'd never forgotten her first smell of the mines that spring as they all rode up out of the woods and into the barren landscape of slag heaps and smoke.

The next day Raht had given her and Frank the grand tour.

When she thought of the mines she always remembered the mule, treading its lonely circle. It had opened up an old, sad chamber in Clara's heart. The animal followed a sanded path and turned a creaking drum by means of a crossbar connected to its harness. High off the ground, the drum wound a thick rope, which stretched over and into a tall wooden shed. Not for the first time, Clara made to cover her nose and mouth. She stopped herself. There was no point: the stink of sulfur was everywhere, even on her hand.

'The mules become well trained,' said Raht. 'She'll stop or back-up on command.'

'Can we try it?' asked Frank.

'Not right now. She's winding the cable in, so she's lifting copper ore or men up the mineshaft. We wouldn't want to send them back down again.'

The mule's head was low to the ground, her forelegs snapping straight with each forced stride. A muleteer sat against the shed, his face hidden under a slouch hat, a long whip laid across his lap. The whip must have done its work another day as the mule worked without encouragement.

The mule prompted Clara to think back to her sister's labor. She'd stood by the bed and her sister had smiled between contractions; a cycle of pain and effort that got the baby nowhere. Clara had been ushered out and had run to the woods, returning only when the screams had stopped. Someone should have been tending the room. Someone should have stopped her finding her sister bloodied and still.

Their horses had been abandoned for the morning, Mr Raht telling them that it was easier to walk. Despite the calls on his time, Raht insisted that he would personally show Clara and Frank the mines. Taylor and Trenholm had their own business to discuss. Raht had taken her and Frank to one of his supply stores and requisitioned suitable boots for them, and then they'd come over to the nearest mine.

'How many hours will she work?' Clara asked, desperate to unhitch the mule, to take it somewhere else, somewhere it could choose its own way and discover more than an endless circle of sand.

'There are usually two or three that take turns working the one whim,' said Raht. 'That's what we call this contrivance. Most of the time they'll be waiting on the ore to be loaded below or unloaded up top.'

A call came from the shed, the whip man whistled and the mule stopped.

'They're well-tended,' said Raht. 'No sense in ruining an expensive animal.'

He must have sensed Clara's sentiment. She'd have to get better at hiding it.

'Let us go and see the steam hoist over at the Buena Vista.'

Ducktown, Raht explained as they walked, was a misnomer, referring rather to a district separated into square divisions, each of which was populated by its own mine. What town did exist – little more than a village – was called Hiwassee.

Raht was easy company. She was grateful for his steadying hand on the wooden paths that meandered over the untidy landscape, the miners having added a great many hillocks and ravines to the ones nature intended. While the 'town' was far more spread out than she'd expected, the scale of the mining operation was striking. Clustered around the Isabella mine were several dozen wooden buildings. Raht enthusiastically pointed out a lumber house, the blacksmith and the assayer's office, as well as mule stalls and ore sheds.

'Do all the other mine captains work for you?' Clara asked, as he helped her start up a steep slope, Frank trailing behind.

'That's right,' he said, 'one captain for each mine. There are a dozen mines, consolidated into three companies. I run the operation for all three.'

'And this one belongs to Comrie?'

'The Isabella? Well, it used to. I helped open it up for your fiancé's father, Mr Ridgmont Senior, bless his soul. But when the Union Consolidated took it over, Comrie was given a stake in the whole company, as well as a tidy sum.'

Wealth had ever been the natural state of things at Ridgmont; Clara never had a reason to query its source. But it gave her a certain satisfaction to understand the copper mine's link to Comrie; as if she understood better a character in a story.

They climbed a low, treeless ridge. Below was a small creek with water the same color as the mud. Children were playing down there, waving up at them. Beyond the creek was a second ridge, its crest crowded with two rows of sheds, open on all sides but roofed with corrugated iron.

'Roasting sheds,' said Raht.

Each one held its own mound of dark, broken rock. And each mound exhaled a slow, constant breath of smoke.

'Inside every roast is a wooden core to start the burning. They run for weeks. We have to get most of the sulfur out of the rock, otherwise it won't smelt.'

Clara looked above the sheds to where the smoke from each merged, losing its form, blurring into a pervasive, yellow-brown haze. The sulfur dried her throat and the smoke stung her eyes. She made a slow full turn, counting in the near distance at least a half-dozen more sets of sheds, all sacrificing earth to sky. The only sounds were man-made. Not a bird wanted to share this corrupted air.

'Mr Raht, Julius. Is it like this every day? How can you live here?' What had she expected? Taylor had tried to warn her, but she'd wanted to come – wanted to see what was at the end of the Copper Road.

'When there's more of a breeze it's not so bad.' Raht coughed as he led them off the ridge. 'The air is heavy today, holding it all low... I suppose I've got used to it.'

They stepped down to a wet road, Frank sliding on the loose earth where he could, one hand for balance, another for his hat. She found it hard to talk to a boy of fourteen. It would have been easier if he'd been a couple of years either way. She'd had no younger siblings to practice on, no one to care for as her sister had cared for her.

After the Buena Vista, Raht walked them to the Eureka Mine. A column of white steam marked out the hissing furnace. A wooden race, several hundred yards long and supported by an assortment of scaffolding, delivered a constant flow of water, which tumbled onto a wheel far bigger than those of the grist mills nearer Comrie. A single cog at its center caught the end of a giant set of bellows on each dependable turn, squeezing air inside a wide chimney, which belched steam in thanks. Clara felt a warm blast of air.

'There is a smelting furnace inside,' Raht shouted over the water and the steam. 'We have to smelt the lower grade ore as it's too expensive to transport it raw.'

Frank was smiling. He stood as close as he dared to the wheel, looking up. 'Does it run all the time, Mr Raht?'

'As long as there's smelting to do, otherwise we divert the race and stop the wheel. Be careful now.'

There was no beauty here, thought Clara; perhaps a certain sad wonder, a collective ingenuity throwing water, fire and rock at each other. But like the mule, something was trapped, kept captive from its natural course. She could write about in her next letter home – to Ridgmont. Maybe it would provoke a reply.

Raht collected a brown, irregular ingot from a heap nearby and handed it to Frank.

'So heavy!' Frank said, turning it over.

'Almost pure copper,' said Raht, as if he were talking about gold.

Clara took her turn and despite the forewarning was surprised at the weight. The metal was cool but coarse and pocked. Here then, were the riches of Comrie; this lifeless crop. A whistle blew at the closest mine head, others answering from further away.

'Time for the gathering,' said Raht. 'We should hurry. They can't start without me.'

The wooden church stood atop the bare hill, as if the Ark itself had just been set down after the flood. A single bell called out into the thick air. Clara followed after Frank. Any number of other workers, women and children climbed alongside them. Frank ran on, wanting to be first up. Clara might have joined in, but the hem of her dress was heavy with mud and the air was acrid. And it wouldn't be seemly as Taylor's fiancée. Raht was breathing heavily as he struggled up behind her.

When they reached the top she discovered no one was venturing up the wooden steps and into the church, but instead to its side where there was a great brush arbor. The boughs that were twisted to make a crude roof were tainted yellow, as dead as the soil they'd once grown in. A crowd of several hundred surrounded the arbor; far too many for the church. A square of four boxes had been fashioned into the smallest of stages. Taylor and Trenholm were waiting beside them. Once he'd recovered, Raht left Clara and Frank at the front of the crowd and hauled himself up to speak.

The speech was attentively listened to, concerning everybody as it did. Clara thought it well-delivered. Raht hoped that the war, and therefore the slowdown, might be short-lived, but they would need to start storing the copper until the markets came back. There could be no more hiring and he'd speak with the individual captains as to how many men needed to be let go. There was no applause. Why would there be? He stepped down and came back to stand with Clara. Taylor took to the stage and swept off his hat, met the crowd with a level eye and waited for them to settle. The sight of him could do that, thought Clara – quiet a crowd.

He explained that if men were laid off they could find employment in the new Confederate Army being gathered to repel the Yankees.

There are times in history when we cannot see far ahead, where the waters move slowly and one day is akin to the next. This is not such a time. The lines are drawn. We can see clearly what this abolitionist president and his administration will do. They will repeal the fugitive slave laws. They will undermine and outlaw slavery in the territories. And in so doing they will devalue our property and our very prospects, until we are so weak, that we will submit to their will and their way of life.'

Clara looked around at the unanimated crowd, not a black face amongst them. Last October, after arriving in America, when she'd stayed with Trenholm in Charleston, there was a presidential rally at the South Carolina Institute Hall. She'd insisted on going along. That day, she'd come to see men's hats barely for wearing at all, rather as devices for celebration. The length of the hall had been a sea of arms waving top, bowler or broad-brimmed hats, randomly tossed into the air. Here in Ducktown, tired dusty hats stayed firmly on heads.

Taylor paused, looking like he felt that the crowd owed him something.

'We ain't seceded yet,' a man called out. 'Tennessee ain't in no war.'

'It will come,' shouted Taylor. 'And if the Yankees insist on war, we will give them their war.'

Raht spoke quietly to her. 'I fear your fiancé has not considered his audience. A few might consider themselves *of the South,* but many are not long from Cornwall or Wales, or are German like me. For them, slavery is not something to defend.'

Clara bristled on Taylor's behalf. 'You have slaves though, Mr Raht. We met one today. Edom.'

'You are quite right, though I only have Edom. I bought him along with a six mule team in '59.' He glanced at her. 'Yes, I know. Even to my faded European sensibilities it was odd to buy a man along with the beasts. But he will be free come October. I signed a deed to free him after two years. Please don't tell Taylor. He has his father's mind on slavery. Robert always prided himself on being the largest slaveholder in Polk County.'

Clara considered that owning a man for two years still seemed at odds with a stand on principle. But Raht was right; living at Comrie, Clara was hardly in a position to criticize.

On the stage Taylor gave way to Trenholm. It was as if a

benign headmaster had taken over from the head boy.

'Maybe George can recover some lost ground for Taylor and myself,' said Raht. 'I don't think either of us has hit any high notes.'

Trenholm had one hand holding onto the breast of his coat, the other by his side. 'My friends,' he said, 'I fear I have no good news to offset the bad. And though this feels like a good spot to preach from, I don't intend to.'

Clara sensed a new attentiveness on the hill. Trenholm had a manner that made it seem as if he was speaking to everyone in person. He was almost casual, but his voice carried clearly.

'I know you are proud working men, not slave-owners at all. So why would you consider fighting for men who are? You are, though, free men. Men building a life and a town. Slavery will pass in its time. I have no doubt of that. It may be right that it should pass. What should not pass is the will of the southern states to govern their own affairs. And to not have them run from Washington, New York or Boston. It is our will that is at stake.

'We do not trust Mr Lincoln. We trust his abolitionist party still less. But Lincoln is no fool. He believes he can play a long game. He will outlaw slavery in the territories which will, in time, become states with Electoral College votes of their own. Our southern society will not be able to expand into the west as the Yankees will. We will be like a small-hold farmer, unable to purchase new land – surrounded, a backwater, in time to succumb to the wider will. This is why so many of our sister states have seceded. We need to test the Yankee will *now*.'

Trenholm paused. Clara could hear the breeze moving through the arbor.

'The war is a question of psychology – a poker game, if I may be so crude. The North has to believe we will fight a hard war for our independence. If they do not, they will simply advance south to conquer us. We have to make them see that their interest is best served by letting us go. The North may believe in the Union, but I don't think it's so strong an impulse as to make many men march to battle – to kill other Americans. And abolition is a sentiment, not a cause. White men won't fight to free the Negroes... We ask you to take up your gun, as you would if a vagrant or a thief came to your home. Put it down again when he turns and walks away.'

He left it on that image. No euphoria swept the crowd, no cheer went up, but around Clara there was a ripple of applause. Men turned to talk to one another, some pressed forward to reach up and shake Trenholm's hand.

'Well I think he did as much as there was room to do,' said Raht.

'Have you been to Ashley Hall, his home in Charleston?' Clara asked.

Raht said he hadn't.

'Comrie would fit into it three times,' she said. 'It's almost as big as Ridgmont – my home.'

'Your old home. We all have to leave Europe behind sooner or later. But you are right, George is a wealthy man. Much of that wealth will be risked in this war. Still,' he dropped his voice, 'money can be made in war as well as lost.'

They waited for Taylor to collect a couple of dozen names. It would have been fewer but for Trenholm. They all walked together back to the Raht house, and after a late lunch prepared to go their separate ways. Trenholm was to take the road on to Murphy and Ashville, North Carolina. Some surveyors and a geologist in his pay had come up that way and were to travel back with him.

'I promised Frank we'd cross the mountains together. What Ducktown needs is a railroad through these hills. Perhaps it'll have to wait on the war's end, but perhaps not. We'll see.'

Clara and Taylor said their goodbyes to Raht too. After that they started back down the road, the fresher air a relief once they reached the river. She was alone with Taylor again. The trip to Ducktown had loosened something in her and it was rattling around inside: some shapeless disquiet. When she'd not seen the end of the Copper Road, she could paint it with any number of possibilities; let it merge with her imagination. But the burning ore, the steaming furnaces, and most of all the fetid air, had put an end to that.

Later, without a word, Taylor eased his horse into a trot and disappeared around a bend in the road. Clara lagged behind, enjoying for a few minutes being entirely alone with the rushing river. She'd hoped the trip to Ducktown would allow her to get closer to Taylor. Love, it seemed, didn't yet involve the friendship she'd imagined it would. Perhaps that would come with real intimacy, after the wedding. He was romantic at heart, she knew that. After the hunt at Ridgmont he'd asked for the blue ribbon from her riding hat. Months later, before he'd left England, they'd walked to the lake, Miss Stuart chaperoning them at a respectable distance. Taylor had produced her ribbon as a 'paper of pins', and proposed. They were all shapes and sizes, some simple and practical, others with colored or jeweled heads. It must have taken him all summer to collect them.

When she caught up to him, Taylor was inspecting Clay's hoof. There was blood.

'It must be deep,' he said. 'I can lead him to the Halfway. It ain't more than a mile. We'll have to see if they have some lodgings.'

Or a spare horse, thought Clara.

When they reached the Halfway, the paddock was busy with teams. Inside the inn itself, every table was occupied, though one was quickly given up for Clara. Taylor came back to her after a long chat with the proprietor carrying lemonade for them both. 'A horse can't be got for love or money, but Charles has one good room at least. He's having it made up for you. If I can't ride Clay in the morning, I'll walk home and leave him here to rest up.'

'Where will you sleep?'

'There's a bunkhouse, or if it's a fine night I'll find a spot in the paddock.'

It was as small a bedroom as Clara had ever used, but it was clean and had a wide wooden bed with a patchwork quilt. A Bible lay on the bedside table. Once alone, Clara look off her riding clothes and tried to wash Ducktown from her hair and body. The water was so cold it might have been drawn straight from the river. She had to wear the dress she'd worn to dinner at the Rahts the previous night. As she drew it over her head there was the stink of sulfur.

They took their meal and some wine – or what passed for wine – back in the tavern, which soon filled up with smoke and noise. George Barnes, on his way back up to Ducktown, gave his regards to Clara and wished her the best for her wedding. The men were drinking away the bad news from the mines. Later on, George took up his fiddle and had the men swapping arms and dancing and yelling around each other. Clara laughed with them and Taylor brought more wine. He took her hand across the table and held her gaze. She recalled another evening full of music and wine, one Christmas Eve, years ago, caroling with the estate workers and Shire. She felt herself color at the memory and had to look away. She'd escaped being a duke's daughter that night. Right now, she felt she'd never been one at all.

George Barnes announced a waltz in their honor, and they took to the floor alone, cheered on by the hauliers. The rhythm was quicker than she was used to and the wine must have been strong. She had to rely on Taylor's strength to help keep her balance. When George bowed the last long note, she laid her head on Taylor's chest. He helped her to her room, closed the door and put the candle on the table. She sat down heavily on the bed and laughed.

He sat next to her, slipped his arm around her and pulled her to him. She enjoyed the sweet whiskey of his kiss. They fell to lie on the bed. Clara was rolled onto her back and Taylor's weight settled heavily across her. She'd waited so long: a year apart, the slow winter. She stroked his back through his shirt, teased it upwards until she could feel his soft, warm skin and the vale of his spine. The fiddle played faster back down the hall, men clapping.

Taylor kissed her cheek and her neck. She pushed her face into his blond hair and took a deep breath of sulfur. Her eyes opened.

'Taylor, we should stop.' She tried to lift herself. Hadn't he heard her? 'Taylor.'

He took her right wrist and pinned it above her head. His other hand was lifting the layers of her dress. She felt his hand on her thigh.

'Taylor! No!'

He took his hand away but only to undo his belt. Clara reached to the table with her left arm and clutched at the Bible. Taylor was above her. She couldn't grasp the book; it was too wide and heavy. She knocked over the candle and it went out. Finally, she got a grip and heaved the Bible up in a swinging arc to the side of Taylor's head. The book fell onto her face and she cried out. Taylor cursed. She couldn't see him; only hear his deep and slowing breath. She sensed some restraint returning to him. The grip on her wrist eased. He climbed off her and his weight left the bed. She heard the pull of the leather as he buckled his belt. There was a brief light as the door opened and closed to leave her weeping in the dark.

Though Clara rose early, all the wagon teams were gone from outside. Clay was fine to ride. Grey clouds had come over in the night and the road was darker, colder. The events of the night before sat heavily amongst her other disappointments: Ellie gone, her parents unable to travel, the uncertainty of the looming war. Once they were away from the Halfway, Taylor made a poor attempt at an apology, blaming the drink rather than himself and saying that after Clara had lifted his shirt he'd got carried away.

She caught herself trying to excuse his behavior. She had drunk too much as well and should never have let him past the bedroom door. She tried for a moment to see it as comical, hitting him over the head with a Bible. But the humor wouldn't take. What if she hadn't managed to strike him? He was yet to ask for forgiveness.

'I guess I thought we're only weeks away from the wedding.'

'Is my honor an approximation then? Does it diminish the closer we get to the date?'

'No, I only meant...'

'Who knows what might happen? Your precious war might take you away and have you killed. You'd leave me unmarried and shamed.'

'Killed,' said Taylor. 'Is that what you think? Those Yankees'll be better at dropping guns than shootin' them. It'll be over before the year's out.'

The war again, everything subjugated to the war. 'I got a letter before we left Comrie... from Matlock.'

'Why from Matlock? What did it say?'

'That my parents can't travel, none of my family will. They must have decided before the war started.'

A familiar dog barked up ahead. They'd reached Greasy Creek and the McGhee ferry. A team and wagon were disembarking on the other side. They waited in silence. The mule at the Isabella mine went round and round in Clara's mind, her own thoughts trapped with it. Once McGhee was close, he used a pole to slow the ferry. He had a fat boy with him, dressed as raggedly as he was. He looked no more than twelve.

'The war does change things some,' Taylor said. 'I doubt we'll get so many up to attend from Charleston now things have kicked off there. It's a long journey, war or not.'

The idea of marrying in America, away from Ridgmont, had excited her. She couldn't have anticipated the war, that it would so decimate her wedding.

'Jist hop on for me,' called McGhee.

Taylor led them as far away as he could on the flatboat and spoke in a loud whisper. 'What does it matter so long as we're married? We'll make it a smaller affair, local friends and such.'

'*What does it matter?!*'

Taylor looked over at McGhee and his boy.

'Taylor Spencer-Ridgmont. I have not come half across the world to marry you by jumping over a broom or whatever it is you have planned. If you are so sure that this war will be over before it starts, I'll wait on that happy day.' She wanted to ride away but could only turn her face from Taylor as they were pulled slowly to the other side.

When they came to get off, Taylor slapped a coin into McGhee's hand. McGhee smiled and Clara heard him say, 'Seems like that was an expensive crossing for you, Mr Ridgmont. My sympathies, sir.'

They rode on, Taylor closed and taut and further ahead than was polite. When they reached the mud sink, they found another stuck wagon, only this time there was no fiddler. A black muleskinner was tugging at one of the lead mules, while his partner whipped them from the wagon. Neither was making any impression and the wagon started to lean as it settled deeper into the mud. On its side was painted *Comrie*, in large red letters edged with black. Taylor leant from his saddle and took the other lead mule by the bridle to see if it would follow Clay. The mule was having none of it. Taylor took his own whip and set about the animal so hard that it reared in its traces. When it still didn't move forward, he struck at the shoulders and head of the standing muleteer, cutting him across the face and chasing him behind the wagon. Clara screamed at Taylor to stop. He ignored her, as he had last night, and she cantered away down the Copper Road until the roar of the river was enough to cover the poor man's cries.

Ridgmont – November 1862

Shire refused to go to choir practice. He didn't give a reason and Father didn't argue with him, just left for church in the fading light. Shire would have two hours.

There was little enough to pack: a change of clothes, another smarter set, a book or two. He came downstairs and found Father's treasured atlas. How odd that he'd be the one to make use of it. He cut the string binding so he could take out the page that showed America; the states like multi-colored fields reaching across a half-finished farm. It was harder still to take the money; pound notes and guinea coins that they kept in an old vase of Mother's. The newspaper told him the cost of a third-class fare. He took enough to get there and back, and as much again. His more bullish side reasoned it was his to take, since they were saving towards his teacher training at Culham. But at his core he knew it was theft, plain and simple; theft and deceit.

He started and restarted a note to Father. In the end, he could only move on when he let go of any resentment or moral high ground and asked for forgiveness instead. He promised to write from Liverpool once he knew the shipping line. Father could write through them if he needed to. And he'd be back as soon as his errand was done.

He climbed the stairs to collect his pack but stood looking at the long, angled scratch on the outside of his bedroom door. They'd varnished it since that scratch was made, but neither of them had suggested sanding away the scar. He traced it with his fingers and heard it made once again. He'd been seven. Mother had been ill only a week. His father had come to his room and told him that she had passed away in the night. He'd lain in bed, hearing comings and goings downstairs. Quiet low voices, doors opened slowly and shut softly, then many heavy feet on the stairs. He heard them go into his parent's room. Instructions were given, as if they were moving furniture.

'Owen. You're to stay in there.' He'd heard Father go down the stairs.

He pulled the blanket over his head and held his hands to his ears. But it wasn't enough to shut out the count to the lift. A shuffle of feet, a bump and a harsh, slow scrape on his door.

'Got it?'

'Yes. Alright my end. Keep her level if you can.'

He stayed in bed until he heard the front door close and the gate swing. When he stepped from his room, he'd stroked that long scratch.

He should be gone. He took his pack down to the small kitchen, placed the letter in the middle of the table but then heard the front door. Father stepped in from the hallway, snow on his shoulders. He straightened up at the sight of his son and his pack.

'I didn't feel so well,' Father said. 'I left Samuel in charge.'

Isaiah Matlock took off his wire spectacles, pushed away the accounts and rubbed his eyes. To say that the results informed his mood would be to miss the point. It would imply a degree of separation between the numbers and Matlock that simply didn't exist.

He preferred to work in the private apartments when the duke and duchess were away, which was to say most of the time. He could use the duke's personal crested writing paper and seal. While he had a duplicate seal in his own rooms, having convinced the duke that it would help to guard his authority in his absence, it was better to sit here. It gave him an elevated view to the front of the abbey – the manicured view. The light outside was fading and, though it was only early November, it was beginning to snow. He couldn't see to the far side of the lake. The great oaks and elms, each artfully placed in its own considered spot, had become no more than dim shadows in the falling flakes.

He'd always found comfort in numbers or, more precisely, accounts. At the end of each week and month he would make the entries and balance the books. Only it had been some years since the final result had troubled the credit column. He could barely remember what it had been like to relax at the end of his ritual and make his plans for the surplus. There was no point in going over the figures again; he wouldn't find anything to rescue them. The years of plenty, when it had been possible to slide money to himself at the duke's expense, were gone. In fact, in recent times, the flow had reversed, and he'd fed his own stolen savings back into the estate to ward off any reckoning. But then he made scant distinction between the estate's wellbeing and his own.

At least now Harland was dead. That was one less risk. It was a mercy that the man had died suddenly. There'd been no opportunity for pangs of conscience at death's door. Only the daughter left to deal with. That would be an end to it. He put his spectacles into his jacket pocket and collected up the ledgers.

All seemed clean and in good order as he paced the red carpet in the Long Gallery. Either side of him were oversized portraits of dukes, duchesses or beatific, blue-eyed children; Hanoverians, Stuarts, and Elizabethans, everyone as much an ancestor of his as they were the duke's. It was easier to run the estate when 'His Grace' was away. He knew the dealings of this place far better than the duke ever had: every room, every servant, every trader. They all had their place in his accounts. His was the greater care.

The estate and its farms, while profitable in parts, were not self-sustaining; far from it. He could run the estate as tightly as he liked – he paid his workers less than others hereabouts – but the balance of the books was determined by the duke's investments elsewhere. He stared up at some Jacobean forebear and thought of the forestry interests in Scotland: they made a small contribution. The shares in the growing railways made a better one. But it had always been the interests in the New World that he had relied on to guarantee a surplus. Not so since the war had started, not since the blockade of the new-born Confederacy.

He came into the staterooms, only ever used for visiting nobility or, on rare occasions, royalty. They were hardly on his way but he liked to see all was well, liked to privately enjoy the gilded and coffered ceilings, the Canalettos, the treasures variously plundered or rescued from a turbulent world. In the state bedroom was a four-poster bed where the blue silk covers rested higher than his waist. He never passed it without recalling the laundry maid who, looking for advancement, had made her availability clear. He'd brought her here and bent her over the bed of kings and queens. Afterwards he'd looked into her service and, finding it lacking, got rid of her. That was a long time ago. These days he had little desire for physical intimacy and he'd never married.

More pictures wound their way down alongside the grand staircase. Here lived the duke's great uncle – Matlock's too – who had sailed to America, backed by Ridgmont. If only chance had taken him north rather than south; much of the current difficulty could have been avoided. From the slave cotton estates that Great Uncle had established, the revenues grew year on year and a healthy percentage fed back into Ridgmont. In time the revenues became more various: railroads, banking, mining. But Great Uncle sired only daughters, and though the American Ridgmonts hung tenaciously onto their name, the percentage came ever more grudgingly. The blood, while thicker than water, began to thin.

A portrait of Clara was at the foot of the stairs. The artist had caught her honestly, her dark hair looking to escape from the pins and combs that held it high, a determined set about her brown eyes. Sitting for a portrait would have been a chore for her. Well, she'd got away now. That was what the girl had wanted, wasn't it? To escape.

The visit from the American cousins three summers ago was a chance to thicken the blood. Neither party needed much encouragement, but Matlock had used what influence he had with the duke. The wistful, old fool had a soft spot for the American

South at odds with common sentiment, even before the war. He'd invested there heavily.

Matlock stepped outside and tightened his eyes against a flurry of snow. He hurried across the square that sat between the two long wings behind the abbey. The great stables stood a small way up the hill, built of the same sandstone. Despite the failing light they looked oddly yellow in contrast to the snow. They were large enough to hold a regiment; he imagined in the past they probably had. But they were still stables. And his rooms and the rooms of the other staff were in the same building. Noble blood or not, Matlock was no more than the head servant.

He let himself into the narrow hall and then into his rooms. The walnut panels reflected the glow of a frugal fire. He had only the one small window. The curtain was pulled across to hold in the heat, but he liked it that way even on warmer days. On the wall behind his desk was a portrait of his father, the steward before him. It held no hint of resentment. When Matlock worked here it brooded over him, a quiet overseer, at times approving, more often not. Next to it was his grandfather, whose fate had steered Matlock's own. He saw himself reflected in them both: a certain sobriety in the eyes, a flatness in their expressions that suggested they expected no adventure in life. And no beard or moustache between the three of them. That would be a dalliance, hint at an inner need for change.

An illegitimate son of the duke of the time, his grandfather had been kept close to home, schooled and given the position of steward. It was no secret that Matlock was related to the duke's family – closely related at that. 'Matlock the Third', he'd heard some of the servants joke. In his rare lighter-moments, he could smile at the thought.

He put the ledgers onto his desk and sat down. He poured some water into a tea cup he'd borrowed from the state dining room, soft paste porcelain with gilt flying birds on blue lapis.

Grace should be here soon. Matlock had despaired when

Harland raged into this office and told him she was pregnant by Taylor. He'd seen all his hopes for shoring up the American income headed for ruin. He argued long against the secret marriage, offered all he could to persuade Harland to take Grace away. But you can never reason with a man who thinks he has God on his side. It was left to Matlock to persuade Taylor that he had to go through with it. It was the only way Harland would agree to keep Taylor's indiscretion secret from the duke. No one else was to know. Then Harland had complicated matters by producing Abel as the second witness. Matlock had suggested to them both that it would be easier to break Taylor and Clara's love match once Taylor had returned to America. But when the time came, he had done nothing. That was Taylor's business. Then came the betrothal, blessed by the duke, who was happy to spend his daughter in Tennessee. Matlock only had to hint at the advantages; the duke saw them clearly enough. The wedding would be in America, and Clara had left Ridgmont for the New World.

The false marriage to Grace was a sham anyway. No one had seen fit to marry for the sake of Matlock's grandfather. If they had, Matlock might be living in the abbey and not in this stable.

He smiled to himself. He had led them all a dance. To Taylor he wrote of a possible annulment, especially after the child's death. Harland could do nothing. He would have damned Grace and himself if he'd confessed to the duke. And Matlock placated him: 'Taylor would not challenge God and go through with it. The match was failing and she would return home.' And then came the war. No commodities – no revenue – no percentage – no comfort.

There was a knock on the door. There were things he could do now that Harland was dead. Lesser moves he could make, while waiting for the main chance.

'Come in.'

It was Ocks. He made a good foreman and Matlock was glad to have the use of him. It wasn't necessary to like the man as well. Ocks' army experience provided a brand of intimidation that

Matlock lacked. His heavy coat stretched across broad shoulders, so long that it almost hid his boots.

'A cold evening, sir,' Ocks said, crossing to the fire uninvited and blocking its warmth.

Matlock let it go. Ocks did what he was asked to do and never brought Matlock any problems. They all got sorted at source.

Ocks held his huge hands towards the coals. 'All's done for this day and maybe for a few days if the snow thickens,' he said.

Matlock had no mind to talk weather and left Ocks to read his mood.

'Your visitor is in the hall, sir.'

'I'd like you to wait outside, to see her home afterwards.'

'Very well.' Ocks seemed content at the prospect.

Matlock wanted Grace quickly away from the staff after he'd spoken to her. 'Show her in.'

Ocks stole some final warmth at the fire before complying. He ushered Grace into the room, stepped out, and closed the door.

'That note for me, is it?' asked Father. 'Is that all I deserve?'

For the first time, Shire felt the full weight of his decision.

Father ignored the note and kept his coat on. 'What hope do you have of finding her? You read the papers. The South is cut off – blockaded. There'll be no passage.'

Shire found a small voice. 'I'll trust to chance. It's not a young war. It may end soon. I'll choose my way carefully. I have to go.'

'Why? She's not your care. What are you hoping for, boy? She's above the likes of us. She always has been. No matter how well you know her. You'll be alone.'

'We've had a hand in this.'

'You mean I have.'

'Who else will tell her?'

'What's at the end of this? Who'll be better off? Clara may already be married for all we know.'

'But that's just it.' Shire looked straight at his father. 'She won't

63

be, will she?' He picked up his pack. 'I've had to borrow some money.'

'Borrowed, is it?'

'I'll save it again when I'm back.'

'You think I'll keep your place open at the school? It's your future you're walking away from. And Grace, have you thought about her?'

'I don't plan to announce it from the pulpit. I'll try to let Clara know myself. She'll have to decide what to do. I'll call on Grace on my way.'

Father put a hand on his shoulder. 'Wait a day. Let's discuss it in the morning. One day can't hurt.' He looked old – worn.

'It won't get any easier.'

'And the duke? He doesn't want you anywhere near Clara.'

'That was a while ago, and he's hardly in possession of the facts.'

Father sat down, pushed the note away. 'And what of me?'

This was the hardest part. 'I'm coming back. Fail or succeed, this is my home. Errand done, I'll be on the next boat. I'd sooner go with your blessing.'

Father's voice hardened. 'It's a fool's errand. I forbid it. On your mother's soul I forbid it.'

Testing himself against that invocation, Shire discovered the depth of his resolve. He'd always obeyed Father before, but his course was set. 'Goodbye, Father.'

He walked out into the dark and the falling snow. Each step felt harder than the one before.

'Owen!'

He turned and his father hurried to him. Breath steaming in the cold air, he reached awkwardly under the neck of his jacket and pulled a leather cord over his head. The ring it held caught the light from the open door.

'Take this.' He held it out to Shire. 'I want you to take it.'

'I've taken enough. I can't take Mother's ring as well.'

'Please. I can't give my blessing, but I can give this.'

Shire put down his pack in the first settled snow and reached for the rose gold wedding ring. He put the cord over his head.

'You're as stubborn as she ever was. Sell it if you have to.'

'I'll bring it back,' said Shire. 'I'll be in Liverpool tomorrow. I'll write to you from there, and as often as I can from America.' That sounded so strange.

'You must tell Clara, if you find her, I regret my part in this. Make her understand that.'

Shire shouldered his pack only to put it down again for a last embrace. When he walked away he looked back just the once, but the falling flakes and the darkness had hidden his father and his home. All he could hear were his own footsteps pressing on the snow. When he faced forward, a cold breeze made his eyes water.

'Please come to the fire,' said Matlock. 'You look cold.'

Still in her mourning dress, Grace wore no outer coat. Her forearms were bare. As she moved unsteadily towards the fire, Matlock could see she was pale. Two weeks since her father's death, she'd not yet returned to her work at the abbey. He brought a chair to her. She sat without thanks, choosing to gaze into the fire rather than at Matlock, who stayed standing. He wanted to get on with things but felt obliged to ask after her wellbeing.

She raised her face to look at him. 'I'm well,' she said, but her voice betrayed her, as did her tired, unfocused eyes.

He could smell the drink on her. Best to get this over with. 'The bishop has written to me. They will appoint a new vicar soon, and of course he will need to take up residence at the vicarage.'

'Where would I go? There's much to do,' Grace protested. 'Father's belongings, his writing, I've not put things in order.'

'Indeed.' Matlock ploughed on. 'But the parish must have its vicar and he must have a home. Sometimes these things are not made easier by waiting.'

Grace's unhappiness barely touched him. She'd been the cause, her and her father, of so much of his trouble. After the child died, Harland had obliged him to find her work at the house and he'd employed her as a second needlewoman. Hardly the right status for a vicar's daughter but no one else would have her. 'To return to work here may be hard for you. I've found a position as a housemaid, on the Scottish estate.' He waited for a reply. 'It will be easier for you away from Ridgmont.'

'So I'm to Scotland, out of the way where I can't whisper your secrets. Is that it?'

'Yes,' said Matlock, 'it is.'

'You were to look after me. I was to have a home. I'll speak out first.'

There was no longer a need to be anything other than direct. 'It was your child that was to be looked after. And that child is dead, along with your base father who visited this blackmail upon me. Without him, who will listen to you? Pity you more likely. No child, no parent and never a husband in the first place. Little wonder she turns to fantasy and to drink.'

He watched her anger fade to despair. There was no strength in her.

'But they're still all here,' she said, 'at the church. I can't leave them. And Abel... Abel knows.'

'Abel.' Matlock smiled. 'His word would be turned easily enough. His own son was long suspected the father, so he'd have an interest in backing another candidate. And have you no care for him, to drag him into this as your father did?' She wouldn't force Abel to back her, though he thought that Abel might. It was time to soften again. 'Look to reason, Grace. There's only sorrow in this place for you. Leave them to their graves, well-tended and well-remembered, and for you a new start. And there *is* no marriage in America. Not yet. Taylor may die in the war. And if that happens, no harm was done and you will be free again.'

'But Father's things?' Grace said.

'What you value you may take with you. I'll see that someone is released from the house to help you put things in order.' He was almost there. Once more he'd found a path others wouldn't have seen. He'd need to write to the bishop when she was gone. That old goat would take a year and a day to appoint a new vicar if not pushed. Grace was sobbing. He stood her up and walked her to the door.

'Ocks.'

'Sir?'

'Please walk Miss Rees home.'

He could see that Ocks had troubled himself to find Grace a shawl. She allowed him to place it on her shoulders. There was a draft from the hall. Matlock closed the door and moved to the fire.

Shire had every intention of going to see Grace, but he had another farewell to make first. There was less snow within the woods, but the weight of his pack made his feet slip and slide more than usual in the sandy earth. He was starting a new journey with an old one.

No one was at the farm; it was too late for that. He let himself into the stable block and stroked all the horses on his way to Old Tom, who was lying down. He usually slept standing. Shire sat down next to his head and Tom snorted. He seemed alright.

'That's all the welcome I get, is it? I suppose it'll have to do.' He'd brought an apple with him but left it in his pocket, thinking Tom would want to get up to eat it. Let him rest. He gathered some straw and made himself comfortable then stroked Tom's ear, pulling it gently through his hand. 'It's odd, Tom, that in going to help one person, I have to stop looking out for others. I'm sorry, old boy.' In truth, Clara had left his care. She'd come to the school, right in the middle of class to say goodbye. He knew she'd done it that way so it wouldn't be drawn out. He couldn't blame her for that, having himself just tried to leave without seeing Father at all. And Clara wasn't allowed to visit him. A single kiss, that's all Miss Stuart had seen and reported one Christmas Eve. It was enough for the duke to forbid Clara from seeing him at all. Shire smiled. What would the duke have done if he'd known what came before that kiss?

When she said goodbye, Clara hadn't mentioned their promise. He'd thought she might have. It had been her idea after all.

'What is love, Tom? What is love but a constant promise?'

The great horse didn't answer. He never had. Shire fell in time with the old horse's breathing and drifted into sleep. He dreamt of mountains wreathed in white smoke, of a high steep ridge crowned with cannon. Men with muskets were racing past him but he held nothing more than his Father's atlas. A general waving a sword on a sweating black horse stopped beside him and ordered him up the ridge. Cannon fire shocked him awake. He guessed he was in the small hours of the night.

It was far too late to go and see Grace.

Ridgmont – November 1862

Matlock stepped outside the vicar's office and back into the chancel to allow Dr Warren and Constable Foxton some space. The low autumn sun speckled through the stained glass. On another day, he might have paused to enjoy the peace, the stillness, but there was much to consider here. He needed to tread carefully. The loud clatter of the latch on the church door made him turn and look down the length of the nave. Abel came hurrying towards him, snow on his boots, his tall form a little bent. Matlock didn't want to talk with Abel until he knew his ground, so instead he knocked on the office door and let Abel follow him inside. Dr Warren stood back from his examination to let Abel see.

'Dear God,' said Abel, and put a hand on Matlock's shoulder.

Grace lay on a pile of vestments to keep her from the cold floor. She was still wearing her mourning clothes. Her knees were drawn up as if she was a young child who was cold in bed. Dr Warren spread more vestments over her. Above her right eye there was a red graze in contrast to her deathly pale face.

'She's alive?' Abel asked.

'Barely,' said Dr Warren. 'She's lain outside all night as far as we can tell.'

'A young boy found her,' said Foxton. 'Out to bring fodder to the sheep, he saw her from the hill. He was too small to move her so came running for me. She was lying on the grave of her son. I carried her in.'

Matlock had known Grace since she was a child and watched, with others, as tragedy after tragedy heaped upon her. Any human touch was a rare experience, and Abel's unconscious weight on his shoulder stirred in him again the brief sadness he'd felt when he'd arrived. He put an arm around Abel in feigned compassion. Abel looked up and pulled away, clearly shocked that he'd unwittingly relied on Matlock for comfort. Matlock was unmoved. He couldn't deny the whispering hope that Grace would quietly slip away and end the risk he'd suffered with these last years. Last night's dealings had been a necessity. He'd given her the chance of a new start. If she'd rather die instead, the better for all concerned.

'The mark?' asked Abel.

'It looks worse than it is,' said Warren. 'No way to tell how she came by it. She'd been drinking.'

'The snow had covered any footprints,' said Foxton. 'But there was some water on the floor in the church, so someone was in an' out. And this was hanging on her mother's grave.' He handed Abel a blue eggshell locket on a silver chain.

'This was Harland's,' Abel said, looking sadder still. 'He kept it in his desk. One lock of hair from his wife and one from his grandson.'

'Unlikely someone else would know of it and go to the trouble,' said Warren. 'She must have made her own way.'

'She's never been right since Harland died,' Abel said.

Matlock tried to keep ahead of the conversation. If he had reason for hope there was also a new problem. Could Ocks be responsible for the mark? He was a hard man, but Matlock wouldn't have put him down for this. It wouldn't do to lose Ocks. He regretted asking him to see Grace home. Regardless, it would be common knowledge that she had come to the abbey. 'She came to my office yesterday, early evening,' he said. 'We spoke of her future. She wanted to move away and asked me to find service for her elsewhere.'

'She said nothing of that to me,' said Abel.

'You're not her employer,' Matlock said. 'She'd been drinking, I'm sure. I could see it was hard on her but counselled her to stay a while yet, until her mind settled. I asked Ocks to see her home.'

Constable Foxton looked up at the mention of Ocks.

'He returned soon enough... This is not his work,' Matlock insisted.

'No, sir, but best I have a word with him, nonetheless.'

Matlock looked over to Abel, sensing something was wrong. Abel was disheveled; he'd probably dressed in a hurry. But the earlier shock seemed to have made room for thought and worry. Matlock followed his instincts. 'Did you not think to bring Shire?'

He was rewarded with a look of barely guarded hatred. It was unlike Abel. They had a shared secret here, shared guilt, though no doubt Abel might feel it sharper than himself. His own conscience had higher walls. When Abel didn't answer, Matlock pushed the point, 'He was close to Grace, was he not?'

'Shire went away yesterday,' Abel said.

'Away? I'd not heard he'd be absent from the farm.' It was disingenuous of him. He knew that Shire only helped out when he could, but it kept Abel cornered.

'He'll have let Aaron know. A friend of mine up near Chester has taken ill. Shire has gone to help on his farm until he's better.'

Matlock shared a glance with the constable, but otherwise felt he'd made some ground and let it lie. Ocks could be involved in this, but with him still here and Shire gone, it would plainly look the other way.

'We need to move her,' said Warren. 'There's no warmth in this church. Can we take her to the abbey?'

'No,' said Matlock, a little too quickly. The last thing he wanted was the duchess fussing over her. 'No. Surely her own home, her own surroundings would be better? I can release someone to look after her.'

'The fires will have died there,' Abel said. 'I'll get over and see to it.' He left the office but moments later returned with the altar cloth and laid it over Grace. 'Bring her on in an hour or so. She'll need a covered carriage.' He turned to Matlock and said pointedly, 'You can manage that, can't you?'

'Yes,' said Matlock. 'And some furs. We wouldn't want her to get any colder on the way.'

Comrie – November 1862

Clara woke at first light. She took a shawl and went to sit by the window and waited while the shadow of the mountains drew back towards her and revealed the fall color. It was November 5th and three days to her wedding. The view eased her mind. Before coming to Comrie, she'd never imagined there could be so many colors in the world. How far could she see? Fifty miles, perhaps? Some of the faded ridges in the distance were beyond Chattanooga. And nothing but trees. She knew there were many farms down there, held secret by their coves or valleys. The rivers and roads were hidden and every last piece of high ground covered by the trees. The war was almost entirely conducted within one great forest, she thought; that thin layer between earth and canopy. It made it seem of less consequence, but it was there: an infection, a rising fever.

She recalled a day in June last year, not long after she'd postponed the wedding. A day when she'd ventured a short way out into the world and realized that the war was not just distant news, but would come ever closer to Comrie.

'It jus' don't seem right you sitting up here beside me,' Hany said. She'd been saying it all morning. 'No, miss, it don't. White ladies like yerself ride in a fine carriage pulled by horses. Not up in front of an ol' wagon an' behind ol' mules.'

Clara used both hands to grip the sprung bench as she was bounced along the dusty road towards town. Hany sat in the middle, as animated as an auctioneer, hands used to support her constant babble. Grey-haired Moses was on the other side, hunched forward holding the reins and saying nothing, familiar enough with the wagon to let the bumps and ruts do with him as they would.

'What would Master Taylor say if he knew you was off riding on a wagon with us? He ain't pleased at your choice of me anyhow. Ain't no special shops in Cleveland, neither. Lady like you needs to go all to Chattanooga on the train if you wants fancy things.'

Clara had got herself up early and enjoyed surprising Hany and Moses by clambering up onto the open wagon beside them. They had come down out of the steeper hills and onto gentler, rolling land. Farms were spaced along the roadside between fields wrestled from the woods. The summer sun rose up behind, warming Clara's back. People worked the fields – white people. She smiled at the sight of a small child sat backwards on a sleeping horse.

It was from these farms, and from the hills above, that Taylor had been trying to raise a regiment. Yet it began to look as if he'd manage only two or three companies at best, and have to settle for becoming a captain or a major rather than a colonel. He'd been irritable for weeks. She wasn't sure how much it derived from her postponement of the wedding and how much from the dearth of recruits. At her daily tea with Emmeline the wedding was barely touched upon. When it was, it was always obliquely, like mention of some sinful relative.

She had a letter to post to Shire. It was a sadness to her, but she'd asked him to stop writing. It wasn't that there was anything improper in their correspondence; his letters were a comfort, containing warmth sadly lacking in the rare notes from Mother. Yet they felt illicit. She shouldn't keep secrets from Taylor – at least not about the present.

It had been a mistake to give Shire the address at Comrie. She'd gone to the school. There was too much common weight in their childhood for her to leave without saying goodbye. And it was one small act of defiance. What could Father do? The children were there, all quietly standing at their desks, so they were hardly alone. Shire had looked betrayed, obviously hoping for something more, some private moment. She'd laid the address on his desk. It was a poor farewell.

There were other things she missed besides Shire. Like the open land to the front of the abbey with its lakes and scattered trees. She missed her parents, rare as their presence and attention had been. She missed the solid, square stone of the abbey itself, but she didn't miss its collective weight: the press of generations of dukes and duchesses that had sat over her, the expectation, the obligation. Here it was more bearable, and if she wanted to she could ride into town on an old cart, no matter what Hany said. She was in a new nation, yet to be won and built, rather than one being preserved and pickled.

She still missed her sister. There was no escaping that.

They moved through the village of Ocoee, named after the river, and crossed into Bradley County. Clara interrupted Hany, who was still criticizing her choice of company. 'Is it so bad that I want to spend the day with you?' Hany would like the allusion to friendship. 'I need some cloth and I want to meet your little sister. You talk about her so much. Can that please be an end to it?'

It couldn't.

'People'll think less of you. Seeing you up here with a couple of black folks. It ain't right.'

Cleveland was the county town, much smaller, she understood, than its Ohio namesake. On it two rail lines converged, one coming up from Dalton, Georgia, and another out of Chattanooga itself. They joined to run north to Knoxville, all the way through the mountains and on into Virginia. She'd like to take that journey one day. It was to Cleveland that the copper was hauled from Ducktown. Where it went from there she had no idea. They'd passed several wagons hauling supplies up the other way.

The town square held a defiant Union flag waving on a smart, white pole in front of the courthouse. The place was busy. A train had arrived with a large regiment from Mississippi, the soldiers on their way north but disembarked for a time. They were spilling loudly into the square in their new uniforms, coloring it grey and looking to spend their Confederate bills at the market stalls. As

Moses looked for somewhere to set them down, Clara watched a trader being harangued after refusing to accept anything but U.S. dollars. A clump of soldiers were gathered in front of the courthouse to look up at the Union flag, hats pushed back and hands on hips. Many of the traders were starting to pack up.

'Should I keep right on, miss?' asked Moses.

'Hany. Where do you normally meet your mother and sister?'

'Right here.' Hany stood up, searching amongst the soldiers. 'There they are.' The wagon hadn't stopped, but she bundled past Clara and jumped down.

Clara let it go: Hany was just excited. She watched her, arms spread wide, welcoming a committed charge from her sister. When Moses pulled up, Clara waited on the wagon, unsure what to do without a step, but he shuffled round to help her down. Hany's sister couldn't be more than three or four. She was trailed by an older lady, neatly dressed and carrying a basket. Her questioning eyes moved from Clara to Hany.

'Miss Clara, this is my mother, Sarah.' Hany raised her sister to her hip. 'Miss Clara surprised us, coming into town with us today.'

'I'm pleased to meet you, Sarah.'

Sarah moved her stare to the ground. Clara was still not used to these one-sided pleasantries with slaves.

'And you must be Cele.' She stroked the child's hair. Cele tucked her head into Hany's neck. 'You're a deal quieter than your sister, and what a pretty dress.'

'She likes to dress pretty when I visit,' said Hany.

'Have the soldiers been here long?' Clara asked.

'No, miss,' Sarah answered. 'There's a whole heap of 'em coming up from the station. I'd rather we was someplace else.'

Cele was leaning from Hany and pointing. 'The willigig! The willigig!'

Hany's face lit up. 'Oh, the Whirligig Man! I ain't seen him in years.'

Hany let Cele loose and the little girl raced off across the grass.

Clara followed to where Cele was jumping up and down next to an old white man who was laughing at her excitement. Other children were gathered round too, all looking at the strange contraption which stood beside the old man, about his height, the like of which Clara had never seen.

It was joyfully crafted in wood; bright red, white and blue. The lower half was as the base of a tower, vertical slats of alternating colors leaning in towards the center. Above that was a wonderful tangle of cogs and gears, wooden flags and windmills, all colored in their turn, some with stripes, some with stars – turning and spinning, driven by the breeze so that barely a piece was still. Bells, hidden somewhere within, tinkled in pace with the motion. The whole upper half swiveled like a weather vane, and atop was a wooden soldier, his arms driven to march whichever way he was pointed.

Cele reached up to the swirl of color as if she wanted to be a part of it.

'How wonderful,' Clara thought out loud.

Even Moses was smiling. 'It's a marvel ain't it, miss? He comes by every year or two. I sat with him once. Told me he'd been to every county in the state. And ev'ry time I see the whirligig he's added a piece to it, so it gets bigger and bigger.'

'What's it for?' asked a young white boy who was poking a hazel switch in between windmill panes to raise a clatter.

'It ain't for breaking,' said the Whirligig Man, moving over a step and lifting the stick up and away.

Clara noticed he dragged a slow foot behind him.

'But what does it do?' the boy whined.

'What does it do?' the old man said. 'What does it do? Why, it don't *do* nothin'. Leastways nothin' of substance. It don't grind corn or wheat. It don't raise no water – but it does make things.'

'What does it make? I can't see nothin'.'

'That's 'cos you is lookin' in the wrong place. You needs to look away from it.'

He bent down and, placing an arm around the boy, pointed at Cele. 'Look at that smile. It weren't there but a minute a go. And see all these fine people. How their smiles is growin' as we watch. You see, the whirligig is mostly happy as long as it's making smiles. That's what it aims to do.'

Cele, pleased to be part of the show, moved over to the man. 'Is it happy now?' she asked. 'How can you tell?'

'That's an intelligent question, little miss.' He went to Cele and bent low, putting both hands on his knees. 'Happiness is at the root of it, wouldn't you say? Mostly, though, it likes to be busy; that's how to tell. When the windmills are spinning so fast that the colors blur and the bells are good and loud, that's when I think it's happy. Then it don't have to think. And it don't care overmuch which way it's pointin'. Just where the wind blows. Do you like it?'

Cele nodded.

'Good. That makes *me* happy.'

They watched a while longer. Clara gave the man a full quarter then shared a wave with Cele, who left with Hany and her mother.

Moses was talking with the Whirligig Man. 'Maybe this ain't the best place for you today. Not with all these soldiers.'

'Why? They got pennies too, ain't they?'

'I'm thinkin' they might take offence. At the Union colors I mean.'

'Same three colors in their new flag last I heard.'

'Miss,' Moses said, 'it ain't friendly today. We shouldn't stay long.'

More men were arriving from the direction of the station, filling the streets. 'We've come all this way. They're our soldiers after all.'

Their soldiers or not, she had to endure them to get across the square. Some turned on their heels as she passed by, some only half-heartedly got out of her way. There were whistles and propositions. She reached the drapers and slipped inside.

She took her time choosing a cloth. Two ladies were trying on bonnets, but also watching her. She exchanged smiles with them. She found a swatch of material checked light and dark blue and asked the storekeeper to cut her a length from the bolt, which he went away to find. She picked up some hooks and eyes and put them on the counter. He returned, measured off seven yards and prepared to cut it with a large pair of shears.

There was a sharp crack from outside, like the snap of dry wood. Clara recalled the same noise from the woods at Comrie: a musket. Four or five more shots came in quick succession, followed by shouting. Her heart racing, she followed the shopkeeper to the window and the two ladies pushed up closely behind them. Civilians were hurrying from the square, traders too, abandoning their stalls. Surrounding the flagpole was a crowd of soldiers, more than fifty, some with muskets raised and aimed at the flag. There was another ripple of shots into the sky. Officers were berating their men to stop, barking orders, pushing musket barrels to the ground.

'Dear Lord,' said the shopkeeper. 'I never thought to see this day.'

The musket smoke dissipated and a pair of officers climbed the steps to the courthouse and went inside.

'I think it's over,' said Clara, scanning the square for Hany or Moses. 'The soldiers had no muskets earlier.'

'Short walk back to the station for an angry man. The guns were stacked there, I'd guess.'

They watched while companies were formed up and marched away. The civilians edged back and the officers emerged from the courthouse with a short man dressed for business. They marched him to the flagpole. He took off his black stovepipe hat and set it aside. He untied the cord and began to slowly lower the Union flag.

Clara turned at a catch in the shopkeeper's breath. A tear trickled down to lose itself in his beard. 'Now ain't that a sad sight,' he said.

'He's doing the right thing,' said Clara. 'There's no sense in anybody getting hurt over a piece of cloth.'

'Piece of cloth!' he said. 'Miss, that's my country's flag the mayor's being forced to take down.'

'I'm sorry, I mean no disrespect. I – '

'You're Taylor Spencer's lady, ain't you? From Comrie.'

'Well, yes. Do you know my fiancé?' Clara didn't like his tone.

'Ever'body knows your fiancé, him trying to raise a regiment for the *cause*.'

The two ladies looked on, making no pretense of minding their own business.

'Only in this county we ain't for his damn cause.'

'How dare you curse at me, sir.'

'This town is for that flag.' Glaring at Clara, he pointed a shaking finger to the newly empty flagpole. 'Bradley County ain't like Polk. We voted to *stay in* the Union, same as any number of others in East Tennessee. It's people like your Taylor Spencer as lead to days like this.'

Clara lifted her head and her voice. 'My fiancé is loyal to his state.'

'Huh,' he laughed. 'Here's a young girl from England telling me about loyalty. What do you know of it? Have you ever had to ask yourself where your heart is? Mine's where it always was, whatever flag flies outside my window. I don't understand how people can attach themselves so easily to a new one.'

Clara moved back to the counter, fumbling for her purse and for the right words to put this shopkeeper in his place.

'I'll tell you what,' he said, 'you keep your money and I'll keep my piece of cloth.' He rolled up the bolt.

Clara left as slowly as she could manage and without another word. They should start for home. Hany had been right; this trip was a mistake. She saw townspeople surrounding the whirligig. Maybe Moses would be there.

When she reached the crowd and stepped between the onlookers, she saw only the base of the whirligig was standing.

The rest of it had been taken and smashed into a mess of disconnected and broken pieces; still red, white and blue, but no longer together. The old man sat on the grass, crying, with the ruined soldier in his hands. The crowd was so silent, as if at a graveside. She wanted to help, but everything was so completely shattered it was hard to know where to begin. She found a piece of the soldier and offered it to the Whirligig Man.

Liverpool – November 1862

Shire rubbed a small circle into the condensation on the window. His hand came away wet and greasy. Looking out became only marginally easier as the other side of the pane held its own coating of cold, Liverpool grime, and it was dark. All he could see was that in the offices opposite his inn they were working on into the evening; light fell from a second floor row of windows out into the street. As he watched, curtains were drawn across each window in turn. He surreptitiously wiped his hand on his trousers.

His lodgings were a couple of streets back from the docks where he'd spent this day and the last looking for passage to America. He'd have to wait a week for a berth he could afford but was hopeful of finding something sooner. At least that's what he told himself, rather than admit that he could simply buy a ticket for home. That he could put his tail between his legs and again watch damp England slide by outside the train window.

A raucous laugh drew his attention back inside the half-lit inn. It was warmer here than in his small room upstairs. He'd seated himself away from the bar which was crowded with dockers. The acrid smoke wasn't quite enough to trump the sweaty smell of their day, or maybe their week. They were big, hard-looking men. Their rowdiness seemed ever on the verge of escalating into something more. He envied them. They were together; physically and in their intent. For him, the evening would be spent alone, nursing his thin beer and his misgivings.

He thought of Grace. He should have gone to see her. Perhaps she'd never need to know. Maybe he'd not get to Clara, or find the match broken.

A man sitting alone caught his eye and raised a glass to him. Shire glanced away as if he hadn't seen. When the man moved to the bar Shire looked him over. He wasn't a docker. He wore a jacket, cut short, that matched his trousers with a dark green and yellow check that brought to mind a stage performer. His black shoes were polished and his sandy hair combed close and neat. The man collected two beers from the bar and came over. 'Mind if I join you?'

An American. Shire nodded.

'I'll get my hat.'

His bowler retrieved and laid on the window sill, the man took a seat and slid a beer across the table. 'Didn't seem right letting the local boys have all the fun. My name's Dan.' Dan delivered a single, firm handshake.

'Shire. Thanks for the beer.'

'It ain't the best, but you get used to it.'

Dan made small talk and Shire began to relax. He finished his old beer and reached for the new one. There was a roar of laughter from the dockers. Dan let it play out before he sat forward and said, 'I've a proposition for you.'

'I'm not looking for work.'

'It ain't work. I'd like you to deliver a note for me.' He held up a small, unsealed envelope. 'To that office over the way.'

'Why can't you deliver it?'

'I'm not of a mind to,' said Dan. 'I'll give you five shillings.'

'Do I look that hard up?'

'No, you don't. But it would pay your lodging here for a night. Easy money.'

'What makes you think I'm lodging here?'

'Because you came into the bar from the stairs. I notice these things,' said Dan, as if Shire should be impressed.

Shire's first inclination was to say no. But if he was going to get on in places further flung than Liverpool, he'd have to be open to opportunities, even small ones. Otherwise he might as well go home. He sipped more beer. 'Do you have a dollar?'

'Planning to travel? Sure, we can make it a dollar.'

Shire reached for the envelope, but Dan drew it back.

'You're to give it to Mr J. D. Bulloch. Name's on the envelope. Only him.'

'What if he's not there?'

'Just ask for him. I'll look after your beer.'

Shire stood and took the letter. His coat was upstairs but he only had to cross the road. He stepped out into the cold empty street and into the now familiar brackish smell from the docks. In the dim lamplight he could make out 'Fraser, Trenholm & Company' stenciled in large letters above the first row of windows. He climbed the steps to a smart door, feeling foolish, awkward. Maybe he should read the letter first? He looked back to the inn where he could make out Dan, who'd rubbed a spyhole to match Shire's own. There was nothing to this. He rapped the knocker. The door opened more quickly than he expected.

'Yes?'

'I have a note. For Mr Bulloch.'

'I'll take it.'

'I'm to give it to him personally.'

'Best come in then.' The man stepped aside, let Shire in and then closed the door.

A short while ago he'd been drinking alone, minding his own business. Now, there was a feeling of bewilderment, like he'd stepped off a train and found he was at the wrong station. He followed the man up noisy wooden stairs and into a large open office. It was as brightly lit as a summer's day with lamps on every desk. A small army of clerks worked away at bills and ledgers, a constant scratching of pen on paper.

Shire took off his hat and trailed along through the office until they reached two blue office doors, one open. Between the doors, in a glass case, was a great model of a three-masted frigate. Around him every wall was lined with paintings of all manner of ships.

Shire's guide knocked gently on the open door. 'Excuse me, Mr Proileau. This young man says he has a letter for Mr Bulloch.'

Inside, a man put down a pen and removed his glasses. He rose from behind a desk stacked high with papers, came to the door with his waistcoat unbuttoned. Watery, red eyes took Shire in. Shire sensed his aggravation.

'I'll take care of it,' Proileau said abruptly and held out his hand.

Another American. Shire was tempted to leave and collect his dollar. But he'd made a deal. He squeaked out a reply, 'Begging your pardon, sir, I was asked to deliver it to a Mr Bulloch... in person.'

Proileau's jaw tightened. He didn't look like a man who had time for this. 'And I said I'd take care of it.' His hand was still out.

Shire was on the verge of handing over the letter when the second office door opened.

'What's this, Charles? Taking care of my mail for me?'

Yet another American. Was Liverpool full of them? Bulloch was taller with trimmed whiskers and a moustache. A military man perhaps, though the uniform was lacking. 'I'm thankful enough to use your offices, but this is too kind.' He had a southern drawl, as did Proileau. He turned to Shire with a smile and took the envelope.

'Just trying to save you any disturbance, James,' said Proileau.

'And I appreciate it. I really do. But I'm already disturbed. Maybe this'll be some good news for once.' He opened the letter. 'Huh. But then maybe it's no news at all.' He limply held up the note, which was entirely blank.

Shire felt a jolt of shock. Everyone was looking at him.

Proileau grabbed him by the collar. 'You think this is funny, boy? Damn Yankees.'

'Easy, Charles,' said Bulloch. 'He ain't no Yankee. Who asked you to bring this?'

'A man at the docks, sir.' Shire surprised himself by lying. He didn't want them all marching across the road. 'Just up and asked me. I didn't know him.'

'But you're to go back to him, right?' said Bulloch.

Shire nodded.

'How much will he pay you? Let him go, Charles.'

'A dollar, sir.'

'Why a dollar?'

'I'm taking a ship. To America. I thought it might be useful.'

Bulloch walked back into his office and returned with his wallet. 'Here's another,' he said, looking sternly at Shire, 'to avoid him.' He handed Shire a banknote. 'And my advice would be to wait a year or two before taking your trip. '62 hasn't been a good year to visit and '63 doesn't look likely to get any better.'

'Yes, sir. I'll think on it, sir.'

'Is that it?' said Proileau. 'Yankees send spies in here and we pay them for the privilege? What would Trenholm say? I gotta tell you, James, we're not that well off.'

'If this is the best idea they can come up with, I don't think we need to worry overmuch.' Bulloch returned to his office and closed the door.

Proileau waved an arm. 'Get him outta here.'

Two men took hold of Shire; each bent an arm behind his back and gripped a shoulder. He was pushed through the office, the clerks all watching. Instead of turning him out into the street, he was taken to another door that opened onto a back alley. One man let go and drove his elbow into Shire's lower back. While he was twisting in pain, they threw him out and he piled into the wall opposite. His shoulder jarred, and his face scraped the cold stone.

After the door slammed closed he stood there alone in the dark, holding his shoulder while the pain and shaking subsided. He had no choice but to return to his lodgings. He expected Dan would be gone. Perhaps he better had be. Finding his way out of the alley, he did a cold turn around the streets to come at the inn from the other side lest anyone was watching. When he stepped back into the warmth, Dan was sat smiling at the table.

*

Later, much later, taking a small lamp from the barman, Shire hauled himself upstairs to his room, fumbling the key into the lock with one hand. He squeezed inside. It was so cold.

He drunkenly congratulated himself. The evening could have gone worse. At first he'd remonstrated with Dan, but when he saw it was attracting the attention of the dockers, he'd allowed himself to be pulled into a chair. Once convinced that Dan was genuine in his apology, he'd accepted several more beers. Thin as they were, they'd started to tell as the evening wore on, easing the pain in his back and shoulder. They'd got to speaking about America. Dan had a cabin booked to return to New York in a couple of days. Shire had just enough wits left not to let slip his own reasons for going. In a final, beer-induced, act of apology, Dan had suggested they go to the Cunard shipping office tomorrow and see how much it would be to share a cabin. If Shire could fund the difference, they could travel together.

He'd paid Shire his agreed fee too, a coin. As he sat on his bed, he remembered his other dollar which he pulled from his pocket. The coin from Dan showed Liberty seated over a shield on one side, an eagle clutching arrows in its talons on the other. The paper Confederate dollar from Bulloch was more curious. English pounds, which Shire had seen once or twice, were much larger. This note had a simpler design, the word 'Richmond' towards the top left. Beside it was an oval portrait of some well-bearded gentlemen, below which it read, 'Confederate States of America.' Shire smiled. Go North or South, he had a dollar for each.

Comrie – November 1862

Clara watched Hany push back the pale green, folding double-doors between the parlor and the study to make one large reception room. With the doors also open to the study and the library, there would be ample space for tomorrow's guests. The fires were burning in every room to warm the house through. Emmeline was giving orders to Mitilde, and Mitilde was passing them instantly to anyone within shouting distance; except Clara. The excitement that coursed through Comrie flowed around her, as if she were a lonely rock in a fast river. She found a damp cloth and went into the library where she'd be out of the way. Books covered the wall on either side of the door to the grand dining room. One at a time, she pulled them from the shelves and wiped away the dust.

To postpone the wedding a second time was unthinkable. Taylor's honor wouldn't wear it. She must either marry tomorrow or somehow find her way back to England and remake her life there. She'd seen so little of Taylor since the war started that sometimes it felt like she was going to marry her memory of him rather than the man himself. Or that she was marrying Comrie. Was that so unusual? That she should feel almost as affectionate to the place as she did the people?

She reached the Comrie ledgers, two dozen or so, conspicuously lodged amidst the literary works of old Europe and young America. 1863 was already appended to the sequence. She guessed that Emmeline must have added it; an empty year – waiting. Emmeline had first shown her the ledgers in September and ever since Clara had helped to keep them up to date. Looking back she could see now how Emmeline had used them as a gentle tea-time snare.

Without tea, Clara wondered how she would have come to have known Emmeline at all. She was hardly an open book; Clara had to make do with glimpses of the occasional page. Their daily ritual seemed important to Emmeline. Perhaps it reminded her of her younger life in Virginia. There was a prescribed time, but no fixed place, and they would variously take it in the drawing room, the dining room, or Emmeline's dressing room that had a fine view of the gardens to the north. Sometimes they set up on the lawn or within the colonnade. Once, when everywhere else had been too hot, they used the hallway itself, sitting above the cool black and white stone floor. But on that September day, barely two months ago, Emmeline had suggested the study.

It was one of the last truly hot days. Mitilde set the tea-tray carefully down on the table next to the lamp. There was just room, between the two stacks of large, brown, leather-bound books.

'Can we please open the curtains?' asked Clara.

'Once you let the heat in you won't get it out,' said Mitilde.

'But I can't bear to drink tea by lamplight when the sun's shining. Shall we go outside?'

'I just this minute carried the tea in here. I won't risk it down those steps.'

Emmeline cut across the fuss. 'We'll let the light in for once.'

Muttering all the while, Mitilde drew back the heavy curtains and opened the window, allowing the room around Clara to take on some color. The wallpaper showed its gold and blue, the painted bookcases their pale green. Ancient faces emerged more fully from portraits as the mirrors multiplied the sudden windfall of light.

Mitilde left them alone. Children's shouts came from outside the slave huts. Clara glanced towards the window.

'I can get them to go inside if you like?' said Emmeline, with the musical drawl Clara still enjoyed, even after all this time. Once or twice she'd heard it in her own speech, single syllable words unaccountably stretching. She had been here almost two years. Taylor had never once suggested another wedding date. The war served as their tacit excuse. She had no idea if the fighting was nearer its end than its beginning. Nobody did.

'No, I like to hear them. And those huts are too hot for them in the day time.'

Emmeline stirred the pot in silence. Despite the scarcities she spared no expense to replenish the tea-caddies with Earl Grey and Darjeeling. The silver tea-pot had lain polished but unused on the mantelpiece for two winters and well-nigh two summers; Emmeline insisted that the tea tasted better from the china. Her dark blue dress was buttoned tight at the collar. Her hair, tied simply with brown lace, might once have been raven black. Clara had only ever seen it progressing towards grey. What she had once taken in Emmeline for coolness, she'd come to see as a profound sadness. She still searched for its oldest roots, somewhere beyond the loss of a child and a husband. On some days, the tea was taken with almost no conversation, but when brighter, Emmeline would occasionally let slip a snippet of her past. These were yet to coalesce into a complete picture. There was no lack of empathy, how could there be? They'd both come to Comrie as young women, to an isolated life away from the societies of Virginia and Ridgmont.

The tea poured, Emmeline became business-like, as if they were at the beginning of a long chore and needed to gather their energies. 'Well now, my dear. Have you the mental vigor for this task?'

'Oh,' said Clara, sitting up straight and setting both hands on the table, 'I'm sure I'll find it.' It was good to see some life in Emmeline's face. Too often she was tired and spent before the day was started. For once her green eyes had some warmth to them. Emmeline reached for one of the books. Clara made room between the tea cups.

'Each of these is a Comrie ledger covering one year. We start a new one each January.'

Clara could see *1858* embossed in gold lettering on the spine.

'Robert had them made up as far as 1875. Quite hopeful of him.'

'And you do the entries yourself? My father never used to concern himself with accounts.'

'These are the master ledgers. And yes, my dear, I maintain them. I did even before Robert died. They are only summaries. Our business concerns keep detailed accounts in their own books. Similarly with the household – we don't detail every minor item in the ledgers, but have a balance for the kitchen, or the stables and such, each month.'

'Don't you find it a chore?'

'No, I never did. But I don't want affairs to decline for lack of my assiduousness. I'm not as young as I was. And if I fall ill a while, you can attend to it.'

Clara surrendered inside. 'Of course. I'm happy to help.'

'Well now, let's see.' Emmeline opened the first page.

The accounts were laid out in the form of a monthly balance sheet, each business having its own cost and revenue entry and the difference showing as a monthly profit or loss. Significant sales or purchases of land, property, and occasionally a new business had their own line entry. It all looked so mundane. But as Emmeline took her through 1858, Clara found herself becoming engaged despite her misgivings. Here in the dry pages of a ledger, she learnt more of the relative value of Comrie's different enterprises than she ever had in all their halting conversations together. She realized that she had underestimated Comrie's reach and how various were its interests.

Some entries were set alongside names.

Charity – Credit	*$325*
Cloe – Debit	*$600*
Sam (died) – Debit	*$400*

Clara had no excuse to feel so shocked. As far as she was aware, there had been no sales or purchases in slaves since she'd arrived. Maybe that was the war again and Taylor being away. But seeing it in a ledger, next to the other commodities... There were similar entries, credits, with the number five, ten or fifteen against them in brackets. Some of these were slaves she knew who worked in the house, or their children. 'What are these entries?'

'Well now, when a Negro child reaches five we give it a nominal value. This is revised at ten and then at fifteen.'

Clara had started to school some of the children last summer. But when Taylor became aware he instantly forbade it, just as Emmeline had said he would.

After all the months of 1858 there was a summary for the year, showing the annual profit or loss for each business and, in addition, a large debit against the entry *Ridgmont*.

'We pay my father?' asked Clara, her finger stroking the word.

'Yes, dear. Did you not know? I used to deal with Matlock mostly, but not since the blockade. We've been supported on and off through the generations from our English cousins and Ridgmont still owns an interest. We could buy it out easily enough, but we don't see it as a debt so much as a duty. A tithe to our past. Who knows when we might need it to flow the other way again? And now they have invested you.'

Clara straightened. 'Am I a commodity too, then? Perhaps you should enter me in your book.'

'My dear, I meant it in love only. You would be the most valuable credit in all the ledgers.'

Clara managed to smile and looked at all the books. 'And Taylor, he wouldn't object to me helping with the accounts? I'm not his wife yet.'

'Meaning, if you'll forgive me, that the transaction's not yet complete?'

Clara said nothing.

Emmeline replenished the tea. 'How well do you know my son?'

Clara was nonplussed. 'I love him.'

'Hardly the same thing.' Emmeline sipped her tea before putting it down. 'They are secretive men, the Spencer-Ridgmonts. Robert was, and Taylor was schooled by him. And though George, Mr

Trenholm, encourages him in business, Taylor has small interest in the numbers.'

Emmeline sighed. 'When Taylor was a very young child he was hard to get the truth from. Boy's pranks mostly. Whereas William would confess and take the punishment, Taylor would stay quiet. As he grew up I started to question even the littlest things he said or did. So when he came back from the woods, on that worst of days, screaming and pointing, I didn't hold him. Regardless of my own distress I should have done that.' Emmeline reached over and tidied a loose hair that had escaped Clara's hairnet. 'I'm sorry, my dear, but it's as well you understand. His father had the grave dug where we could never forget it. Not for a day. And afterwards Robert could hardly bear to be here and I could never be away. Taylor needs someone to trust him. And that falls to you. If you attend to these books, you'll know his business and you'll know Comrie.'

It was such a strange proposition from a mother. Emmeline had said that Taylor needed trust, not that he deserved it.

'My dear, will you think again on the marriage? Where better to learn a man's secrets than on the pillow. Everything is so uncertain in this war. It's as if we can't breathe until it ends. Marry him soon... Well now, I've said more than I should have. Forgive me. I've not yet tended to William today.'

Clara could think of nothing to say that wasn't either encouraging or discouraging – a commitment or a rejection. She stood, kissed Emmeline's brittle hair and fetched Mitilde to help her outside. Then she looked down at the books, puffing out her cheeks.

Her long determination to outwait the war was corroded by Taylor's absence and his pride. Without him here, she sensed she'd reverted to the flawless adoration she'd held for him when they were an ocean apart. That night at the Halfway House now seemed injudicious, no more than that. Should she plan a trip to Charleston to stay with Trenholm, get away for a while, meet people again?

She'd been here so long and what did she have to show for it? But she had drawn a line: that she would not share a marriage with a war that had a greater call on her intended husband than she did.

She fingered the books, thinking to find the current year, 1862, to see how business lay now. No, that was unsatisfactory. If Comrie had a story she should understand it properly and start at the beginning. The ledgers on the table began at 1850 so she moved to the library to find the earlier ones. The very first was for 1839. She knew that the year itself wasn't spurious, but followed the removal of the Cherokee by treaty to lands over the Mississippi. Robert had bought various allotments when the old Cherokee lands were parceled up and auctioned off.

She took 1839 and 1840 to the desk and browsed through them. There was little income. They were more a log of the expense of building Comrie, which was considerable, given its scale and remoteness. She replaced them and took the next two, finding them easier to understand. There were far fewer entries than the year Emmeline had shown her, and mostly they concerned the household, some income from local farms and many slave purchases. The entries were in block capitals. As she proceeded from book to book, looking mainly at the yearly summaries, she saw the story of Comrie emerge from the numbers. A few grist mills at first, using the steep streams that ran into the Ocoee to support the emerging farms. And then in the middle '40s the cotton revenues began from their holdings further west. Later in the '40s, Emmeline's more flowing hand started sharing the entries. In 1850, Comrie took a big stake in the East Tennessee and Georgia Railroad and at the same time, in the setting up of the bank in Cleveland, Bradley County. A credit from Ridgmont had supported both. The bank started to make profits almost immediately, the railroad later when it reached the town. All the entries were now in Emmeline's hand. Still later, beginning in '54, the money from copper. It was a trickle at first but then grew exponentially until, in a few years, it trumped everything else.

The sun angled low through the windows and Clara realized it was almost evening. Mitilde had been right about letting in the heat. She reached for her fan – at home they'd been no more than ornamental, but not so here. Why did she still think of Ridgmont as home? One repeating entry confused her. On the summary page, there would be a single entry before the final balance, always a credit, marked simply as *Adjustment*. The amount varied greatly from year to year and occasionally it was absent. In fact the last one was in '56. It was usually substantial, sometimes tens of thousands of dollars.

She returned all the ledgers to their homes, weary from the concentration but somehow satisfied, then climbed the stairs to her room and sat on her bed. Opening the drawer to her side table, she took out and unfolded a muslin cloth. Inside was her long blue ribbon of pins, her engagement token from Taylor. She smiled. No two pins were the same. Her eye was drawn to the prettier ones, their twinkling colored or jeweled heads. But the plainer ones in between were the ones that she'd used, the pins that mended and made.

She walked back downstairs, through the hall and into the colonnade. The view gave her pause, the forest holding onto its green, even this close to sunset. Above was a wide strip of the palest pink beneath the blue. Knowing more of its history she saw it afresh. It was an easy place to love. If she was mistress she'd have more say. Perhaps she could persuade Taylor that stone houses for the slaves would be warmer in winter and cooler in summer.

Emmeline was sitting next to the grave in a wicker chair. She was reading under a shade. Clara imagined her, brought from her settled life in Virginia with her two infant boys, to these hills, still less peopled back then. She'd succeeded and endured nevertheless, only to lose a son and a husband. Clara walked down to her.

Emmeline let her book fall into her lap. 'Well now, my dear, you have studied a long time. Have you come to tax me with questions?'

Clara seated herself on the warm grass. 'Only one. What is the adjustment entry, in the summary?'

'Ah, you went back in time rather than forwards. Well, I was quite a catch. My father gave a dowry of sorts, but to me rather than Robert. Shares in our interests back in Virginia, as an insurance, in case Robert's ventures failed. The adjustment is the profit of those interests transferred from Virginia each year. Once we were thriving here, I sold them off, so there are no entries anymore.'

Clara wondered at the gaps, the years when the adjustment didn't appear and was about to ask, but Emmeline's thoughts had moved on.

'Do you think I should get a tree planted here? It would furnish the shade itself, and would hide this old headstone. Though I love him dearly, William isn't the most welcoming sight for our visitors.'

'That's a lovely idea,' said Clara. 'We can choose it together if you'd like. We can plant it before the wedding. I don't want to wait any longer.'

Comrie – November 8ᵗʰ, 1862

Clara sat in her wedding dress, its train bunched beside her on one of the stone benches lining Comrie's large hall. The seats were interspersed with white marble statues, as thoughtful as chess-pieces on the checkered floor. It was all cold stone, with the doors wide open to the November air.

Almost everyone had gone on ahead to the church, even the bridesmaids: a daughter of the manager of the Cleveland Bank and the niece of a friend of Emmeline's from church. Both were picked for their ornamental value. So it had been Mitilde and Hany who had helped Clara from her room and down the wide, spiral stairs to the hall. She was glad of that. The steps had been dusted and washed yesterday, the bannister polished twice over to the very top floor. Mitilde had lifted her wedding dress to be safe, lest it pick up the tiniest blemish. Then they had abandoned her to go and help in the parlor. Clara could hear Mitilde's brusque orders, a pitch higher than usual, accompanied by the clatter of crockery and the occasional ring of crystal.

She was thinking how she'd missed Harvest festival at Ridgmont, or rather forgotten to remember it. It would have been several weeks ago. She felt the chill. All the curtains were open today, the lamps lit too in the chandeliers, despite the morning hour. She wanted to rub her forearms to warm up, but they were covered by the fine, white lace of her gloves.

Footsteps from the study made her look up. They changed from the creak of wood to the cool echo of stone as George Trenholm, suited in dark grey and with a high top hat, entered the hall. His hands were gloved too, in a pale grey, and he held a black cane with a polished brass end that clicked once on the stone as he placed it, holding his other arm wide. 'Why, what's this?' he said.

'A bride left alone on her wedding day? This won't do.' He walked towards her smile and sat close. 'And it's myself at fault. I should have been the one waiting.'

'You're forgiven,' said Clara.

'I wasn't asking for your forgiveness, merely expressing my regret,' said Trenholm, 'that by my own tardiness I have shortened my time alone with a princess in need of rescue in her cold castle. Should I fetch you a blanket while we wait?'

'No. Thank you. There's a wrap in the carriage when we go.'

'We should give them a while yet. It won't hurt Taylor to wait some more. And how, may I ask, have you spent your moment of peace?'

There was much Clara wanted to say. George had been here a number of days and she'd enjoyed his exaggerated attention. Even with his connections to Taylor's family, it was still a compliment that he would take time away from Richmond and Charleston to attend the wedding. She knew that she was sitting next to one of the wealthiest men in all of the South, and was grateful that he'd come. But she'd chosen her own bed. It wouldn't be right to share how she missed her parents, how she'd have preferred to pick her own bridesmaids. Nor could she tell him of how in her waking dream she had seen the whirligig, its colored sails turning and spinning in the falling snow, and how on top Shire had been the soldier, marching towards her.

She adjusted her gloves and said instead, 'Just on a little ironic reflection. I never wanted to be matched to a bishop or a politician or a soldier. And here I am, off to marry a soldier after all.'

'But one by necessity,' said Trenholm, 'and not as a career. Taylor won't stay in the army a day beyond the war.'

'It was only a muse.'

Trenholm took her hands so she was compelled to look at him. 'I take my duties seriously today, Clara. Heaven knows I have enough of them. As well as being Taylor's bondsman, I'm also in your father's place, which I know is sad for you.' He stilled Clara's weak protest. 'So if anyone, other than the groom, has a care to this marriage and to you, it is I. And I will hereafter assert myself as family, with all the obligations that come with that. If ever you have need of my help, I will give it, even unasked-for.'

She could see he was in earnest and she kissed his cheek.

Trenholm fetched Mitilde and with Hany they helped Clara outside and to the top of the steps. As the mistress of Comrie, this view, these colors, would be hers forever.

*

Colonel Taylor Spencer-Ridgmont stood outside the church with Major Jasper beside him. Most of the guests had passed inside. This was the first day Taylor had worn his new uniform, three stars on either collar proudly announcing his elevated rank. He straightened his grey frockcoat, which reached to his knees, adjusted the wide green sash at his waist to be free of the golden buttons arrayed in two vertical rows. What would the army do without buttons? There were three more, purely ornamental, on each cuff. He shooed away Jasper's hands which were brushing at his shoulders.

He'd have preferred the service to be at Comrie, though the chapel was pretty enough. It sat amongst the woods and atop a rise within earshot of the Ocoee River. Its white wooden slats had a fresh coat of paint, as did the steep, light blue roof. At one end perched a modest bell tower from which four narrow windows looked out, one at each station. The tower housed a single bell. Below it was a round spirit hole for the departed, above it a simple spire, a taper of copper, painted to match the roof. A handful of gravestones rested amongst the colored leaves on the slope below. They had no imposed order, there being yet an abundance of room.

Here came the Thomas boy with his young wife, his corporal's uniform patched up for the occasion and the left sleeve pinned to his chest. Taylor acknowledged him as he passed by into the church. Mother, as soft as ever, had found the boy a new job at the bank since he was no longer any use at the grist mill on Cloud Creek. Taylor doubted that he had the intellect for bank work.

'I remember my wedding day,' said Major Jasper. 'Nervous as a hog in October I was. It's a day you see yourself more clearly.'

Major Jasper was also in a new uniform, though his stocky shape didn't show his off quite so well. Or more likely he'd not had the funds to get it fitted. Taylor had recommended him for major when he'd vacated the position himself. He was dependable and an organizer, used to running the rail depot in Athens. So what if Jasper didn't have Taylor's quality? He knew the men from McMinn County better, and Taylor would be able to get him to do all the paperwork that was such a waste of his own time.

Taylor's promotion had been some time in coming. Polk County could only muster three companies. He'd tried and failed to get the regiment named for Comrie or even Ridgmont. It was he who'd supplied the funds for the uniforms and the guns after all. Yet he was only elected a major. Half the companies came from McMinn rather than Polk, and the men had voted to be called the Hiwassee Volunteers after the river that ran the border between the two counties. They'd spent the last year posted in and around Knoxville and latterly at the Cumberland Gap; left to hold closed the Confederacy's back door while Bragg and Kirby-Smith marched into the Bluegrass of Kentucky, hoping to convert the state to their cause. Though the chances for glory had largely marched with them, Taylor's advancement had come as a result, casualties at Perryville making space for his old colonel's promotion, and thereby his. He was glad of it, but still felt behind schedule in terms of rank.

'Here come the bridesmaids,' said Jasper, as a two-horse open carriage drew up the hill. 'We should go in.'

The pews were packed tight with the well-to-do people of Polk County and beyond. There was a loud buzz composed mostly of welcomes and gossip. Smiling faces turned to them as they marched slowly to their places at the front. Taylor looked over the guests. Many of them wouldn't be here but for the war and want of a grander wedding. These were the lesser lights, local friends or people in the employ of Comrie, hence their excited chatter. It was a step up for most of them. Mother looked happy for once. She was one pew back, chatting to her church friends. They were, no doubt, content with both their forward seats and Comrie's gift of the new paint, inside and out. She was too generous. And why come all this way to the church anyway when the minister said he was happy to conduct the service at Comrie? But Clara had insisted, and mother had admonished him to learn the art of compromise.

Would a wedding at Comrie have kept him further from God? Maybe he would have need of His intervention before the war was over. If the Almighty was guiding the shells and picking the long lists to join him, then no doubt this service was a provocation. His other wedding, in another country and in the dead of night, he'd put aside long ago. It was under duress. God had made his pronouncement on that marriage by taking the child.

When last he'd heard from Matlock, many months ago, he'd been satisfied that his secret was well kept. Surely if that blackmailer, Harland, was ever going to speak out, he'd have done so at the time of the betrothal. But no letters from Matlock had come through the blockade this fall; there was no way of knowing what that vicar and his frigid daughter were doing. The passing pleasure he'd taken in Grace hadn't been worth the trouble. But Matlock could be relied upon to keep a lid on things. That man knew his business.

What he did today was good. Clara would nurture his better self, though the last year had been nothing but frustration. His visits home had always followed the same pattern: a happy reunion, a day or two of bliss, Clara's rejection of any real intimacy and a mixed parting. It had become so predictable that when offered a furlough two months ago he'd turned it down, preferring the monotony of army life to another cycle of romantic advance and retreat. More than once, he'd needed to slip from camp and take out his frustrations on the local whores. No more of that after today. She couldn't deny him tonight. This was the true marriage.

A quiet washed forward through the crowd. Trenholm and Clara were at the door and all heads turned and drew a breath as they walked in. The congregation, more recently used to loss and fret, united in hope for the colonel and his English bride.

*

Shire stood on the starboard foredeck. The sea and the sky were different shades but the same mood of grey. His memory of solid land was edging away along with the Irish coast. The wind was cold, humming through the rows of taut ropes, each stretching up to its own destination on the mast above. There were pulleys to match each rope's girth, some enormous, as big as Old Tom's collar; some no larger than a cricket ball. Shire felt the power, imagined it invisibly translated from the sails to everything else: to this long, smooth deck, clean as a dining table; to these climbing nets, narrowing black webs reaching for the safety of the platforms; to the huge side-paddle wheels which assisted the sails by churning away at the sea, hunting for purchase in the swells.

He preferred being outside, but his visits were necessarily short before he was seduced back to the warmth of the fore saloon or to his cabin. It was a few hours since they'd departed Queenstown, County Cork, on the second day of the voyage from Liverpool. The ship, *The Scotia*, over three hundred feet long, was a marvel.

Had he made the right decision to sail on her with Dan? There was no steerage, only first class. Though he'd only paid the difference for a shared cabin, Dan effectively subsidizing him, it was still vastly more than he'd have paid on a lesser, slower ship. That was two thirds of his funds gone. Not a fact he'd mentioned to Father in the letter he'd posted in Liverpool. Was it because he was sailing above his station that he felt more comfortable outside, away from disapproving looks? Dan had made fun of him more than once for stepping aside for the crew.

The Scotia was a new ship, and one of the fastest. Shire had learned that, since coming into service at the start of the summer, she'd come close to setting the fastest westbound leg to New York. At least he was getting to America as quickly as he could. When he was able to put his misgivings aside, he could feel his guts tremble like the *Scotia*'s engines. He'd once been as far as London, but here he was, sailing west, waving goodbye to Ireland and racing towards the New World. There was no turning back. He couldn't know how he'd fare in America, things might not turn out quite as he hoped, but he indulged himself, reveling in the simple purpose of the task before him. It wasn't often a man could be dedicated to a single end, and one so in tune with his heart.

Another ship was heading towards them, bound for Cork. Unlike the *Scotia* it had no side-wheels so must be driven by the newer screw propellers. It had made use of the space amidships for an extra mast but was otherwise similar in size and shape. It passed by on the starboard side, between Shire and the rocky Irish shore, and a yellow canister was thrown from the stern. It bobbed up with a small, red flag stretched instantly straight by the wind. Dan joined him at the rail.

'Taking the air again, young Shire? I guess since you've paid to travel well, you might as well make the best of it. Come back to the saloon and I'll buy you a beer.'

'I'm not cold enough yet. I thought I'd take in the view while there's still something in it.'

Dan was Shire's first Yankee; he'd only previously met southerners. He was probably around thirty, Shire guessed, smaller than himself and always turned out smartly, if you liked check.

'Any idea what that's all about?' Shire pointed to the canister, which was being approached by a tiny sailing boat now the other ship had passed.

'That's the news,' said Dan pulling his coat closer to his neck and leaning on the rail. 'Some enterprising soul has trailed a telegraph wire from Cork down to the very southwest corner of Ireland. The canister's taken ashore and the news and telegrams in it transmitted quicker than you can skin a leprechaun. It means all the people that matter don't have to wait for the ship to put in at Liverpool or wherever. Shaves a whole day off the news. Still leaves your country nine or ten days adrift of the action.'

'Yours too,' Shire had to raise his voice over the wind.

'All the action's on our side just now. You'll find that out soon enough. Clever though, ain't it? They laid a cable right across the Atlantic before the war, but I heard some poor fool busted it with too much electrical power. That must have been a hard one to break to the boss. Hah!'

As Dan talked, the small boat bobbed skillfully in and gaffed the canister, dragging it aboard then setting sail for shore.

A foghorn bellowed from behind them and Shire turned. It wasn't the *Scotia,* it was another ship off their port side that had been keeping pace with them since they drew out of Queenstown.

Dan made for the port rail and Shire followed, determined to emulate Dan and keep his balance without taking a hold. The ship broke a wave and he fell into a cluster of coiled, black-pitch ropes. He conceded the game and when he went forward again he put a hand on the thick, forward mast. He joined Dan at the rail. The other ship was bearing away. The blast on the horn seemed to be a goodbye.

'They've no business being so friendly,' said Dan. 'You know where that ship's headed?'

'I heard Savannah but they were being tight-lipped about it.'

Dan looked surprised. 'You're smarter than you look.'

Although similar in her arrangement, the ship was two-thirds the size of the *Scotia.* Shire knew her from Liverpool when he'd been checking out his options. She was a blockade runner looking to slip or race past the Union Navy and into the South. As such she was a more direct route for Shire to Clara, but the price of passage was astronomical.

'It's all cozy this end but people die at the other,' said Dan, staring after her. 'Your country should stop building ships that keep the war goin'.'

Shire read the papers. And he'd seen more than a few Confederate flags flying in Liverpool supporting the South. 'The cotton reserves have all gone,' he said. 'People are dying in poverty in Lancashire on account of the cotton blockade. That's why support for the South endures. We build ships for the North too.'

'They all mostly come to us in the end if we don't sink 'em. It ain't your war, I guess. It just sticks in my throat.' He nudged Shire. 'That office I sent you into – Fraser, Trenholm & Co – all the Rebel shipbuilding and purchases are organized from right there. I reckon there's more money passing in and out of that office than most of Liverpool. And not only blockade runners. They want a fighting navy too.'

Shire was surprised at Dan's candor. 'Are you spying then? Is that why you were in England?'

'Not exactly. Not yet anyway. I buy arms for the Union Army. Rifles, munitions. So I move in similar circles to Rebels doing the same. I make a report after each trip to the army. It's all official, but I ain't an agent. I wanted to be able to tell them for sure if Bulloch was there. He's the big fish. Works for the Rebel navy. I figure if I give them good information, one day it might lead to something.'

'Couldn't you just have watched to see if he came in and out?' Shire stroked a phantom pain in his shoulder.

'To be honest I don't know what he looks like. And I didn't want them to get to know me. I didn't think they'd hurt an English boy.'

Shire smiled. 'I'll live.'

'You cold enough yet?'

Shire nodded and followed Dan to the saloon.

*

Clara's smile was beginning to tire. Not from any lack of joy on her part, but through overuse of muscles accustomed to much shorter bursts of happiness. The conjoined parlor and study at Comrie was full of guests, many of whom spilt over into the hall. The slaves moved amongst them. Those from the fields Clara knew less well, but they'd been liveried today for house service. The hall door had been closed on the night and it was warm inside, with lamplight cast and reflected into every corner. It was so good to see Comrie full of people. Emmeline was sat receiving visitors near the parlor fire. For want of summer flowers, she had arranged for the most colorful leaves to be dried and sprinkled over the tables and sideboards; even over the piano. So autumn had not so much been shut out as invited in. On the table there were sugared plums, stack cakes, bourbon cakes, venison and chestnuts. Clara collected a wink from George Barnes who was leading a clutch of fiddles that were matching melodies to the mood. It felt as much like Christmas as a wedding.

Since returning from the church, Clara's day had been made up of innumerable encounters. Each meeting demanded a smile of welcome, a smile of interest, and a smile in parting before beginning again with the next. She observed Taylor had followed a similar dance and only occasionally did chance bring them close enough for a shared word or a kiss, as it had now. As soon as their lips parted there was company again.

'Why, George,' said Taylor, 'can't a man get more than two moments with his wife on his wedding day?'

'In all honesty, no,' said Trenholm. 'The day is to celebrate with the rest of us weary travelers who've braved the late season and a war to attend. Even Julius here has come down out of his hills.'

Hany arrived between Raht and Trenholm carrying a silver tray heavy with glasses of red wine. She looked her usual pretty self but her smile was buttoned down. Taylor placed an empty glass on the tray and took a fresh one. He dispatched most of it right away. Taking two glasses, Trenholm pointedly passed one to Clara and the other to Julius Raht. 'Now, Clara,' said Trenholm, 'is Julius looking in on you while Taylor is away winning the war?'

'He is,' said Clara. 'He's our most frequent guest.'

Raht, now holding wine as well as a pastry, inclined his head. 'It is always my pleasure.' The drinks before this one seemed to have sharpened rather than slurred his German accent.

'Well,' said George, 'since your fine husband is duty-bound to leave again within two days, and we're not sure which way the armies will tend in their little waltz, I've taken the liberty, as your father by proxy, to ask Julius here to look in on you and Emmeline just as often as he can. You can trust to his judgement.'

Clara was quite happy to trust to her own judgement. 'I'm sure we'll be fine, but Julius is always welcome.'

'Sir,' Taylor was addressing Trenholm, though mostly watching Raht. 'I think you may safely leave my wife in my own care.' Though it was said with a smile, Clara detected Taylor's annoyance.

If Trenholm did too, he ignored it. 'Have you tended to it then?'

'The war is well away from this corner of Tennessee. I'm sure General Bragg will keep it so.'

'We can only hope,' said Trenholm. 'By my count he has only two corners left.'

There had been a tacit understanding that the war was to be kept from the day, but the rule broken, Raht waded in. 'Where do you see the next battle, Taylor. Now that Bragg has retreated out of Kentucky?'

'Withdrawn, sir,' Taylor corrected, 'withdrawn. He won on the field and carried off half the produce of the Bluegrass. If it was Lee, we'd call it masterful. As to your question, Rosecrans is concentrating at Nashville and Bragg is matching him south-east of there, blocking the path to Chattanooga. My regiment is redeployed from the Gap to join him and is marching while I marry. I wish I could stay longer. You don't plan to join us, Julius?

There are generals older and rounder in camp.'

'I know it is not brave of me, but I will do more good for the cause by getting the copper out of these hills.'

George Barnes and his fellows ended a fast reel and received some gloved applause.

'The time might come when you don't have a choice. Are you convinced of the cause, being so new to the country?'

Clara had heard the rumors, delivered through Emmeline, wondering at Raht's southern loyalties.

'We are all new to the country, the country being so new,' said Raht, with no sign he'd taken offence. 'I make no secret that I think the war should never have started, but here it is. And as long as George needs my copper I'll be happy to get it to him.'

Trenholm had established a new arsenal in Atlanta. He'd promised that, one day soon, Clara could visit. He put an arm around Raht's shoulder. 'You should be grateful to Julius. Not only do you make profits on the copper he sells me, but I supply your army with percussion caps made from that same copper. Mr Bragg wouldn't get far without those. But enough of the war. I'll take my friend where he'll not be interrogated and leave you two to resume your kiss.'

But as they left, the next smile took their place.

*

Matlock ground his way through the old snow which was crusted from several cold days and freezing nights. Yellow light escaped around the edges of curtains and reflected off the ice, but as far as he could tell he passed unnoticed through Ridgmont village.

The marriage had died this morning.

The laundry maid he'd sent to care for Grace, picked for her discretion rather than any nursing skills, had returned early with the news. He'd already given instructions to the gravediggers. Grace could lie between the grave of her blackmailing father and her ill-

110

conceived son. To others it might be an unhappy end; to Matlock it was just tidy.

He'd rather be warm in his rooms, but a nagging worry had chased him out into the cold. He'd spent the afternoon at the vicarage and then the church. There should be a marriage certificate, he'd signed it himself. Grace or Harland must have hidden it somewhere. The only other connection was Abel. He'd visit him now, soon after her death and try to catch him off guard.

He beat his gloved hands together as he walked. He wondered when it would be prudent to let Ocks return. The day Grace had been found in the churchyard, Matlock had searched him out. He was working alone in the woods; unusual for a foreman. There was a red scratch across his left cheek. He said he'd gained it while thinning the trees. Matlock told him that Grace had been found, close to death, and that Constable Foxton wished to speak with him. He judged Ocks' shock to be genuine, and Foxton had been satisfied enough, but the local tittle-tattle was another matter. People were aware Ocks had walked Grace home and that Shire had left that same night. Matlock had thought it best to send Ocks away until the gossip died down. But now, with Grace dead, he doubted people would talk of anything else.

Abel's cottage was at the far end of the village, a small way on from the other houses. He let himself through the low wooden gate, stepped up into the small porch and knocked. When Abel opened the door he didn't appear surprised at so late a visitor.

'Abel.' Matlock took off his hat. 'A sad day.'

Abel widened the door and stood aside. 'The parlor is cold,' he said. 'You'll have to make do with the kitchen.'

The room was lit by a single lamp and warmed by a small stove. Abel cleared the table of books and letters while Matlock looked about. There was preserved affection here: a dresser showing off mediocre crockery, dried herbs hanging by the window. Abel's long dead wife kept a presence.

He waited to be offered a chair. Abel looked old, he thought, or perhaps just careworn; small wonder with recent events. He'd not expected a warm welcome but sensed something more than antipathy.

Abel sat down and half-heartedly waved Matlock to do the same. 'It's a little late for tea,' he said. 'It's been a long day. I'm tired.'

Abel looked anxious as well as tired, thought Matlock. He sat and put his hat and gloves on the table. There was no need to waste any time. 'With all that has happened, I thought it best we speak.'

Abel's face was instantly guarded. 'What is there to say?' he said.

'Little indeed. In the end it seems the worst was not realized and we can let things go on as they are,' said Matlock. 'I thank God that no law was broken.'

'*The worst was not realized?*' Abel echoed. 'Perhaps you should have been there this morning as I was, to watch Grace follow her father into death so soon, herself broken and no care left for her own life...'

'Forgive me,' Matlock held up his hands in supplication. He'd been clumsy but was surprised at the strength of Abel's ire. 'I meant merely in the matter of the marriage there was no bigamy.'

'Are you sure of that?'

'I can't be certain, there being scant news from the Confederacy, but an American marriage would have to have been very recent.' Matlock paused. 'It would still go ill for both of us if the truth escaped.'

'You more so than me perhaps,' said Abel.

Matlock ignored him. 'There was a certificate. It's not at the house or the church.'

'You think I have it? When did you think to start covering your tracks? Did you wait until she'd died? You're a hollow man, Matlock.'

'I'm a practical man. And I believe they are *our* tracks.'

'Did you never think to take a wife? Or acquire a close friend.

Either might have held a mirror up to whatever it is that eats away at you.'

Matlock chose to note the unsuppressed anger rather than consider the thought. 'I'll remind you that I had no more hand in Harland's scheme than you did.' Matlock returned Abel's stare, used his own calmness as a goad. There was something to unearth. 'The license would sink us both.'

'I don't have it.' Abel broke the stare and stood up, 'Why would I?'

Because you and Harland were as thick as thieves. 'No matter. Perhaps you will think on it? Where Harland may have kept it? You were closer to him than I.'

'You're not close to any man. Neither of us spoke up when Clara planned to go to America and marry but there was a difference, then and now. Then, I kept quiet for my friend. You kept quiet for your own interests. And now... now I regret it bitterly and you thank the Lord it's over.' Abel's face had colored. He turned away, an arm against the sideboard.

'Has Shire not returned yet? Constable Foxton is eager to speak to him.'

It was a lie, but as intended, it was too much for Abel. He rounded on Matlock. 'Where have you sent Ocks? Scratch healed up yet has it? Hard to keep a secret in this village. Tried to force himself on Grace, didn't he? Only she'd been there once before with Taylor and she wasn't having it again.'

'Harland told you this?' Matlock was more interested in what Abel was implying about Taylor than about Ocks. 'Surely not. You're guessing. He wouldn't have married them.' He stood up.

Abel backed away, unsteady. 'Maybe he didn't know.'

Matlock returned to the matter of Ocks. 'It could have been Ocks. It's as likely she just fell. I'm not sure.' It was true enough. 'In fact half the village is not sure with your son away. But the right word from me can steer Foxton's mind.' He advanced on Abel. 'Perhaps I should dismiss Shire from the farm? That would tilt the balance.'

'You leave my boy...' Abel said, but he slurred his words, as if he was drunk.

Abel groped towards him with one arm. Matlock stepped back and let him fall heavily onto a kitchen chair and then to the floor. Matlock knelt beside him and rolled him over. Abel was struggling to speak. His right eye was unfocused, the white around the grey shot through with bloodlines. Matlock had seen this before, in his own father – some form of apoplexy.

He knelt there as the seconds and minutes drew out, wondering what was best to do, what to say. He went through to the parlor and found a cushion to put under Abel's head and arranged a coat over him. Abel was watching him but seemed unable to speak at all. His one focused eye might have shown gratefulness or wariness, it wasn't possible to tell.

'I'll get help, Abel. I'll get Dr Warren.' He moved around the table to reach the door. But instead, he found himself looking through the papers that Abel had tidied when he'd first arrived. There were two letters written in two different hands, one unfinished. As he read them, he walked slowly back to where he could see Abel lying. The unfinished letter was to Shire. It told of Grace's death and Abel's suspicions of Ocks. It was just one line that caused Matlock to sit gently back down.

To me it seems little good can now come of you finding Clara.

He read the second letter from Shire telling of his ticket for the *Scotia*.

'Oh, Abel. What have you done?' He heard his own voice, soft and calm. 'Let your lovesick boy away into a war on a fool's errand.'

Abel was agitated. He was fighting to lift his head from the cushion, his working eye open wide.

'And what should I do now? I think the matter of Grace will be settled when it's discovered he has run to America. There'll be no home for him here.'

Abel made an anguished moan.

'And perhaps I can forewarn Taylor in time. No need to worry over a return then, I think.'

Abel stiffened then relaxed, both eyes closed. His breathing, which had been quick and shallow, slowed. Matlock looked into the cupboards. He found brandy and poured himself a glass.

'It does make you wonder on the providence of things. How, within a few weeks our secret is literally dying amongst us; even if your little hero has run away with the evidence.' After sipping more brandy he took the coat from Abel and hung it up. Next he retrieved the pillow and let Abel's head down onto the cold tile floor.

He doused the lamp and sat there in the dark, listening to Abel's breath, willing it to stop. He put more wood in the stove. He could leave, but it wouldn't be long, and he'd like to be sure. He turned his mind to Shire while he waited. He lost track of time, it was measured only by Abel's slow and enduring breath. Later he could hear the snow crackling outside as the cold came on deep and hard. When he moved and collected the pillow again, he realized there was no choice left to make. He'd already decided, somewhere back in the darkness. He felt his way and knelt down beside Abel.

'Do you know the meaning of your name, Abel?' he whispered. 'No? I do. You find you study strange things when, as you pointed out, you have no friends and no wife. Abel is from the Hebrew and means *breath*.'

He laid a hand on Abel's chest, which rose and fell lightly but evenly. He placed the cushion fully over Abel's face and lent forward. There was no struggle and soon the breathing ceased.

Matlock rose and stood there until his trembling began to subside. He took the cushion back to the parlor, then put on his coat and tucked the letters into his pocket. Quietly, he let himself out into the cold night to walk back to his estate.

Comrie – November 1862

The day after the wedding, Clara retired early to her bedroom, leaving Taylor and Major Jasper to their after-dinner drinks in the hunting room. All morning and afternoon, as the various overnight guests had departed, she'd worn a veneer of conviviality and she wondered if it had been convincing. Hardest of all was when Trenholm took his leave and she'd not been able to detain a lonely tear, which he'd gently wiped away. She suspected he'd taken it to be given wholly in affection.

She'd seen little of Emmeline who, with rare energy, was busy setting Comrie to rights. Not even Taylor had spent any time with Clara, instead preparing to depart the next day and attending to minor business matters.

Hany was helping her to undress. 'It sure was a fine weddin', Miss Clara.'

She wasn't sure that she should be called *Miss* anymore, but was too tired to think on it.

'After all the guests were gone or in bed, we had our own cel'bration, though I didn' oughta tell. It was too cold to be outside, but we used Mitilde's cabin, it being the biggest, but we was all tight in there. And we had the leavings from the weddin', and there was plenty too. And old Moses, he brought out some shine and we made a punch, though I mostly drank birch beer, and I tell you, Miss Clara, I ain't had but two hours sleep.'

Clara stepped out of the hoop and let Hany gabble on while she unlaced the corset.

'If you want to sit down, I can do this just as easy?'

'I'll stand, thank you.' Clara rested one hand on the bedpost, her body taut and apprehensive of Hany's hands. Hany stopped attacking the laces and took things more gently.

'Are you hurting, miss? I can get more hot water brought up if you want a bath?'

'No. What there is will be fine. I'll tend to myself tonight. You must be tired too.'

'Master Taylor drank a lot yesterday, didn't he?'

Clara didn't answer. The corset was finally off.

'When the war is done, and he's home for good, you'll make a fine gentleman of him, miss. I guess it must be hard on him having to go right away again. And the war, I can't imagine what that's like. You'll make a fine gentleman of him, miss. You want me to wash your back?'

Clara was thankful to Hany for sensing her mood, but wanted no more sympathy, if that's what this was. She dismissed her and took herself into the bathroom. Her undergarments were bloodied and it was painful to wash. Once in bed she read a while, wondering how long Taylor would stay downstairs. She doused the light and tried to sleep, but thoughts of last night kept her awake: how her encouragements and then entreaties to tenderness had been brushed aside, how he'd rutted on her again this morning.

When he arrived, she wasn't sure how long she'd lain there. She opened her eyes as he unsteadily put down his own lamp and began to undress.

'There's my wife,' he said, 'still awake for me.' He struggled with his boots.

'Did you and the major enjoy yourselves?'

'Enjoy? Well yes, I suppose we did. He's a good man. Worked for the Georgia and East Tennessee Railroad before the war. In awe of Comrie I think. And of you. But I'll enjoy myself here more if I can get these damn boots off.'

'Taylor, I'm tender. After last night. And tired too.'

'I understand,' he said, 'but your husband is off to war again tomorrow.'

'In the morning then. When we're rested.'

'I'm rested just fine.' Taylor stripped off his shirt and trousers and got into bed. His heavy kiss tasted of cigars. His hand pulled up her nightgown.

'Please, Taylor. In the morning.'

'I'll be quick.'

He rolled her onto her stomach.

'Taylor!'

A practiced knee placed inside hers pushed her leg away and he felt for her roughly, his other hand and his weight between her shoulder blades. She cried out once, then sank her face into the pillow.

Atlantic Ocean – November 1862

Somewhere in the mid-Atlantic it became impossible for Shire not to tell Dan what he was doing. He put this partly down to the confinement of the voyage, but also to the several whiskeys he'd been softened up with.

'You wanna go *where*? Are you out of your imperial English mind? That's the other side of the war. You'd have done better being on that blockade runner we sailed with.'

'I didn't have their price,' said Shire.

Dan stared at him, wide-eyed. 'So what is your plan exactly?'

Shire rubbed the back of his neck. 'Well, I imagine I'll head down to Washington, see the lay of the land and look to get safe passage south.'

Dan's eyes widened further. 'It's only a short word. Which part of *war* isn't getting through to you? Virginia's been a battle site for a year and a half. You can hear the guns in Washington half the time. The armies sweep up and down and east and west and there's barely an acre not picketed.' Dan held out both hands and shrugged his shoulders. 'And anyway, lately the war's been north-east of Washington in Maryland. So don't trouble yourself going south, the war'll come to you if you wait awhile. Either side'll happily hang you first and *not* ask questions later. There *is* no passage and nothing's *safe*.'

'Well, out west then,' countered Shire 'They can't picket all the way to the Pacific.'

'They're doing their darndest. And if you get much past the Mississippi the Indians do the picketing. But there's a whole second war out that way every bit as vicious. Maybe more so. At least in the east, folks have generally made up their minds north and south. You head out west and it's all mixed up and they're happy to shoot each other even when the army's not around.'

Shire stared into his whiskey. He'd expected a reaction from Dan, but not one quite this impassioned. 'I thought perhaps I could join up. The army has to go south sometime.'

'They've tried going south alright, but so far they've just bobbed back up. And not so many as went south to start with, neither. I don't see you helping much by getting killed.'

Shire had nothing left to say.

Dan topped up his glass. 'I can see you're sweet on this girl, but why not chalk this one up to experience and head home to your father? For all you know her paramour is dead. They're dying regular on that side too.'

Did Dan really think he was crossing this ocean only to sail back again because he couldn't quite see his way forward? 'She needs to know... has to know. Even if she's married him, it's not legal. I'm her friend.'

'Friendship, is it?' Dan smiled. 'Seems an errand based on hope plus nothin'. But persistence is a virtue. In my experience it pays off better than anything else. If you're not shot, that is.' He was looking at Shire thoughtfully. 'Well if you're set on playing the hero, here's a plan,' he said. 'In my line I know the companies that ship goods to the army. Stay with me in New York a while, I'll see if I can find you a job with one of them. They tag along pretty close behind the army but usually out of killing range. That way if the Union starts south again you can catch a tow.'

It was a way forward at least. They chinked glasses. Shire dug for a smile.

'You see,' Dan said, 'persistence has paid off already.'

Later, the rise and fall of the Atlantic rocked Shire to sleep and he dreamt he was flying. Waves of high wooded hills colored bright red and yellow blurred beneath him. He floated down to a white weatherboard church with a tapering metal spire. Beneath it was a round hole that could have been made just to allow him to fly inside. The congregation was nothing but soldiers, blue on the left, grey on the right. With their backs to him and their hats under their arms, they were chanting the Lord's Prayer. At the altar his father was presenting the bride to the groom. Shire screamed but no one turned to hear what he had to say.

PART II

New York – November 1862

Shire walked north along Broadway. It was his fourth day in New York and well into the afternoon. As with all the previous days, he had nothing to do. Dan had no time to be with him in the day, and had repeatedly advised him to stay in their shared hotel room, and certainly not to go any further than the area around Battery Park. 'New York,' he said, 'was about as safe as the ninth plane of hell, most of the police having been promoted to the eighth.'

But Shire needed to get on. He'd lost the sense of advancement he'd felt each day on the *Scotia*, the breeze in his face that had been a measure of his progress towards Clara. Sitting in the hotel would get him nowhere.

Though the pavement was wide, he found himself sidestepping those more assured of their destination than he was. It was bright and, he assumed, warm for New York in November; certainly warmer than you'd expect at home. The buildings were high; often four or five stories, and kept a full half of Broadway in shadow. He crossed to the side in the sun.

The street opened onto a small park which fronted City Hall. Shire backed against some railings to stop and watch. From here a number of streetcars, some horse-drawn and some steam, started and travelled away north. Hooves competed with the hiss of the engines. Everybody wanted to get somewhere in a hurry. People spilled from the cars and busied up and down the wide, white steps of City Hall. He felt conspicuous just standing still.

Dan had taken him no further than the hotel bar. He seemed more interested in the results of his report on Bulloch than in finding Shire a job that would take him south. 'They say they know Bulloch's there most of the time. They want to know who else comes and goes, from which shipbuilders and which finance houses. They gave me two hundred dollars to use the best way I see fit next time I'm there.'

Two hundred more people Dan could get beaten-up, thought Shire.

'They're interested in how many blockade runners Trenholm is buying as well as any navy ships commissioned. He's a rich man they tell me. Had offices here in New York before the war started.'

Shire had a hangover to contend with each and every day. It made him edgy and lowered his mood. In the daytime Battery Park commanded a great view of the ships that entered or left the Hudson, but they served only to depress him further. They were moving and he was not, some heading back east, towards home. And every evening, at some point, Dan would shake his head at what Shire hoped to do. It had begun to rub off on him. New York was no more than a new starting point, and it was time he got started.

He reached inside his shirt to touch his mother's ring. He was momentarily shocked to not find it before he remembered he'd hidden it in a tear in his mattress at the hotel along with his two earned dollars from Liverpool. He'd kept the rest of his money with him, splitting his risks. Or had he doubled them? It felt safe enough just here, there were plenty of policemen. He bravely accosted a passer-by, a man in a tired suit who didn't appear to be in such a hurry as everyone else. Shire asked him if there were any army offices close by.

'There's a recruiting office up on 3rd and 46th. Might be there's one closer but that's the only one I know. You can get the car as far as 34th and walk from there.'

I generally find the next thing to do is right in front of you. Aaron had usually meant the next pile of horse shit, the next bridle to hang up or bit to clean. But Shire felt it applied here as well. He'd have to cut out on his own sometime. He asked where he should get on the streetcar and was directed across the park. He found one waiting. Inside were rows of wooden seats, room for two people each side of the aisle. He slid into a place by the window. As they moved off, he tried to keep his bearings by reading the street names chiseled high into the stone of the corner buildings. They left Park Row and then started down Centre Street. This carriage was horse-drawn at walking pace, so did little to speed Shire's journey, but he reasoned he'd bought some safety as well for his twenty cents. Dan had told him about the poorer wards, and in Shire's sketchy mental map of New York these were somewhere to the east of Broadway. They were no-go areas even for the police, Dan said; run by gangs that had enjoyed a free rein on the lower east side for decades. It was supposed to be better uptown.

The route the streetcar had taken away from City Hall meant that Shire was already a few blocks east of Broadway, running north. Centre Street seemed smart enough, but as he looked away down the roads that went further east, he could see it was darker; the buildings appeared to lean in towards each other. The fetid smell reminded him of the one time he'd travelled with Father to London. He was glad to be in the car.

'Blocks' had entered Shire's vernacular. He didn't much care for them. Instinctively he distrusted anything so geometrical, so planned. It looked unnatural to the eye. He much preferred the gently winding lanes and byways of Bedfordshire. In fact, he didn't much care for New York at all. No one seemed at home. They were either immigrants waiting to move on or businessmen on the make. He imagined that those who lived here must do so grudgingly, too poor or too hopeless to strike out. The grand buildings, statues and wide streets, couldn't mask a city uneasy with itself: desperate and disparate Europe rubbing up against hard American vested interest and coming off second best. Maybe there was a better America beyond the Hudson.

The journey took much longer than he'd expected. Eventually, the car trundled up Lexington and turned east on 34th Street where he got off. Here was another entirely new place for him to assess. His hotel and Battery Park suddenly acquired a better aspect as somewhere he at least knew. He asked his way again and was pointed to 3rd Avenue. From there it was just a matter of counting off the blocks. It was airier here. The avenue was as wide as Broadway but the buildings were lower. Aside from a couple of clumps of men at the street corners, it was less crowded than anywhere he'd been since he'd arrived. What carriages rumbled by were able to move at a trot.

At 46th Street the place was easy to find, 'U.S Army Recruiting Office' proclaimed in big black letters over a door and barred window-front. Inside was a clean room, mostly empty with a low bench under the window. The smell was polished too, not dissimilar to a tack room. Two men sat at either end of the bench, hats in hands, waiting. One wore shoes, the other what might once have been shoes. On a large poster opposite the entrance the ubiquitous American eagle, with its wings spread above tall bold print, invited 'Good Men' to join the 165th New York Volunteer Infantry. Beside it was an open hatch with a closed wooden door on the other side. Leaning through the hatch, and largely filling it, was a bull of a sergeant.

'What have we here then?' The accent was Irish. He held a hand up, palm out. 'Now stop. Don't tell me. I like to guess how many days.'

'How many days?'

'Off the boat. I can always tell a fresh one. And not a bad boat either, I'm thinkin'. God knows we'll need t' feed up those two poor souls.' He nodded towards the bench. 'And you have a good set of clothes, so you've not been here long enough to fall on hard times.'

Shire made to speak, but the hand was back up. 'Not a word!' There was a short silence during which Shire could hear a strange arrhythmic tapping in the back office.

'Foive.'

'Sorry?'

'Foive days since you landed?'

'No.'

'Damn. How many?'

'Four.'

'Bloody close though, so I was. Sorry, but I have to entertain myself somehow in this wee office. So you'll be wanting the forms. I assume you can write? You look bright enough.'

'Forms for what?'

'Oh. Maybe not so bright. To join the 165th.'

'No,' said Shire. 'I just have a question.' He scratched the back of his head. 'If I wanted to pass through the lines, to the South I mean, who do I need to get permission from?'

The sergeant looked dismayed. 'We're all wanting to go south, me lad. That's the whole point. *On to Richmond* an' all. Best thing you could do is lend a hand with some of the pushing as, generally speaking, Jeff' Davis is not taking visitors just now.' He slid some forms and a pencil across the counter.

'Sign up and I'll guarantee you'll be heading south before the month's out. Couldn't say where exactly. Washington, Virginia, might be New Orleans.'

'Might be six foot south,' someone called from behind the sergeant.

'Quiet... South one way or the other. I'd like to head that way meself but they keep me cooped up in here.' He appeared genuinely regretful.

Shire was wondering how best to pursue his question when a soldier from the office pressed a note into the sergeant's hand, then saved him the trouble of reading it. 'Telegraph from Downtown, sir. Marked urgent. Says there are gangs massed around 2nd and 44th and we should be ready. They're sending help.'

'More than one gang?' said the sergeant. 'Bad news when they get together. We'd best close up for the day. You boys will need to stay here too.'

Before Shire could object, he heard shouting outside. One of the recruits turned and knelt on the bench to look out of the window. He jumped back as it shattered, an iron bar crashing through and then wrenched back.

The sergeant charged from the office towards the outside door, but too late. It burst open and two men rushed in. Without breaking stride he punched one full in the face to send him reeling back outside, then grabbed the other by the hair and threw him after the first. He reached to close the door and shouted to his men. 'Find the bloody pistol!'

Shire, with no way out, backed towards the far end of the room. More men pressed in and the sergeant was forced back. He readied to throw another punch but was clubbed on the side of the head and went down. A screaming mob surged in, some made for the office door and others for the hatch. A soldier raised a pistol but was overwhelmed before he could fire. From the office came hurried cries of desperation, even supplication, silenced by cruel bone-breaking blows. The man who'd felled the sergeant returned to the front room, eyes bright with violence, and pushed his way towards Shire and the recruits.

'Are yer soldiers yet?' he screamed at them and raised a truncheon over them. 'Are yer?'

'No,' answered one of the men and was struck across his raised arms.

'Then you're lucky boys.' The accent was Irish too. 'But soon enough we'll all be soldiers whether we want to or not, won't we, sent to fight other poor boys and to free the niggers. Only you don't look quite the poor boy.' He was looking straight at Shire.

'Michael!' A younger man grabbed Michael's arm. 'We'll not be having time for introductions. They'll be coming soon enough.'

'Alright, Thomas.' He turned back to Shire and the would-be recruits. 'You boys get yourselves outside. This office is about to close.'

As Shire edged his way towards the door he saw men heaping papers in the back office. A telegraph machine was smashed to pieces. The sergeant and the soldiers, either unconscious or submissive, were dragged out through the door. Shire pressed his own way outside.

132

The street had transformed. It was packed in every direction with a hateful, screaming mob. Shire was forced out into the road by the weight of men. Everyone around him carried a weapon, some sticks or spades, but others with knives or drawn sabers. A few had muskets. Amid the chaos he registered that many of the men had green and white hooped socks worn outside their trousers. He could gain no control over which way he was carried, and concentrated instead on not getting hurt. He'd lost track of the two recruits. He was just one of the mob. Smoke began to pour out of the office door and window. When it was joined by flame the crowd recoiled further into the road. He heard more glass shatter and saw the next building along was also ablaze.

The cries and shouts about him were disorientating, every face a mask of anger. He turned around again and again, tried to suppress his panic and think which way to go. Did it matter as long as it was away from here? He began squeezing himself down the street, back the way he'd come only a few minutes before. He made slow headway, using his strength carefully so as not to antagonize anyone with a weapon. Then he was almost free, finding himself on the edge of the throng with clear road to the south. The crowd was in a line right across the street, facing that way and jeering. Shire saw why. The police were advancing up Third Avenue.

They were precious few compared to the mob but they were organized. They spread out. In front was a spaced line on foot. The nearest smiled and tapped their truncheons on their palms. Behind them was a rank of mounted police, struggling to hold their horses in check. No more than fifty in total, but determined-looking men. The captains were barking orders and had their pistols drawn. The crowd yelled abuse and stood its ground as the police began to advance steadily from a hundred paces away.

Shire had a wild thought to run into their lines, but watched as a looter backed out of one of the shops close to the police. Two officers set about the man with their long sticks and left him a twitching, crumpled mess on the sidewalk. In desperation, Shire turned and tried to tunnel back amongst the crowd, but it was as solid as a brick wall. He had to face the police again. They were getting closer. The crowd screamed at them from the road and from the windows and roofs of ransacked shops and houses. He looked for a way of escape. Beside him he recognized the smaller gang member from the army office, the one called Thomas. He held a short iron bar at head height while inviting the police to come on. He seemed to recognize Shire. 'This enough like fighting for yer?' He thumped Shire hard on the back.

There was a musket shot from somewhere behind, possibly one of the second floor windows. Shire couldn't tell. It galvanized the police. A sharp order and the horses stepped to the front and charged. The officers fired pistols into the crowd. Close by Shire, a man clutched at his neck and fell forward, blood pouring through his fingers. The mob broke, trampling each other in panic, but there was no space or time for the front row to get away. Shire faced a horse that bore down on him. At the last second he threw himself to his right only to find someone fully in his way. He knocked them to the ground. The horse passed over. They both scrambled up. It was Thomas.

The foot police reached the crowd. They grabbed anyone they could from the line and set into them with unrestrained ferocity, clubbing them more about the head than the body. Shire was pulled towards the side of the street.

'C'mon!'

He'd almost made it to the sidewalk when he was struck hard across the back of his neck and went down on his knees. He raised his hands expecting further blows, but Thomas had stayed with him and brandished his iron bar at the policeman, who was persuaded to find an easier victim elsewhere. Shire was lifted to his feet, bundled onto the sidewalk and through a door. He was dazed and in pain.

'Keep moving,' said Thomas. 'They'll be into these houses once they get more men. We'll get out the back and away.'

They tumbled through a series of halls and rooms in a private house. Others escaped alongside them. A door, a gate and they were in a narrow alleyway. Shire followed without question, wishing to God he'd heeded Dan's advice. The noise of the riot subsided behind them, but the smell of burning stayed in the air. They stopped, breathless. Shire rubbed his neck.

'Thomas.' Thomas offered his hand.

'Shire. Thanks for saving me.' The strong handshake momentarily steadied Shire's hand.

'I didn't catch the bastard. But I should be thankin' you. That bloody giant horse was going to knock me clean out of Manhattan. Did you say *Shire*?'

'Yes.'

'Odd name, but I like it. Uncommon names tend to go well round here. Fresh off the boat, I see, so you'd better stick with me a bit 'til we get clear. English is it?'

Shire nodded, and then wished he hadn't. He rubbed his neck again.

'Shame. But one good turn an' all. I'll be heading back to downtown. That suit you?'

'It does.'

Anywhere but here would suit him.

'Good. It'll mean crossing behind those blue bastards.' Thomas pulled his trousers out of his socks to hide the green and white stripes. The bar found a home inside his jacket. 'Try not to nurse your neck. You'll attract attention.'

He had just seen a man shot and been charged by police horses, but there was no time to think. As the light began to leave New York, Shire followed one step behind Thomas, trying again to follow the street names. They crossed over Broadway and down 7th Avenue, but Thomas used the smaller alleys to avoid the police, who guarded the junctions, never in groups fewer than ten or more. He realized they were heading back east when they crossed Broadway again at Union Square. Thomas told him they were in

The Bowery. Dan had mentioned this area; it belonged to the gangs. Shire stuck close, too afraid to head off on his own.

Thomas seemed more relaxed on his own ground. To Shire it was another world which in the growing darkness tightened around him. The alleys were all narrow, unpaved, no more than stinking dirt and mud. The buildings on either side were ramshackle, practically derelict. Women and children shouted and swore from the doors and windows. He soon lost any sense of the way back. It was as if he was walking along a foul drain. It coated the roof of his mouth and the back of his throat. He wanted to stop and retch but needed to follow Thomas.

'No police,' said Thomas. 'This is home turf.' As he spoke the alley ended and they stepped out into an open junction where five roads angled together, the buildings all narrowing to the joins. In the center, children fed a great, untidy fire. 'Welcome to Five Points.'

Shire swallowed dryly. The name had notoriety beyond New York. Something else burnt above and behind the fire. As they got closer he felt a sick horror rise through him. A man, he'd been a black man, hung from a lamppost, only a few feet off the ground. He was burning.

'Don't mind him,' said Thomas. 'Sure we had a party to get us going before we went up town.'

'What did he do?'

'He didn't do nothin'. Didn't get away is all. The women, they like to burn them once they're up there. I've no idea why.'

By the firelight, Shire could see beneath the low-hanging corpse were three women. He should look away. One of them reached up and stabbed into the dead man's leg, then carefully poured oil into the wound. She touched it with a taper, as if lighting a candle in church.

'Why would anyone do this?' Shire wasn't sure if he'd spoken out loud.

'Come on,' said Thomas, as if maybe he'd seen it afresh himself. 'We don't need to stay out here.'

Before Thomas took a step there was a shout.

'Thomas!'

Shire jumped.

It was Michael, the leader from the army office. He walked towards them, bloodied and smiling. 'That was a fine fight, was it not? One less army office to take our boys away to the niggers' war. Did we lose anyone?'

'Some went down in the charge. I don't know if they were ours.'

'But it was us who burnt the army office. So it's our glory. It was a tight job getting back. The police may want to make a show.' Michael looked at Shire. 'Is he wanting to sign up with us now then? English is he?'

'Aye,' said Thomas.

'Has he started telling you what to do yet?'

'He doesn't say much at all.'

Michael stepped uncomfortably close to Shire. 'A convert. He looks fit and well. Have you decided against soldiering, boy?'

'It wasn't soldiering I was planning, sir.'

'Sir, is it? We'll not be needing your *sirs* here.' He edged closer, looked Shire coldly in the eyes. 'So what was you doin' there? Mistaken it for a brothel maybe, what with it full of whore Irish soldiers who've lost their way?'

'I was looking for a way south.' Shire used his farm accent. 'I have business there.'

'Do you now? Well let's just check if we have some business *here*, shall we?' He grabbed Shire by the front of his jacket.

'Can we not leave him be?' begged Thomas. 'I'd be lying on that road if he'd not saved me.'

Michael kept his eyes on Shire. 'You've a soft heart, Thomas.' Tobacco juice spittled Shire's face. 'If he's fresh off the boat he won't mind paying an entrance fee.' He padded Shire for a purse.

Shire tried to close his jacket. With no change in expression Michael simply took one step back, still holding Shire with his left arm, and clubbed him with a swinging right fist to the side of his head. Shire would have hit the ground hard if Michael had not held onto him. His head was nothing but light and pain. He vaguely felt the purse taken from him and then he dropped to the floor.

'That'll do then,' Michael said, assessing the take.

'Michael, please? It's enough.'

Shire struggled for vision. Looking up, the first thing he saw was the knife gripped in Michael's hand.

'Don't you get it? He's the same. The same bloody English as them, as Lincoln or Lee. They start a bloody war and expect us to die in it. And for what? For their bloody ideals. Free the darkies, keep the darkies? It's not our fight. And this fool looks like he might be full of fuckin' principles given half a chance.' He jabbed a booted foot under Shire's ribs and swapped the knife into his right hand.

'Michael!' A new voice. 'Michael. The police are crowding up on Chatham, a bundle of 'em. They're coming this way.'

'You've seen them?'

'I've just run from there.'

'C'mon then. We'll teach them not to bring their uniforms in here.'

Shire heard their footsteps race away. He sat up carefully with his back to a wall and nursed his ribs. The fire at the center of the Five Points reached up into the cold sky. Blood came away when he felt above his ear. He was alone, all the inhabitants of Five Points, even the women and children, gone to battle the police. The chill air turned the sweat cold on his skin. 'Use what strength you can, Shire boy.' Somehow it was easier to speak than to think: to pretend to be outside of himself. 'Or they'll never be any news of you to Clara or Father.'

He stood and started to stumble back in the direction Thomas had brought him. His legs were weak and his balance shot so he scraped his weight along the wall. There were some railings, they were easier to manage and he did better. Looking ahead, he saw his way would pass the hanging, burning corpse. The hands were bound behind the poor man's back, the noose cruelly up under the chin and beginning to cut through the skin. He edged closer. There were tins of oil on the ground amongst pools of fat that had dripped down to congeal on the cold pavement. If he was to hold onto the railing he would have to pass behind the body so close he must touch it. Praying for his lost balance and strength he got as close as he could bear, then pushed off to take a half-circle and gain the railings on the other side. Immediately he slipped in spilt oil and fell sprawling on the sidewalk amongst the tins and fat. Struggling, he rolled onto his back and found himself directly below the hanged man, looking up the length of his charred body. The rope creaked and the corpse slowly twisted, the clothes all burnt away. The tongue was a blackened spike between fully exposed teeth. As Shire lay there, a large gob of fat dripped down onto his right cheek. He twisted away as it burnt into his skin, the pain overwhelmed by the horror. He scrambled away on all fours, until he was again clutching at the railings where he vomited through the bars.

He had no idea how long it took him to stagger to Worth Street. The street lamps were lit here. After a few blocks, and with a burst of relief, he discovered he'd reached Broadway and knew his way home. He emerged at City Park, to see police guarding City Hall. No one came to help him and he kept on. After what felt an age, he made it to Battery Park and to his hotel. They tried to turn him away, but he asked for Dan who was called down.

'Sweet mother of God, what in hell happened to you?'

When Shire woke and stirred, he found Dan had pulled back the curtains and was sat looking out.

'Well, good morning,' Dan said, but didn't turn to look at Shire. 'It's another fine autumn day, though you might want to stay closer to home on this one.'

Shire sat up, worked on a neck that was stiff as new leather. There was a small dressing on his burnt cheek and a scab on the cut over his ear. His clothes of yesterday were in a pile next to the bed. Washed or not, he'd never want to wear them again; though there was no money to replace them.

'I'm sorry, Dan,' he said.

'Where did you get to?'

'A recruiting office on 3rd and 46th. It was attacked.'

'You were there? That's where I heard it all kicked off. Were you joining up?'

'No. No. I was just... researching.'

'Well, you picked a hell of a day for it. Some numbers dead.'

'In the office? There was a sergeant.'

'I don't know. Let me get you some coffee.'

While Dan was out of the room, Shire retrieved his mother's ring from the mattress and held it in his palm. The rose gold sparkled in the light through the window. It was all he had left. He would have to sell it to get the fare home. Or did he still have a little inherited stubbornness left to spend? He slipped it over his head as Dan returned with eggs as well as coffee. The coffee was strong. He'd have preferred tea. It woke him up at least.

Dan was gazing out of the window again.

'Dan,' said Shire. 'I've lost all my money. I shouldn't have taken it.'

'Well, truth be told, you're as likely to have it stolen in here as out there. I keep mine with me.'

Shire was quiet for a while, then said. 'I suppose I'll have to join up. I can't see what else to do. I don't want to stay in New York.'

Dan said nothing.

'Are you alright, Dan?'

'I'm sorry,' he gave his attention to Shire at last. 'Truth is we both had kinda big days yesterday. Some mail reached me from home, from Ohio to the office here. I've been drafted.'

'What?' He'd read about the draft in the papers.

'Drafted. They passed some law to raise the army numbers

and tried it out back home. It's what they're afraid of happening here. Because I'm from Ohio my name was in the hat. Looks like I'm gonna get going south before you do. Thing is, I'm not that keen.' His gaze wandered back outside.

'But you can pay your way out, right? Exempt yourself?'

'I could. Don't seem too manly though, does it?'

'Doesn't your work count for you? You help by getting the arms, surely?'

'Perhaps.'

Shire slowly turned over their mutual sad state of affairs. 'Where would you join up? Here?'

'No. Back in Ohio.'

'The Western Army?'

'Likely, yes. But some Ohio regiments come east. Some stay out west. Why?'

Aaron's old advice came to Shire once more: *I generally find the next thing to do is right in front of you.* Sometimes, it seemed as if he'd brought the blacksmith along with him.

He swung his legs out of bed and winced at the pain in his ribs. 'I'm broke and need to go south, so in all likelihood I'll join up. You're drafted but don't want to join. What you need is a substitute. That's allowed, isn't it?'

'Shire, you don't know what you're saying. I don't want you dying for me.'

'But I'm going to join anyway. This way, I can save you the trouble and start out west where I may get south all the quicker.'

He waited for Dan to catch up.

'You really want to do this?'

'I think so. I know I want to get out of New York.'

'I'd have to pay you the exemption. I won't do it otherwise.'

'I'll need paying,' said Shire. 'Otherwise I don't have the fare to Ohio.'

Ridgmont – December 1862

Matlock stepped into The Drover's Rest and closed the door. The smoke hung in distinct sedimentary layers, heavy enough that it was barely disturbed by his arrival. Not half the lamps were lit. They glowed dimly into the haze, like lightships in a fog.

Matlock saw Ocks, alone as expected, at a table set into a stone alcove at the back of the room. Though it was December, this was the first inn Matlock had visited all year. It wasn't the most discreet or pleasant place for this evening's business, but it would work better than a summons to his office. Ocks would feel more comfortable on his own ground. Tonight Matlock would play nearer the friend than the master, uncomfortable though that was. With a few days yet until Christmas, the place was quiet.

As he approached, Ocks sat up, as solid as the wall behind him. He had an untidy week's growth of whiskers, flecked grey in places.

'Why, Mr Matlock. Have you lost your way?'

'Morally perhaps. At least my father would think so to find me in an ale house for no good reason. May I join you?'

Ocks opened a scarred and calloused hand, inviting Matlock to sit opposite. 'Do you have a bad reason?'

Matlock laid aside his coat and ordered ale for them both. Ocks was affable enough, dispatching his drink in anticipation of another. For a while they discussed nothing more than minor matters on the estate. Matlock sipped at his ale and refilled Ocks' tankard. After he ordered a second jug, and Ocks was tamping tobacco into his pipe, he felt the time was ripe. There was only so much amiability he could stand. Though they were alone at this end of the room, he lowered his voice. 'There was something more I wanted to discuss.'

'I didn't doubt it.' Ocks said around his pipe as he sucked it alight.

'I've been thinking it may be time you moved on. You've never looked to be a favorite here. That's not been your job. But the business with Grace has hardened opinion against you.'

If Ocks was surprised he didn't show it. 'Are these my marching orders then? Not quite your way to let a man go over a drink.'

'Don't you feel it? Even with Shire leaving the night before Grace was found, people are more inclined to think ill of you than of him.'

Ocks smiled and blew out a stream of smoke. 'When you've had Russian guns and cannon blazing at you in the Crimea, the gossip don't sting too much.' He put his pipe back in. 'Why don't you tell me what it is you want?'

What Matlock wanted was the result of reading two newly arrived letters, neither of them addressed to him. The first was from Shire to his father. Following Abel's death, there being no family, Matlock had insisted on managing Abel's estate himself. Any letters therefore came to him first. This one told of Shire's plans to travel to Ohio and join the Union army. The boy's tenacity was concerning. The second letter was from Clara to the duke. It was an easy matter to read it and reseal it. Her letter had been delayed by the blockade, so announced her plans to wed in November. She'd have been married for several weeks already.

Ocks didn't need to know everything. Matlock gave him a half-story: how Taylor was the father of Grace's child, but not that they had secretly married. Neither did he think that Ocks had any reason to know of the more recent wedding. The duke was due back on Christmas Eve. The wedding news would out then. He needed to set Ocks on his way, '...and now the fool has it in his mind to find Clara and tell her.'

He stopped speaking as more beer arrived. When they were alone again it was Ocks that picked up the thread. 'And that would put paid to the match. And leave the duke, and perhaps you, a little hard up.'

He was taken aback at Ocks' precision, but kept his face relaxed. Ocks might know that the estate relied on American revenues, but surely not Matlock's own entanglements? Nobody knew. He tried to deflect the conversation away from himself. 'It's the duke's reputation that concerns me.'

'Tosh and nonsense,' scoffed Ocks. 'The nobility knocks out bastards more often than family. You of all people should know that. And so what if the duke has to sell off some family silver to balance the books? He's plenty to spare. No, I can see clearly where the troubles would come home to roost. Especially as you kept this from him while he packed his daughter off over the ocean — your whispers in his ear.'

There was no profit in denying it. Matlock leant back. 'The question remains, what should we do about it?'

A cheer went up from a game of cards the other side of the bar.

'We? How do you wrap me into your muddle?'

'Like it or not, people are thinking you had a hand in Grace's death. That maybe you pushed her the last yard.' Ocks' face soured and Matlock held up a hand. 'But there is a different way to see this. An opportunity for you.'

'Paint this opportunity for me then.'

'The war in America looks set to run a while yet. Men with fighting experience are needed. You miss the army, am I right? But war aside, there's land for the taking in the west. I could find a sum to help. And if not a pioneer, I'm sure Taylor will need an overseer on his estate or for one of his other concerns. I have influence there... Take your pick.'

'And what is it exactly you want me to do?'

Matlock held his gaze for a while but looked away as he spoke. 'The boy is out of date. He doesn't know Grace is dead. He doesn't know his father is dead. Both may have a bearing. Catch up to him. Persuade him to another course. I have his letters to his father. He is travelling to Cleveland to join the Ohio infantry. Which regiment exactly you'll have to find out. The duke has interests in the North, too. A letter of introduction to the state governor should more than suffice if you need help.'

The inn's old wolfhound padded over and rested its head in Ocks' lap and he stroked it behind the ear. Matlock could see his proposal had struck a chord.

'I don't see how Grace's death or Abel's changes much. Shire in the army. Hah. That would be a sight. He's no fighter. Likely the war will do your work for you if he strays too near the front.'

'Maybe. But I'll not trust to that.'

'And how far should this persuasion go? I have no quarrel with Shire.'

'You have no quarrel with most of the hands you persuade here. But we need to be sure. He may have some evidence. Letters perhaps.' If Ocks discovered the wedding certificate once there, so be it. 'I'll pay better if we are sure.' It was lightly said — but hung in the air with the smoke.

'We'll have to see how we find things,' said Ocks.

'You'll go then? You'll need to go soon.'

'Let me sleep on it. Things here aren't quite as I'd have liked them to be.' Ocks was subdued, reflective, but then lent forward and his tone was harder. 'And you might want to keep a mind to yourself. Abel was well liked. It's no secret you visited him before he died. Perhaps you put him in as much melancholy as you did Grace when you told her to pack her bags.'

Matlock swallowed dryly and reached for his ale.

'Aye, she told me that much. Death has kept close behind you of late, Mr Matlock. I'll trust you right enough, but don't look to cross me. The boats sail both ways.'

Camp Cleveland, Ohio – December 1862

In the center of the square, under the American flag, a loose halyard slapped the pole, out of rhythm with the swirling wind. The gritty snow, sharp as sand, had taken up residence in the air and sucked the color from the scene. To Shire, the surrounding brown barrack huts, a tied bay mare, the blue uniforms, were all shaded towards grey. If ever the snow met the ground, it was soon collected into short-lived eddies and whipped back up to prickle his hands and face. He half closed his eyes against the sting, tried not to lick his cracked lips; it only made them colder. It still felt strange to be marching beneath that flag.

'Right face!' shouted Sergeant Bluffton.

The whole of Company B swiveled ninety degrees.

'Forward!'

Half the men – the 'ones' – stood still, while Shire – a heartbeat late – and the other designated 'twos', stepped forward and to the right of the man in front. The company was magically converted from two lines for battle into four lines of column.

'March!'

Step off with the left leg. Keep your distance constant to the man in front. Don't give Bluffton any excuse. Shire could feel the shape of his scar. The freezing wind defined it for him. The rest of his face was raw, a dull ache under the skin, but the scar itself felt wet. He recalled a kiss from his mother in some other life, long ago.

Could he call it a scar yet? Had it finished healing? At first the burn had wept a clear but constant discharge. But by the time he'd travelled with Dan from New York to his parents' home in Medina, Ohio, it had crusted red and yellow. He'd tried not to pick at it but it itched, inside and out, keeping fresh the memory of the burnt man, twisting slowly above him. The scab had only yesterday come away completely, leaving a glassy red tear, the size of his thumbprint.

'Left wheel – march!'

Don't try to anticipate; Sergeant Bluffton mixes up the orders. This left wheel took them nonsensically at a barrack hut before a quick right wheel set them straight again. To think at all was ill-advised. Just drill until your body did whatever Bluffton said. March, turn, stop, present arms, march again and try to forget it was Christmas Eve.

A lone, lanky soldier was standing outside the commissary store, watching them. What was he about? Bluffton halted the men. The bay mare, tied outside the officers' mess, defecated wetly, steamy warmth wasting into the air.

'Fix bayonets!'

Shire pulled his bayonet from the sheath attached to his belt. His numb fingers vaguely registered the deeper cold of the barrel as he slipped the bayonet ring into place. Next to him Ned's older hands were slower still.

'Trail arms!'

Ned was last to get into position, but earned nothing more than a glare from Bluffton. He was supposed to look out for Shire, so Dan had said. Maybe Dan had intended it the other way around. It felt like that sometimes, though Ned had at least a dozen years on him. But it was good to have one friend at least, even if he was a bit broken.

'Shoulder arms!'

Dan had returned to New York the same day Shire had left for the army. Parting was almost like walking away from home again. Dan had been his only friend this side of the Atlantic, and would himself be back in Liverpool soon enough. Everyone who mattered was so far away. He imagined his friends at Ridgmont; the church with the nativity set out, the farm with the horses all stalled, the school empty for Christmas – Father alone at home.

No letters. He'd hoped one might have come through the

shipping line, having left Dan's address with them for forwarding. It was hard sometimes to feel the same impetus with which he'd set out to keep his promise. He'd tried not to let this show in his latest letter home. And he'd written that he'd enlisted for nine months, not for the three years which was the only option. The war couldn't last that long.

'Order arms!'

Three years. Fighting a war that wasn't his, to keep a promise made sitting in a tree when he was seven. He moved his rifle to his right hand and rested the butt beside his foot, holding the barrel lightly. A clatter of tin came from the kitchen hut, followed by some prize cursing. Bluffton scanned the line, daring anyone to so much as smile without his permission, then turned his back. Shire relaxed. At last he'd got through a drill without a mistake, despite his wandering mind. Perhaps that was the trick.

Someone behind kicked the butt of his rifle. Shire dropped it on the hard dirt. He heard laughter and spun round on a burst of anger. Cleves was wearing a stifled smile in his weasel face. Tom Muncie and Mason, both big men, stood either side of him. Mason made the slightest nod towards Cleves. Shire didn't need it – it was always bloody Cleves. When he turned back, Bluffton's face was barely an inch away, his brown beard almost up to his scowling eyes. Shire felt as if he was about to be mauled by some great bear. Though the bear would likely have had better breath.

'Why have they sent me this ass-backwards Englishman, who'd drop his piss-proud cock before breakfast if it wasn't so small?'

Spittle flecked Shire's cheeks and lip. He tried, but failed, not to flinch.

'Extra fatigue duty,' Bluffton spat. 'You must be getting good at digging latrine ditches. Let's see if you can hang onto a shovel better than a rifle.' The sergeant turned away.

More hours out in the cold. Shire picked up his rifle and wondered how many more weeks Cleves and Bluffton would keep this up.

The sergeant called over the soldier outside the commissary store. The tall man had no rifle and his uniform was too short, an inch of pale skin showed above his boots. He had an odd gait as he walked, rather than marched; his lower legs and forearms appearing to swing past the usual stopping point, as if a vital ligament was missing. He came to a stop, arms relaxed by his sides, slightly hunched as if he were sitting back on a fence rail.

'This one's from Kentucky,' said the sergeant to Company B. 'I don't know why we can't fill this company from Ohio, as it should be. And I don't know why this boy hasn't seen fit to join up with his own kith and kin. What I do know is I ain't got the time to teach him the drill. Stand to attention, boy.'

The Kentuckian, untidy dark hair under an ill-fitting cap, straightened himself; though to Shire's eye it wasn't a stance that came naturally to the man. He gained two or three more inches in the process, a proportion of which translated to his trousers and showed off more skin.

The sergeant looked down. 'You planning on turnin' heads with those pretty white legs?'

There was laughter in the ranks.

'Commissary store didn't have a fit, sir. Said they'd see what they could do.'

'You address me as *Sergeant*. Corporal Lyman!'

'Sergeant?'

Amazing how the corporal could strip any hint of energy or enthusiasm from a single word.

'This man will replace Rittman in your section.'

Rittman had deserted with his sign-up money a week ago; bounty jumping they called it.

'You're to teach him the Manual of Arms and the drill.'

Lyman's heavy sigh didn't carry past Shire. 'Yes, Sergeant.'

'And take him back to the commissary hut and get him some gaiters or longer socks. Our Kentucky boy might be feeling the Ohio cold.'

There was more laughter, tolerated by the sergeant. Shire smiled too. The new recruit was shown to the spare place in the section, immediately to Shire's right, still drawing amusement both on account of his height and trousers.

'Shoulder arms!'

He was keeping a neutral face, and Shire felt for him. But he was sick and tired of being the company's whipping boy. It was time for someone else to take a turn.

'Left face!'

The poor man was facing straight at him. Despite a nugget of guilt he couldn't quite escape, Shire broke into full-throated laughter along with the rest of Company B. He looked up at the hapless man, received a thin smile and a raised eyebrow. Only then did Shire realize the Kentuckian was facing the same way as everybody else.

Shire stepped in from the dark. The men in the closest bunks swore at him and told him to close the door. He welcomed the rank concoction of three dozen sweaty men. Anything to be inside where his hands wore the air like warmed gloves. He picked his way down the narrow space between the three-tiered bunks, squeezed past standing men and through their blown smoke, edged round those sat reading or writing. No one made it easy for him and no one had a pleasant word. He stepped over Cleves' leg as it predictably shot out to trip him and reached his bottom bunk at the far end. Someone's newspaper lay on his rucked-up blanket. He moved it to one side and sat down, held up his raw hands to inspect his blisters in the lamp-light.

'Hey, Shire,' said Corporal Lyman from above, 'would you mind going back out to take a shit for me?' Lyman's voice was as lazy as he was, never troubling itself to get up out of a low register. 'No point me getting frozen as well.'

Shire struggled to slip his coat off his stiff shoulders, then sat waiting for his hands to warm up so he could untie his muddy boots.

Ned was sitting on the middle bunk opposite, cleaning his own boots. He gave Shire a nod and jumped down. 'Give me your mug.' He took it and disappeared down the hut.

Tom Muncie was pointing his usual big smile at Shire, like a welcome home dog. There was no harm meant, but Shire picked up the paper rather than acknowledge him. *The Cleveland Leader* was a week old. In the second column there was a succession of headlines which anticipated the report below. *The Battle of Saturday, Rebel Works Almost Impregnable, Retreat a Military Necessity.* The battle, at somewhere called Fredericksburg in Virginia, had been a bad loss. There'd been papers in camp all week, but nobody had offered him one; he'd had to listen instead. At home, in their snug kitchen, he and Father had made a study of the war, *The Times* spread across the table. He knew General Grant had moved early in the year, steaming up the two great tributaries of the Ohio – the Tennessee and the Cumberland – to take much of middle and western Tennessee. But Eastern Tennessee – and Clara – were safely behind the Confederate Army. An army confident enough, under General Bragg, to drive deep into Kentucky as late as October. From his eavesdropping, he'd discovered many men had joined because they felt the need to defend the North, rather than fight their way south. Maybe the war would last three years.

'This paper's for sale, not for loan,' said Lyman, snatching the paper up to his bunk. 'Anyhow, it don't make encouraging reading for someone who can't hang on to a rifle.'

'And is my bunk for loan?' said Shire.

'It's the bottom bunk. Stands to reason we're gonna use it. 'Sides, you were out digging in the fresh air.'

'Looks like the Rebels were well dug-in if you read that report,' said Mason in his baritone from higher up.

There was a small commotion down the hut as two washer women entered and men handed over their dirty clothes. Shire fingered his own flannel shirt, stiff with mud, but was too exhausted to undress. Besides, who was there to dress well for tomorrow? Only Bluffton.

Ned returned and handed Shire his tin mug, half-filled with coffee, and sat down next to him. 'See that fella?' he said, for Shire's ears only. He motioned with his thumb at the next top bunk, where a pair of large feet in woolen socks extended well off the end. 'The new boy, from Kentucky. Reckon he won't stay longer than Rittman. He'll bounty jump for sure. Why else would he join an Ohio regiment? Probably already jumped in Kentucky. Man could get rich on that trade.'

'Only if he doesn't get shot for desertion,' said Shire.

'He don't say much. I'll bet you fifty cents he's gone before New Year.'

Ned made no move to return to his own bed and Shire struggled for something to say. Before he'd introduced them, Dan had told Shire how Ned had lost his farm in the spring, adjacent to Dan's own family, after Ned's wife and child had died of cholera. The farm belonged to his father-in-law who'd taken it back. It seemed a mean-spirited thing to do. So Ned was driven by necessity just like he was.

'You alright?' asked Ned, leaning a few inches closer than Shire was comfortable with.

'Thinking of home. Christmas... you know?'

Ned looked older than Dan had claimed. Maybe a year ago he'd have looked five years younger. His eyes seemed to look out at a world he was afraid of.

'Yeah... I'm trying not to think on it myself. Though I expect the colonel will have us out singing carols in a blizzard tomorrow.'

Shire's plan to become a substitute had gone awry. Dan's employer won him an exemption on the basis that he was helping to supply arms. So Shire had gone along with Ned and signed up as a straight volunteer. The sign-up money was three hundred dollars.

Ned leant closer. 'You got that money sewed up tight? I don't trust that quiet boy.'

153

Shire said he had. He'd sewn half the money into the jacket lining of his new uniform, though he suspected probably half the company had done the same. He'd put the other half in the Phoenix Bank in Medina before coming on to Camp Cleveland with Ned.

A drummer set to practicing at the other end of the hut, working through the signals until someone snapped and cursed him quiet.

Mason leant out over the top bunk to talk down to Lyman. 'I think Burnside will go after getting kicked out of Fredericksburg.'

'Probably,' said Lyman. 'Seems to be the way of it. New general, lost battle, fired general. Lincoln don't suffer fools.'

'Well I wish he saw them comin' more clearly. Perhaps we'll be shipped east to help out.'

Shire found he was rubbing his scar. If they went back east, he might as well have signed up in New York.

'Maybe,' said Lyman. 'No tellin' which way we're headed. But so long as there's a ready supply of fresh meat signin' up straight off the boat, I'm thinkin' we'll stay west. I don't know what business they had fightin' this late in the year. Armies didn't oughta fight in the winter. Reckon Shire's got until spring to learn to shoot straight.'

Stone's River – New Year's Eve 1862

Colonel Taylor Spencer-Ridgmont worried that he might never get into the war as the last day of 1862 ebbed away. The guns and muskets continued to crash and rattle in the cold air as they had all morning and on well into the afternoon. Battle wasn't as he'd imagined it: all neatly laid out in lines and squares on a summer's day, dotted with puffs of white smoke. Instead there was hardly any open ground and the fighting was hidden amongst the trees. Within them the lines extended for several miles, mostly to his right. The ground was nearly all flat, what gentle rises there were barely enough to give an advantage. Only the noise gave him a dubious orientation, an incessant roar that pervaded the woods, never dying altogether, but rising and falling like a winter storm. His pristine grey uniform was unsullied by any hint of battle, and he feared it might remain so.

For months on end the Hiwassee Volunteers had been held in reserve, away from the fighting and the glory. And today had been like his year in miniature: frustrating. They were moved to the left, again and again. This time they'd been asked to move with more urgency. The battle had become fluid, the Yankees rumored to be retreating steadily in an arc to the north and east, so that the ground his horse trod became ever more littered with the dead from both sides, sometimes alone, but often in rows, where they'd stood to fight. It was hard not to look at them. So many. The smell was of gunpowder and raw meat.

They were moving faster now, over a rare piece of open ground, his regiment strung out behind him. A staff officer reached him, saluted and pointed to a low ridge perhaps four hundred paces to his front and left. That was to be the brigade's objective when all the regiments were up. At last they would fight. He acknowledged the order and angled the regiment that way, still in column, quickening their pace. He looked either side for the other regiments of his brigade, but could only glimpse them back in the trees. Should he get in line of battle and wait for them to come up? No, not yet. Keep the lead.

The target was no more than a gentle rise with a litter of tall pines on top. It was occupied by a battery of Union artillery, firing into hidden units somewhere to his left. There was no Yankee infantry support that he could see. The battle was strung out, units out of line and exposed. If he moved quickly he could take those guns without waiting for the brigade.

He ordered the regiment into line and sent a dispatch of his intent to his brigade commander, begging a counter-order if one was needed. But he wouldn't wait for the reply – it was for form only. He should have been colonel of this regiment all along. Here was his chance to show why. Turning his horse he saw just three companies in line, the rest further back. 'Major!' he shouted to Jasper above a new wave of noise from the right, 'I'll take these companies forward. When the rest come up, you follow me to those guns. Is that clear?'

'We were to wait for the brigade, sir.'

The companies on hand were C, D and F. Ignoring Jasper, Taylor summoned their captains to him. Company C and D were from McMinn County, which had voted last year to stay in the Union. Company F was from Polk, many boys from close to Comrie, some even worked for him. Taylor made the only logical decision, 'Company C on the left and Company D on the right, in line abreast, will advance and take those guns. Company F will form to their rear and advance in support.' Why risk men that he would need after the war? 'Be quick now, while there's no infantry with those guns.'

Jasper, on foot, came to stand beside Taylor's horse. 'Can we at least wait for the rest of our own companies, Colonel?'

'Just do what I tell you, Major.'

The first two companies stepped out and accelerated to the double quick. Polk County fell in behind. Taylor rode to and fro in front of the line, sword raised, encouraging his two hundred men. They didn't love him, he knew that. But if he could give them a prize today, something for the flag and the regiment, perhaps they could start to get a reputation. And at this moment in his life, his reputation and that of his regiment was one and the same thing.

They were moving forward smartly enough but ahead was a corn field, abandoned and unpicked, decaying in the winter. Dry, brown stalks stood in rows across their way. It slowed them and made the line uneven. Taylor pressed his horse through, riding above the stalks. He saw that four of the six Yankee guns were being turned in their direction.

When they emerged from the corn stalks and stopped to dress the line, the men eyed the guns that now pointed at them. These troops had seen skirmishes up near Cumberland Gap, but had never come under cannon fire. Neither had Taylor, and despite the cold day, he felt dribbles of sweat run down his back. They started forward again. Straight away the cannon fired and the balls screamed overhead; all but one of which drove into the soft ground before them, spraying cold soil. Fifty paces more and they could charge home. He was close enough to see it was round shot being loaded again. The gunners were adjusting the elevation. His line would not escape unscathed this time. Why were the cannon not limbering up? Not racing to safety? They fired again. Three solid balls of metal ripped holes in the line, men disintegrating and their shattered, splintered bones blasted to wound those closest. Taylor's horse twisted beneath him and he wrestled with the reins, but he couldn't take his eyes from the carnage. Like a single, sentient animal the line wavered and then stopped. But the sergeants and lieutenants pressed them, beat them forward of the corpses and the dying. Taylor's insides were knotted. He couldn't breathe. He tore his eyes forward, only to see blue infantry running across the guns to form a line of defense below them. Not so many, maybe two companies. It must be now. He lifted his sword and ordered a volley. The range was long but he had other plans. They fired as companies, two blasts. The smoke was too thick for Taylor to gauge the effect. Regardless, he ordered a charge. Almost in relief, the men obeyed and for the first time, the regiment sent up the Rebel yell as they sprinted forward. He took off his wide hat to wave them on, the air cold as it blew on his sweat-soaked hair.

He yelled and screamed with his men. He sheathed his sword and took out his pistol. Thirty yards away the Yankees fired their volley and men around him fell like dumped sacks of grain, but not enough to break the charge and they rushed in. The blue coats rose to meet them and the all-embracing yell changed to an unholy mixture of profanities, cries of terror, effort and pain. Taylor sat amidst it like a god, viewing the mortals around him, somehow immune and detached. The momentum of the charge had carried them well up the rise. The Yankees were giving ground steadily and behind them the guns were limbering up to escape.

'On!' he shouted. 'On!'

His horse was shying and stamping, but he managed to move it forward with the men. He must get those guns. Those guns might get him a brigade. He fired two shots over the brawl and into the nearest team. An artilleryman snapped into an arc before falling. His line swayed back down the hill and suddenly Taylor found he was forward on his own men. Two Yankees came at him from the left. One, a boy, grabbed his bridle, the other lifted a bayonet. They were so close. Taylor hurried a shot in desperation and the bayonet fell away. Looking forward, he leant from his saddle to see the boy still holding his mount. He couldn't shoot with his horse's head in the way. He dug his spurs in hard and the horse reared, twisting to pull the bridle free. The boy backed away. As the horse righted itself Taylor took aim at his chest, but as he fired the boy tripped backwards so took the bullet in the face.

The grey line was edging forward again as the reserve company pressed up in support. Taylor's horse screamed as a bayonet was thrust into its flanks. He fought to control the animal as it reared in agony. Together they collapsed sideways, Taylor landing hard but clear of the writhing horse. Winded, he struggled to get his arms beneath him and discovered himself face to face with the boy. Only there was little face to see, just a mess of teeth and jaw. There was a desperate life in the eyes and the boy twitched and clawed at Taylor, clutched at his jacket. A sharp memory of Taylor's dying brother flashed for a split-second, fused with the image before him. There was something in the boy's hand: a knife? Finding his balance, Taylor beat at the bloody face and stole the weapon before scrambling backwards. The boy lay back, moving less, his dying strength spent, and Taylor was left gripping a bloodied drumstick.

'Away,' he said, quietly at first but then louder. 'Away! Fall back!' He sat there shouting, faces passing by him that he knew, from home – from Polk. They didn't understand. It wasn't his fault. He must get away. He stood and grabbed a sergeant. 'Back! Get the men back!'

Major Jasper was there. 'But, Colonel, we got 'em whipped. All the companies are up.'

Taylor struck him backhanded across the face. 'Damn you, I said retreat.'

It was easier said than done with the lines enmeshed. But the order spread and the grey soldiers backed away, the tired Yankees taking pot shots at them to hurry them on. The artillery was gone, and a few minutes later the blue soldiers left too, the rescue complete. So that when the next regiment in the brigade came up, they were able to claim the rise.

The Ohio River – January 1863

The band finished playing 'A Glory Gilds the Sacred Page', and the last note fell flat in the cold air, leaving in Shire a melancholy residue. The train, back at the station, whistled farewell. Moving in column towards the boat landing, Shire's thoughts were constrained by the rhythm of the march; short, pointless observations that led nowhere. How the rank in front were in crisp unison but his rank were out of step. How Tom Muncie's sheathed bayonet bounced on his thigh with each stride. How the colonel kept his horse's head up to match his own chin. Colonel Opdycke had spent some time ensuring that they were smart and well-ordered at the station, for what looked destined to be only a short march. Shire sensed the river up ahead, there was a muddy scent, a more honest constancy to the breeze.

Lyman's advice to the generals not to fight in winter was obviously being ignored. Back in Camp Cleveland, Shire had heard constant rumors of Rebel cavalry raids in Western Tennessee. Corporal Lyman had offered odds on which town the Rebels would show up at next, but the gamblers fared no better than the Union Command. News came through that General Sherman had failed down in Mississippi, and of a bigger battle, fought over New Year outside Murfreesboro in Tennessee. Stones River they were calling it. Shire had mentioned it in another letter to Father. He'd posted it yesterday, January 3rd, the day they'd marched from camp and off to war. Maybe their movement was brought on by that battle; no one could tell him. Only that they were to board a boat here at Cincinnati.

The band started up again but the regiment halted.

'I should've taken your bet,' Shire said to Ned. 'Tuck is still with us.' He didn't know if Tuck, quiet as usual in the rank behind, was aware he'd been so christened without his input.

'I got the time wrong is all,' said Ned. 'Easier for him to jump once we're out of Ohio. They were gettin' smart to it in camp.'

Shire had to admit some sympathy with Ned's prediction; Tuck only ever spoke if spoken to. On the crowded train from Cleveland, the man had somehow made his own space and kept himself to himself. If he did jump, they'd have learnt precious little about him. As it was, Shire had seen the company 'thin' through December, transfers and sickness adding to desertions. He'd overheard that the new regiment was barely six hundred men yesterday when they'd set out. Six hundred men had proved more than enough for the train, so early this morning, despite the cold air, he had been glad to tumble from the cramped passenger car that had rattled him across Ohio through the night.

The march resumed and soon the road emerged from the scrubby trees to a wide boat-landing on the riverbank. Ordinarily the sight of a four-storied river steamer would have drawn Shire's eye, but the Ohio River itself demanded his attention; it was at least a third of a mile to Kentucky on the other side. He'd seen nothing to compare back home. And this was merely a tributary of the great and distant Mississippi. There would be so much to tell Father when he went home.

Boarding by company was slow. As Shire's turn came to step up from Ohio, a sergeant yelled from the top of the crowded gangplank for the men to wait. When they did make it aboard, Ned led him to the uppermost deck. 'Might as well use any sun as shows itself.'

They found a place at the stern, backward of the two side-paddles. Shire dropped his pack and slumped down, his back instantly uncomfortable against the wooden balusters, the planking cold and hard through his trousers. He took his rolled blanket and pushed it behind him. The deck quickly filled up. Forward of him rose twin, black steam stacks, dark smoke billowing from their red thistle mouths. They brought to mind the steam train that took him to Liverpool. Ned sat down beside him.

'Are you homesick?' asked Shire.

Ned winced and Shire mentally kicked himself. 'Sorry, Ned... I wasn't thinking.'

'I know... What I miss ain't there no more. Anyhow you're a deal further from home than me. You ready for it?'

'At least we're moving south.'

'You think that's a good thing?'

The paddles started their first turn and they moved off into the current as if powered by a pair of waterfalls. They were noisy enough to mask the engine, which was relegated to a deep throb delivered through the wood. Around them men were talking, smiling; more content with the boat than the train. It spun on itself mid-river, for a moment drifting helplessly with no steerage. But as the bow came round, the paddles found their grip and the boat shot forward to manufacture a stronger breeze that made Shire twist on his cap. His boot was kicked hard.

'You're in my spot.'

Shire squinted up at Cleves. His pockmarked face wasn't a friendly sight from any angle.

'This ain't no theater,' said Ned, answering for Shire. 'There ain't no spots for nobody.'

'You talking for your English pet now? C'mon, Sir Shire.' Cleves kicked him harder, above the boot.

Shire had no thought to hit back. Only a sick weight in his gut.

'Tell you what,' said Cleves. 'I'll give you three shots at the State of Kentucky. If you hit it, you can stay. Even you couldn't miss a whole state.'

'It's out of range, don't you think?' was all Shire could manage.

Cleves snatched Shire's cap and hit him around the head as he struggled to get up.

'Why don't you get out of my range before I drop you in the Ohio.'

Shire collected his blanket-roll and gear. He awkwardly caught his cap which was thrown at him as he left.

Ned caught up to him. 'You're gonna' have to hit that son of a bitch.'

'What happened to his face? Was it a disease?' Perhaps there was a reason Cleves behaved like he did.

'Not disease. Burns. He used to work in the steel works in Cleveland. They laid him off, so he came out to Medina to work the farms. One hit'll do it. He ain't a big man. Corporal knows he's got it comin'.'

Shire had been beaten up either side of the Atlantic. He wasn't in a hurry to add to the collection. 'Guess I'm not the fighting type.'

'Well, forgive me if that's not a mite concernin' given our new profession.'

They found Mason, Lyman and Tom Muncie in the prow where it was quieter away from the paddles, the boat drawn along, it seemed, by no more than the suck of the river. Shire looked ahead. The water was lent a muddy green by the reflection of the trees, Ohio right, Kentucky left. A heron launched itself from a low branch, its feet hanging for a few beats and then raised up behind, gliding so low to the water that Shire expected to see wet lines drawn by the wingtips. Except for the chill – and Cleves – it was an idyllic way to drift towards war.

Such a big river. The sheer enormity of America was re-enforcing his unease. Travelling from New York by train had taken two long days. And though he'd crossed Ohio, all of Kentucky and Tennessee was still between him and Clara, not to mention the Confederate Army. He felt again the urge to open up to Ned. There was no one else and it might be a good time. What was stopping him? He wondered if Ned might tell the others. They'd have fun with that. The sun slipped behind the ridge ahead, the trees atop silhouetted, like a thin line of defenders. The real cold was coming on and Shire sat down and huddled inside his coat.

Beside him Ned slyly lifted a bottle of whiskey from his

backpack and dropped his voice. 'You don't mind do you, Corporal? I procured it from a boy on the train. It'll keep the chill off.'

'I don't mind so long as you're sharing,' said Lyman, laid out with his head resting on his blanket roll. 'Only keep a look out.'

'I... I must've met the same boy.' Tom Muncie, a wide smile in his round face, showed off an identical bottle.

Shire knew Tom to be a year or two older than himself, but they all treated him like a younger boy. Perhaps it was the red hair, just now trying to escape sideways from under Tom's cap, or maybe the freckles. Father might have said that Tom wasn't quite the full shilling.

'You want some, S... Shire?'

'No thanks, Tom. We're not supposed to.' Shire scanned the crowded deck. It was so cold though, he thought – and here was someone being friendly.

The first thing Shire became aware of was a constant, deep buzz. He rejected the notion of opening his eyes and instead stretched his dry mouth, feeling his jaw move on cold wood. Somewhere in the fug of his brain he concluded that his face must be pressed to the deck. He peeled it free and heard himself groan, then sat up, a numb hand across his eyes. He was scared to open them on what he anticipated would be bright sunlight, but when he edged the hand away, as if it might reveal the shining Angel Gabriel, he discovered only a flat, metal sky. The buzz revealed itself as the throb of the engine. He tried to make sense of this new world, in which emotion seemed to have been swapped for dumb pain. Kentucky and Ohio were sliding by either side of him, keeping pace with each other.

Around him on the deck were shapeless lumps of grey, the blankets' occupants betrayed by the odd escaping limb. Only Shire stirred. The boat took a gentle turn. Shire felt as if he hadn't turned with it. He needed to stand. Pushing off his blanket he struggled up like a new-born foal. Mercifully, the rail was close. He bent over it, failed to focus on the brown water far below, and retched, the puke dropping away and backwards into the Ohio.

He spat away the drool and, wishing he was unconscious again, found his canteen and fumbled with the stopper. The water was cool and he forced himself to swallow. Where was his jacket? Why would he have taken it off? He looked under his blanket and coat.

It wasn't there.

He shook what he took to be Ned, but got a curse from Lyman instead and tried another blanket. 'Ned. Ned wake up. I can't find my jacket. Do you have it?'

Ned propped himself up on his elbows. 'Now why would I want another jacket when I have my own?'

That didn't help. 'My money's sewed in it. Remember?' A desperate thought struck him and Shire put his hand into his shirt. He pulled out a cut leather cord. His mother's ring was gone.

His hangover instantly forgotten, he frantically searched amongst the sleeping men close by, but was rewarded with only groans and curses. 'I'm going to find Captain Yeomans.' He picked his way between the bodies.

'Hold on.' Ned followed him. 'Think about this. What's the captain gonna do? And besides, you should report it to Lyman first.'

Shire could think of nothing but his mother's ring. How could he tell Father he'd lost it. 'Lyman will do nothing but talk to the sergeant and he'll do nothing at all.'

'And you think the captain will?'

Shire dodged a thrown boot after treading on a sleeping arm. 'Watch where you're going, you English piss-pot!'

'Look, Ned,' said Shire, finding it hard to keep a lid on his anger, 'you don't have to come with me. I can fight my own battles.'

'I know,' said Ned. 'But Dan asked me to look out for you. An' I aim to.'

The captain was awake, sat with his back against the wheelhouse and wrapped in a blanket. He had both hands around a cup of coffee.

'Sir... Captain,' said Shire. He'd never addressed the captain before.

Ned gave up on trying to tug him away.

Yeomans sipped his coffee. 'What is it, Private?'

'I've been robbed, Captain. My jacket's gone. I lost money and valuables.'

'That's unfortunate.' Yeomans didn't appear overly concerned. 'D'you know who took it?'

'No, sir. It was taken while I was asleep.'

'Then there's nothing to be done.'

Colonel Opdycke rounded the corner of the wheelhouse, smart enough for a dress parade, his moustache looking as if he'd trimmed it before sun up. Yeomans struggled to his feet and pulled his braces over his shoulders. Shire and Ned stood to attention. While Opdycke waited for Yeomans to put himself in order, he looked Shire up and down. Shire had never been this close to the colonel before. He didn't think he'd ever seen eyes so intense, so impatient. He should be told about the theft. He'd do something.

'We'll be at Louisville within the hour, Captain. See that your men are ready to disembark. Why is this man not wearing a jacket?'

For half a second Shire held his tongue, but it was too much. 'I've been robbed, Colonel.'

'The colonel wasn't addressing you, Private,' snapped Yeomans.

'Robbed of a jacket?'

'Yes, Colonel. It contained money. And they took my mother's wedding ring. Gold, sir.'

'You're dealing with this, Captain?'

'Yes, sir. But what's to do even if we found it? One gold ring looks much like another.'

'How much money?' Opdycke addressed Shire.

'One hundred and fifty dollars. Half my sign up money, sir.'

'And you were fool enough to keep that amount on your person? You should have lodged it with the pay-sergeant.'

Most of the men had sewed it into the lining just like he had.

It wasn't his fault. 'The ring, sir, it's rose gold. It has a strong red color to it. We could tell it apart, sir.'

The boat eased into a bend. Shire's nausea returned and he took an involuntary step towards the colonel, caught his balance and staggered back.

'You have puke on your shirt, Private. Captain, this man has been drinking.'

Shire couldn't muster a denial. Surely that wasn't the most important thing.

'You.' The colonel turned on Ned. 'Have you been drinking too?'

Ned was as steady as if he was fitted to the deck. 'Oh no, sir. I don't touch the stuff since my wife and child passed away. It brings on too much emotion.'

Shire looked at Ned and wished he could lie so easily. He half believed Ned himself. 'But, Colonel –'

'Captain,' said Opdycke, 'have your entire company paraded on deck, jackets off, pockets turned out. Have the officers and sergeants search for this ring. I'll not have theft in my regiment.'

Shire sighed in gratitude.

'Deduct the cost of a new jacket from this man's pay. Have him stripped and drenched. This regiment will fight for God, not for the Devil.'

Louisville was close off the prow, spiked by a handful of church spires so that it might have been Bedford or Oxford but for the vast Ohio. A long row of warehouses sat ready and eager, close to the wharf. The steamer was abuzz on every deck with preparations to go ashore – except on the top foredeck, where, in front of Shire, Company B of the 125th Ohio stood in their flannel shirts, each man with his kit laid out piece by piece in front of him.

Shire would happily forego the money if only he could find the ring. He knew most every man in Company B was going to make him suffer for this; at least if he recovered the ring, there'd be a point to it.

The colonel was hovering nearby, so the captain was doing a thorough job, taking a personal interest. While the 1st lieutenant inspected the men lined up on starboard, Captain Yeomans led the inspection on the port side. He insisted Shire and Ned walk with him. The sergeants shook out knapsacks, emptied canteens, felt the lining of kepi caps. Shire had ample opportunity to suffer every man's disdain. He could see it in the tightness of their hands, in the sour set of their mouths. Each man looked as if he was thinking up trouble for Shire's future. Why, oh why, had he drunk the whiskey? Surely he'd have woken up, but for the whiskey. In front of the stern colonel, the captain had already tipped two bottles of 'Old Harmon' into the Ohio, collected three decks of cards and a set of dice.

There was a gentle jolt and a few men took a step backwards as the fenders cushioned the boat against the wharf. Theirs was one of a half-dozen steamers, some like their own, sending up black smoke to drift south over the warehouses.

They'd reached Shire's section. Lyman let out a sigh and Yeomans took a step towards him. The captain favored a clean upper lip so his black beard looked like some sort of bushy chinstrap. He pushed it close to Lyman's face. 'Something wrong, Corporal?'

'Well, sir, with respect, I ain't gonna steal from my own men. Not even Shire. What kind of a corporal would that make me?'

'I'm sure you're the kind of corporal that wants to share his men's hardships.'

'Besides,' Lyman pressed on, 'no fool's gonna leave anything stolen in his kit once he was ordered to lay it out. We're standing in the cold for nothin'.'

The sergeant tipped up Lyman's knapsack and a pack of cards fluttered to the deck. Yeomans half smiled. 'Private Shire. Collect these cards and throw them in the river.'

Lyman sighed again as Shire did as he was asked. He was probably right: Shire was going to suffer for nothing.

A gangplank banged onto the wharf. Shouted orders, boots on wood. The officers' horses were soothed ashore. A derrick swung a wagon through the air.

It was Tom Muncie's turn. He wore the same mild smile he always did no matter what the circumstance. Shire knew like everyone else that it was only born of his eagerness to please.

'Something funny, Private?'

The sergeant put Yeomans right. 'He has a stuck smile this one, sir.'

Shire didn't worry that the sergeant barely glanced into Tom's pack. The last man was Tuck, a head taller than the captain. The lieutenant was finished on the starboard side. This was Shire's last hope. Ned stepped closer and looked down into Tuck's kit.

'You have a particular interest in our friend from Kentucky, Private?' said Yeomans.

'I wouldn't like to say, sir,' said Ned. Then did. 'Only he keeps himself to himself. None of us really know him.'

'Why, you little runt,' said Tuck. 'Just because a man has something to think on, you take him for a thief. I don't see your gear turned out.'

'What's this?' said Yeomans, toeing something amongst the kit.

Shire spent his last burst of hope, but saw only what appeared to be an enamel doorknob, patterned with colored flowers and discolored on one side.

'A keepsake, sir.'

'Strange keepsake.' Yeomans bent down and picked it up. 'Fire damaged too. You collect pretty doorknobs, Private?'

Tuck's normally neutral face was painted with concern. He watched Yeomans toss and catch the doorknob in his hand before throwing it to him. Tuck caught it as if it were crystal and held it like a two-day chick. Shire met Tuck's eyes and his heart sank. This man was no thief.

The sergeant finished going through Tuck's things, leaving them in a mess. 'Nothing, sir.'

'Alright.' Yeomans glanced over and got a stiff nod from the Colonel. 'Private Shire, strip to your drawers. Corporal Lyman, take a man and pull two buckets of water from the river.'

Lyman took Cleves with him. The men were allowed to break ranks and formed a half circle. They started to jeer and whistle as Shire took off his clothes, passing them to Ned along with the last of his self-respect. He shivered from the humiliation rather than the cold and held his hands under his arms and backed against the rail.

'Stand to attention, Private,' barked Yeomans.

The company made way for Opdycke.

'You men will go into battle soon. And you will go in sober with the Lord at your shoulder. Let this be a warning. The next man caught drunk or hungover will be court-martialed.'

Opdycke stepped aside, and to the laughter of the men, Lyman threw his bucketful of freezing water at Shire's chest. Shire couldn't breathe. Then a leering Cleves stepped towards him and tipped the other bucket over his head.

Louisville – January 1863

'We figured they died in the smoke, which is a comfort. Ma's arms were wrapped around Pa, her head on his chest.' Like Shire, Tuck had pulled a crate close to the stove that was yet to fill the high, conical tent with much heat. 'But it was a horror really. Flesh melted together. So burnt we couldn't separate 'em. But weren't no reason to. We asked old Thackery to build the casket a little bigger and we dug the grave a little wider.'

Tuck's accent, now Shire was getting a longer sample of it, was new again, much slower than New York and somehow lazier than Ohio. The words were strung out, as if they had no hurry to get anywhere. And the events of the day had let free in Tuck a good supply.

'I'd have been there when it happened but for the trial. Cousin Orville had got himself beat up two weeks back – over nothin'. Pa reasoned it'd be good for him to have family along. Orville's not the sharpest neither. Why, one day, I seen him try an' drive in a fence post with the sharp end aiming at the sky. Judgement went for him. I thought it best to bring him back home, keep him out of Millersburg a day or two. And we could always use an extra hand. Even Orville.'

'We could have used some extra hands setting up this here tent,' called Lyman, laid down on the opposite side. 'It was heavy work for three men.'

'I don't recall you doing much heavy work,' said Mason, sharing a look with a nodding Tom Muncie, both sat on their straw beds. The wind got up another rush and flapped the cowling above the tent's only pole.

'Set a light will you, Tom,' said Lyman. 'It's getting dark out there.'

173

Tom, ever eager to please, stirred himself and lit the lamp that hung from a tripod next to the pole. The cream canvas took on a warmer yellow. The Sibley tent – for all the world like the wigwams Shire had only ever seen sketched in picture books – was large enough for several more men, but they had it to themselves. Ned had never arrived.

Tom sat back down and Tuck picked up his story. 'When we come ridin' up, a few neighbors were pickin' through the ashes of the house. The barn was gone up as well, horses an' all. That irked me. Still does. Like it was wrong to steal horses on account of the law, but fine to burn people on account of principle.

'Slave house burnt too, though I didn't oughta call it that no more. Adam came out from the woods once he'd seen me. He'd got out somehow and told us what happened. More'n ten men, he said, shootin' and hollarin' so Ma and Pa had to run inside. He said no shots came from the house, which puzzles me. Maybe Pa figured they'd be let alone if they turned the other cheek. Or maybe Adam is plain wrong. He said the men lit the house with pitch front and back, shootin' all the while. He couldn't hear nothin' from the woods, not above the fire and the guns... I don't like to think on it... but it comes unbidden. I wish I'd not seen them.'

Shire felt the least he could do was listen. He owed Tuck that, even if it had been Ned that singled Tuck out at the inspection that morning; probably to distract attention from himself.

Shivering, he'd waited with Ned and Tuck on the dockside while the rest of the regiment marched away. They'd been ordered by Captain Yeomans to wait for and accompany the supply wagons. There was really no need for a guard, not this far behind the lines. He said they should use the opportunity to make their apologies. It was a couple of hours before the wagons were ready and they'd set out, trailing along at the rear as they passed through Louisville. Ned had made his peace with Tuck, apologized straight up and Tuck had appeared accepting of it. They'd walked on while clouds had crept darkly down from the north.

It had started to snow when they came out into the country and they'd sped up. Ned complained of a stone in his shoe, told them to keep with the wagons while he attended to it. Ten minutes down the road Shire and Tuck got concerned. They'd gone back as far as the crossroads where they'd left Ned, but there was no sign of him. The wind got up and the snow had started to thicken.

'Well,' Tuck had said, 'at least we know where your money went.'

Shire had screamed into the sky.

Lyman crawled to the tent flap to spit out some phlegm he'd been busy hawking up. Mason shook his head.

'You want I should spit it in here?' asked Lyman.

Tuck held his hands out towards the stove, pulled his crate even closer, his knees up under his chin. Sat next to him, Shire felt he'd been scaled down. His troubles seemed shrunk too. At least he still had a father. Tuck had lost both his parents at once.

'I figured to stay at first. Thought it was *right* to stay and that's what they would have wanted. But my heart weren't in it. We held a barn raisin'. Some folks helped. Others I'd known from a boy didn't come to the funeral. People we'd taken a meal with. I don't think it was neighbors who done it. Adam didn't recognize no one. But somebody must've brought them, showed them where the farm was.'

Straw, escaping from under Shire's blanket, raced over the ground, blown by breezes gaining entry between the pegs. The odd snowflake made it in too. The wind pushed the slack in the canvas this way and that.

It had taken the rest of the walk into camp for Shire to begin to accept the truth about his money and the ring. His one friend; the person he trusted the most. It would be hard without the money. But he'd go back to the bank in Medina and give up the other hundred and fifty if it would get the ring back. And to get one good swing at Ned. He'd have to think what to tell Dan. He felt hollowed out.

When they'd reached camp they had to report Ned's desertion to the sergeant who took them to see Captain Yeomans. So it was into the afternoon before they found Lyman sat directing Mason and Tom Muncie in erecting their new home, the snow swirling around them. Short of hands, they were the only ones still at it. No one had offered to help, all snug from the growing storm in their own tents. Once they were settled in and had the stove lit, Shire told them about Ned.

Mason had put a big paw on Shire's shoulder. 'If it's any comfort, none of us saw him as a jumper.'

It wasn't.

Then Tuck evidently had a need to spill his own story to Shire, which he still wasn't done with. 'Pa hadn't made a show of freeing Adam. He'd never truly felt right ownin' a slave and even before Mr Lincoln's proclamation, it was plain which way the wind was blowin'. Adam had a wife and child thirty mile away after their folks moved. So Pa set him free. He was going to join his family when the harvest was all in. After the fire he kept sayin' how sorry he was and how it was his fault and weepin' and goin' on. It got to me. I cuffed him and told him to quit it. Never once struck him while he was a slave, but as a free man I felt he had a right to it.

'But it weren't his fault. And it weren't Pa's fault for freeing him neither. It sure was the fault of them who did it, and our maker'll take care of them, but even that ain't the root of it.'

Tuck had the look of a man listening to his own argument.

'In the end you have to figure it's *slavery's* fault. *There's* the sin and the evil. And sore as this war is, it draws the line pretty straight. If you want to fight slavery, you're able to point a gun right at it.'

He sat up, finally looking at Shire. 'Took me a whole year to figure that out. General Bragg helped my mind some, comin' up right into Kentucky so close to home. Started to look like we was losing the war. That tipped me. I gave Orville my horse rather than let the army have it. It's a deal smarter than he is, so may keep him out of trouble. I didn't much care which state had me, just not Kentucky. Felt like it had a hand in killin' my folks on account of not seeing it's way to fight with the Union sooner. Ohio appears to be of sounder mind, so here I am. And here we all are, back in Kentucky.'

'I hope to hell I ain't in the line between you two,' said Lyman, speaking up to the canvas. 'One's out to defeat slavery single-handed and one can't shoot straight. Heaven help us.'

'Heaven might not be enough with you in charge,' said Mason, 'what with you being so discouragin' an all. What'll your call be as we charge at the guns? *C'mon boys! I done told you we're all gonna git shot. Now take it with no fuss.* And on the other side, you'll be complainin' before you get in. *Howdy, St Peter. You know these gates ain't hung quite right if you need 'em to last a while.*'

'I'm jist sayin' we need boys who can shoot straight, is all,' said Lyman. '*Why* you fire the gun don't matter a heap once the fighting starts. Tuck don't need no head full of high thoughts and Shire needs to remember to hold the wooden end and hope they don't come in ones and twos, cus' he'll need to have at least a whole brigade to aim at.'

'I'm planning to master not getting shot first,' said Shire.

'Given a choice though,' mused Lyman, 'I'd stand next to Shire. You're more apt to get killed next to a hero than somebody who knows when to skedaddle.'

'Listen to our leader,' said Mason. 'Thinking on runnin' before we've had a chance to be shot at.'

'You just watch your red skin don't run before the rest of you.'

Shire looked at Mason. What did Lyman mean?

Tuck tapped his arm. 'I'll fix you to shoot,' he said. 'Pass me your rifle.'

Shire lent over to his bed, but before he could reach the gun, the wind climbed to a new intensity. Beyond his bed, the skirt of the tent lifted so he could see the snow lying outside. The wind raced in and the muddy pegs began pulling clear.

'Douse the lamp!' shouted Tuck, then jumped up to do it himself.

Shire's loose mattress disintegrated into the snowstorm that was suddenly inside the tent. The pole began to lean. His only thought was to throw himself away from the stove. He heard a scream that might have been Tom's and put his hands over his head. He felt the cold canvas land on him and then start to ripple and slap. It was so heavy that he couldn't press up onto all fours. He had no idea which way was out until he realized his left hand could feel the wind and snow. He struggled sideways, the weight of canvas easing, until his head emerged into the cold air.

Mason was next out and together they lifted the canvas away from the tipped stove. Tuck, none the worse, emerged and pulled out what pegs were left so they could drag the tent clear. They uncovered Tom Muncie, red hair first followed by a smile. Lastly they found Lyman, still prone on his bed.

Faces peeked from between the flaps of the nearest tents and laughed at them. They were offered all manner of unhelpful advice, much of it aimed at Shire, while they wrestled the tent in the snow and the wind. Finally, the Sergeant took pity and ordered their neighbors out to help before the last light faded. It was grudgingly given. The stove was broken, and once the tent was back up they were left to endure a long, cold night.

Louisville – January 1863

Shire endured January in cold and tedium. It was as if his old life had closed behind him. He settled into a level gloom, his waking hours governed by bugles and drums. They drilled six hours daily by company and battalion. Added to that, fatigues, guard duty and dress parades kept him occupied and tired. In the middle of the month it became so wet that even drill was suspended.

The prospect of the army delivering him to Clara began to seem wildly hopeful. There was no shape to the war that he could discern. If the generals wanted to move south they would have to bring on another battle. And he saw evidence daily of how much that cost: more than once he was in a funeral escort for officers who'd died from wounds gained at Stones River. The cold and the proximity of the soldiers took a toll in his company too: men became sick with consumption or fever and were too weakened to stay with the regiment. Some died in the camp hospital before they could be shipped home. There appeared to be many ways to die in this war.

There was still no letter from home. He'd stand outside the scrum when the mail arrived, no longer expecting to hear his name. There should have been news by now. He began to doubt his mental list of excuses: letters could go astray, Dan's mother could neglect to send one on, his own letters might not have found their way home. He'd lie awake, listening to the rain on the canvas, imagining darker reasons. Perhaps he should write to Aaron and ask after Father.

Approaching the end of January they heard that the 125th had been assigned to the 34th Brigade of the 10th Division, commanded by Brigadier General C. C. Gilbert. On the 28th they broke camp and marched to the river at Portland, outside Louisville. As he saw the vast Ohio once more, one man amongst thousands, he was reminded how insignificant his troubles were in the grand scheme of things. They were squeezed on board the steamboat *Jacob Strader*, cheek by jowl with two other Ohio regiments. They were forbidden from going ashore and each company had to take its short turn using the ship's galley. To begin with it was bearable; the anticipation of movement overriding the cramped conditions. But after a night in port and no sign of departure the next day, the men became fractious, taking offence over anything and everything. Shire kept his head down.

In the afternoon he was with the squad below decks, confined to an airless companionway. To avoid being jammed shoulder to shoulder, the men alternated which way they sat, backs against opposing walls. Even then Shire had to sit with his knees up. Opposite him Tom Muncie had his jacket off and was hunting lice, popping them then wiping his hands on his trousers. Shire closed his eyes, wishing he was somewhere else.

It was almost two and a half years since he'd seen Clara and he knew nothing of her new life. If by some miracle he made it to her, he might find her content. He couldn't imagine any circumstances in which the certificate he carried would be welcome. And what would she think of him? He saw himself through her eyes: a little boy come all this way with a forlorn hope.

There had been a constant trickle of deserters since Ned. Shire wondered, not for the first time, if he should abscond himself. He could collect what remained of his bounty money from Medina, make for New York and take a ship. He might be home with Father by Easter.

Down the companionway, a few men had started to quietly sing a hymn, almost whispering the harmonies so they didn't antagonize anyone.

Clara had come to sing in the Ridgmont choir, just the once. She'd not told him she was coming, just turned up at his door on Christmas Eve dressed in her maid's winter clothes. Her parents were away for the season and her governess was sick in bed. She'd stolen out without permission. Her carriage had pulled away without her, leaving Shire no say in the matter.

The choir was meeting in Eversholt and they had to walk there together through a dusting of snow, Shire carrying a lantern to light their way down the cut lane. 'My cousin is only thirteen. Why would she visit without family on Christmas Eve? You'll never pass for her.'

The trees ended and the road rose level with the fields. The stars stretched to every horizon. Clara walked ahead, staring up at them, turning and pirouetting to pick out the constellations. 'Cassiopeia,' she said, her breath puffing upwards. 'My sister showed me that one. She was a queen. Cassiopeia, not my sister. And her vanity caused a lot of trouble, so she was put up there.'

'It's me that'll be in trouble. I'll catch it from Father. There's plenty who work at the house in the choir. They'll recognize you straight off.'

'Do you think I'm vain?' He was used to Clara ignoring him. 'I think we nobles get vanity ingrained into us. The very idea of nobility is vain, don't you think? But tonight I'm like the rest of you.' She was wearing a simple woolen dress and black coat. She'd also borrowed plain gloves and a scarf, but the bonnet, Shire thought, must be her own; fine black wool with silk edging.

She stopped and he almost bumped into her.

'Who's going to gainsay me? You don't have to make introductions. I just want to join in for once, rather than be tiptoed around.'

Why was he bothering to warn her? She was plainly going to do as she wanted. She always did. Clara kissed the end of his nose, as she might a favorite nephew, then marched away to resume her heavenly survey. He stayed rooted where he was for a while, holding the lantern, then hurried after her.

They crested a low rise, small spinneys silhouetted against the stars like looming behemoths. A fox barked. From somewhere distant church bells tolled – carried on the cold, they struck the seventh hour. A few lights escaped from the hamlet of ahead. As they walked gently downhill, he heard the first few notes from a violin being tuned in the winter air. Clara tied the bow under her chin and pulled the silk edging forward of her face. 'There,' she said.

When they reached the Drovers Arms people were spilling outside. There were trays of spiced wine and they each took a glass. Father was handing out song sheets for those that needed them. A viola joined the violin.

'Ah, there you are,' said Father. 'You could have handed these out. I've enough to think on. Who's this young lady you're with?' Shire saw the recognition in Father's eyes before he'd finished the question.

One of the choristers stepped over. 'Abel, will we be singing before moving off?'

'Samuel, how are you?' said Shire. 'This is my cousin Elizabeth. She's come to sing with us.'

Clara nodded her bonnet, and Shire grabbed a song sheet from Father. He heard Samuel's question as he pulled Clara away and into the crowd.

'I thought your niece Lizzie was a deal younger?'

'So did I,' said Father, knowingly, but then joined in the deceit, 'but the years get by us quicker and quicker, don't you find, Samuel? We'll sing "Angels from the Realms of Glory".' He called for the carolers' attention, chided them to finish up their wine and formed them into an arc with two rows. Shire stood behind Clara. The viola took up the bass and the violin the treble.

Angels from the realms of glory
Wing your flight o'er all the earth;
Ye who sang creation's story,
Now proclaim Messiah's birth.

He knew how well Clara could sing. He remembered, when they were very small, Clara bossing him to sing with her in front of the duchess. Now, she sang out with the best of them, holding the song sheet up to Shire's lantern and backing into him.

They sang one more, 'The First Noël', before they set off into the cold. An array of lanterns, frail wisps in the darkness, bobbed on ahead. By a roundabout route through Birchall's Wood, they made their way back to Ridgmont village from where he and Clara had started out earlier. On the way they stopped at farms and houses, whispering when they got close until they struck up. Without exception the occupants would come out with offerings; mulled wine, beer, cider, hot mince or meat pies and, in one case, warmed slices of honeyed gammon.

Clouds drifted across the stars and a light snow started to fall. Clara and Shire trailed along behind. Carolers would drop back to be friendly, or perhaps to see just who it was on his arm. He would artfully lower the lantern to leave Clara's face in darkness, but he could hear the gossip: her secret was out. But the crowd seemed happy to have a stowaway amongst them.

They finished in Ridgmont village and headed out into the country again. Father came to find Shire. 'Don't you think your young cousin might be getting cold? You should take her on home.'

Clara answered for him, 'But, Mr Stanton, it's still early.'

Father talked to her across Shire as they walked. 'The duchess may have words with me when she returns home if she comes to know you've been out unaccompanied. She certainly will if I keep you to a late hour and bring you home drunk. We've a few calls on the way to the estate church. After that we'll finish up, as always, at Ridgmont Abbey for midnight. Am I right in saying that you're the only family home this Christmas Eve?'

'You are,' said Clara. 'Sad, isn't it?'

'That's as maybe, though there are folk a lot sadder. Now we expect to be welcomed at the house. And by my reckoning, that'll be down to you. So I'd suggest you borrow Shire and hurry directly back. Then we'll see you on the steps in time for Christmas Day.'

Clara stopped and turned to Shire. 'My feet are a little cold,' she said.

'Fine,' said Father. 'I'll make your excuses. And straight there mind. My nose says there's more snow to come.'

They stole away and headed towards the estate drive. Soon the snow began to fall in earnest. The flakes thickened in the air; a new breeze sent flurries sweeping across their path. As they reached the drive the snow was heavier than ever. It was the best part of a mile to the abbey.

'Let's take to the gatehouse until this passes,' said Shire. 'Armitage and his wife are with the choir, but he never locks up.'

The gatehouse had one small turret next to the drive entrance. Fighting the snow, Shire led Clara past the stone eagles atop the gate pillars and round to the back. There were no lights inside, but the door was unlocked as he'd expected. They stepped into the dark scullery. Clara shrieked. When Shire brightened the lantern there were a brace of pheasants dangling by the wall, one gently swinging where Clara had walked into it. She laughed and put a hand to her chest, then untied her bonnet. A rabbit and a hare hung nearby. The room smelt like cold, meaty soup.

'He's more a gamekeeper than a gatekeeper,' said Shire.

They went into a warm kitchen and took off their boots and socks. He opened a door onto a small sitting room. It was perfectly round, being the base of the turret. The fireplace always looked oversized. 'The fire heats the whole turret.' He gestured at the thin set of steps that hugged the wall and curved upwards. A small window looked out forward of the gate.

Clara stepped from the cold stone floor and onto the thick rug. The fire had been banked up to outlast the caroling. He poked it into life, giving it an extra log before he sat down next to her.

'I'm warming up everywhere but my toes,' Clara said. 'Help them out will you?'

Shire didn't move.

'Go on,' she ordered, 'before they drop off.'

Shire got onto his knees, unsure of quite what to do. He gingerly took one foot and rubbed it between the palms of his hands.

Clara squealed. 'Be gentle.' She offered her foot again.

This time Shire used his thumbs to press and circle into her heel and then moved slowly up to her toes, which he then held between his hands to warm. Clara had always teased him. That was nothing new. But for once he didn't mind.

She let him attend to the other foot. 'That's much better,' she said. 'Now come and kiss me.' She took his hand and pulled him to lie next to her.

'Clara...'

'Shhh,' she stopped him with a finger on his lips then followed it with her mouth. She tasted of Christmas. For long minutes the only sound was the crackle of the fire and their snatched breathing surrounding this one long kiss. He realized Clara was unbuttoning her dress at the front. They should stop this. She took his hand to guide it, a little awkwardly, under her chemise and onto her breast. He tried to pull away, but only weakly. Together they caressed her. Clara led him, the hardness of her nipple surprising him. Her kissing became harder, more urgent; his hands began to find their own way. The fire cracked loudly as the new log caught and their lips parted. He should have just kissed her again. Instead, he sat up and glanced at the window. 'It's stopped snowing,' he said.

Clara said nothing. She buttoned her dress with fumbling fingers while he stood and pretended to look outside.

'We'd best get you home.'

On the way to the abbey their lantern gave out. But the stars were unveiled again, spun a little way around the North Star. After a while Clara held out a hand. They circled to the trade entrance. Shire stood while she climbed the step and turned to say goodbye. She bent and kissed him on the nose as she had hours before. He wasn't having that. He pulled her to him and for a few heartbeats they kissed as they had before, before Clara let herself in.

As Shire walked away, a yellow light shone down onto the fresh snow and he looked up. At a second floor window in one of the abbey's wings, a curtain was held back. A woman in a nightgown and cap held a small lamp. She made no attempt not to be seen. Shire hurried away to find the choir.

The soldiers finished their hymn. Tom Muncie offered Shire half a cracker and he took it. He wasn't about to desert. He'd just have to hope this ship would head off in the right direction. As he sat there, he quietly struck a unilateral deal between himself, God and the Union Army. He'd stay and fight for the North – and in return he'd be taken to Clara.

That evening, the 125th were taken from the *Jacob Strader* and boarded instead onto the *Clara Poe*. It could only mean that God and the Army were in on the deal.

They were held in port for three more days. Two full divisions joined them, some arrived by river, some overland, and all were squeezed onto an assortment of transports. When at last they swung out into the brisk air on the Ohio, Mason said the word was that they were headed for Fort Donelson, up the Cumberland, from where General Grant had evicted the Rebels last winter. This was a deal closer to the front, a fact re-enforced by the gunboats that took station in front of the flotilla.

The Ohio was nothing short of colossal. He marveled that any device of man could endure on so wide and strong a river, despite travelling with it as they were. It didn't run fast; just slow, heavy and invincible; flat silver reflecting a grey, winter sky. On the third night afloat, his sleep was fitful. Lyman had to shake him awake and he found himself nervous as well as tired. Before mid-morning, they turned up the Cumberland and into the current.

'Turning south,' said Mason. 'Look out, Tennessee, Ohio's coming to visit.'

Tributary as it was, the lesser river nevertheless swallowed the flotilla whole, though the gunboats and transports were obliged to close up and proceed in single file. They were close enough to the shore for Tuck to point out the huge snapping turtles hauled out onto the muddy bank.

After noon, Shire's company and one other were called onto the foredeck and ordered to load rifles. From up the twisting river, muffled by the forest, he could hear gunfire. The occasional deeper boom of cannon overlaid the rattle of muskets. One gunboat steamed on ahead – presumably to lend its own guns – rude, black smoke rose above the trees to mark its winding progress. The company stayed silent, and like Shire, looked forward as the land slowly revealed itself around each bend. A steady flow of logs and branches betrayed the true speed of the water. The gunfire died away before he saw Fort Donelson, perched on the right bank, empty and unused, the forest stripped from its surrounds. The *Clara Poe* moored up opposite the modest town of Dover which lived beyond the fort.

They were kept on-board while their surgeon and a small detachment were rowed across to the town. He could see on the far shore that the town was lively with soldiers and horses. News came that there had been a fierce attack that afternoon. It had been repulsed, the gunboat arriving just in time to assist.

This was not to be their garrison, but they were to wait for more transports to join them before pushing on to Nashville. And they were allowed ashore. The locals pressed their own skiffs into service and charged ten cents per soldier to row them over. Tuck brushed off Shire's weak protests and insisted that they should visit the battlefield. They walked east along the southern bank with Mason. The fight had not been at the fort captured by Grant last year, but on the opposite side of the town. While back across the river the forest was half-dressed in enduring winter foliage, on this side the trees had been cleared to give the defenders a long field of fire.

Tuck found a corporal in the 83rd Illinois, the only regiment that had been here to defend the town. He told them there'd been two brigades of Confederate cavalry in the attack. They all agreed it was small scale, but the evidence was no less grisly for that. The dead of both sides were still on the field, mutely marking out the battle.

When a child, he'd visited his own mother, pale but peaceful in her coffin. But this was no parlor vigil and only the fear of ridicule kept him from turning back. Here, he found, the dead were not reconciled to their new state, but untidy in their agony and despair. It was hard to detach it from his own possible future. The Union men lay together, often behind a fence or an earthwork, on their backs where they had been rolled to be known. Some had barely a mark; others, with saber cuts to the neck and face, lay open-eyed in fear. Shire walked quietly through the scene, appalled for them but terrified for himself.

There were far more Rebel bodies. They were scattered and intermingled with horses. Some, killed by cannon fire, Shire didn't go near. The cold air swept off the river, but couldn't remove the smell of guts, feces and the beginning of corruption.

It looked like most of the 125th had come over the river to visit. Sergeant Rice was out in the field with a private Shire didn't know. Shire watched him draw his knife and kneel beside a dead Confederate officer to cut the buttons from the grey uniform. He couldn't begin to imagine why a man would want such a memento.

Shire approached a lone, dead horse, a white mare that in its familiar attitude could have been resting. Its muzzle on the hard ground held its head upright, ears flat as if at ease. Only the right hind leg was at odds, angled away from the torso and broken. He stroked her mane.

Mason came to stand with him. 'The horses make me sadder than the men.'

Shire felt a soreness in his throat. 'It's easier to put your heart into a horse. They were either whipped here or came out of loyalty.

Either way, there's no fault in them. Men can look after themselves.'

'You've a lot of sentiment in that head. I guess this is a good place to use it.'

Shire looked around at the dead Rebels. 'Or perhaps a horse is an easier path for the sadness to take, like lightning through a tree. Maybe it's too hard to go and put your hand on a dead man.'

'Maybe,' said Mason, looking with him. 'But I won't waste my own feelings on men who fought for slavery. It's a bad cause to get up for.'

It was an odd moment for it to come to mind, but Shire had been meaning to ask Mason something since they set up camp at Louisville. 'What Lyman said about red skin, what did he mean?'

Mason turned to look at him, as if he were weighing him up. 'It means that Lyman has a big mouth.'

Tuck came to join them and whispered amongst the dead. 'Why aren't they buried yet? At least our boys. I wouldn't like to be left lying to be looked over by anyone with a mind to it.'

There were no burial parties to be seen. They left, fearful they might be put to it themselves. When they were being rowed back over the river, Tuck said to Shire that he was sorry he'd pressed him to go, and wished he'd not gone himself.

Franklin, Tennessee – February 1863

The chestnut mare passed so close to Shire he could have reached out and touched her. The staff officer hauled on his reins and drew up facing the colonel. He saluted. 'Colonel Opdycke. Colonel Reid requests your company.'

Opdycke trotted away up the column.

'Something's up,' said Lyman. 'Looks like we might have some work to do before supper. I said the day felt ugly.'

'And when don't your days feel ugly?' said Mason, but got no reply.

Shire and Company B were at the head of the 125th, but the regiment was in the middle of the strung-out brigade. Ahead was the 98th and the 113th, behind the 121st and 124th. Today had been Shire's longest march yet, all the way down the turnpike from Nashville. He had a lightened pack but it had become heavier with each passing hour. The earlier snow had warmed to a freezing drizzle, and he felt the cold more deeply now that they were stood still. News filtered back down the line that there was Confederate cavalry up ahead in Franklin. He stuffed his hands deeper into his coat pockets and searched for warmth that wasn't there.

When the Colonel returned he summoned his captains. Shire leant out of line to see as well as hear. Tall in his saddle and clean-shaven but for a modest moustache, Opdycke looked every inch the soldier. Shire remembered his punishment on the Ohio and felt colder still.

'Gentlemen,' Opdycke spoke as if he was running for mayor, 'we're ordered to march to the front of the brigade and to clear the town. I want Company A on the left, and Company B on the right, deployed as skirmishers. The remaining companies will be in column behind.'

'Are any other regiments going in, sir?' asked Captain Yeomans.

'No. The honor's all ours.'

Shire had once been told it was an honor for him to read the lesson in church. He preferred that sort of honor to this one.

'Do we know what's up there?'

'Cavalry. We don't know the numbers. The rest of the brigade is on hand, but our job is to clear the Rebels out, so we won't stop at their picket. Understood? You keep the boys moving.'

The colonel wheeled his horse and Shire felt a surge of excitement or fear, he couldn't tell which. Right now they seemed much the same thing. Bugles sounded all along the column. The regiments ahead were ordered off the turnpike to let the 125th forward at the quick. Their collective breath steamed up into in the cold air. Men from the other regiments called out as they passed by.

'Save me a room at the best hotel in town.'

'Don't get messy up there, 125th.'

'Give my regards to Jeff Davis.'

Once they were in front, Company B was thrown into skirmish formation on the right, told to load and take intervals of twenty paces in groups of four. Mason and Tuck took the lead, Lyman, though he was the corporal, followed on with Shire. They started forward into the trees.

Shire's stomach felt hollow, his bladder heavy. He had no time for regret; his mind was keyed into each moment. Every tree, every scrub bush, every fold in the ground drew his eye. He found that he could distinguish between the footfalls of his companions, that he could smell the earth that Tuck's boots threw up in front of him. And he prayed to God in earnest, that they would find the enemy gone.

When they crested a low hill, the trees thinned, and he could see a small town below them held behind a loop in a river. There was an angled column of white smoke this side of the houses.

'I can't see no Reb's,' said Mason.

'Someone made that smoke,' replied Tuck. He moved ahead,

his musket held across his stomach and they all followed.

When they got closer to the river, the reason for the thinning smoke became clear. Both the rail and the road bridge had been destroyed. The company began to converge. Shire stepped more slowly, wary of the houses on the other side. The blunt order came to wade across.

'The Reb's won't need any bullets,' objected Lyman. 'They can just watch us freeze to death.'

For once Shire agreed with Lyman. They all stood and looked at the water.

'C'mon boys.'

He recognized Corporal Barnes.

'We can't roust them out from this side.' The corporal jumped down the bank and started into the water. Tuck followed. Shire heaved a breath. He copied the others and took his leather box of percussion caps off his belt. He held them high along with his rifle and cartridges and waded into the freezing water. By the time it reached his waist, his breath had tightened to nothing more than a rapid and shallow puffing. The soldiers called to each other, guided those coming behind to where it was less deep. He was midstream when he heard the first shot. It came from the town and was followed by more. Up to a dozen soldiers in grey advanced towards the river along a house lined street to his front.

He'd found the enemy then. And the enemy had found him: terrified, and stuck in a river with his hands in the air. He stopped. For a moment he considered ducking under, gun and all. He should go back. Tom Muncie moved past him. He turned around and the colonel and his horse were splashing towards him. The horse looked no more pleased than Shire.

'Captain!' the colonel called back over his shoulder, 'cross the column here! It's shallower here!' And then to Shire. 'On you go, boy. The Rebels are this way.'

He turned back and started forward again, his mind momentarily wiped blank by the shame, by the thought that he might have looked a coward to his colonel. On the far side there was a scruffy looking grey officer on horseback. The man drew his pistol and aimed at Corporal Barnes. He fired once, hit nothing but cold water, before he was chased off by a handful of shots from the Union side. The grey foot-soldiers halted and started to edge back, still shooting. Shire struggled on, pushing as hard as he could through the water, thinking how mad it was that he was fighting to get closer to men who were trying to kill him.

He watched Barnes make the bank first and help Tuck up after him. Other groups got out and took cover. Shire wanted to catch up to Tuck and dragged himself out of the water. He was nothing but dead and heavy from the waist down.

'Take a pot,' Tuck said. 'It keeps 'em mindful.'

Shire shivered violently but knelt to the side of a tree and aimed his rifle down the road. He fired in a rush at the first movement he saw.

'That's my boy,' said Mason, reloading. 'At least you aimed south.' The big man's presence was reassuring and Shire gave him a frozen smile.

He struggled to strap the percussion box back onto his wet belt. Behind him the column was taking time to cross and, to protect them, the men already over were pushed on away from the river.

Shire didn't see any more Rebels until they reached the town square where they found cavalry; forty or so in a tight bunch, retreating down a wide road that led south. For a moment Shire thought it was over, that he was safe, but the horses wheeled and the Rebels levelled their rifles and fired. Bullets smacked into house timber; every one like the strike of an axe. A window shattered. Corporal Lyman, from behind a porch support, gave his first order of the day, screaming at them to return fire.

Shire fumbled for a cartridge and bit into the paper to empty the powder into his barrel. His hand shook so much that half of it fell to the dirt. He dropped in the ball, but the guns were firing around him: Tuck, Mason, Tom and Lyman with half a dozen others. The cascade unnerved Shire still more and he dropped his ramrod. When he finally brought his gun up, the Rebels were riding away down the road. His hammer clicked but the gun didn't fire.

'I find those work a deal better with a percussion cap,' said Lyman. He was smiling at Shire, so was Tuck.

'Keep movin', boys.' It was Captain Yeomans. He urged them on up the street and after the Rebels. When they stopped, further down the road, Shire reached with one hand into his cap box. The new leather was stiff and scraped on his cold fingers as he pushed them inside. He swore, groped around, eventually singled out a cap and tried to force his hand steady to place it on the nipple. He mustn't miss the next volley. The Rebels had turned to fight again. A few dismounted to fire back at the half of Company B that was up. Their bullets kicked off the road in front of Shire and buzzed on passed him. All his muscles tensed, anticipating an impact. He tried to shrink into himself: as if some childhood bully was about to thump him.

Lyman gathered a dozen men together and called for a solid volley. They raised their guns up and fired on his command. Shire's gun failed again, probably from lack of powder, but this time only Tuck noticed. The range was long but at least one man went down, clutching a shoulder before he was lifted into his saddle to canter away with the rest.

Soon after, the remainder of the 125th came up, and they were held there, freezing, until after dark when they were relieved. They learnt that the cavalry belonged to Bedford Forrest.

'Forrest's Cavalry. You hear that, Shire?' said Tuck. 'We done chased out General Bedford Forrest!'

That it was barely more than a handful of Rebels wasn't mentioned. There wasn't a wound in the whole regiment. Cold and suffering though they all were, Shire was surrounded by excited talk as they marched back into town to find a fire. He didn't deserve to join in. Lyman was already making a story out of Shire's missing percussion cap, one he was certain he'd hear again and again in the days ahead.

'One shot,' he said quietly to Tuck. 'I got off one shot.'

'You went forward, didn't you? I'll bet not everyone gets to do that first time out.'

But Shire recalled that moment in the river, when the cold water had numbed everything but his fear. He would have gone back. He would have run away if the colonel hadn't been there to push him on.

London – March 1863

The eighteen dukes gazed down silently into the House of Lords, where a nineteenth was making his plea. Dressed and armored in grey stone, they were only marginally less animated than the assorted nobility that populated the wide, red-leather benches. Matlock, perched in the Strangers Gallery, was further from his master than the statues that lived beneath the gilded ceiling, their dukedoms inscribed under them. Closest at hand were Winchester, Hereford and Norfolk. Down below, standing in the fourth tier, Matlock didn't think that the Duke of Ridgmont cut quite so martial a figure.

'My Lords, is the issue in doubt? The Confederacy has tried to raise a loan of three million pounds, secured on the promise of cotton. And it is subscribed instead for nine million. The capitalists of Europe, then, recognize the Confederacy for purposes of trade. In denying them the corresponding political legitimacy, we put this very trade at risk. Reports that I credit tell me that last year cotton was planted in the South when there was hope for recognition, but that it was ploughed back under when that same hope died. And it is that lost hope that is transmitted here, and then translated to distress in the mills of Lancashire.'

Matlock considered his cousin's delivery. The intonation rose and fell in all the right places to color his long argument. He slowed or paused skillfully to lend emphasis to his case. Yet it retained the air of a theatrical performance rather than that of a political speech, though perhaps those two were not such strangers. Having sat for an hour, Matlock's awe at his surroundings was on the wane. The studs on the seats were too widely placed, meaning he could only get one buttock comfortable at a time. He didn't like being this far away from Ridgmont. If he was honest he never liked to be away from the estate at all. He wanted to meet with the duke and then get back, but it was too late today. He'd have to take a train in the morning.

Tiring of the duke's slow arguments, he began instead to wonder whether there was any backing for the speech, and for the notion that the British government should recognize the Confederacy. There was the odd murmur of approval, an occasional half-hearted 'Hear! Hear!' from those sat close to the duke, but the wider audience remained subdued.

'By withholding recognition, Great Britain *does* declare against the right to secede, *does* label the South as illegal, *does*, by its glaring tacitity with the United States Government, take leave of her neutrality. By denying our harbors to both sides we favor the North, whose own harbors remain unmolested, and compel the Southerners to instead burn their prizes at sea instead of raising privateers.'

Matlock fancied he could make a better fist of the argument. He carried the same heraldic blood as the duke, so why not? More facts, man, more facts: as to trade, as to losses. Less of a history lesson. The duke dwelt at turgid length on past examples of British recognition in favor of fledgling states. Many lords unashamedly read their papers. Some, seduced by the soft, wide benches, dozed off altogether, their glorious gluttony pointing ever higher as they slipped ever lower. Mercifully the duke returned to the present day and his arguments were all the more cogent for it, but Matlock feared he'd lost his audience if, indeed, he'd ever found them.

'We could debate, ad nauseam, whether the desire to end slavery was the root of invasion, as well as if the vaulted objective of extending it was the reason for succession. This will be forever hidden in the hearts of the many that have taken their sides. More pertinent is what the immediate, devastating effect would be of a freed slave population, on themselves as much as their masters.

'But if separation were recognized and realized, for that may be the order of it, the South could look again impartially at the question of black labor, without the provocation of the northern abolitionists inflaming it to a point of honor.'

The Duke of Ridgmont sat down amidst a small circle of approval. Lord John Russell rose from across the House to make a response, dark intelligent eyes in a face flanked by luxuriant greying mutton-chops. Whether derived from his high office of Foreign Secretary, or from his long experience of debate, to Matlock he appeared the master of the duke as soon as he began to speak. While observing the polite conventions of the House, he paid little respect to the duke's analysis.

'My Lords, I imagine there is no member of this House who does not wish for the civil war in America to end, not only for the resumption of harmonious commerce, but to end the suffering of the American people. Yet no man who has knowledge of the sizeable forces arrayed against Charleston, Savannah, and those making slow progress in the west, can claim that the issue is settled and that the Union will not one day press a victory. Therefore, for the present, I perceive it is our duty not to proceed to an act so unfriendly to the United States as the recognition of the South.'

Matlock was not a student of geography. Unless a location could be translated to a line in his ledger, it held no interest to him. And as Lord Russell proceeded to list many cities and states in his reply, Matlock had only a sketchy mental map for reference. Somewhere amongst them Shire had run with his stolen secret, and Ocks was chasing. While the stakes were high, the outcome wasn't in doubt. Ocks had written from Columbus. He'd determined Shire's regiment, and had letters from the governor's office sufficient to gain him a place in the same. Ocks had never failed before in acts of persuasion. Once Shire learnt of Abel's and Grace's deaths, surely Ocks could divert him – or find a more permanent solution. What was evident from the debate below was that the armies of the North were moving ponderously at best, and victory might still be gained by either side.

Lord Russell reached his peroration. '...In consideration of the termination of any conflict, the principles on which we feel ourselves compelled to intervene, would only be for the cause of the liberty and freedom of mankind, as demonstrated by our conduct throughout history. In regard to this American civil war, such a moment has not yet been attained and we must therefore continue our impartial and neutral course.'

As Russell retook his seat, the Speaker stood and shouted to make himself heard above the chatter of the Lords as they rose, many initially from semi-consciousness, slowly and stiffly to their feet. 'The next item, Number 51, pertains to the Salmon Exportation Bill, the Earl of Dalhousie to propose an amendment to the Bill.'

Matlock watched the aged exodus, the Lords clearly more interested in consuming salmon than exporting it. He took up his ledgers and hurried out. Once downstairs, he found a runner to take a note through to the duke. Half an hour passed while he waited in a vaulted hallway. Old men, men of empire, came and went, shuffling their shoes across the cold tiled floor.

The duke finally appeared. 'Ah, Matlock, there you are.'

He'd been there all along.

'Good man. Follow me.' The Duke led him through a high wooden door, down a long portrait-lined corridor and into a small but comfortable office. A single arched window let in grey, late afternoon light that bounced weakly off the Thames. 'You've brought some ledgers.' The duke slumped into a chair at his desk, swigging from an oversized sherry glass. He waved at the other seat, which Matlock pulled closer to the desk.

'Yes, Your Grace. For the Americas only. As per your instructions.'

'I only need a summary.' The duke squeezed the tiredness out of his cheeks and mouth with one hand.

'It was a fine speech, Your Grace. Very... comprehensive.'

'You think so?'

'The House was attentive.'

'The House was half-asleep. You'd hope they would perk up when there's a war on the agenda. Nothing will come of it. Russell has his position set and only events will move him. But we must fight our corner, Matlock. For our friends, even if it's a tight one.'

He sat up and refilled his Sherry glass. 'Now, I'm to meet with some of those friends. And although the discussion will range broad and wide, I may gain from them a clearer view on the way things tend in the war, how we might protect or enhance my interests, North and South. You understand?'

'Of course, Your Grace.'

The duke drew himself to the table and took up a pen expectantly. Matlock arranged his ledgers on the desk. It was never a good thing for the duke to know more than he needed to: it limited Matlock's 'flexibility' where the accounts were concerned. No, the duke must be kept at arm's length; though it might mean another painful trip to London. Better that than to let the duke take a blundering hand. Matlock had a practiced method and employed it now. One at a time, he went into excruciating detail on their investments, muddled them with accruals and deferrals, tax levies and rebates, share purchases and exchanges. At the end of a long hour the duke put down his pen, his ink undipped, and rose to look into the darkness that had settled outside.

'It's no good, Matlock. I'm a politician, not an accountant. I'll have to take you along.'

'Why, of course, Your Grace. I'll be at your service. When is this meeting?'

'Oh, in six weeks or so.'

'Here in Parliament, or at Ridgmont?'

The duke strode over and gripped Matlock by the shoulder. 'In Nassau... The Bahamas, man.'

Charleston, South Carolina – March 1863

George Trenholm wandered away from the house, beyond the manicured part of the garden, to the pond. The dying March sun cast long, still shadows over the water from the oak trees. It was good to be at Ashley Hall, good to be in Charleston. The town houses and estates he owned throughout the South – and those estranged in the North – were comfortable enough, but Ashley Hall was his home. He'd held to his long habit and protected the half-hour before sunset for himself. No merchants, no dealers, no congressmen; the gardeners stayed out of sight, even Anna and the children knew to keep indoors. Anticipating this time kept him sane on the hardest days, when business, politics and family life all sought him out. It wasn't that he didn't enjoy the bustle, he did: to steer every deal or opportunity to the good, whether for himself, his children or the Confederacy. But his next meeting was a chore. There was absolutely no profit or benefit to be gained. And it required him to put his honor to one side. He stole in under the Spanish moss that hung from the trees, made himself invisible.

Taylor had arrived just before Trenholm came outside. He'd had him put in the drawing room without seeing him. Let him stew there for a while and wonder why he'd been pulled away from his regiment and the war.

He sucked in the cool evening air and filed away the events of the day. The purchase of the rolling mill in Atlanta was almost through. It was a risk, he knew that. If Tennessee fell, then Georgia would be attacked next. But Atlanta had to hold. And those in the west shouldn't have to beg everything they needed from the east. It would be within a few miles of his arsenal; the two would work together.

The orphanage at Orangeburg had requested that he pay them a visit, meaning they wanted more funds. That was fine. He hadn't set it up to abandon it. And he was richer than he'd ever been, as long as the South survived. He'd take Anna with him. She'd like that.

Reluctantly, he left his refuge and started back to the house. There'd be more color soon. The dogwoods and azaleas were waiting for some warmth. What to do with the garden? He always liked to have some scheme in hand to enhance it. Maybe he should forgo it this year. There wasn't the time. And the effort, both his and his gardeners', was needed elsewhere, to plan and build defenses for the town and the harbor. The war had started here. They could hardly expect to be left alone.

Light shone out from random windows on all three floors of the house. The shutters should be closed earlier. He would talk to Anna. Wealthy as they were, they shouldn't waste the oil and the heat. He took a last deep breath and went inside.

As Trenholm entered his drawing room, Taylor slid a soldier's boot off the chaise longue. Trenholm pretended not to notice. Taylor stood, holding a glass of whiskey.

'It's still a shock to see you in uniform,' said Trenholm.

'I must ask your pardon, sir. It has suffered since my wedding. I've not had the opportunity to change.'

Trenholm charged his own glass then raised the crystal. 'To your marriage.' They settled onto opposite ends of the chaise longue. The boy looked as worn as his uniform. He'd lost weight and there were shadows under his young eyes. Perhaps it was as well he could gain a few days' rest.

'I wondered if you might visit Clara, come via Comrie and ride over the mountains. They're good for the soul.'

'In my new profession I get enough riding, though the train took two days.' Taylor stretched and rolled his neck. 'This whiskey's good.'

How sad, that a man married only a few months didn't take the opportunity to visit his wife. Could things have soured already?

'A Bowmore Single Malt from the Scottish Isles. I have enough laid down to survive a while yet, but could get more at need. One advantage of running the blockade.'

'Business is good, then? There were queues outside every shop as I came from the station.'

Taylor seemed at ease. Usually this room, with all its arches, curves and domes, the sheer size of it, gave Trenholm an advantage. But then Taylor wasn't a stranger here. Trenholm had offered him the room for his wedding. It would have been a bigger affair than in Tennessee. Taylor had declined. That was a blessing at least, thought Trenholm: that it hadn't happened here in his own home.

'Business.' He considered the word, gently spinning the whiskey in his glass. 'I guess it is business, but of a strange sort. You build or buy a ship, usually overseas, and run the blockade. Cotton out and just about anything in, though we keep a mind to the army. One run will pay for the ship. Just one, mind. After that it's all clear profit. We average eight or nine runs before being caught or sunk.

'Then there's my office in Liverpool. All Confederate bonds and contracts pass through that office for any purchases or sales in Europe. Sales being nearly always cotton, purchases mostly boats and arms. And Fraser, Trenholm and Co takes a percentage for providing this heroic service to the Confederate government.'

Irritatingly, Taylor wasn't showing any sign of asking why he'd been called here – summoned really – all the way from Tennessee. Not that the boy was a big wheel in Bragg's army, but a regiment needed its colonel. Trenholm had wired Taylor's division commander to ensure he was given a furlough.

'But we are not immune from the war,' Trenholm said. 'I was in Richmond last week. More than sixty poor women killed by an explosion on Brown's Island.'

'Truly?' Taylor picked at a loose thread on his jacket.

'They were making ordnance. I heard the explosion from my office. What sort of war is it that sends our own wives and daughters to die like that? We should have more care for our women.'

'We didn't bring on this war,' said Taylor.

'Didn't we? Our orators, our fire-eaters were eager enough. They were never going to cut a deal with Yankee abolitionists. But we must fight for our side, mustn't we, each in our own way.'

The fire cracked loudly and Taylor jumped, almost spilling his drink. 'I'm sorry. I must be tired.'

Trenholm noted how Taylor's hand shook as he placed the whiskey down.

He would bait him a little longer. 'How goes the war out west?'

Taylor sat forward. 'Bragg holds our line around Tullahoma while we recover from Stones River. Both sides were badly beaten up.'

Trenholm had made sure he knew all about Taylor's failed charge. It had no real bearing on the battle, but had stopped any prospect of Trenholm pushing to get Taylor a brigade. Although maybe it wasn't in the country's interests that he should push. A man needed sound judgement to manage so many men.

'We ain't strong enough to advance, but it appears Rosecrans ain't either. The officers are split over Bragg. The war will have to be won in the east if they can't send us more troops. I'm hoping we'll keep it away from Comrie.'

'Oh, Comrie's a good way behind the lines. And the copper Raht hauls out of those hills is almost as lucrative as blockade running. At least you and I can say our interests are lucky in this war.'

There was no point in more of this chat; Taylor had outlasted Trenholm's patience. 'But come, you'll want to change and dinner will spoil. There's another matter to discuss.' He collected a letter from the table. 'This came into my possession some weeks ago. The contents are not entirely clear. I'm hoping you can help.' He hesitated before handing it over.

Taylor looked up when he saw the opened envelope bore his name. He stood, his voice rising with him. 'Why, sir, this is addressed to me, at my regiment.'

Trenholm stayed silent and let Taylor read the letter from Matlock. He'd read it several times himself. An Englishman called Shire had joined a Union regiment in Ohio, the 125th. Another, called Ocks, was dispatched to catch him, to tell the boy that his father and someone called Grace had both died. Ocks was to stop the boy – 'at all costs' – from reaching Comrie with a license.

'These are private matters.' He waved the letter at Trenholm. 'How did you come by this? You presume too much in your care of me.'

'The crest is that of the Duke of Ridgmont,' Trenholm said, calmly. 'Letters for the army are censored. You know that. And one from an English duke, or his lackey, attracts attention. You should be grateful that once it had climbed the chain, it found its way to me on account of my connections with you.'

'And you should have forwarded it. It is of no interest to the army or to you.' Taylor started for the door.

If only it was as simple as letting him go. 'Sit down, Taylor. There's more at stake here than has dawned on your western wit. Sit down!'

Taylor returned, but went to stand and stare at the fire.

'Now,' said Trenholm. 'Simply explain to me. Who are these people? And what license is this?'

Taylor said nothing.

'Dinner really will spoil if we wait on your invention. This Grace, you married her?'

Taylor spun round.

'Well what other kind of license makes sense?' continued Trenholm. 'And one that has to be stopped *at all costs.*'

Taylor made one last attempt. 'Sir, it is a personal matter that is mine to deal with. If you will...'

'I say it is not,' Trenholm shouted. He banged his glass so hard on the mantelpiece that the whiskey spilled onto his hand. He pulled a cloth from his jacket and tried to regain his composure.

'I've had time to think on this. You can only have married in '59 when in England. Am I right?'

Taylor closed his eyes.

'Am I right?'

'Yes... Yes.'

'There must be a child. I can see no other reason. Conceived while you were courting Clara?'

'He died, before his first birthday. I'd barely met Clara.'

'I'd extend my sympathy if I thought you deserved it. And now the mother is dead too. God's almost covered your tracks for you, hasn't he? But here's the nub of it. When did she die, Taylor? When?'

'This last November.'

Trenholm drew closer to Taylor and placed a firm hand under his chin. He lifted his face to look him in the eye and said slowly, 'before or after your wedding?'

'Matlock never shared the exact date. Before, I think.'

'And you haven't thought to enquire?' How could he not? Or was he as good a liar as his father?

'What does it matter? A few days makes no difference.'

Trenholm walked back to the chaise longue and collapsed onto it. 'Dear God. I've credited you with too much intellect.' He'd have to take what Taylor said at face value for now. 'It will decide if your marriage is legal. If it is, it's by pure fortune on your part. You couldn't have known of this Grace's death when you married Clara. Indeed, you'd planned to marry sooner. So you are a bigamist by intent at least. What would your father say?'

'Father? Father was never one to let the law get in the way? You knew that.'

'This is not the same. Have you no care for your soul? Or for me. I'm your bondsman!'

Taylor looked like a child caught up to no good, yet still intent on avoiding the punishment.

Trenholm continued. 'We must look into it. Can this Matlock

208

be trusted to tell the truth? No, I thought not. Let me paint this a little wider for you than your personal indiscretions. The Duke of Ridgmont shares a number of our business interests. And those connections will end, for good, should he find out his daughter has been treated so dishonorably. But that's as nothing compared to the politics of the matter. The duke is the Confederacy's last voice in the British Parliament. He speaks for us in the House of Lords. He works his offices to allow us to buy ships and arms, somewhat from self-interest, but also from loyalty to his family. That would be you.

'Now the British have themselves dead set against joining us in this war. Yet wars can turn on a penny. There will be an election in the North next year. If our armies remain successful, perhaps they'll vote in someone with less guile than Lincoln, less inclined to fight. Or maybe some Yankee will accidently sink a British ship and they'll get all prickly. Do you see where I'm heading? If this boy, Shire, gets news to Clara, and the duke learns of this, then the Confederacy loses its last best friend in England. And your shame and ridicule will be nothing besides that.'

When Taylor next spoke, there was no hint of contrition. 'This Ocks fella, I know him. He's a brute... He'll catch up to Shire. I know Shire too. He's just a boy. Not a fighter at all. He won't last in the army. I don't see what else you want me to do.'

'You don't? Then how you command a regiment is a mystery to me. *I'd say* you ought to take an interest in the 125th Ohio. I have. They're in Rosecrans' Army, 34th Brigade, somewhere around Franklin on your front. I've registered an interest in their movements. *I'd say* if they start to get anywhere near to Polk County you should move Clara south, to Atlanta, or to here. And don't underestimate this Shire. He's already in Tennessee. He's the only one in this sad story that has acted with any honor. But the boy appears to have made the mistake of putting on a blue uniform, which gives us the privilege of shooting at him. So you'd best get busy at that.'

Franklin – March 1863

Shire waited with his squad in the cold yard of Shannon and Buchannan's store, as they'd been told to. Company B had used it as their kitchen since they arrived in Franklin six weeks ago. There was a large, open pot hanging from a tripod in the lee of the building, steaming into the cold air. About Shire's feet were littered several broken-up beehives. He sat on a crate, gently working stolen beeswax into the leather of his percussion cap box. If he could soften it up it wouldn't chaff his hand every time he needed to load.

'The colonel's sure to make examples of us,' said Lyman. 'Me especial' as a corporal. I wouldn't be surprised if I lose my stripes. We should never have listened to Tuck.'

'Aw, quit your whining,' said Tuck. 'You saw the captain back us. We got to stick to our story. And your jacket's so dirty, no one can see your stripes anyhow.'

Tom Muncie sat whittling disconsolately with his shut-knife. There was no shape emerging from the wood, he was just murdering it with unhappy slices. They'd been caught red-handed with the hives, so Shire was inclined to agree with Lyman. Mr Dickson, the erstwhile beekeeper, had found them out somehow. He'd interrupted them as they broke the slats apart for fuel. When Captain Yeomans was summoned, Tuck had claimed that they were sold the hives.

Mason nudged Shire's elbow. 'C'mon. It ain't so bad. We're all in it together.'

'You think so?' said Shire. 'More likely it'll be the Englishman who gets singled out again. I should never have gone along with it.'

It had felt both right and wrong at the time: wrong like scrumping for apples, right to be one of the boys. Now Mr Dickson had dragged Captain Yeomans off to see the colonel. What would it be this time?

Loss of pay? Extra picket duty? That was no small matter with Rebel cavalry swinging by every day and taking pot shots. At best, they'd get extra work detail building the fort, the bane of their lives. His hands were calloused from the labor and ached from the cold. It wasn't just being picked out and picked on as the only English soldier in the regiment that was wearing on him; it was also that as each week had passed in Franklin, he'd neither heard from Father nor moved any closer to Clara.

Across from him the new company undercook, Jordan, was at work. Freshly enlisted, he was the first black man in Company B. Shire knew he wouldn't be allowed to fight – only to cook.

'It ain't a smart story that's for sure,' Jordan said. 'You don't harvest honey in March. It's 'bout as far away from harvest time as you can git, and that's a fact.'

'Don't you think I know that?' said Tuck. 'I thought there might be enough old honey to flavor those flat rocks you feed us as biscuits. My Pa taught me a man's gotta right to try and improve his circumstance.'

'Not by thievin' he ain't. And you don't need to go lookin' in the army handbook to get told that, there's a Lord's rule for it. Your Pa not show you that?' Jordan took a ladle and leant around the steam to skim fat off the stew. The same fat would be put out in place of butter tomorrow. It was hard not to agree with Tuck.

Another squad came into the yard, leant their rifles against the wall and came looking for food. Cleves was first to find a tin plate and hold it out.

'Tain't done yet,' said Jordan.

'C'mon, Three-Fifths. You're supposed to have a meal ready if men come off duty. Is it three-fifths done?' He drew some laughter from behind. 'Now spoon up.'

Jordan tasted the stew. 'Five minutes.' He tipped a full cup of salt into the pot.

Shire spoke aside to Mason from where they were sat watching. 'What's Cleves talking about?'

'It's an insult,' said Mason quietly. 'A surprisingly educated one coming from Cleves.'

Shire was none the wiser.

'Our esteemed forbears,' said Mason, 'had a disagreement after they formed our constitution, concerning voting rights. Each state gets a voting value on account of its population. The southern states wanted to include slaves in the count. After a long debate, the convention settled on a value of three-fifths for each slave.'

Shire was confused. 'Three-fifths of what?'

'Three-fifths of a man... Kinda rubs it in, don't it. First of all they're a slave so not free to do anything, leastways vote. They get assessed the value of three-fifths of a man. And then the value of their vote is given to the state that enslaves them.'

Shire considered it. He nodded at Jordan. 'You think he understands?'

'I'd say from the way he looks like he wants to gut Cleves, he understands pretty good.'

Mason looked thoughtful. He leant in close to Shire. 'As we're talking fractions, you asked me once about my red skin.'

'I shouldn't ha – '

'It's alright. I want to tell you. See, I'm an educated man much like yourself. A lawyer... I thought you'd be surprised.'

'Well, no I – '

'I started on the court circuit in Ohio.' Mason drew out a small figure tied on a leather cord round his neck and showed it furtively to Shire.

Shire touched its smooth surface. 'Is it bone?'

'It is. It was white when my grandmother gave it to me. It's a panther – and she was half Iroquois Indian.' Mason tucked it back down his neck. 'Which makes me one eighth Indian or seven eighths white, depending on how you look at it.'

Shire wasn't quite sure how he was supposed to look at it.

'Often I'd get a client and it'd all be fine until someone whispered in their ear I was part Iroquois. They didn't even tell me sometimes. I'd pitch up at the courthouse for the trial to find they'd hired someone else. One judge flat refused to let me prosecute an Indian boy who'd stolen a saddle. Like I wouldn't do a proper job on him. I quit it after that.'

'Does the army know?'

'I never brought it up and they ain't asked. I want to fight. Perhaps then we won't have to think of people as fractions of this, that and the other. But there are plenty of outsiders in our little club, not only you. Tuck's not from Ohio. I have my own secret. And we're all better off than Jordan over there.'

Before Cleves could get his meal, Captain Yeomans appeared around the side of the store, Sergeant Matthews trailing behind him. Shire was first to stand to attention. The captain got up close to the five accused men.

'Don't you poor excuses for soldiers ever make me lie for you again,' he barked.

Shire respected the captain but wished he'd grow a moustache above that beard. It never looked right. He wanted to ink in the captain's upper lip.

'Next time, I'll step neatly to the side and let the colonel do his worst with you.'

Were they actually going to get away with it?

'Do you understand?'

'Yes, Captain.'

'Sergeant.'

'Yes, sir.'

'I need you to volunteer two of these honey-scented men to wait on table for the colonel and his guests tonight.'

'Shire and Mason, sir.'

They were both too wise to protest the injustice of it. It was still a let-off.

'Are you sure?' said Yeomans. 'I suspect our chirpy corporal and the Kentuckian were more likely at the root of this.'

'Well, sir, I'm thinkin' this way. Shire speaks well if spoken to, and Mason knows his manners.'

Tom Muncie, it seemed, was never in the running.

'Alright. Make sure they're looking smart.' He started to leave.

'Beggin' your pardon, Captain.' It was Jordan. 'What about these here hives, sir? Can I burn 'em?'

'Well they're no use to Mr Dickson or his bees anymore. Do what you want with them.'

The captain gone, Cleves was straight back at the pot and looking at the newly appointed waiters. His dabbed scars, born in the Cleveland iron foundries, rose with his smile.

'Make sure you dress up nice for dinner, Shire.'

Jordan slopped a miserly portion onto Cleves' plate and his smile disappeared.

'What the hell do you call this, boy?'

'Three-fifths,' said Jordan.

Shire leant against the wall of the brick kitchen and enjoyed the evening air. This didn't feel like a punishment. He'd just brought out the dinner plates and was waiting for the dessert to be ready. There was probably half an hour of daylight left. He looked around and compared the farm to the one he'd known so well at Ridgmont. It was a different setup altogether. There was a house here for a start, a handsome one, with a red tiled roof and stepped gables. It was capped with stone at either end and shaded by tall cedar trees. The roof extended out over an L-shaped porch which was fronted with a smart, white fence. The garden was as well-kept as the house, set to grass in front of the kitchen, and behind was a long, ordered vegetable garden. There was a smokehouse and various outbuildings, including slave huts. None of those back home. In his back and forth to the dinner party he'd had to dodge any number of children, and there were many blacks about, cooking or working the garden, their own children running along with the white ones. He decided it wasn't like the farm at Ridgmont at all.

He'd met Moscow Carter, the eldest son, before. Company B had helped him work some cotton through the gin that was a couple of hundred yards up the Columbia Pike. Moscow had been fair with them, when you considered they were occupying his town. He'd brought them coffee and warm biscuits. All in all, if you put the slave huts aside, you had to admire the place.

The dinner party was to thank the regiment for its assistance with the cotton. Though he didn't recall any of the officers, sat here enjoying the Carters' food, being there at all. There was a call from inside the kitchen. Shire straightened his new jacket and stepped in. The quartermaster had agreed that he and Mason could draw new trousers as well if they were going to wait on table. So the punishment was edging towards a reward.

'Now don't you go dippin' those Yankee fingers in this pie.' The black cook handed him a tray with six bowls. She'd been strict with Shire since he'd arrived.

'No, ma'am,' he said. 'I wouldn't dream of it.' He put on what he considered to be English charm, with the sole hope that he might be given a slice before the evening was over. They certainly didn't seem to be suffering privations. He could smell apple somewhere under the cream. They must have dried them over the winter.

He walked over and up onto the porch, then took the steps that led directly down through the porch floor into the basement. It was a curious place for a dining room, but it was easy to get to from the kitchen and he supposed it kept cool in the summer. Here in March there was a fire going, and the warmth welcomed him in when Mason opened the door. Bending his head to allow for the low ceiling, he served the Carters first as the captain had told him he must, despite them being the hosts. They didn't appear to object to being treated as guests in their own home with their own food. Moscow's father had the equally unlikely name of Fountain. Shire moved on to serve Colonel Opdycke, Major Wood and Captain Yeomans. He wasn't sure whether the regimental surgeon, Dr

McHenry, outranked Yeomans, but served him last anyway. Mason stole the tray from him and went up the steps. He was left to attend to the wine.

He thought the diners' polite interaction curious. Most days, a few miles to the south, pickets and cavalry would shoot and die in the mud and the cold. Yet here tonight, a certain civilized restraint held sway. So far, the conversation had skirted the war. They talked of the farm, of Fountain's purchase of the land many decades ago and how he'd built such a fine house. Both Fountain and Moscow were widowers and considerable time was spent listing the various children, grandchildren, nieces and nephews that either lived on the farm or had the run of it.

'It's a marvel,' said Dr McHenry, 'that you have such an ordered farm with the care of so many children.'

'We are not without help,' said Fountain. 'And each child becomes a useful pair of hands in their time.'

Fountain looked like a man who would know how to keep order, thought Shire. Grandfather though he was, the man was strong and broad in the shoulders. He wore his grey beard trimmed wide and square. Colonel Opdycke, his own new and rather wispy beard brushed to a point, made the first advance into contentious territory. 'How are you coping on the farm? With the loss of your slaves…'

Shire had heard the colonel preach and lead prayer on abolition.

Fountain sipped some wine before answering. 'We've lost but a few. Most have chosen not to leave what is their only home. The farm still accommodates them and they do the same work for their keep.'

'It's as well for now,' said Opdycke. 'We have so many from hereabouts throwing themselves on the army for food. But your cotton, you were shorthanded there.'

'We were, and we thank you for your help. We've lost more men from the town to the army, my other sons included. That's the deficit.'

'Do you know where they are?'

Moscow, his spoon suspended over his pie, answered in his father's place. 'They're both in the 20th Tennessee, as I was, until captured. Now I abide my parole.'

The cook had told Shire that Moscow had been a colonel. He was clean-shaven and had his father's tall forehead, but Shire thought his eyes were set a little harder underneath.

'That's more than many abide,' said Opdycke.

'I've done my time in the army,' said Moscow. 'In Mexico and in this war. And as the Doctor says, there are many children to tend to. I won't leave them again.'

'You must worry for your other sons,' said Major Wood to Fountain.

'I do. I do. I lost many of my children when they were young. To illness and accident both. All part of God's plan. We have to accept it. I'd hate to lose a grown one to a war I look on as man-made.'

'You think the war unnecessary?' said Opdycke.

'I think it was avoidable,' Fountain replied. 'I think that we were badly led into it from both sides. I was a patriot, Colonel. As was Moscow. But when an army invades your home, what are you to do?'

'There's the nub,' said Opdycke, putting down his glass. 'We don't consider that we can invade what is our own country. We see it as a rebellion.'

Shire thought it a hard word for the Carters to hear from a guest. An awkward silence settled on the room, only the scrape of spoons on near-empty bowls. Though the glasses were mostly full, Shire topped them up as a way of easing the quiet. There was a rush of childish footsteps across the floor above.

Moscow eventually picked up the challenge, not spitefully. 'We're not insensitive to the fact there are different opinions. We're not as you might have us be, ignorant backwoodsmen who never venture off their one-bale farm. My brother Tod is a young lawyer, educated in the classics at our own academy here in Franklin. He did not ride to war lightly. Neither did I. I have seen this land,

Colonel. I've ridden across Texas, worked in Missouri, traveled over New York State. And thanks to my capture, seen the inside of a Union jail in Boston. We know the depth of the arguments. But Lincoln's invasion, the misfortune he has brought on us, has left us no choice.'

Opdycke took in a loud breath through the nose. Dr McHenry got in before the colonel could reply. 'The wine, sir,' he said, 'it's unlike any I've tasted.'

Moscow turned to the doctor. 'It's a local wine. From the muscadine grape.'

'You must forgive the good doctor,' said the colonel, raising his own glass, 'he has an interest in all things medicinal. How do you find it, Doctor?'

'Quite delicious. Very sweet. Perhaps too much so for an educated palate. Closer to a dessert wine.'

Maybe it had sounded patronizing only to Shire's ear.

Moscow was even in his reply. 'It's a grape native to the South. It can only be cultivated in our climate. The sweetness suits our palate and our cuisine. Do you not find, Doctor, things thrive best in their own place? A transplanted variety might not take to the soil so well.'

The doctor stayed silent.

The colonel reverted to the earlier exchange. 'Is it as a misfortune that you think of us? To you perhaps, but not to the slaves, surely.'

'Do they seem so fortunate to you as they arrive to call on your charity? Many were made homeless as well as free in this winter. Free to go hungry. I would call that a misfortune, yes.'

Captain Yeomans supported his colonel. 'If it were us, would we not accept poverty over bondage? They're now free to improve their lives and we are ready to help.'

Shire recalled a black man he'd known only in death. One who lived in the helpful North – in New York. He kept his hands stiffly by his side to stop them wandering to his scar.

'The assumption is,' said Moscow, 'that there has never been prospect of change in the South in regard to slavery. But our struggle has been to conceive a way to change while preserving the things we value most.'

'With respect, sir,' Opdycke smiled, 'it is an extremely slow conception, and one that has borne no fruit. What change was afoot in regard to slavery before this war started?'

'I'll concede there was little. Yet in pushing the argument for so long and so sharply, the North has encouraged an opposing view, rather than allowing our society to discover its own answers. It's harder to find the right prayer when you're ordered to kneel. We're not all alike. Tennessee is not Alabama. Franklin is not New Orleans. But you have made us one in our purpose. And now our pride and honor are at stake. And our armies do well, despite your advantage in numbers.'

Opdycke wiped his mouth with his napkin. Shire decided it wasn't the moment to clear the dishes.

'If you were ever going to win this war,' said Opdycke, 'then it had to be at the start. The North can afford to lose many battles, dismiss many inept generals, and yet remain stronger than you. The Confederacy, on the other hand, must inevitably retreat to preserve its army. You can choose to give up men or territory, but you cannot keep both. The bear is very nearly chased up the tree. If we misjudge you, then the favor is well returned. We do not do this only for the slaves. We fight firstly for the Union. Yet many of us see slavery itself as the corruption. If slavery is your society's foundation, what pride is there in what you build upon it? We would free you from slavery as well.'

'Why, Colonel,' it was Fountain smiling now, 'it is a strange rescue which lives in my town by force of arms. And we exist in a wider world, from which this continent is not entirely immune. Your politicians and navy are clumsy and may yet offend the English enough to side with us. Then the lines would be drawn quite differently.'

'I think that unlikely in the extreme,' said the colonel.

'Why, sir,' said Yeomans. 'We have our own Englishman who may afford us an opinion. Private Shire here.' Shire's comfortable place as an observer evaporated. All eyes turned on him.

'If I'm right, Shire,' said his Captain, 'you were in England just last fall?'

'Yes, sir.' Shire half wondered how the captain knew this, but had to attend to the conversation.

'What is the sentiment then? Will England go to war with the South?'

'No, sir,' Shire said, quite sure of his ground. 'Though there is great suffering and starvation in the north of England where the cotton mills are idle. There you might find support for the Confederacy among the poorer people, but it is not shared in the south, our south, or in London. We settled our own argument with slavery more than half a century ago. No government could stand that supported a Confederate state that would preserve bondage.'

'Well answered, Private,' said the Colonel. 'You seem well-educated for a man in the ranks.'

'I'm a teacher, sir. And my father's a schoolmaster. After the war I plan to return home and finish my training.'

'I'm curious then how you find yourself here?'

Shire was caught. Surprised to be in the conversation at all, he'd come away from his usual story of an immigrant fallen on hard times. Captain Yeomans unwittingly saved him.

'Why it appears to be a trend, you English coming over to fight for us rather than the Rebels. We have that new man joining us, sir. You'll recall the letter from the Governor's office?'

'Oh yes,' said Opdycke. 'Most peculiar. The governor asking us to find room for a corporal. An ex-sergeant in the British army we're told. What the Governor would have to do with him, I've no idea. But we'll take as many trained soldiers as he wants us to. Curious name too. What was it?'

'Ocks, sir,' said Yeomans, 'Corporal Ocks.'

Franklin – March 1863

Spring had been forced into retreat by a last foray of winter. The very first light started to filter in amongst the trees, illuminating patches of snow. Shire could at last see Tuck, if only in outline.

'I done told you,' Tuck said, 'just up an' go see him? Seems the plain thing to do if you ask me, which you 'pear to be doin'.'

Shire knew Tuck was tired. He was too. The company was on picket duty and stretched out in a long line of pairs two miles south of Franklin. He'd been here more than four hours with no fire and was achingly cold. Mason and Tom Muncie were unseen somewhere to their left. There had been no hint of the Rebels. All the same, they were wary and spoke in whispers.

Shire considered Tuck's suggestion. 'I guess I don't want to know why he's here. It means something. It has to. Why else would he pick this regiment?'

It was a week since Shire had waited on table at the Carter house, since his old life had caught up with him in the form of Ocks. His mind hadn't stopped churning since. Ocks had duly arrived two days later and been assigned to Company A. He'd made no effort to find Shire, who'd begun to doubt Ocks knew he was there, until yesterday, when Ocks had given him an unsmiling nod at the end of regimental drill.

'You want me to go see him?' prodded Tuck. 'Is that it? Or come with you?'

Shire knew he was being unfair. He wanted reassurance from Tuck, but Tuck didn't know why he had come to America. He'd not shared it with anyone since Dan. 'You don't know Ocks,' he said. 'He ran the estate farm as tight as a tick. If anyone crossed him, they got something to show for it.' Why would Ocks come away? He was well set. He must know what Shire was up to. He realized that Tuck was staring at him though the half-light.

'You know,' whispered Tuck, 'you're gonna have to tell me the whole tale sometime. I can see you're holdin' on to the nub.'

Shire kept quiet.

'It's your business, but most troubles do a little better with an airin'.'

'It's complicated.'

'*Complicated* usually means *confused* in my experience.'

Tuck pulled a small bottle of whiskey from inside his coat. 'I've been nipping at it in the dark, but there's enough left to cover a story.'

Shire felt the damn break inside him. He edged closer to Tuck, who listened patiently as the truth spilled out. If ever Shire threatened to dry up, Tuck passed the bottle one more time. Before long, Shire had told him everything: why he was here, his childhood with Clara, even of their kiss and caress in the Ridgmont gatehouse that Christmas Eve. He'd said too much. Embarrassed, he grabbed the whiskey and finished the last half-inch.

Tuck was quiet for a while. 'Well,' he said, 'I think you're doing the right thing.'

'Truly?'

'I'd say so. It's the honorable thing to do, and I'd do much the same. Seems to me the good Lord has set this duty squarely on you. Ain't anyone else looking out for Clara. She's your friend and your sweetheart... And this Taylor's a damn snake.'

Shire fought down a powerful urge to hug Tuck right there. He'd come to doubt himself so much.

'How you're going about it is another matter. Circumstances steer us all, I guess. But hitching up to this army?' Tuck shook his head. 'It has its own pressing concerns. One thing we can do.' He sadly took back the empty bottle and tossed it into the woods. 'Next time we're let off the leash, we'll find you a friendly whore. You touch one titty and come chasing over to America in search of the other one. It ain't healthy. First woman can cloud a man's judgement. Second one gives a mite more perspective.'

Corporal Lyman crept up behind them and whispered fiercely. 'You boys makin' weddin' plans or somethin'? 'Cos I'd hate a Reb' to have to shoot you just to shut you up. Is that whiskey I'm smelling? Damnation, Tuck, the captain will gut us all... Now, the lights comin' on and they're apt to clear their barrels soon. Don't be shy in shootin' first if you see anything. Find a tree, get behind it, and quit yackin'.'

Shire did as he was told. Lyman was right: this was the most dangerous part of the day. When not on picket, it was common for Shire to be turned out with the whole regiment at dawn. The Reb's liked to get up a scare to keep the Union boys on edge. But he felt the whiskey and his confession had smoothed his own edge a little.

The light came on. A few snowflakes drifted down hypnotically between leafless branches. Shire tried to put his thoughts aside and rally some concentration for the last hour of the watch. He squeezed and stretched his eyes, looked as far into the trees as the light would let him.

A twig snapped somewhere ahead and there was movement. He threw his rifle to his shoulder, cocked and fired. The discharge fractured the still air.

'What d'you see?' hissed Tuck.

'I'm not sure.'

'Deer, like as not.' Tuck's rifle was at his shoulder too.

Lyman was right back. 'Was that you, Shire?'

'Yes, Corporal.'

'Then I'd best check for casualties on our side,' he said. 'Reload.'

Shire was fumbling in his cartridge box when a larger man came up behind the three of them, apparently careless of the alarm.

'Good morning, Corporal.' His voice was deep and he didn't bother to whisper. Shire knew the accent, or rather the lack of one to his ear.

'If you'll pardon us, sir, we've got a scare on,' Lyman whispered. He'd clearly taken the man for an officer.

'Oh, I don't think there's much out there for you to worry about,' the new arrival said loudly. 'It's not good ground for an attack on this side of the pike. If I was them I'd come up on our left. Wouldn't you? You won't mind if I borrow Private Shire for a few minutes. You can fill the line here.'

Lyman gave way to the easy authority. 'Alright. If you could you bring him back loaded please, sir.'

Shire knew his time for speculation was at an end. He shared a worried glance with Tuck and then followed Ocks back behind the lines.

Tuck turned back to the front with Lyman. He saw nothing and began to relax until, a few minutes later, Shire charged back between them and raced straight on into the woods and towards the Rebels.

Ocks came up more calmly. He stopped as he reached them.

'What in hell's name did you say to him?' demanded Tuck, stepping towards Ocks.

Ocks didn't even look at him. 'I just brought him some news from home,' he said, before he turned and walked back towards town.

Shire raced between the trees, heedless of any danger. The rip of grief and a new reality tore through him. The smells and noises of the forest were lost to him. Minutes before, after firing his rifle, his senses had been sharp, attentive to any sight or sound that might betray the enemy. Now, he heard and saw nothing, only ran on uphill, relentlessly uphill; as if solace waited for him at the top. The snow deepened and he was forced to slow to a walk, frantically using his rifle butt to lever him upwards.

He'd died alone, Ocks had said. Three months ago, with no one there. All this time he'd been in America, his father had been dead and in the ground. All his prayers entreating God to care for him had been pointless. And Grace dead too. He hadn't waited to hear more from Ocks, just ran away despite Lyman's calls. And it was rage that fueled him. Rage at himself, that he had left his father, betrayed him, to come on this fool's adventure an ocean away. He used it to dismiss the burning in his legs and lungs as he climbed further until, utterly spent, he collapsed where the hill levelled out. He lay for long empty minutes, his face half-buried in the snow.

At last he rolled onto his back. Tall bare trees surrounded him, seeming to angle inwards towards an unseen zenith lost in the mist. He reached for the comfort of his mother's ring, before he remembered it was gone. Slowly his dizziness eased and his senses began to return. He rose awkwardly in the squeaking snow, looked onto a white world that was muffled and still. Leaning on his rifle, he tried to get his bearings. And it was stood there behind him, just thirty paces away: a stag, sideways on, not moving but for his head, lifted on a stretched neck to sniff the windless air. His dark brown coat was the only color in the scene, framed between grey, bare trees and against the canvas of the snow. His antlers were a crown, a badge of majesty. He was magnificent.

The head turned towards him with calm knowing eyes. They stared at each other, intimate, their alternating, steaming breath reaching closer. Shire wanted empathy, wanted comfort, but instead felt only judgment, as if there was wisdom here beyond his petty sorrow; as if he was out of place and his crisis had no bearing. He struggled for some meaning, some relevance, but touched only the remains of the rage that had driven him here and sparked it anew. He needed death. Death had visited him, but only by proxy from another time and place. He needed it to be here, now, so he could feel it, commune with it. Defying the cold, his fingers worked unconsciously. He grabbed a cartridge and bit it open, poured the powder into the muzzle. He took the ramrod and pushed the ball home.

All the while the stag was calm. It didn't react to the movement or the metallic scrape of metal. It wasn't primed to move; there was no tension, no readiness to spring away. Shire took a percussion cap and fitted it. He was taut with fury. He wanted only to summon death to him, to take this creature in spiteful revenge. He raised the muzzle and aimed for the heart. A small cry somewhere deep inside slowed him, gave him pause. But the anger prevailed and he pulled the trigger.

The hammer snapped shut, punctuating his madness, but the gun didn't fire. He screamed in frustration and finally sparked the stag to motion, but not to escape. Instead it charged, and Shire's rage was transformed to fear through an icy bolt of adrenalin. There would be no time to replace the cap. Just enough to cock the trigger, fire again, and hope that having invited death into the scene, it wouldn't leave with him. His thumb slipped on the hammer and he looked down to the gun, the sound of hooves in the snow raced towards him. He pulled up the barrel, breathless with terror, to nothing... nothing but an empty scene with a sudden heavy snowfall half obscuring the trees.

Rage and fear both spent, he gave into grief and wept for he didn't know how long, until they found him. Tuck laid a hand on him. Mason and Tom were a few paces back, anxious to be away.

'C'mon, Shire,' said Tuck. 'Whatever it is, we need to get you back to the lines. Before the watch changes and they put you on a charge.'

Nassau – May 1863

The four men waited in silence. Their small talk had all been used up during the voyage across the Atlantic and in the days spent in Nassau since. Matlock stood and walked across the white plank platform to the rail. He preferred the silence, only occasionally disturbed by the duke's newspaper when he turned a page then snapped it straight.

It was an odd place to hold a meeting: fifteen feet from the ground, perched within the limbs of a bulbous Silk Cotton Tree. Its branches spread out almost flatly; branches that were the girth of a normal trunk. The square platform rested in between. They'd climbed here, somewhat precariously, by way of a single flight of steep steps. The curiously shaped Royal Victoria Hotel was a stone's throw away: four floors, long and thin, both ends shaped like the rounded stern of an ocean steamer.

He'd feel easier once these meetings were over and he was aboard a steamer back to England. Not that he relished the idea of being at sea again, having been sick for most of the outward voyage. At least he'd be on his way home to Ridgmont. There he could sort out whatever state of affairs he found waiting, be in control again. These few days on shore, waiting for this damned American, had relieved his nausea, but not his anxiety. He wasn't made for travel.

Below him was a large, clipped garden that might in time foster shade for the hotel's guests. And beyond, falling down the slope to the busy harbor, was an assortment of red rooftops interspersed with wide palm fronds. A pleasant breeze brushed through them on its way up to the hotel, mixing the sweet scent of the gardens with that of the sea. The first clouds of the day, seeds of the inevitable afternoon downpour, were starting to build over the town.

Half turning, he caught Stringer's eye and was rewarded with a salesman's smile, all width and no sincerity. That man was ever on the make. Once he'd worked out that Matlock was the key-holder for the duke's purse, he'd cornered him at every opportunity: arriving for breakfast in the ship's salon just as he did; coincidentally promenading on deck. Matlock remained closed to him. The estate had no interest in building or operating ships. Stringer had gone as far as implying Matlock could receive a discreet finder's fee if the duke were to invest. But there was no need to deal with outsiders to profit from the duke. Matlock had an endless private opportunity to redistribute their inheritance.

Stringer would be like a dog on a leash today with so much wealth at hand. But he was merely in the employ of W.S Lindsay and Company. Sitting next to him was William Lindsay himself, a much more admirable figure: a banker, a member of Parliament and the biggest ship-owner in England. He was also, Matlock had learnt, a confidant of Napoleon III. His tales of the emperor's court were quite fascinating. They'd been a bright spot on an otherwise arduous voyage. How on earth had he come to pick Lindsay as an associate?

Where were the Americans? The hotel and the garden were quiet, unlike the evenings. The accepted daily routine seemed to be to sleep off the night's excesses, rise after lunch, and commence them again before dinner. Everyone in this hotel was profiting in one way or another from the war: diplomats, British and Confederate naval officers, blockade runners, newspaper correspondents and a host of lesser rogues. All reveling into the small hours; all looking for a share in the money generated by the trade of blockaded goods through Nassau.

There was laughter below. Vibrations on the steps transmitted through the platform. A head appeared, and the duke and his companions stood.

'My dear Duke.' A grey-haired man, not old, dressed smartly and with a black necktie, climbed up and gripped the duke's shoulder while shaking his hand. Most Americans were over-effusive in Matlock's, blessedly limited, experience.

'Why, Mr Trenholm. George,' said the duke, 'how good to see you.'

'May I introduce Charles Proileau, who runs my office in Liverpool,' said Trenholm.

Proileau, balding and spectacled, looked suited to an office life.

The duke took his turn. 'I believe you know our member of Parliament, William Lindsay. The Lower House, but we won't hold that against him, and his associate, Mr Edgar Stringer.'

'Oh, Mr Lindsay and I are friendly fish in the same big pond.' Trenholm greeted Lindsay just as warmly, his voice deep and melodic. 'And he's known as a strong supporter of our cause. We have many ships trading thanks to you and Mr Stringer.'

Lindsay took the lead for the pair. 'I only wish our government would allow us to do more, sir, for you and your countrymen.'

Matlock absented himself from the introductions and stood to one side. The duke made no effort to include him. A tray of iced rum was served and everyone took their seats in the cushioned wicker loungers, arrayed in a friendly circle. Matlock preferred a more upright chair behind the duke, where a small table would allow him to make notes.

Trenholm bridged the gap to more serious discussion with an apology. 'Please forgive me for detaining you, gentleman. The Union navy has no sympathy for the timetables of ships leaving the Confederacy. We had to wait on the best conditions to run the blockade, but here we are. I hope you don't mind the venue. There's little chance of a discreet meeting on this island.'

Matlock looked over the rail. There were a couple of heavyset men down on the path to discourage anyone from lingering.

'I suggest that, for today, we tend where we will. We all have commercial, political and personal interests. Those, I humbly maintain, will be best served if we are open and frank in our assessments. I can also assure you, though I'm not a representative of the Confederate government, I will report directly back to our Secretary of the Navy, Mr Mallory, on matters that merit his attention.'

Matlock couldn't fail to be impressed by how Trenholm then expertly summarized conditions in the South, both military and commercial. The duke asked general, open questions, and it was left to Matlock, by way of a whisper in the duke's ear, to promote the more pressing ones that had a bearing on Ridgmont's finances. Since he'd been dragged here, he should at least look to profit from it.

Trenholm's advice was ever pragmatic. 'Where you have property or a business that is threatened directly by the Yankees, my advice is to co-operate with them. It's what I tell my own people. This war waves back and fore. Yankee dollars are more accepted than our own; we can't deny it. My only wish is you charge them to the hilt. If their armies are to come at us, let us at least try to bankrupt them for the privilege. What is the sentiment in Britain? I have the view of the good Mr Proileau, but we have both your Houses represented here. Do the British steer away or towards us?'

The duke deferred to Lindsay. 'Let us rather say they are at anchor. There is no mood for intervention or, at this time, recognition, despite speeches from myself and the duke in our respective chambers. I still believe there is wide sentiment for the South, due in no small part to your feats of arms. We are ever supporters of the underdog. If the war started to tend northward, more formal support would follow, I believe.'

'Understand, George,' added the duke, 'there is much to preoccupy our government. Europe has its own woes, and the French emperor, as ever, tries our patience. Much as we here might advocate it, the British government doesn't want to get committed in America and thereby tie its hands elsewhere.'

'Should we look to France then to build our ships? I believe you have the emperor's ear, Mr Lindsay?'

'I have had the honor to meet him on several occasions,' said Lindsay. 'But dictators are capricious and any investments would be subject to his whims. Britain, at least, is a liberal democracy. If we act within the law, we are protected by it, even from the government.'

The waiter returned to recharge the glasses. There was such a studied silence that Matlock felt obliged to stop the scratching of his pen. A woman's squeal, followed by a recovering giggle, escaped from one of the hotel balconies.

'May I?' Stringer asked Lindsay, once the waiter had descended from the platform. Matlock anticipated the easy patter of the salesman, soothing contentions that steered ever to the positive. Whether they were selling greengages or ships, they were all the same.

'It helps to separate the matter of naval and commercial vessels. For the latter there is no question of interference from the government. Quite the opposite. As you'll see from the number of British naval officers in Nassau, we want to trade with the Confederacy. The Union dollar may be the stronger currency, but Confederate cotton bonds are stronger still and will fund all the blockade runners you need.'

'I understand,' said Trenholm. 'And I'll be happy for Charles to conduct more business with you on that score. But what should I tell Mr Mallory regarding the prospects for his navy? Charles tells me that before you sailed, the British Government seized the *Alexandra.*'

Matlock was familiar with the scandal. A ship under construction in Liverpool was claimed to be intended for war rather than commerce. The British government, not wanting to antagonize Lincoln, had it under guard.

'We believe they have made a mistake, sir,' Stringer sat forward. 'And, with respect, I believe the *Alexandra* is merely impounded.'

'Is there a difference?' said Trenholm. 'Charles is pretty anxious as it's his name on the order. We made him into a British subject for the privilege.' He reached over and patted Mr Proileau on the shoulder, drawing only a frugal smile.

'It will be made a test case,' continued Stringer, 'as to whether the *Alexandra* breaks our Foreign Enlistment Act. But the government's choice of vessel is poor. Apart from a reinforced structure, there is nothing they can point to. And if they lose this case it will be harder for them to bring another for a more obvious fighting ship. Your navy will have its ships, sir. Just like the *Alabama*. We'll get them to you.'

Matlock thought that neither Trenholm nor the duke looked convinced. The *Alabama* was let loose last year. Things had changed since.

The afternoon wore on, the conversation meandering between the commercial and the political. Matlock observed, in the case of both Trenholm and Lindsay, these were often closely aligned. He took notes only where there was a Ridgmont interest. When the meeting broke up, Lindsay and Stringer left with Proileau, all carefully negotiating the steps. Trenholm provided a cigar for the duke. Matlock stayed at his station.

'George,' said the duke. 'I was honored to have you take my place at the wedding last autumn. What must Clara think of me?'

'The honor was mine, sir, truly. She is a wonderful girl. Of course she was disappointed you couldn't come, but she understood.'

'Have you seen her since?'

Matlock made a show of busying himself with his notes. He hadn't quite understood how close Trenholm and the duke were. Certainly not that it was Trenholm who had given Clara away.

'Just the once. She came to Charleston before Christmas, after the wedding. Sadly, without Taylor, whose duties keep him in the field. It's lonely for her while this war lasts. Does she know you are here?'

'No,' said the duke, clearly embarrassed. 'I feared it would place an expectation on me. Perhaps I should have asked you to bring her?'

'Running the blockade is not without its hazards. She's safer where she is.'

'Is she though? Half of Tennessee is gone.'

'I have a friend who looks in on Comrie. If the war gets close, I'll get her out of there.' Trenholm paused. 'Of course... you could return with me? An English duke in the Confederacy would be big news. Your support matters to us a great deal. You and your man could take a closer look at all your interests, and you could visit Clara.'

Matlock looked up from tidying his notes. He wanted to leave Nassau but sailing safely east, not try his chances with the Union Navy.

'Hah!' laughed the duke, 'What d'you say, Matlock? Shall we venture further from home? Your face is a picture, man. Don't worry. Mr Trenholm is toying with us. He knows I couldn't risk it. Not unless I want to burn my bridges entirely with our government. No, we'll have to leave it to George to watch over Clara.'

Matlock was relieved but saw that Trenholm's smile had weakened.

'Matlock? Is that the name?'

'Yes, sir. I'm sorry we weren't introduced earlier.'

'You've taken a bundle of notes, Mr Matlock. We wouldn't want those seen outside our circle.'

'They are for the duke's interests only.'

'Don't you worry about our Matlock,' said the duke. 'Soul of discretion, aren't you?'

'Yes, Your Grace. Sometimes your business is so discreet, I don't even tell you.'

The duke laughed, but Trenholm just puffed his cigar.

Fort Granger, Franklin – May 1863

Shire slid a last wet shovel of dirt and rock into the barrow. He evened out the load to make it easier to push. It wasn't cold, but the air carried a fine drizzle and held the smell of damp earth close to the ground. His clothes were muddy. He wiped his forehead with his sleeve and his own stink made him blow out his cheeks. He lifted the barrow with straight arms and set off again. Father's death was present in every step and breath he took. Had he done twenty-five or twenty-six loads? What did it matter?

It was a punishment. On regimental parade this morning, Captain Yeomans had bawled at him. His uniform was a disgrace, buttons tarnished, his rifle dirty. The result was four hours of fatigue duty. The few other people around earlier had blurred into the murk, before leaving one by one. He wasn't glad to be here, but it didn't trouble him much either. At least he was away from the chatter and banter of the company. The monotony of this task fitted his mood, a physical penance. It might help him sleep.

Fort Granger was nearly complete. Its three bastions faced east and north, while behind them the long wall looked west above the steep slope that fell to the Harpeth River. The fact that all the walls were built made Shire's round trip all the longer. His lonely task was to take out the spoil from the powder magazine that was being dug deep in the middle of the fort, expanding the cellar of a house they'd demolished. The barrow-load had to be wheeled behind the middle bastion, through the sally port and, with aching shoulders, around the northern end, before he reached the slope above the river. It gave him plenty of time to think, not that he made any progress. As he twisted his hands underneath the arms of the barrow, pushed it up and watched the dirt slip and slide down towards the river, he was no nearer any resolution. He started back on the lighter return journey. There would be matters at home; the house, the school. What had happened in the months since? What could he do from here?

He passed back through the sally port and into the fort again. There was an oversized robin perched atop a pick-axe that had been left standing – an inverted T. Shire looked at the bird with disdain. It was all wrong. He longed to see a robin from home, in its proper proportion, with the right length of tail and singing the right tune. He was homesick for people no longer there. His loves and friendships lived inside him like so many lost spirits. Only one stood out from the others, Clara, who still lay ahead of him.

His thoughts for Grace were drowned in guilt: guilt that he could find no room to grieve for her alongside the loss of his father, guilt that he hadn't gone to her the night he left, and guilt that he was thinking on the implications for himself and Clara rather than about poor Grace. Perhaps he could have saved them both if only he'd stayed home. Her marriage to Taylor had died with her, so he was reduced to carrying a tale of what had been, not what was. The matter hung on whether Clara had yet married and, if so, when? If her marriage was legal, would he really chance Clara's happiness with his secret? What if she'd married earlier? In either case there was still a duty to open her eyes to Taylor. But it was when he brought his own feelings for Clara into the equation it all fell apart. Their promise to each other was exacting a heavy toll. He'd read back through all her letters, hoping to find in them something that would encourage him to go on. Her very last letter he'd left with his civilian clothes at Dan's home. He had no fondness for it; it had asked him to stop writing. But he remembered it: '*Taylor would not understand, and I will have no secrets from him.*'

Back at the intended powder magazine, he took up his shovel, resigned to his mind going back and fore with the barrow. The only consolation, if it could be called such, was that there was no decision to make, at least not now. The regiment had been in Franklin for almost three months and showed no sign of moving, as evidenced by his present task. It was the army that would decide if he would get any closer to Clara.

He looked at his dirty, blistered hands and then up at what passed for sky. The drizzle had taken on a darker shade. The sun must be going down somewhere out there. Lyman would come to fetch him back soon. He'd make this his last load, corporal or not. The barrow full again, he rested the shovel along its length and set off, navigating the detritus of the building site, until he was once again outside the fort and rounding the north bastion.

'You're a sorry sight for a soldier, Owen Stanton.'

Shocked by the sudden deep voice, as well as his real name, Shire dropped one arm of the barrow and the load spilled out onto the grass, partly burying the shovel.

Ocks sat on a boulder just up the slope and half in the mist, his greatcoat pulled up about his neck. 'I thought you might've looked me up before now,' he said. They hadn't spoken since he'd visited Shire on the picket line some weeks before. 'Thought you'd be curious as to the details.'

Shire's heart beat in his chest, but he wouldn't run away this time. 'What difference would it make? Both still dead, aren't they?' He rescued the shovel, righted the barrow and began to refill it.

'I was away for her funeral but I heard it was a quiet affair, her having no family. But then neither did your father at the end.'

Shire kept shoveling, trying not to rush.

'I'll tell you since you won't ask. Grace was found in the snow, by her son's grave... after you disappeared. She lingered a few days. I suppose she had nothing left to live for.'

Shire stopped shoveling.

'Paints a picture, don't it. You and her such good friends an' all. The only talk in the Drovers was about the two deaths and what the link might be. Your father sick from worry or gossip, people said. Did you see her to say goodbye? Given what you're up to it seems the least you could have done. Maybe that's why she lay there?'

'No,' said Shire. 'I couldn't.' He wished he had. If he'd only gone to her that night, it might have changed everything. But he'd convinced himself it was easier on her not to know. Now he saw it for what it was: cowardice.

'Uh,' Ocks grunted, 'Might have been better.' He stood up and came down the slope to stand close to Shire, closer than he needed to.

'Changes things though, don't it. With her gone, there's no one to say who the father was. Who's to back you up? Harland dead, Grace dead. Your father, if he ever knew, dead.'

Shire pushed past Ocks to start to shovel again, gave himself time to think. Ocks didn't know about the wedding. Matlock hadn't told him. It gave him something at least, something over Ocks. And he wasn't going to give it away. 'He's still not fit to marry Clara.'

'Perhaps not. You looking to step in, are you?' Ocks snorted. 'We're not allowed to dream of that, Shire. We're barely good enough for a vicar's daughter, you and I.' He grabbed the stem of the shovel in one hand, stopped it and looked Shire in the eye.

'Leave it, Shire. No good'll come of it... not for you. This isn't our fight, two poor boys, two Englishmen.'

'It's Clara's good I'm thinking of.'

'You don't think I'll let you get that far, do you? Not once this army gets moving. It won't stay here forever.'

'What's in it for you, Ocks? What's Matlock bribed you with?'

'Just looking after the interests of my duke, I am.' Ocks smiled. He let go of the shovel and walked away into the mist.

Nassau – May 1863

Trenholm emerged with Proileau and Lafitte from the Nassau customs house. He squinted into the bright morning sun. In unison they put on their wide-brimmed hats and crossed the wharf.

'Well, I think we got about what we expected there,' said Trenholm. Was it too early for a cigar? The harbor held a kaleidoscope of aromas, not all of them pleasant.

'I think I'd prefer to deal with pirates rather than those freeloaders.' Proileau was ever quick to anger. 'At least pirates have to put to sea to rob you.'

'Chances are they're descended from pirates,' mused Lafitte as they walked, 'and not too distantly.'

Trenholm had sent John Baptist Lafitte out from the Charleston office to take control of business and was staying at the Lafitte home; so much more relaxing than the Royal Victoria. You couldn't be in that hotel more than two minutes without some hawker trying it on. Lafitte was one of his best men. It had been unlikely that Trenholm would improve on the trade terms that Lafitte had previously secured.

'I guess they're entitled to their pound of flesh like everybody else,' said Trenholm. 'Not so different from us.'

He'd threatened to move his operation to Havana or Bermuda if they couldn't get a better deal. The number of vessels they ran in and out of here certainly merited asking the question. The game had changed last year. Previously he'd run cargo straight to Europe. But they did better sailing smaller boats in and out of the Confederacy, then transferring the cargoes to bigger transatlantic ships, using the island ports near at hand. The smaller ships were faster, with shallower draughts. They could dodge and hide from the Union blockade in the mazy coastal waters of the Carolinas.

But they weren't so suitable for crossing the Atlantic. Trenholm could see Nassau had grown in the few months since he was last here. The authorities were getting rich hosting the sale of cargoes and the transfer of goods.

'The deal's no worse than the other ports,' conceded Lafitte. 'I guess they know that.' His white hair was brushed back and his beard was cut short; little more than stubble. He appeared at home. Perhaps he was turning pirate himself, thought Trenholm.

A small barefoot boy, no more than ten, pushing an oversized handcart stacked with shoddy crates, squeaked by in front of them. The wharf front was crowded with a mix of the low, fast blockade-runners and the larger oceangoing vessels. All were either loading or unloading using derricks or ramps. A few local fishing boats bobbed nervously between the larger hulls. And almost every bit of land was taken by stacks of boxes and barrels, some under the shelter of open-sided warehouses, some covered by tarred canvas, and still more at the mercy of the elements. This port was operating at capacity, thought Trenholm. They didn't need to attract more business.

For once his mind wasn't wholly on the present. It kept casting back to Comrie and the undertakings he'd made to a girl sat in her wedding dress, how he'd said he'd always help her, even unasked-for. He wasn't doing so well by her.

Lafitte led them through the maze of boxes.

'Cost-cutting isn't our main concern,' said Trenholm. 'It was worth a try while I'm here, but it's throughput we need. We're making a mint on every load. So we hire the best crews, you tell the captains that. I don't mind high wages if they're good. Same goes for the captains themselves. And if you can get British ex-navy, hire them on the spot.'

They came alongside a vessel that was casting off.

'She's a beauty, ain't she?' said Lafitte. 'Not one of ours though.'

'The *A. D. Vance*,' read Proileau. 'Named for a friend of yours, I believe.'

'Old Zebulon, from North Carolina,' said Trenholm. 'He picked a fine one. Maybe I should run for governor.'

'Ha.' Proileau smiled. A rare thing. 'The poor man has just the one named for him, George. Hell, half the other ships here are yours. Trust you to take a liking to one that isn't.'

Trenholm ran an experienced eye over the sleek shape. Two small masts, one each fore and aft, to assist the side-mounted wheels that did all the hard work. Two funnels, back of center, tilted gently backwards so as not to challenge the wind. She'd be fast. Out at sea she'd burn the best anthracite to keep the smoke to a minimum, but right now she pushed out thick, grey smoke. She must be well over two hundred feet long. A harbor tug pulled her clear of the wharf. Then she engaged one paddle and turned on the spot. Finding her aim, the second paddle kicked in and off she sped. One more ship couldn't hurt. 'We should see if she's for sale.'

There were raised voices behind them. He turned to see a cluster of black men, shoving and slipping over a carpet piled with walnuts. Beyond them, he saw a familiar solitary figure.

'Forgive me, gentlemen. I have some business to attend to with Mr Matlock there. It won't take long. I'll meet you back at the house and we can go through the Liverpool accounts.'

Following Matlock, he came away from the main wharf and into an area set aside for the drying and wholesale selling of sponges. Acres of them were laid out on the floor to dry in the sun and the breeze. Yet more spilled out from warehouse doors. Trenholm had to ignore the businessman in him. He had other people to do his buying. He slowed his pace, waited until Matlock was away from all the vendors and moving out towards the edge of the harbor. The man had a slow, slightly stooped, meandering gait. He didn't give the impression of someone who walked often for pleasure. 'Mr Matlock.'

Matlock turned and looked surprised. He took off his hat and bowed slightly.

Trenholm laughed. 'You don't have to bow to me, Matlock. I'm no duke.'

'Did you want to discuss business, sir?'

'No, no. I have a private matter.' Trenholm preferred to be direct. It was the best way to get a telling reaction. 'I need to know when Taylor's wife died... His first wife.'

He was good, Trenholm would give him that. Not so much as a twitch. He had the face of a butler.

'To whom do you refer, sir? The only Taylor I'm aware of is the duke's son-in-law.'

'I'll save us some time, shall I?' said Trenholm. 'A letter of yours came to me, rather than to Taylor. I've met with him regarding it. I know of the wedding, of Shire, even of your man Ocks. So there's no need to pretend. I need to know that date.'

Matlock's innocent mask fell, but not into distress. Trenholm instead saw his eyes sharpen and a tightness come to his mouth. 'The duke. He doesn't know.'

'I understand,' said Trenholm. 'Shall we walk on?' They started forward again. 'What I'm trying to ascertain is whether I'm going to have to tell him?'

'To what purpose?' asked Matlock. 'Who would that serve?'

'I would think the truth stands on its own where his daughter is concerned. Beyond that, there's the law. I gave his daughter away on his behalf. Took her hand and placed it in another's. Yet half a year later, I find I don't know if she's truly married.'

'There is no issue in law, sir. I can reassure you as to that. The wedding, in Tennessee, was on November 8th, yes?'

'It was.'

'Grace Rees died on the 7th. I saw her body that very day. Strange, I know, but it appears the Lord took an interest.'

Trenholm felt some relief, but chose not to show it. 'I only wish he'd taken an interest sooner. Or that someone had. Taylor tells me you were at this secret wedding. How could you watch the match with Clara continue after that?'

Matlock stopped and spoke with some anger. 'That is all I could do – watch. You think I invented this, sir? I say the invention lies elsewhere. It was Taylor's indiscretion. And the girl's father that insisted on the wedding, farce as it was. They never saw each other after that day. It was blackmail, pure and simple. And Taylor pursued the match with Clara against my advice.'

Trenholm ignored Matlock's case. 'I knew Taylor's father. Not a pure man himself, but a friend of mine. I know Comrie. I know its business and its links to Ridgmont. That was your risk. And you put that money before a bigamous marriage. Is the duke so hard up?'

'The duke's interests are my own. At no point in this have I been free to act. But what of you? You've known this how long? Since you read Taylor's letter, so a matter of months. And yet you have not written, or yet spoken to the duke? No. You were pulled into the same web as me. The duke's money and voice are important to you and your new little country. You wouldn't risk that. Not even if I'd told you Grace had died after the wedding.'

Trenholm hadn't expected such confidence, such assertion. And Matlock was painfully on the mark. Trenholm could afford to lose the duke's patronage, but his country couldn't. Not while there was the slightest chance of Britain supporting the Confederacy.

'Who else knows?' he said.

Matlock turned and started to walk them back towards the dock. 'Only Shire. And whoever he's told. Nobody in England but me.'

'What about Ocks?'

'He knows of the child, not the wedding. I think Shire may have the marriage license, but it proves nothing now.'

'On the contrary. It proves Taylor is a liar. It proves he risked her dishonor. The effect on the duke would be much the same.'

'I can do no more.' Matlock held his palms upwards. 'It will be played out in America. Ocks has joined the same regiment. He will deal with Shire if your armies don't first.'

Trenholm considered he'd already done his best to ensure the armies did. He knew many senior officers in Bragg's army and had asked that if the 125th Ohio put its head up, that it be roughly treated. He hadn't been able to give anyone a reason. Luckily he had enough authority not to have to. He held back from telling Matlock any of this. Instead he tried one last time to regain some authority. 'If anything changes in England, I need to know. You understand? Send any word via Proileau and the Liverpool office. That'll get to me sooner.'

Trenholm left Matlock amongst the sponges and walked back up the hill to Lafitte's home. Proileau was eager to take him through the Liverpool accounts. It was all good news. On average, only one in eight trips through the blockade had been stopped. Business in war was more lucrative than out of it.

Despite the profits laid out before him, Trenholm's mind wandered. Matlock was easy to dislike but harder to read. Though he played the victim in Taylor's affairs, Trenholm's gut wasn't easy. He was so obviously distracted that, after he'd finished, Proileau had asked if anything was wrong.

'Oh, nothing much, Charles, nothing much. When you get back to England, I want you to send a man or two down to Ridgmont, on the quiet. There's something there I'd like checked.'

Murfreesboro – June 1863

Shire hurried on behind Tuck through the dark and the rain. His feet kept sliding out from under him on the slick road; he'd nearly fallen several times. Perversely, the whiskey helped his balance, kept him loose, where stiff-limbed sobriety would have had him on his backside in no time.

His feelings were slippery too. He tried to grip the excitement, the anticipation, to push away misgivings and guilt. The latter pair had no backing or authority, at least not from anything on this earth. With Father dead, he was alone and his own master. Besides his own conscience, which he'd been negotiating with all day, the man skidding along in front of him was now his moral lead. And, though their current assignation was anything but moral, Shire trusted to some hard-to-define, earthy wholesomeness in Tuck. He had little evidence to support this: Tuck procured them whiskey on a regular basis, he swore well and often and his bartering bordered on theft. Yet Shire trusted him as he would a big brother; to get him into trouble, certainly, then to do his best to get him out of it. Right now Tuck was busy with the former.

Shire looked back over his shoulder to their new camp outside Murfreesboro, where the battle of Stone's River was fought last New Year, and where the Union army was concentrating once again. Hundreds of lights blurred together in the rain. Ahead of Tuck, a much smaller number could be seen a way up the road.

'Why don't we wait until the pay arrives?' called Shire, 'I'm down to my last few dollars what with the map.'

'I got you a good price for that there map. Don't you go complainin' at me.'

'I'm not complaining. I'm grateful. Or at least I will be when I get it. It's just I don't have much money.'

'Well, what you have'll do more for you before pay day. Once the army's been paid, they'll double the price. I hope you ain't thinking on Clara again?'

'No.'

Shire certainly was. Now that they were putting into practice what he'd previously taken as a flight of fancy from Tuck, Clara was suddenly very real. As if they'd parted last week rather than three years ago.

''Cos there's a battle coming sometime soon and, well... Even if you do get to her, you'll be better armed this way. Trust me. But you let me do the talking. Just now, they'll be down on their luck and we can cut a deal. You hear?'

'Fine.'

Their destination was a dozen or so unhitched wagons gathered untidily to the side of the road, each lit from within. Stretched from the nearest was a large awning, and Shire made out at least two figures sat under blankets or large shawls. Tuck stopped and Shire bundled up close behind him as if he was taking cover.

'What the hell are you doing? They ain't gonna shoot ya. Stand up straight.' He handed Shire the whiskey bottle. 'Now follow me and shut up.'

Shire trailed Tuck out of the dark and they approached the awning.

'Good evening, ladies,' said Tuck, touching his cap.

Straw was scattered on the floor. A black pot steamed atop a small stove. A thin chimney ran up through a contrivance in the canvas. The familiar smell of coffee mixed with sweeter scents.

'Hello, boys. Step inside,' said one of the girls, her tone as soft as her smile. Then, less pleasantly, she yelled back over her shoulder. 'Minnie.'

'Hold on,' the answer came from the adjoining wagon.

The rain was noisy on the canvas, but Shire could hear activity from around the camp, some of which he cared not to. No coffee was offered. Minnie, who was anything but, emerged from the wagon down some creaking wooden steps placed at its rear. Immediately behind her, and belting his trousers, was a young officer.

'You take care, Lieutenant.'

He disappeared into the night and the rain.

Tuck set to bartering and Shire to squirming. It was painful enough that they were here at all, but to haggle over such a thing only drew it out. If the price was too high, he'd sooner head back to camp. At least part of him would.

'Well if that's all you're paying, I ain't gonna waste two wagons on you,' said Minnie, taking the dollars from Tuck. 'And you be quick too. Fanny, take these big spenders and see if Violet's done. If she ain't, that corporal's getting overtime.'

Fanny stood up. Bypassing a smiling Tuck, she reached out from under her shawl and instead took hold of Shire with a soft hand. 'C'mon, you. Your friend's on the tall side.'

Shire, who felt like a boy caught stealing toffee from a market stall, was led through the gloom between the wagons to the one furthest away. Tuck followed.

'Violet. You done in there?'

'I am. Poor boy was up and out quicker than a sinner on a Sunday.'

'We gotta share the wagon.' Fanny put her head in through the untied canvas.

'Alright. Help me get the sheet up.'

She disappeared inside.

Tuck thumped Shire's arm. 'Now take your time. They'll shoo us out soon enough, but there ain't no sense leaving any fun behind.' 'Okay, boys, in you come.'

Once inside, Shire and Tuck were steered either side of a white sheet that ran down the middle of the wagon. Fanny was undressing.

'What you waitin' fer? The clock's runnin'.'

Seeing his hesitation, she helped him out of his coat and

jacket, but Shire turned away to undo his belt.

'Hey, Violet, I think I got me a first-timer. That right, boy? What's your name? Shire? What kind of name is that? Lie down here. C'mon, I won't bite, not unless you want me too. What regiment you with? Now, ain't that warm? You don't sound like you're from Ohio. England? Hey, Violet, I got me an Englishman.'

'They built just the same I 'spect.'

'Appears to be so. But he's a gentleman. Very polite an' all. Hang on, he's starting to find his rhythm.'

'Ladies,' it was Tuck. 'I'd take it as a personal favor if you could stop conversin'. It's off-putting.'

'Don't feel to me like you're put off none.'

'I'll take that as a compliment.'

Shire spread out the map on an upturned crate. He pored over it as if it contained a lost treasure. Tuck had stepped in from the rain and dropped it in his lap, then set up to shave.

The map was a fascination to Shire. There was a healthy trade in them around camp, but until now, the best he'd been able to do was find maps in newspapers or in Harper's Weekly. Usually these were centered on some battle site elsewhere, giving him little clue as to how close he might be getting to Clara. And like the page he'd taken from Father's atlas, they were too small-scale. This map was quite different. It was labelled *Kentucky and Tennessee by Johnson and Ward*. The two states had thick red lines to mark their borders. Outside of that, it was all black and white, but inside, each county was colored alternately pale green, pink or pale pink. The effect was to make each state appear like a patchwork quilt: Tennessee as if the bed was made, almost oblong, with neat square counties; Kentucky as if the bed was just slept in, untidy, with counties irregular and all bunched-up. The county names were given prominence, so you had to search behind their thick ink to find cities, towns or rivers. The red northern border of Kentucky was the Ohio River. Shire found where they'd joined it, back in January. He traced it down to Louisville and to its junction with the Cumberland, on to Fort Donelson and Nashville, then the short march to Franklin. Now they'd come over one square to Murfreesboro, Rutherford County. Just one county – in four months. Polk County, he knew, was somewhere beyond Chattanooga, the town where the railway lines converged. And there Polk was – pink – lodged in the bottom right hand corner of Tennessee. He counted seven counties between, depending on the route. Around one hundred and fifty miles as the crow flies. But armies didn't move like crows; not as straight, and not as quick.

Sitting up to take in the whole map again, Shire realized this was probably his finest possession. It was a melancholy thought. Smart as the map was, it made him miss all the possessions he'd left at home. He wondered if he would ever see them again.

'It cover where you wanna git?' said Tuck, speaking with the half of his face that was away from the razor.

'Yes, it does. Thanks, Tuck.' He had to raise his voice over the rain drumming on the canvas.

He didn't like to admit it, not to himself and certainly not to Tuck, but last night's trip out of camp had shaken something loose in him. He'd hinted at feeling ashamed to Tuck who'd said, 'Well, are you gonna insist on feeling ashamed?' Much to his surprise, Shire had decided not to. Somehow he could look at things afresh, and he tried not to question it too much. Maybe he was getting his impetus from the army. From the news, and the evidence right outside his tent, it was apparent that Rosecrans had assembled his army and would start to push for Chattanooga. Unless Bragg was prepared to back up out of the state altogether, a fight couldn't be far off.

So, whether due to the prospect of battle or because of Fanny's purchased affections, lying next to the map were three letters. The first was to Aaron Turney, his friend on the Ridgmont estate farm. It explained that Shire had only this spring learnt of Father's and Grace's deaths. By necessity he needed to give his address as the 125th Ohio Infantry, latterly moved to the Third

Brigade, 1st Division, 21st Corps, Army of the Cumberland. He decided not to mention Ocks, but was glad that at least someone at home would know he was alive. He enclosed a second letter, for Messrs Proctor & Jones at Bletchley, authorizing them to act in the matter of Father's estate.

His third letter, addressed directly to Clara at Comrie, had taken more thought. He'd written as if he was a distant cousin who found herself travelling with her husband in the North. She wished Clara well, said her thoughts were with her at this troubled time for Tennessee. They'd been too long apart, since their caroling at Christmas many years before. She hoped to visit Clara soon to keep their promise, should the war allow. His mood light with the relief on taking a hand in affairs, he'd rather wistfully signed it, *your affectionate cousin, Fanny*. He'd regretted it as soon as he'd written it, but there it was.

'Tuck?'

'Yeah.'

'I need this letter to get out. And I don't want it held up, or torn up, by our censors. Can you do that for me? This other one doesn't matter so much. It can take its time.'

Tuck, half his face soaped up, turned and looked at Shire with his letters and the map.

'Well,' he resumed his shave, talking into the mirror, 'someone's all busy and bushytailed. What d'you think brought that on?'

'Can you do it? I wouldn't want to ask Lyman.'

'Now don't try and provoke me with dumbness. Might cost a few cents. I'll have to be quick though. This army's got a buzz about it.'

Suddenly, Tuck took issue with something in the mirror. He spun round and collecting up the letters, tossed them behind his kit bag.

'Hey!' said Shire.

'Hello, Corporal Ocks,' said Tuck loudly, ahead of Ocks stepping wetly into their tent through the open flap. 'Whoa, pardon me, but looks like you have an extra stripe there. I'll try again. Hello *Sergeant* Ocks. What brings you to visit our fine company?'

'I came to give Shire some good news.' He looked pointedly at Tuck and nodded outside.

'Why, Sergeant, I'm just getting myself smart before we take the road south. You're welcome to take Shire outside if you want a little English chitchat in the rain.'

Shire folded his map. He didn't want Ocks to see it, and he didn't want him shaking his damp coat all over it. 'I'm sure the sergeant can tell both of us.'

'You'll stand when I'm talking to you, boy.'

Shire resisted the impulse to leap to his feet. Instead he got up as slowly as he could.

'I'm sorry, Sergeant. Only the news you usually bring me isn't much to get up for.'

Ocks smiled. 'Oh, you'll like this. You too, Tuck. There's been a re-shuffle, what with your company sergeant being in the wars, as it were.'

The rain outside intensified. It was as noisy as standing behind a waterfall. Shire inwardly sank, and Tuck's razor arm fell to his side.

'I've come over to Company B. And I'm your new sergeant.'

Comrie – July 1863

The letter was from Shire. Clara recognized his handwriting on the envelope. She didn't want to read it in the house; she was certain of that, though she had trouble understanding quite why. She went outside, past the kitchen and the smokehouse to the stables. It was a strange time of day to receive a letter, coming on to sunset, but they arrived spuriously these days, on the rarer occasions that someone travelled out of town and into the hills.

Despite the month, it was cool. There was a peculiar light about the place. The low sun illuminated the clouds from below, lending the sky a gentle phosphorescence. It was usually sheltered here between the house and the great wooded slope that rose steeply up beyond the stables and the slave quarters. But today the wind stirred dust off the dry yard.

Moses, never too far from the horses, emerged from the stables, carrying a pail. With his eyes down to avoid the dust he nearly walked straight into her. 'I's sorry, miss. Thought I was the only one out here. It ain't a pleasant evenin'. Storm on the way. You'd be better off inside.'

She held closed her shawl.

He looked at the letter in her hand. 'You got news from Master Taylor?'

'I just wanted to see the horses.'

'Huh. Well you might as well feed George for me.' He held out the pail. 'If you've a mind to, that is. You want I should get you the oats?'

Clara smiled. 'I know where they are.' She didn't mind Moses telling her what to do, but as she took the pail, a low, enduring moan rose in the air high above them. It was unearthly, climbing a note in pitch then falling back again, once louder, then softer. Clara looked to where the wind raced off the top of the hill, a stream of cloud moving fast, clipping the trees and washing past them, so it looked for all the world as if the forest itself was moving away. She crouched, leant into Moses.

'It's alright, miss. Don't fret.' His old pale eyes were open wide.

'What is it?'

'There's a pass up there. On top. Narrow, with cliffs both sides. When we get the wind out of the east, sometimes it howls. Not often though. That's all it is. That's all. Ain't heard it for a couple of years, and never this loud. We call it the Cherokee Wind.'

'Why?'

Moses shuffled his feet in the dust. 'Some, not me, but some, think it's the Cherokee spirits, mourning for their people that were driven out from their own hills. We don't like to go up that way much. Mitilde'll fret if she hears it. I'll feed George, miss. You go on inside.'

The moan died away and there was nothing more than the sound of the wind in the trees, like pebbles after a wave. 'I'm alright.'

The stables also acted as a carriage house, wide sliding doors below high gables. There was a double row of stalls, twice what was needed. Clara understood the urge to be ostentatious, but you needed an audience. Ridgmont, settled in the time-sculptured fields of the English shires, adorned with its own past, could trumpet its wealth. Comrie's stables might, she imagined, be at home in Virginia or in parts of Kentucky; but here, in Appalachian Tennessee, they were oversized, incongruous.

George was waiting by the feed bag and she fetched his oats. He was a big horse, good for the plough as well as riding, but he was still small compared to the working horses at home – Shire's horses. Her eyes adjusted to the gloom of the stable. She read the letter, one hand absently stroking George.

Shire was here – in America; to what purpose it didn't say. Clearly it was meant only for her as he purported to be a non-existent cousin with the unlikely name of Fanny. It was strange to think of him away from Ridgmont. She read it again. *To keep their promise,* he said. Why was he here? He couldn't know of her unhappiness. He mentioned the caroling. That night had, she realized from this distance, marked the end of their childhood friendship. She remembered walking into the pheasants in the dark, remembered the cold kitchen stone on her bare feet, and the perfect little round sitting room with its fire and its thick rug. But for that rug, maybe nothing would have happened.

She stretched her feet closer to the fire and wished that the room had corners. It was gently turning above her in a way that was quite new, courtesy of the Christmas cider and spiced wine. 'I'm warming up everywhere but my toes. Help them out will you? Go on, before they drop off.'

Shire was too clumsy and it tickled, making her sit up. The room steadied. 'Be gentle.'

His second attempt was much better. She enjoyed teasing him. She always had.

'Now come and kiss me.' She pulled his unsure weight to lie next to her.

'Clara...'

'Shhh' She kissed him and for a while, lost in the new sensation, forgot that it was Shire.

Afterwards, when they were walking back to the abbey she caught herself pretending that Shire had unbuttoned her, and that she had pulled away. But that wasn't fair. But for Shire, they might still have been in the gatehouse. But then that's why it was safe to tease Shire. He'd always forgiven her: when she'd blamed him for a Chinese vase she'd broken, when she'd shut him in the dark icehouse. Always.

At the back entrance to the abbey, she climbed the step and turned to say goodnight. She bent and kissed him on the nose as she had hours before, tried to return him to the safe place where she'd always kept him. But Shire had pushed back her bonnet and kissed her fully. She didn't resist.

The next morning, Christmas morning, Miss Stuart wasted no time in telling her what she had seen, and that when the duchess came back to Ridgmont, she would have to be told. She wanted Clara to beg, to ask her to keep quiet. But that was a forlorn hope. Clara wouldn't give her the pleasure.

When the time came she was taken to see the duke in his study, rather than to the duchess. To make it all the more humiliating, Miss Stuart took up a position just a few steps aside from his desk. Clara was eighteen; she didn't need a governess.

The duke looked up from his writing and, perhaps surprised at how tall his youngest daughter had become, stood too.

'Well now, we should sit I think. Miss Stuart, you may go.'

'You don't need me to recount what I saw, Your Grace?'

'No, no. I've heard it all from the duchess.'

Miss Stuart closed the door behind her; a small blessing at least.

'Your mother has asked me to speak with you.'

Why couldn't her mother speak to her? Come to that, why did the duke need to be asked? Did he not care on his own account?

'You know why?'

'It was only Shire. Am I not allowed to kiss my friends goodnight after they see me home?'

'A home you'd been given no permission to leave.'

'At what age will I be allowed to decide to leave my own house?'

'It's not a question of choice. It's a question of propriety. The whole village, everyone it seems, knows you walked home alone with the young man.'

The term 'young man' seemed to adorn Shire with the morals of a stranger. 'A young man who has a care to my wellbeing.'

'That is at odds with what Miss Stuart saw.'

'Miss Stuart has a spinster's imagination. She sees what she wants to.'

'I haven't asked you here to malign Miss Stuart. In truth, we should have had this conversation before now. We thought you and Shire would grow apart as you got older, trusted that your station in life would be enough.'

'He's my friend.'

'He was a playmate, for when you were a child. The duchess was fond of his mother and entertained some misplaced sympathy after her death. It should have been dealt with then.' He held up a hand to forestall her. 'I don't want to have the boy stopped from working on the estate, but if you see him again, I'll do more than that. I understand he's begun helping his father at the school. That's not a position for someone who doesn't know his place.'

George nudged her, hopeful of more oats. Her face was resting on his neck. She took a deep breath of his sweet, musky scent. The caroling was a long time ago. She shouldn't have drunk so much.

It was hard to bridge the years; to be precise about how she'd felt after being forbidden from seeing Shire. They were growing older; he was taking up his position at the school. He was just Shire. He'd always taken that promise more seriously than she ever had. But she'd missed him, and remembered thinking all winter about the gatehouse.

When Taylor arrived that spring, he'd turned her head. Here was someone to love. And there'd been the prospect of a new life away from Ridgmont, away from obligation and 'propriety'. Now, she could admit it had been a relief too. It had been easier to leave Shire behind, put him safely in a box of memories with everything else from Ridgmont, and tie up the bow.

It was almost completely dark in the stables. A low moan called again from the hills. She folded the letter away. This then was her escape: to live a lonely life in the hills, waiting for a war to end, and fearful of the husband who would afterwards come home. And now Shire had left the box, and her memories were coming to find her.

Marion County, Tennessee – August 1863

Shire had been checking his map and guessed they'd left Grundy County behind, but Marion County was the same tired green of August. The 125th Ohio was becalmed and had fallen out into the drooping, scrubby grass beside the turnpike. As part of the rear guard, they were yet to start the climb into the Cumberland Mountains. Shire looked up at the blue column ahead of them, many miles in length, ascending in stops and starts. The road it followed switched back and fore to ease the steep grade. On the lower slopes was the main supply train, over two hundred and fifty ponderous wagons each with a complement of horses or mules, dragging heavy loads through the slowly drying mud. The wagons swayed alarmingly as they took the acute turns. Ahead and higher were several strung-out brigades, mostly infantry, but for one single battery of artillery that sluggishly neared the crest. It was almost biblical. As if the Union army, weary of this wet, then hot, Tennessee summer, had chosen to ascend to the Almighty and lay their troubles at his gate. It was another punishingly hot afternoon; the Almighty was making the army work hard to reach him.

Shire sat on the grass with his boots off, easing liniment oil into the mess of blisters. A noisy, black and silver bee, solid as a bullet, fussed around him and he waved at it angrily.

'I wouldn't get ornery with those fellas,' said Tuck, laid on his back. 'Carpenter Bee. Get vexed real easy. Must think you have wooden feet... And I done told you it was a bad day for new boots. You need to ease them in of an evenin' after the march is done.'

'My old ones fell apart yesterday, like they'd lost hope.'

'Should have gone to the quartermaster sooner then, when they was on the way out.'

'He's not going to give me a new pair ahead of time,' said Shire.

'You're too honest for your own good. I keep tellin' you, but you insist on it. Be honest in the big things in life, not the little ones.' Tuck placed a stalk of grass between his teeth, alternately chewing it and rolling it across his mouth. 'Why, I think the commandments generally only pertain to the bigger things. You wouldn't steal a horse, but we'll pick plenty of apples from the roadside when they come on. You might cheat on your girl, but not on your wife. Same applies here. Why I'd 've found a worn-out pair some other fella threw aside and shown them to the quartermaster. It ain't lying, it's just makin' it easier for him to come to the right conclusion. How much did you pay Cleves for that liniment?'

'A dollar,' said Shire, applying it tenderly.

'A dollar!' Tuck sat up. 'Cleves, you spotted skunk.' He tossed a small stone, but Cleves simply smiled.

'Well what else am I going to spend a dollar on? I needed it and he had it,' said Shire.

'Might be some girls pleased to have a change of army up in Chattanooga. Some of them might rub another sore spot for a Yankee dollar.'

Shire didn't answer. While he didn't exactly regret it, visiting the likes of Violet and Fanny didn't seem something to make a habit of.

An old farmer, barefoot and with his hat flopped over his face, carried a pail of boiled corn cobs to the edge of his field. Half the company raced to buy them, Tom Muncie in the lead.

Miraculously, the army was aiming right where he needed to go – to Chattanooga. As best he could tell from the map, Polk County and Clara looked only one or two days from there by horse. Not that he had prospect of a horse. And though he was getting closer, other problems loomed larger. Not least that the Rebel army wasn't going to back-up forever. Rebels aside, how would he get away from his own army when the time came? And most of all, assuming he found her, would she be married and happily at that?

Then there was Ocks, who now held sway over Shire, a

constant presence. How close was he going to let Shire get before he intervened? It was surprising that Ocks hadn't clobbered him already.

A sudden shout went up from nearby. Men stood and there was a general excitement. A rabbit, unhinged by the army that had just sat down in its neighborhood, zigzagged across the grass, not knowing which way to run amongst the men.

'Colonel?' Captain Yeomans called.

Opdycke was sat reading on his horse. He looked up. 'Whose turn is it?'

'Company B, sir.'

'Very well, best be quick though, before it comes to its senses.'

'Sergeant Ocks,' shouted Yeomans, 'Choose your man.'

Ocks took a loaded rifle from his back.

'Shire.' The shout came from Cleves, not Ocks. 'Let Shire have a pop.'

Amidst much laughter the cry was taken up. 'Shire! Shire!'

He stood awkwardly without his boots. This was a matter of company honor, but Shire realized his own company was more interested in persecuting him. The chant continued as he took the gun from a grim-looking Ocks. He prayed the rabbit would go to ground, but it was still there, cutting this way and that, the shouting spooking it further. The men peeled away out of his line of fire, some exaggerating. Bets were quickly made. Tuck sat up and gave him a nod. It centered him. This didn't matter so much; not against his own losses, the war and the cares ahead of him. He brought up the stock and settled it to his shoulder. He heard Tuck's favorite piece of advice – *don't force the gun still, let it be still.* The rabbit followed no pattern, turning this way and that. The shot was impossible, but he knew his arm would start to tire if he waited. Best get this over with. He at least took care to apply another of Tuck's mantras – *don't pull the trigger, squeeze it.*

The rifle kicked into his shoulder and the spout of white smoke obscured his view. There was a moment's silence followed by a collective cheer.

263

'I'll be damned,' said Tuck below him, looking out to where the small rabbit lay. 'All that advice I gave you, and all we ever needed to do was take your boots off.'

'One up for the British,' said Ocks, taking back the rifle with a rare smile.

Shire was having his back slapped and his hand shaken.

'Hey, Cleves,' shouted Tuck. 'How much did that cost you? More 'an a dollar?'

Cleves was sourly paying out on very long odds. 'Why that rabbit had a death wish. He waited for Shire to fire and then ran into line.'

Jordan, as company cook, had the honor of collecting the rabbit and displayed it to Shire. 'It's a biddy one alright, but I'll be proud to put it in the pot. I ain't never seen a shot like that.'

Opdycke had enjoyed the scene that played out beside him; a brief escape from his many cares. He struggled to get his attention back to the field manual while they waited for the road to clear. Always good to see an underdog come through. He hoped it wasn't an omen for this war.

It was too hot these last few days, since the rain let up. The heat had become embedded in the breeze, robbing it of relief. He preferred the hours either side of sunrise and sunset. At those times the air was cool, not just thick, moving warmth, and he could look about him at the gaining or waning colors, without needing to half close his eyes against the sharp brightness. He wished he was back home with Lucy and his son; wished for a day doing nothing more than working at his livery business. He looked at his regiment at rest around him. They'd earned a reputation for discipline and good order, but they'd yet to experience much more than a skirmish, despite months in the field. Surely Bragg wouldn't abandon Tennessee without a fight for Chattanooga?

Back up the mountain the army began to lumber forward once more. They were making a pig's ear of things up there. How hard

264

could it be? He should ride up and take them in hand... Not yet. It would be a few minutes before the start fed back to the 125th, but he would get the men into line. 'Sergeant. Have the men fall in.'

Bugles sounded and the men stirred. There was the familiar clatter of metal and canvas as they stoppered canteens, shouldered packs and rifles, obeyed with little complaint but even less enthusiasm. They collected onto the turnpike, save for the soldier who'd shot the rabbit and a familiar red-haired boy who stood over him. The shooter was painfully pulling on his shoes. Opdycke dismounted, put the manual into his saddlebag and led his horse towards them.

'Private,' he said, addressing the boy on the ground, who hurried to stand to attention. He had only one boot on. 'That's not much use unless you plan to hop to Chattanooga.'

'I'm sorry, Colonel. I picked a bad day to break in new boots.'

Opdycke remembered Shire from the dinner party at Franklin; his English accent marked him out. He didn't trust the nation, but thought he'd better not tar this soldier with so wide a brush. He looked strong, as tall as Opdycke was himself and there was some width to his shoulders.

'Here, I'm well rested. Climb up on Barney, his shoes are sound. You can get back in line, Private Muncie.'

Regimental Sergeant Smith was close by. 'Sir, it ain't proper to put common men up there on your horse.'

'Oh, away with you, Sergeant. This is a modern army, not a medieval one. I'll keep the rules that need keeping. You know that. Barney likes a change of rider and I like to walk once in a while.' It also cut down on stragglers.

Private Shire tied his boots and hung them on the pommel before he climbed up. Tom passed up the man's backpack and rifle, then trotted away down the column. What little Opdycke knew of Shire intrigued him, and as the column got underway, he kept station beside the horse. 'That was a fine shot back there. Seemed some of the men were pulling against you. Might keep them quiet for a while. You find it difficult in the regiment, being English?'

'I imagine it made me stand out to begin with.'

'That accent does. I suggest you soften it.'

'I'll do that, sir.'

Opdycke tried another tack. 'When we spoke, in Franklin, the circumstances were constrained. You never explained how an educated English boy has found his way into our American war. It hardly seems your fight?'

'In my experience, Colonel, there are two types of men in your regiment. Those here on principle and those by necessity. I'm one of the latter.'

'Necessity drove you to cross the Atlantic, or to join the army?'

'The army.'

Opdycke had hoped for more openness having extended the kindness of his horse. 'I'm not sure I agree with your experience entirely. That boy you were with, Tom Muncie.'

'You know him, sir?'

'I know his father. He's a sheriff back in Warren and his other son's a deputy. Tom there, well he doesn't quite have the right way with people to be a lawman, so his father, Garrett, had to tell him he couldn't join the family profession. Got him a job cutting lumber instead. Tom took it hard, so when the chance came he joined up. Didn't even ask his father. Garrett came to see me and begged me to discharge the boy. But he's strong, does what he's told, and we need the men. I didn't see that I was at liberty to dispense personal favors. He's not here on principle or necessity.'

'His own necessity, perhaps,' said Shire.

'Maybe. What brought you to America in the first place?'

'I wanted to see if the grass was greener, though I miss my father. My only relative, or kin, should I say?'

'And now you're seeing a good deal of grass. And the necessity?'

'I was robbed, sir, in New York. I didn't want to stay there and work. It's not a place I took to.'

'You won't see your father until your three years are up.'

'He died, sir. Soon after I left, but I didn't find out until the spring.'

'I'm sorry.'

They walked on slowly. This mud was like molasses.

'And Sergeant Ocks. I understand you know him?'

'I sometimes helped on a local estate farm, when not teaching. I liked to work with the Shire horses, hence my name. He managed the workers for the estate.'

'And knowing you were in the 125th he asked to join us? Were you friends then? He's a deal older than you.'

Shire adjusted his cap. 'Not a friend, sir. I don't know why he joined the 125th in particular. Just happenstance.'

Opdycke was going to express his incredulity at such an unlikely co-incidence, but Shire cut across him. 'Do you think there'll be a battle soon? When we get to Chattanooga?'

'Seems likely. They don't appear inclined to defend these fine hills. It's hard enough climbing them, I'm sure glad we're not fighting for them. The Rebels suffered greatly last month at Vicksburg and Gettysburg. They can ill afford another defeat. If we could beat them here too, in between, maybe we'd start to see the end of it. But Rosecrans is a chess-playing general. He doesn't go looking for a fight, rather to maneuver the enemy out of position. He's good at it too. But we'll have to corner them sooner or later.'

'You'd like a change of general, sir?'

'I wouldn't say that. There are much worse generals than Rosecrans. At some point Bragg's gonna have to fight anyway. He can't just give up the South bit by bit. Do you think you chose the right side to fight for, Private?'

'Oh, I couldn't fight for slavery, whatever the necessity.'

'Sometimes I wonder at how any man can. And fight hard while they're at it. There are things that pass understanding, I guess. But no man should own another. And they, the Southerners I mean, would have us spread it right over this continent. We couldn't have that. It has to be settled here and now.'

267

They stopped again, having barely covered a quarter-mile.

'I'm sorry, Private Shire, but I think I need to go and unpick the mess up there, and I'll need to take Barney with me. Looks like you'll be able to rest your feet a while longer anyway. Can I ask you to watch over Tom Muncie for me? I'd like to take him back to Garrett in one piece.'

Having ousted Shire, Opdycke mounted again and rode forward. The results of his gentle inquisition left him unsatisfied. He would write to Major Moore, back in Ohio; ask him to find out how Ocks had come to be placed in his regiment by the governor. He just couldn't bring himself to trust the English.

Chattanooga – August 1863

Clara stared out of the train window. The ride from Cleveland to Chattanooga was no more than an hour. She wasn't used to travelling alone. It wouldn't have been tolerated in England, not for a lady, and certainly not a duke's daughter. But she was enjoying having the room to think, away from Hany, and politely cut short any attempts at conversation from the strangers seated opposite. The car was full with a mix of civilians and soldiers. It was hot again, and she was glad to be seated on the north side, away from the midday sun. After climbing upwards out of Cleveland, the train had started to descend.

It would be good to see Trenholm. The note had come only yesterday. A boy had ridden up all the way from the telegraph at Cleveland station. Trenholm was in Chattanooga and would be for several days. The press of time meant he could not come to Comrie, but he asked if she would visit him. There was an address. He said he hoped she might see Taylor, as the army was close at hand, pressed back to the southern edge of Tennessee.

Phrases filtered out from the chatter around her. 'Yankee army closer,' 'Knoxville wouldn't be given up,' 'Help would be sent from the east.' But for every person that spoke in hope or anguish for the Confederacy, she suspected there was another who was tight-lipped, not daring a smile or a careless word for the Union. When Moses drove her into Cleveland that morning, they had found it a subdued, edgy place. She'd seen that the draper's shop was boarded up. Not a week passed without some tale of men pressed into the army or incarcerated. At least it felt as if change was coming. Good or bad.

The train jolted round to the left and afforded her a view of Chattanooga, held in a full sweep of the Tennessee River. It was a long name for a small town. The flood plain reached out several miles to its south, but beyond the houses and the river, the mountains rose up steeply. Further west, looming over the river from the south, was Lookout Mountain. She remembered that not long after she'd arrived at Comrie, Taylor had promised to climb it with her. It was one of many things he'd promised. There'd been no word from him, though she knew he was not far away. She learned more at church from families who had their boys in his regiment. She wondered again where Shire was and why he was here. It was fruitless conjecture, but it was hard to set it aside.

When the train pulled in, she let the press of people get off before her. On the platform, incoming army supplies vied with civilian trunks and cases going out. Clearly most of the people of Chattanooga felt it was time to leave. There was no air of panic, more a quiet sadness. She navigated her way around the boxes. Once outside there were no carriages, but she'd been to the town before. She only had a light bag, so was happy to walk and ask her way at need. A gun carriage rattled by, the first she'd seen, throwing up dust into the hot air.

She switched her way across the grid of Chattanooga, coming closer to the river. It only took a short while to reach the address, a private house, not overly grand. Trenholm wasn't there, but a middle-aged lady, a Mrs Croxton, welcomed her inside. Word was sent that she'd arrived. The house was relaxed, with no sign of an exodus. 'You are not planning to leave?' she asked her host.

'We see no need,' and then, perhaps on account of Clara's accent, 'the Union is not a threat to us.' Clara said nothing. She and Emmeline had never discussed what it might mean for Comrie. As if the Union could never reach that far.

Trenholm sent a message to say he would join her presently. But presently stretched through the afternoon and it was, for once, a tired-looking man that found her alone in the relative cool of the sitting room. 'Clara. My heartfelt apologies for keeping you waiting. It's a hard town to transact business in. Every second lawyer or banker has either joined the army or left.'

'Have you heard from Taylor?' she asked. Of all her cares he should be seen to come first.

'I saw him just yesterday. He's returned to his regiment. I'm sorry.'

'No matter. I've come to expect it.' She searched inside for any trace of disappointment.

'The war governs all. You must forgive him.'

'They've taken some of our people too, one in ten, to help the army repair the railroads and build the forts. We had no choice. They just came and took the strongest. We'll struggle with the harvest.'

'That may not be the last of it. But, Clara,' he sat back in his chair, 'you must not stay for the harvest... It's time to leave. Rosecrans is close and it'll be too late to go at the last minute. If the armies come together the trains will be swamped or commandeered. You should leave right away, you and Emmeline.'

'But what about Comrie? We can't abandon it. It's not just Emmeline and I who live there.'

'I don't think the Union army is going to stop and discuss your concerns. That's a Confederate colonel's house you live in. Your people are better off without you. Bring your maid. Take the train straight from Cleveland down to Atlanta and over to Charleston, to my home, until the war's over.'

'They'll burn Comrie, won't they?'

Trenholm didn't answer, but instead left the room. He returned and offered her a package thickly wrapped in brown paper.

'It's a Union flag. Keep it well hidden. When you leave, give it to someone you trust. Moses, he's a wise old bird. He'll know where to hide too, if you get caught there. Tell him, when the Union is close, to fly it, hang it from a window or strap it to a column – anything. Chances are it'll do no good, but if they're in a hurry perhaps they'll move on by. It's worth a try.'

'You are sure then?' she said. 'That Chattanooga will fall?'

'Well, there's only two horses to back. You have to pick one with your head no matter where your heart lies. And I think Rosecrans has the measure of Bragg. Half of Bragg's generals are in this city and not one of them has a good word for him. An army at odds with itself is a losing army. There are any number of ridges and mountains west of Chattanooga he could have defended, but he gave them all up. Why do you think I'm here?'

Clara shook her head.

'To move every asset I've got under a Union name, that's why. I've plenty of acquaintances that never wanted out of the Union. And they're happy to trade for property further south or hold assets for me. Then we all get to take our chances that they don't get burnt by either side. It's why I was so busy today, what with tomorrow deemed a day of "prayer and fasting" by our president. As if we have time for such nonsense. I'd sooner put faith in my own maneuvers. But you must return to Comrie tomorrow and leave as soon as you can. Taylor wishes it too.'

'Does he?' said Clara. 'His care seems as absent as he is. There are other people to think of. And it was Emmeline's home before it was mine. I'll not leave without her.'

Next morning, the Chattanooga Presbyterian Church had on show as many stars as the Almighty had displayed the night before; variously one, two or three on the collars of the Southern officers. Clara heard that Bragg was ill and resting, which allowed comments pertaining to him to be often less than Christian. She was introduced by Trenholm at every opportunity, her hand kissed as if she were royalty, rather than merely exiled nobility. She noted how many of the generals sought out Trenholm rather than the other way around.

A jowly Major General Cheatham, wearing a flawless grey uniform adorned with gold braid and buttons, was one such. 'Why George, I see you are out of uniform again. You'll be hung for a spy if the Yankees catch you.'

Trenholm shook his hand but addressed Clara. 'General

Cheatham has long tried to convert me to a man of the cloth. By which I mean this sort of grey butler's outfit he's wearing. General, this is my adopted daughter-in-law, Mrs Clara Spencer-Ridgmont.'

Clara's hand was worshiped once more. 'My pleasure, ma'am. I know your husband, though he's not in my division. A striking man, but no match for you.'

'Then I fear I have married below myself. Perhaps you'd better recommend a promotion for him.'

'There may be a few positions coming available once the Yankees arrive.'

'And when do you expect them, General?' asked Trenholm.

'Oh, I think you've a week or two to finish up whatever sly business you have, George. We've not spotted them within fifty miles yet. Allowing for the ones that have lived here all along, that is.'

The minister took his place and Clara turned with the congregation to the front. White-gloved hands deprived of swords and pistols, instead lifted prayer books. Enlivened by the congregation before him, the minister practically shouted the opening prayer. 'Matthew it is that tells us, *"And you will hear of wars and rumors of wars. See that you are not alarmed, for this must take place, but the end is not yet."*

Before he could draw his next breath, there was an unholy screech from outside and an explosion.

'It's not possible!' said Cheatham.

Clara looked to Trenholm.

'A shell,' he said coolly. 'It appears Mr Rosecrans is closer than we thought.'

The next shell sounded even closer, and the esteemed congregation started to leave. Trenholm bade Clara not to rush, saying it was likely as safe in here as outside. When they emerged in their turn, squeezed out like sand through an hourglass, people were running in all directions. She held tightly onto Trenholm's arm as they descended the wooden steps, and tried to still her own panic. Another detonation and they were both knocked against the rail. Clara's head cleared only to hear a child scream. Was this how the coming of the Union was to be? There was a young girl, lying in the street, her leg bloodied and clearly broken. Clara followed Trenholm towards her. A woman, a mother, bent to the child. There were enough people there already.

'She'll be cared for. We can't help further,' said Trenholm, and pulled Clara back towards their lodgings. 'They're firing from over the river.'

There were two more deafening explosions – deeper detonations. She looked for them but saw nothing. Cheatham was shouting orders from the church steps. Soldiers raced past them towards the river. Clara wanted to run straight to the station.

'Those were our guns replying,' said Trenholm.

They hurried on as quickly as they could through the emptying streets. By the time they reached the safety of their temporary home, the only cannon fire was from this side of the river. It seemed that the Yankee artillery had been driven off.

'It would appear I'm backing the right horse,' said Trenholm.

'Will we get out?' asked Clara.

'I'm no expert, but I think that was only a small show, a battery that came up unseen. A real bombardment and we'd never have dared to leave the church. They'll be some days yet. The Tennessee River is not so easy for an army to cross under fire. But, d'you see now, Clara? You cannot reason with war. Promise me you'll take Emmeline away. As soon as you can.'

'Yes. I promise.' She pushed her Union flag to the bottom of her bag. She thought of Taylor and what it must be like to run towards those shells. Later, she let Trenholm walk her to the station.

Ridgmont – July 1863

Matlock had waited a long time in the darkness beneath the old oak tree. Like a leashed dog, seeing its quarry, the tense air strained for release and violence. He'd lost track of the hour. It could be either side of midnight. In the late afternoon, looking out from the duke's study, he'd heard the growling begin over the low hills and in the dry dells. He'd walked here without a lantern after the last light faded.

The breeze strengthened and danced around his tree. He could hear the squeak of the arrowed weather vane atop the square tower. The wind tumbled and rolled and he imagined weighty, rain-laden monsters growing tall and unseen into the sky. A stab of light, still distant, was rendered pervasive by the belly of the cloud, so that the church shone momentarily from every flinty wall. The first lonely, overweight drops slapped onto the warm, flat tombs and raised brief, high notes from the metal gate. When they became more populous, they began to rattle the parched leaves above him. Then, freed at last, the deluge arrived. It flattened the thin grass and drummed on the hard ground.

He moved out into the rain and to the gate as quickly as his heavy burden would allow. When he reached from his cloak for the latch, his hand almost recoiled from the stinging rain. He pushed the gate ajar with his shoulder and it swung closed behind him. He looked beyond the tower and, shunning the path, made his way between the graves. The rain battered him and it was impossible to hurry. It felt like he was dragging a withered leg. He wished he was a stronger man.

Three blazes of light, shot in a second, showed him surrounded by graves. Each stone silently shouted a name and an earthly span. The tower loomed then disappeared, a mute witness. He stopped behind a smaller headstone. His cloak fell open and with a straight arm he dragged out the heavy hammer, its wooden handle taller than the gravestone beside it. The squat, heavy head rested on the wet grass. He waited with an angel of stone that defended a tomb nearby.

A lightning bolt ripped behind the church, so close that he cowered. There was no pause before the thunder screamed out from the storm. Too late he reached for the hammer and the wet handle slipped from his grasp. He recovered, shaking, gripped it again with two hands and waited once more.

The next strike was further away. He had time to start the hammer into an underarm swing behind him. As the roar rolled into the dell he brought it forward, drove it with all the strength he had. The metal sparked on the stone, but he heard nothing beneath the admonition of the thunder. He stumbled under the hammer's bounced weight and at the numb shock in his hand. In the wet darkness he collected his balance and gathered his strength again. But when the next flash stuttered across the churchyard, he saw his work was already done. The cheap stone was broken and its name lay flat, drowning in the rain. He pulled the hammer inside his cloak and limped away through the storm and the dead.

PART III

The Tennessee River – September 3rd, 1863

Shire stood on the north bank of the Tennessee and considered the challenge ahead. There was no pontoon bridge, but Harker's Brigade, of which the 125th Ohio was a part, had to cross all the same. The artillery was busy building rafts. What few boats were about had already been commandeered. For once Tuck hadn't delivered. He was unable to get a berth for any of them, only for their packs, stuffed with their jackets and shirts. They'd been ordered to swim.

'Must be two hundred yards,' said Lyman, hands on hips and staring at the far side. 'What if the Reb's turn up when we're only halfway?'

Shire recalled their winter crossing of the Harpeth when they had fought their way into Franklin. The Tennessee River in summer looked far more inviting.

'Just go on complainin' as you always do,' said Tuck, 'and they'll beat a retreat quick enough. Besides, a few boys from the 64th are over.'

Shire shielded his eyes. No more than half a company was on the far bank. How Tuck could tell it was the 64th he didn't know. Beyond them the mountains rose steeply up again, reaching for a Cambridge blue sky.

He turned on hearing a call from Tom Muncie, who had come out of the woods with Mason and Jordan. They each carried a pair of short planks taken from a hut the company was demolishing back in the trees. Shire could still hear the rip and wrench of wood.

'Here you go, boys,' Mason said.

Shire took a plank and used his bayonet to cut two lengths of rope – Tuck had found them this at least – one long, one short. He'd saved a piece of tarred canvas from his pack. Using it, he double-wrapped his few dollars, his letters from Clara and the wedding license, and then tied it all tight with the smaller length of rope. He'd not trust his treasures to the boat or to the character of the men on the other side. Using the longer length he lashed the package, his rifle and rolled trousers to the plank. Then he tied his laces together and wound his boots around the wood too. He set off with his friends, each carrying their own contrivance over the warm pebbles that led to the water.

Jordan was laughing. 'I'm about ready for this,' he said. 'Outside of winter, we'd swim in the river most Sundays back home.' Jordan often found his way to be with the squad and no one objected. It was useful to be on friendly terms with a cook.

Shire found that he too was full of childish excitement. In the past weeks there had been no rain, only a hot, brutal sun beating down as they climbed ridge after ridge towards Chattanooga. Even his underclothes felt stiff with old sweat and dust. He recalled a summer's day rowing on the Great Ouse in Bedford, the oars too thick and heavy for a young boy. Father had laughed as they went round in circles. It was the first time, since Ocks had caught up with him in Franklin, that he'd held a memory of Father and smiled. Smiles surrounded him. Up and down the river the whole brigade was shouting and wading into the Tennessee. Two thousand men, all become boys again.

'Ten cents a man for the first over,' said Tuck.

Everyone was game, except Lyman. 'I'll just be thankful if the good Lord helps me to the other side.'

Tom Muncie was first in. He laughed and waved back at them. The water soothed between Shire's curling toes. He waded in until he could float the plank at waist height on the sparkling surface. Using one hand to steady it, he took a step or two more and leant into the coolness. To start with it was easy going and he kept with the group, but two thirds over, the river picked up. While the stronger swimmers fought hard for the far bank, Shire and Lyman let the current take them and worked with it, back-paddling to dodge other men. They came ashore well downstream and had to walk wetly back up.

'Who won?' asked Shire.

'Cook boy,' said Tuck, jerking a thumb at Jordan. 'I think he's part catfish.'

Shire was content to pay his ten cents to feel fresh for once. They made the best of it, everyone did, by getting naked and soaping up. It was a happier and better-smelling regiment that dressed again an hour later.

'Welcome to Georgia,' said Tuck.

'Not quite.' Shire had checked his map was dry and was consulting it as he habitually did. 'We're still in Marion County, Tennessee. The river isn't a border. And go a few miles south and you might hit Alabama, not Georgia. All three states come together.'

The map had proved a comfort. It measured his slow progress towards Chattanooga – and Clara – but they'd crossed way west of the town, and if Bragg gave it up without a fight, Shire fretted they'd bypass it altogether and head for Atlanta. He'd been so fixated on reaching Clara he'd never considered that they might march right by.

When it came time to form up he became aware of a deeper disquiet as the joy of the swim flowed away. Despite what the map said, perhaps they had crossed a border of sorts. Was it simply that they were in the deeper south, arrived at the harder heart of the Confederacy? Or that he was at least on the same side of the river as Clara, and a moment long awaited was at hand? The mountains, a picturesque backdrop from the northern bank, now looked close and threatening. Way up the valley, a cannon fired and the echo tumbled down off the hills. Perhaps, he thought, it was that there was a battle to fight, and they had all just been baptized before the sacrifice to come.

Crawfish Springs, Lee and Gordon's Mill
September 12th, 1863

The sun had set on Georgia. Inside the mill, there were camp-chairs, crates and a bench for the officers who wanted them. Colonel Opdycke chose to stand, though he leant back against the boarded wall, his weight on one foot to let the day's ache ease from the other. From the smashed window beside him, he could hear the rush of the stream through the ruptured weir. The broken mill machinery had been cleared, from this room at least. The Rebels evidently preferred to destroy it rather than leave it for the Union Army. Their earlier violence had left a fine dust hanging in the air that dried Opdycke's throat. An orderly on General Wood's staff handed him a coffee. Its ashy aroma overlay that of ground wheat. A brace of lamps projected soldierly shadows onto the bare walls. He tried again to concentrate on what Wood was saying.

The general sat behind a small desk, leaning back in his chair. He finished up the divisional business and moved to the wider picture, waving his cigar for emphasis. As it was unlit, no one else lit up either. 'This mill's too close to the creek for division headquarters, so I'm setting up in a house on the hill. From tomorrow we'll meet there. Our corps is consolidating in this area, gentleman. Van Cleve is up the road a little way, so we can rest up. But we'll keep out a strong picket. There's plenty of Reb's about – we're not clear just where. We know Thomas's and McCook's Corps are getting together to the south of us. It seems Mr Rosecrans has determined that the Rebel rabbit isn't running quite as fast as he thought, and that he'd better collect us all together.'

There was gentle laughter amongst the officers, but Opdycke didn't join in. He wasn't slow himself to criticize the higher ranks. Heaven knew, they deserved it often enough. But in private, or in a letter home; not in front of the whole division. Rosecrans deserved more credit. He'd maneuvered Bragg out of Chattanooga with hardly a shot. And as a major general he should be referred to as such. They all knew Wood had fallen out with Rosecrans earlier in the month, but Wood shouldn't display such disrespect.

'And if an order comes down from HQ,' continued Wood, 'we'll jump to it. We wouldn't want to use our own eyes and ears.'

There was more laughter. Opdycke rubbed and stretched an eye. Naturally, they would side with their commander. Wood lit his cigar, which was his way of saying that the meeting was over. Others followed suit but Opdycke decided to leave and said goodnight to Harker. Outside he brushed the dust off his jacket. He'd not brought Barney with him as his regiment was camped nearby, so he walked back alone under the emerging stars. Battle would come soon. With the armies drawing together, it could be any day.

He stopped where the road was at its darkest to take in the perfume of the forest. It was at its strongest either side of sunset, and changed every night if you troubled to get attuned to it. With the summer flowers almost gone, it was the grass that won out, like a hayfield at home, dry and sweet. He was so rarely alone. He imagined himself back at his saddle and harness business in Warren, a businessman again; though he made a good colonel. He might never have known. He'd rather be a good general. His little boy would not be as he remembered him. The last time he saw Lucy and Tine was at the start of the year. He became aware of a cricket close by only when it stopped playing. Toads added their deeper song from over by the creek.

He found his tired mind had turned fallow. So when he started to walk again, he tried to set it to something more orderly and estimate the number of regiments on hand for the Union. The 125th was one of five in Harker's Brigade, though one had remained in Nashville. Wood's Division had three brigades, but Wagner's had been left to defend Chattanooga. That left eight regiments here in the First Division. Most divisions would have more – say ten on average. And Crittenden had three divisions in the Twenty-First Corps and there were four corps under Rosecrans. So perhaps one hundred and twenty regiments. One hundred and twenty colonels like him to play their small part, each with a few hundred men. He'd prefer to have a brigade. That was the real tactical unit in a large battle, as it had been at Shiloh when he'd been a captain in the 41st. He shivered, not sure if it was brought on by the cooling air or his muddled memories of battle.

The free scents of the forest gave way to those of camp, also a comfort in their own way. He called out early to the picket, conscious that they would be nervous. All was well.

None of his men had seen a real battle. He preferred to think of them as men rather than boys. In truth they were both. The skirmishes around Franklin had been good training, but nothing compared to massed musketry and artillery. Now he would discover if they could stand up to it. All that he could pray for was that Wood used them wisely. There was a lone fiddle keening somewhere nearby. Corporal Weirton most likely. He could play. Mustn't lose him.

He found Captain Bates, gave him his orders, then checked on Barney. After that he wished for nothing more than his fire, which someone had tended. The tents hadn't caught up yet so it would be another night under God's canopy, but he didn't mind. He had developed the essential habit of sleeping wherever and whenever he could. He would write to Lucy first. He found some paper, sat down and set it against his Bible.

'Excuse me, Colonel.'

Opdycke looked up to see Yeomans. He had a mulatto boy with him, although it was hard to be sure in this light. 'Can't it wait, Captain?'

'Sorry, Colonel. This boy's come across from the Reb's. When he heard we were the 125th, he asked to see you. He kept on, though I said you was busy. He tells me he was a servant – to General Bragg himself.'

Opdycke put down his Bible. He looked at the boy who twisted his hat in both hands, like he was wringing it dry. It could be a deception: the Rebels often sent fake deserters across to misinform them, but this boy wasn't a soldier. 'Have you something to tell us, son? Is that it? Sit down where I can see you.'

The boy's eyes were unsettled in the firelight. He sat and hugged his knees.

'How long have you been with Bragg?'

'Since the spring, sir. Six months.'

'Why leave him now?'

''Cos you here now, sir. All the Union here. He ain't fightin' my side.'

Opdycke smiled. 'Do you know what he's up to?'

'Not 'xactly, sir. I mean, I ain't no staff officer, but I was there most times when they all met. He means to fight. Maybe here, maybe Rome or Atlanta. I don't rightly know. I know there's men comin' from the east. From Virginia.'

'We've heard those rumors. You're sure?'

'Yes, sir. General Longstreet they said, sir.'

'Well, thank you, son. Captain, I want you to take this boy up to the mill. See if General Wood wants to talk to him. Make sure Wood hears about Longstreet.' Opdycke picked up his Bible again and the boy stood.

'That ain't why I came to see you, sir.'

'What then?'

'A few nights back, sir, General Cheatham, he was with Bragg and a few others. General Cheatham says to Bragg, remindin' him he says, that if we find the 125th Ohio, we're to treat them rough.'

'That doesn't make any sense.'

'I wouldn't normally have remembered. I was handin' out coffee. But Bragg got a temper up. Says he don't have no time for seein' to personal favors on the battlefield. General Cheatham pressed him though, mentioned someone called Trenholm. General Bragg said to Cheatham he would point his guns and muskets where they were needed, and if the 125th Ohio got in the way, that would just be a happy coincidence.'

Chickamauga Creek – September 18th, 1863

Shire knelt down, pushed the canteen under the cool water and let it bubble full. He had ten to do in all. Tuck and Lyman had the same.

'Sure is a pretty enough place,' said Tuck. 'Outside of a war, you'd think to pitch up here for good.'

The stream was no more than fifteen paces wide. With the dearth of rain it was low, but still running. Shire had picked this spot under a willow to keep them shaded from the late afternoon sun. He could see the familiar whiteboard of Lee and Gordon's Mill a half-dozen meanders upstream. Shire reflected that he'd not been into a wooden or stone building since Franklin four months ago, and would dearly love to step inside that one purely for the novelty. These days, his world was composed of forests, rivers and sky, and tents when the baggage train kept up.

Colonel Opdycke had set them here five days ago and had them build breastworks on this side of the creek, while the rest of the army went up and down the LaFayette Road.

'The colonel gives a good prayer, don't he,' said Tuck. 'Sure knows how to edge the Lord to our side. I hope them Rebel preachers and colonels ain't up to much.'

Shire said nothing. Earlier he had stood in a half circle with the whole regiment. The colonel had led them in prayer and song, and demanded that they do their duty to God and country. The rumor was that the battle would come very soon. At the service there had been a collective, solemn intensity. Perhaps the men were trying to make up for other days when the spirit had been lacking. Shire was surprised at his own serenity. Today, he seemed to have stepped sideways from fear, letting it flow slowly by, like this creek.

'Hey, Lyman,' called Tuck. 'Even you must have drawn some comfort from the colonel?'

Shire looked up and saw that Lyman wasn't listening. Instead, he was staring into the creek as if it held a watery ghost. He dropped a canteen, then rocked back and sat down. The canteen started to float away until Tuck stepped into the water to rescue it.

'Damnation. Now my boots is all wet. What's the matter with you?'

'I'm gonna die,' said Lyman simply. 'I seen it all, right here in the water.'

Shire moved over to him. Lyman was the color of his faded corporal's stripes, his eyes were unfocused, every muscle in his face slack.

'It's the prayer,' Shire said. 'It's made you melancholy. Nothing more.'

'No,' said Lyman, with all the certainty of a dug grave. 'I've seen it. No point pretending otherwise.'

Tuck took off his wet boots. 'Aw, quit it,' he said. 'You ain't never once had an ounce of hope in you. Why, if I gave you the best horse in Georgia you'd complain about the rope I led it in with.'

It was as if Lyman hadn't heard Tuck at all.

'I want you to take my money, Shire.' He reached into his jacket. 'You're lucky. You don't see it. But this ain't your war. You'll live through it. There's forty-five dollars to go to my Hilda. My letters I'll keep on me, but take them from me when I'm dead and send them too.'

Shire pushed away Lyman's hands. 'I'm as likely to be killed as you or anyone.' He felt the truth of it. He'd earned no singular protection from God.

Lyman dropped the notes. Shire was left to collect them.

'My playing cards,' said Lyman, 'they're in my pack. I can't have those sent home. Tuck, I'll give them to you when we get back to camp.' He picked up an empty canteen and began to fill it.

Once done, they slung the straps across their shoulders, and staggered like drunk men under the water's weight back up to the LaFayette Road. It was busier than it had been all week. Staff officers, cannon and wagons all moved in both directions.

'Don't seem this army knows which way it's tendin',' observed Tuck.

Later, as the sun touched the high ridge in the west, Shire sat with his squad around their fire. The tall trees of Georgia cast long shadows across the camp. There was the faintest of breezes, and the grass held a light evening dew. The camp was quieter than usual, the crickets louder than the men. All the soldiers had found something to do. They busied themselves with letters home, cleaned their rifles or read their Bibles by the firelight; anything to avoid talking.

Shire watched Jordan put up the tools of his trade. The company cook went about it quietly. He hooked spoons, ladles and pans onto a rope strung for the purpose. He managed it so gently, so reverently, that there was barely a sound, and he wouldn't allow any implement to swing.

Mason was laid close to Shire and spoke quietly. 'What's that fool giving away now?' He nodded towards Lyman who was moving through the company. 'We don't need him telling us death is in the air.'

'Whatever he thought he saw in the creek has got a hold on him,' said Shire.

'I don't see he's got any more right to feel a foreboding than the rest of us. He's just more practiced is all. His Pa had the worst kept farm in Medina County. Land was good enough, only they didn't tend to it.'

'Why did he join up?'

'Way he told me it was to escape his Scandinavian wife. Her folks moved on to Minnesota, but Lyman wouldn't follow, and she'd been nagging him to go ever since.'

Shire thought on the reasons they were all here. Cleves was

at the next fire, paid better as a third rate soldier than he was as second rate farm hand. Mason? Perhaps because he thought he ought to be a better man than he found himself. Tuck? Well, when it came down to it, he was really out for revenge. It was just a question of how wide he was spreading the blame. And Tom Muncie – the way the colonel had told it – he was here because his lawman father didn't think he was sharp enough to be a deputy. Of them all, as a black man, Jordan had the most straightforward reason to fight, but he wouldn't be allowed to. He would have to head off with the baggage.

Shire considered he had the oddest reason of all; it had little or nothing to do with the war. And if he died here, he would have been of no use to Clara. She'd never know why he'd come. He would have done better to stay at home and look after Father. Lyman had been right at the creek; it wasn't his war.

Ocks was coming towards him. 'Nothing to do, Private Shire?'

Shire stared into the fire. 'I've no one to write to, Sergeant.'

'Show me your bayonet?'

'What?'

'Come on.'

Shire took the blade from its sheath. Ocks took it, turned it in his hand. He sat down closer than Shire would have liked. In his other hand he held a whetstone, deeply worn at its middle, and he began to slide it against the long blade. It took Shire back to Ridgmont Farm, to when his friend Aaron Turney used to sharpen the scythes before the harvest.

'Remember,' said Ocks, 'once the blade's in, give it a little twist before you pull it out. Otherwise, it'll get stuck. And you'll want it back.'

Shire looked away. Ocks had only come to frighten him.

Across the fire, Tuck refused to take Lyman's pack of playing cards.

'What's with him?' asked Ocks, still working the blade.

'He says he's going to die if there's a battle,' said Shire. 'Says he's seen it and we can't persuade him otherwise. He's giving everything away, even his rations.'

Ocks put the bayonet down on Shire's blanket. 'Seen it before. In the British Army. And they're most often right. Take his things. Give him a bit of peace.'

Ocks left and Shire stood to put away the bayonet. An oversized beetle buzzed slowly by. He followed its escaping silhouette across the last, thin stripe of a pale yellow sunset. High on the slopes of the dark ridge to the west, signal lamps were busy with news and orders. The breeze had shifted to the north and it was colder. Perhaps there would be a frost. He sorted through his pack and found his valuables: his map, letters and license. All his treasures bound up in a single leather cord. After he was sure they were tied tight, he put them into his jacket and reached for his blanket.

Chickamauga – September 19th, 1863

The guns roared to the north of Colonel Spencer-Taylor and his Tennessee regiment. They'd been roaring all morning. Through a small window high in the leaves, Taylor could see smoke rising into the late summer sky. If General Bragg had a grand plan, Taylor didn't know what it was. From what he had gathered, there were probably as many Confederate troops keeping quiet to the south of him as were fighting to the north. It was past noon. The battle was either intensifying or coming closer – maybe both. The Hiwassee Volunteers stood in line of battle. Most of the uniforms had departed from the smart, dyed-grey of two years ago, washed by the rain to a faded brown. He sat behind them on his horse and considered whether to dismount as Major Jasper had advised. But he liked to be higher than the men, and it was important that they should see him.

'I'd as soon get it over with, wouldn't you, Colonel?' said Major Jasper. 'Standing still is more of a chore for a southern man, I reckon. Yankees are used to it.'

Taylor didn't reply and Jasper walked away to trouble the captains and lieutenants. The forest prevented Taylor from seeing either end of his own line. His regiment had become part of a scratch division under Johnson, so the units to his left and right were barely known to him. It would be hard to keep aligned in this terrain. He couldn't worry too much on that. Let the brigade commander see to it, since no one had seen fit to give Taylor that rank.

Not for the first time, he swallowed down his bitterness at the memory of how he'd pulled his regiment back from the very edge of a triumph at Stones River. If Jasper had kept all the companies tight that day it would never have come to that. It had been hard work recovering his reputation since. Trenholm's influence had been useful. But there had been scant action for the regiment until today. No opportunity to make a new impression. They should have given him a brigade all the same; six regiments and a battery of artillery. He could do some damage with that many men. And the 125th Ohio was out there somewhere. His mind felt for it, cast about as if he were tracking a black bear through the hills. He knew the chances that he'd encounter that one regiment were thin. But if Bragg could win the day and break up Rosecrans' army, then they could roll the Yankees and their little Englishman all the way back to Nashville.

Maybe then he could get over to Comrie and try again with Clara – as a victor. Perhaps she'd prefer him if he was wounded. Some women liked their men damaged. She didn't seem satisfied with him as he was.

He heard the major give out the order for the men to eat whatever they had in their packs. They were to stay in line though. He hadn't troubled to ask Taylor's permission. No matter.

He couldn't afford to be unmanned again. Stones River and the boy; it couldn't be ignored. It had been the shock. The shock of seeing the drummer boy's face shot apart like Will's all those years ago. Not that he'd ever forgotten Will's death. That moving image had come to him daily, asleep or awake, each day since. It was as familiar to him as the view from Comrie, as much a part of his life as trimming his beard. It was with him now, while he sat and watched the men eat.

Will hadn't died instantly. In the years since, Taylor had hated him for that. He couldn't just lay still, not even for his brother's sake. There had to be those last slow seconds, always the same, where his bloody face had struggled to animate itself with what muscles it had left. Taylor had admitted to himself long ago, that his memories of the day were not consistent. He'd see his brother away from him, across a glade, the gun dropped and discharging before Will fell too. Other times he'd be closer. So close that he could feel the blast of the shot, and the sudden spray of blood stinging his eyes. There had even been times when the gun was in his hands. But these were memories of dreams and dreams of memories. They'd been stirred and steered by his mother's feeble questions, disinterred from her over the years like dirt from an unhealed wound. Father had stopped asking after a month or so. Only weeks after Will's death, he'd taken Taylor back into the woods to hunt again. He'd schooled him in life's harsh realities and they never mentioned his brother. He wished Mother had said less and Father more. And there was always the grave. Will's name chiseled above you as you rode up the drive. There was never the option to forget. But something had changed after Stones River. The memory of Will's face and that of the drummer boy's had merged into one. Will seemed a little further away.

Taylor didn't trouble himself with guilt. Or at least what he observed in others and understood to be guilt: an odd compulsion to behave contritely for some perceived sin. He knew that he used to behave that way once. He recalled when he was fourteen or so, he'd shot a hound that belonged to Moses. He'd taken it on a duck hunt, but it wasn't trained like his own dogs, and it wouldn't return the kill. That made the dog useless, so he'd shot it. He'd lied to Moses, told him the dog never came in. Days later he'd sought out a litter and gave Moses the best pup. He could no longer recall the impulse that might have made him do that, like he'd lost the memory of a particular color. Father had schooled guilt out of him. And regret was a feeble, unproductive thing.

It was the fear of losing control that worried him most. He was bound to see the same horror today. He'd seen men hung slowly, seen a bayonet pass right through a man, seen one of his corporals stood holding his own bowels. It was just a shot face that he couldn't deal with.

A shell burst in a tree over to his right and his horse shied. He watched branches fall to the ground followed more gently by a shower of leaves. He got the horse under control and looked afresh at his men, who'd finished eating. They seemed steady enough. Then one man stepped backwards and was sick on the pine straw. No one jeered. A sergeant put him back in line.

As he'd done many times already this morning, Taylor took out his pistol and checked that the chambers were full. Men would die in many ways today. And sure as the sun would come up tomorrow, some would be shot in the face. His breath came faster. He would have no reputation left to recover if he ran again.

Major Jasper walked back to him, one hand on his sheathed sword to angle it away from his legs. 'I wish we would get the order,' he said. 'When we do there'll be no point shufflin' up like a nervous boy to his sweetheart at a barn dance. We should see it for what it is and go in hard.'

'What did you say?'

'See it for what it is, sir. Horror an' all. Only way to go about it.'

It summoned a day with his father at a slave auction down in Birmingham. Will was dead a year by then. Taylor had backed away from the auction block, the whips and the stench of fear. A hand had pressed onto his back and his father had bent to his shoulder. 'See it for what it is, son. That's the way the world is. No use turning aside from it. See it and use it.'

A staff officer rode up. In anticipation, Major Jasper stood the whole regiment to attention. The officer was no one Taylor recognized.

'Colonel Ridgmont. Your regiment is to advance in line with the brigade.'

Taylor stared at him dumbly, his father's long dead voice more assertive.

'At once, Colonel,' barked the rider.

Taylor shouted by way of an answer. 'Tennesseans will advance. March!'

His three hundred men stepped westward through the trees.

*

As he stood in the morning heat beside the LaFayette Road, it appeared to Shire that the whole Union Army was in a hurry to go north. Harker's Brigade weren't invited. Instead they stayed to cover the ford through Chickamauga creek, close to Lee and Gordon's Mill. Shire watched regiment after regiment rattle by and kick up the dust, which never once settled. The 125th needed to cross the road to take up its position, but the colonel was having trouble finding a big enough gap in the traffic. In the end, they hurried across by squads and formed up again on the other side.

Following Mason, Shire waded knee-deep through the ford. He carried his rifle in front of his chest. Dragonflies – red, blue or silver – darted between the men. His boots were heavy as they trudged out the other side. Yesterday, the Rebels had pushed towards the creek. It had taken only a few cannon shots to turn them back. They'd not come within range of Shire's musket. Yet he was wary now and stared into the scruffy woods. Out there were all sizes of oak and chestnut, though they were altered from home. Shire couldn't say how. They were just not quite right. They mingled with tall stands of pine, what he recognized as cedar, and what Tuck told him was hemlock. He sipped water from his canteen to keep his hands busy, and wished he was in the sandy forest he knew as a boy. The guns rose and fell in the north like the promise of a summer storm.

'Feels like we're being leap-frogged by the whole darn army,' said Tuck, as he looked back over the creek.

'Suits me fine,' said Mason. 'I ain't in no hurry to join the ruckus up the road. When I'm old and have a grandson on my knee I'll plain lie. Say we were in the thick of it.'

Noon came and went. Shire began to believe their luck would hold to the end of the day. But then the order came to fall back across the creek. They formed into column and took their own place on the road. Before long, he was sweating out all the water he'd so nervously drunk. The colonel marched them quickly towards the mounting sound of guns. Covered ambulances, coming back south, were obliged to leave the road to let them pass. From under the arched canvas, wide-eyed wounded stared out. Shire marched on through the dust, envious of the injured.

The gunfire grew louder and louder, until at last they came behind the Union line of battle set in the trees to their right. A spent minie ball flicked off the road behind Tom Muncie. Shire knew that the test he'd long expected had arrived. More wounded men spilled from the smoking woods and headed for the rear. The musket fire became continuous, so that a volley or a shot could play out no more than a fraction of its echo before being interrupted by the next. The tumult rose in intensity until, to Shire, it became a single, deafening entity, as real and tangible as the ground he marched on. Bugles fought to be heard. The smoke became thicker. The taste of sulfur was stronger in every breath he took.

A field opened up to their right, and at once Shire could see the backs of the long lines of blue. There were cannon on the high ground, being worked hard. Shire had heard cannon before, but never like this: so many and so near that the detonations twitched at his coat, passed through his bones and his empty gut. He struggled to compose any thought. His mind was used entirely for comprehension. A horse reared so steeply it dumped an officer. A lieutenant pulled a soldier up roughly by the collar and pushed him forward. An artillerist was thrown backwards from a recoiling cannon. When a shell exploded in the blue line and turned a part of it instantly red, Shire snapped his head forward rather than see anymore. His feet trembled as he set down each stride. He should have listened to Father.

Fields were open on both sides now. Officers dressed the lines, shouted into the din. Mixed pines and oaks started on the right, close to the edge of the road. Shire welcomed them like a blanket after a nightmare. They were ordered a few paces into the field opposite, then turned about to face the road in line of battle. There was a log schoolhouse on the other side, its back-half within the trees.

When the order came to go forward, Shire had to catch his balance. *Just do whatever the sergeant says.* They were not sent straight ahead. Instead, they were slanted to the left, so that they would go obliquely into the trees up from the schoolhouse. Shire was in the second rank. He was breathing hard even before they started to move. To his right the trees swallowed the angled line, one man at a time, until it was his turn.

It was darker in the woods. A new world of rationed light dappled the forest floor. The noise of battle changed. It seemed to come from all directions. Shire sucked in the pine scent and tried to breathe more slowly. He was following Mason again. He tried to keep in line despite the trees. There wasn't too much undergrowth. The ground was springy with pine straw and he could feel pinecones roll under his boots. They moved away from the schoolhouse and deeper into the woods. Shire looked past Mason, but he could see fifty paces at best. Their pickets were out there somewhere, feeling for the enemy. The minutes stretched out and Shire wondered how much further into the woods they would go. He looked to Tuck on his left.

Tuck smiled. 'Bet you wish you'd stayed at home now, don't ya?'

Shire forced himself to smile back. It felt like a grimace. He was so hot. His jacket was thick and heavy. Warm sweat trickled down his back. There was a cry up ahead. The pickets fired then fell back to the line. He could see movement in the trees, men in brown and grey moving across their front. *Oh, Dear Lord.*

'Company, halt. Prime.'

Their muskets were already loaded. Shire took a percussion cap from the leather box on his belt. He placed it on the nipple.

'Ready... Aim!'

He brought his gun up; one amongst many. He pointed it towards the moving men. The order came before he'd picked a target.

'Fire!'

The volley ripped across their front and left a whistling tone inside Shire's head. White smoke blinded him. There was no breeze to dispel it. It was impossible to know if he'd hit anything. But as the smoke dissolved, a few of the Rebel forms staggered or fell.

'Load!'

He juggled a cartridge, bit it open too roughly and had to spit out the gritty powder. He poured the remainder into the barrel, then the ball and the cartridge paper. Tom Muncie, loading next to him, was either laughing or crying. Shire reached for his ramrod.

'Aim!'

He wasn't ready. He should aim anyway. Without warning, he was yanked back from the line.

'Fire!'

He was spun around by Ocks, who stole his musket and pulled the ramrod from the barrel. Despite all his training, Shire had been about to shoot the ramrod along with the ball. He'd have had no way to reload. Ocks placed a percussion cap, pushed the musket at Shire and thrust him back into line.

'Forward march!'

A few paces. The forest ahead spat lead back at them as the Rebels got off a lesser volley. Bullets snatched away pine needles above Shire's head. He saw Cleves, the other side of Tuck, back out of formation. Ocks reached out a paw to beat Cleves' head and shoved him back in.

'What's the matter with you?' Ocks shouted. He sounded joyful. 'We've got 'em in the flank. Aim low, boys.'

'Ready!'

Shire had dropped his cartridge and bent to find it. A ball slapped into the tree right where he'd been standing. 'Sweet Jesus.'

'Fire!'

The smoke melted away and the Rebels fell back until there were only trees again. The company cheered and Shire was slapped on the back. Tuck's smile was as wide as the Tennessee River. Shire doubted he'd ever stop shaking.

The colonel rode up behind them. 'Captain Yeomans, did you lose any?'

'One, Colonel.'

'That's the only one in the regiment.'

It was Ocks who pointed them towards Lyman. He was lying behind the line, face upwards. He'd been shot through the throat; front to back. Blood pumped from his neck and he was choking. There was the same sickly metallic smell as when you bled a pig. Mason knelt and quickly rolled Lyman onto his side, then put a trembling hand over the wound. Shire had no idea what he could do. The coughing eased but the blood wouldn't stop pouring between Mason's fingers. Tom Muncie ran to find help. Tuck knelt too. Lyman started to shake like a girl who'd once had a fit in Shire's class.

Tuck stroked Lyman's hair. 'Easy,' he said. The trembling subsided. Lyman lifted his arm and took Mason's hand from his neck.

'We'll see your folks get everything,' said Tuck.

Lyman blinked once, as if he understood. His blood pumped weakly. And then it was just an even flow. Tuck closed Lyman's eyes and stood. Shire had done nothing at all. He watched the blood drain away into the pine straw.

*

Taylor came out of the woods behind the Hiwassee Volunteers and into a wide field that ran slightly uphill. Several Confederate regiments formed a long, grey and brown stripe to his left. There was nothing but trees to his right. The Union held the skyline and their cannon opened up right away, but they shelled the center, well away from Taylor. There were so many men. The other regiments moved to the double-quick, and he ordered the same. He waved his sword and screamed at them. They screamed back and swept up towards a blue wall edged with steel.

They got so close. Some detached, delusional part of his mind started to hope that the enemy would never shoot. The Yankees waited and waited until his men were within twenty paces, then fired brutal volleys by company. Every second as many as a hundred rifles swore down the slope. The Rebel line shivered. As he looked down its long length, he saw it writhe like a snake pinned at both ends.

His own regiment received a volley. It was badly aimed and flew high, but his horse was hit; a hard smack, as if it had been struck with a flat stick. The horse's legs buckled and tipped Taylor so he landed painfully on the corn-stubble, his sword stretched out in front of him. The regiment pressed on. They didn't stop to fire, just yelled and bore into the blue. He drew his pistol and chased after them. No fear, only anger, pure anger. When he caught up, it had become a brawl. There were no free Yankees, so he shot at those already engaged. He emptied his pistol into them, slashed his saber across their backs. He was elated. Yet it was hard for the men to fight up the slope. They began to fall back. To his left he could see all the other regiments falling back too. They left a carpet of men, as if autumn had come early to the field.

Back at the edge of the trees he helped Jasper and the other officers rally the men. Their blood was up as much as his. He could see they were frenzied, that they still wanted to fight. More orders came. 'There's a road ahead,' he was told. 'If we can take it the Yankees'll have a devil of a time getting back to Chattanooga.'

They were directed into the woods on their right to make room for an extra Texas regiment. His men were happier in the trees. They found the Yankees there and drove them. The blue was easy to pick out. He saw Major Jasper had his saber out to push the men, but he didn't need it. The Yankees were stubborn and it was slow going, but his men made ground. Ahead in the trees, Taylor saw a large log cabin, a schoolhouse maybe. There were Yankees in there and either side of it. Taylor moved himself to the front. He loaded his pistol. 'Do you think we can take it, boys?'

'Hell yes, Colonel!'

The Rebel yell sounded to their left and the Texans ran at the cabin. 'C'mon, boys. Texas is havin' all the fun.' Taylor raced ahead, chased by his closest men. Attacked from two quarters the defenders broke and backed away. Taylor looked in through an open window and saw Union soldiers pouring out the front door. He climbed inside. There were two dead Yankees and a young one still alive who sat on the floor and held his shoulder.

'I need to get back to my lines, sir. Please, sir.'

See it for what it is, son. That's the way the world is.

'I'll save you the bother.' Taylor aimed at his chest. Then he raised his arm and shot between the boy's wide eyes.

*

Shire and the 125th fought on through the woods and the late afternoon. His eyes watered from the constant smoke. They were lucky, so he was told. Each time they encountered the Rebels, they found them either disorganized or moving across their front. Colonel Opdycke kept their formation tight, and they were always able to push the enemy away. Shire had never lived with such sustained animal fear. He'd only ever known it fleetingly: in a fall from a horse or in a sudden slip when climbing a tree. Today it was a constant companion that lived and breathed alongside every heartbeat. And each time the fighting stopped he remembered Lyman.

Before dusk the regiment pulled back through the woods. They moved over ground that had seen heavy fighting. There were clusters of discarded dead in blue, grey or brown. Shire stepped over branches felled by shells and was hurried past injured men who begged for water. Away from the regiment he could still hear the battle. He doubted whether in the dying light one side could be told from the other. He lost all track of where he was. Slowly, the guns diminished with the day to only the occasional shot, as if out there was nothing more than a band of friends on a dusky hunt. When the colonel stopped their slow stumble through the woods, Shire could dimly see a log wall a few paces ahead. With a shock he realized that it was the schoolhouse. He'd come all the way back to where he'd started into the woods that afternoon. He watched Mason slump down and push his cap over his face, his shoulders shaking with grief.

The air was cold and still, and the smoke from the day was free to settle into the forest. With no prospect of a hot meal, Shire dug in his pack for hardtack. The biscuit had little flavor at the best of times. Now it had none at all. But he found some unconscious, bovine comfort in the simple act of eating. He realized he was surprised to be alive, and wondered if, from here on, he always would be. Next to him, without asking, Tom Muncie started a small fire. He heaped on a double handful of pinecones and the fire flared brightly. At the edge of its thrown light lay a corpse, or at least part of one. Shire gazed at it with everyone else. He guessed that the man had been struck by round shot. The leg and hip had been carried away along with the small of the back. The one remaining knee was drawn up to the man's stomach, held there by his hands in sympathy with the agony frozen on his face. The body appeared to have kept some latent energy, the muscles taut even in death, as if it might yet exhale a final breath. A canteen was strapped over his shoulder. Shire was short of water – but he couldn't bear to move any closer.

Ocks arrived and kicked out the fire. The light mercifully died. 'Idiot.' He raised an arm over Tom but didn't strike him.

Shire shook his head to try and rid himself of the image.

'I need pickets,' said Ocks.

When no one volunteered, he pulled Tom up by the arm. 'You'll do, and Shire. You must have plenty of rounds left. You were firing slowly enough.'

Shire took up his rifle and followed Ocks into the gloom. At least he'd be away from the corpse. Ocks grabbed his shoulder and pointed into the black woods. 'I want you a hundred paces out. Shoot to warn us if you have to.'

When they moved off, Tom stayed so tight to Shire that he had to ask him to mind his bayonet.

Tom whispered. 'It weren't a good time for me to upset Sergeant Ocks. N...not sure why he picked you out though?'

Shire didn't like to think on that. Fear, so lately put down, returned as a cold sweat. Terrifying as the day had been, at least he'd had all of Company B around him. Now there was only Tom. Shire counted out his paces. They were small, frightened steps. So much so, that when he reached a hundred, he forced himself to count out another twenty. It felt like the bravest thing he'd ever done.

*

Colonel Opdycke trotted beside General Wood. They were half a mile back from the lines. Out of the woods the very last of the light was dying over the high ridge to the west. They climbed a small rise, above the lingering smoke of battle which was beginning to mix with the night's first true mists. The crack of the rifles and the detonation of cannon that had enveloped Opdycke all afternoon were gone. But they had left a high-pitched whine inside his right ear which made it hard to understand the detail of what Wood was telling him. He gathered that the Rebels had tried all day to come around the Union left, so that units had needed to be constantly moved to the north, as the 125th was.

He was pleased to be going to Rosecrans' headquarters. Wood had invited Harker, but he'd demurred, saying there was too much to do. He'd offered up Opdycke instead. So here he was, a lowly colonel off to rub shoulders with the top brass. He hoped when they got there to hear more of the story of the day, and see what plans were made for tomorrow. Yet part of him felt unstrung. He would have liked to have walked amongst his men, to have checked on the injured, the ammunition, the water. Captain Bates could do it all no doubt, but it would have helped Opdycke to settle himself, to smooth away the tension of the day.

Opdycke could see lanterns up ahead outside a cabin. Away from the house were scattered campfires. He sensed a great number of men resting outside the firelight. He followed Wood through a strong guard and they dismounted in front of the house. His feet were sore as they took his weight, and he forced himself straight. Wood was hailed by a man in civilian clothes who held aloft a cigar. It was hard to tell in the lamplight, but Opdycke thought the man's beard might be red.

'Taking the air, Mr Dana?' said Wood.

'That cabin wasn't built to hold so many generals,' Dana replied.

'This is Colonel Opdycke of the 125th Ohio.'

Opdycke took off his hat and offered Dana his gloved hand. He'd heard much about this man. Dana hung on longer than was called for, and took in Opdycke as if he planned to buy his horse.

'How went your day, Colonel Opdycke?'

'Very well, sir. We were late into the fight but pushed the enemy wherever we found them. Our losses were light.'

'Then you may be called on tomorrow. Other units were used up from what I can gather.'

'You think the battle will continue? The Rebels haven't had enough?' Opdycke had wanted it to be over.

It was Wood that answered. 'In truth, Colonel, I think they had the better of the day. For the most part we merely held our line. We shall see what our esteemed major general has planned. As it's crowded, I fear I must leave you outside.'

'A word with you first, General Wood,' said Dana. He put an arm across Wood's back and steered him around the corner of the cabin.

So that was Mr Charles Dana, so often the talk amongst the officers; sent from Washington by the war department to report back on Rosecrans. Not an army man; a newspaper man. Opdycke might debate Rosecrans' strong and weak points, but it was clear to any dunderhead that he'd do better without some busybody clicking off dispatches every time he had to make a tough decision. But then the professional army was arrogant sometimes. It hadn't been easy to get his own promotion: the West Pointers were always first in line.

Now that he had nothing to do, he realized how bone-tired he was. He'd been in the saddle all day. Barney must be tired too. He asked a passing orderly where he could find water.

'There's a barrel for officers at the end of the porch, sir. For your horse there's a pond just out there. Not fit for man or beast. There's been injured boys bleeding into it all day, but it's all they have.'

He would normally tend to Barney first, but the barrel was closer, and he was so thirsty from barking orders in the smoke. There was no dipper so he took off his sooty gloves and drank from his hands. He splashed the last scoop onto his dry face. When he'd filled his canteen he had trouble getting the stopper back in.

The pond was a perfectly round depression, muddied about its dark edge where it had seen traffic all day. A few men collected water while others lay stretched out on their stomachs and sucked it straight in. Opdycke was glad he couldn't see the state of it. Barney wasn't so particular and drank and drank, blowing from his nose.

'Well, we made it through the day, old boy,' said Opdycke. He patted Barney's shoulder with a sympathy he held back from the men around him. Moans and sobs, cries for home and loved ones slid out of the darkness, but he let them float by him and not through him. He'd done well today. It wasn't right in time of battle to have a soft heart. It would be an indulgence. His men and his country were better served by a steady mind, one that knew when to save them and when to spend them. He started to lead Barney back to the cabin by a roundabout route where he hoped to find him some better grass. Where it was darkest of all, they came across a battery of four cannon with no gunners and no guards. Opdycke steered towards one and stroked the barrel which held its heat from the day's sun. He ran his palm along the length of it, smooth and warm like a woman's thigh – like Lucy's. He was amused and slightly shocked at the odd thought, but then fighting was, when it needed to be, a passionate business and not all emotions could be suppressed. He missed her. He was glad to be alive to think of her.

Ahead was what appeared to be a cedar tree, its lowest branches spread wide and flat. It was lit from beneath by a single, hanging lantern. A man was digging there – just one – not tiredly or steadily; he was manic, and dug as if his life depended on it. Stripped to the waist, he attacked the earth with his short shovel and the will of a madman. Two other soldiers stood to the side to avoid the wildly-thrown dirt. A still form lay nearby. Opdycke led Barney closer.

'C'mon, Sam,' said one of the watchers. 'Let me take a turn. Rest a while.' He put out a hand, but the digger knocked it away harshly.

'I don't need no help.' The man was breathing hard. He paused only to wipe his face with his forearm before he started to dig again. Opdycke came level and stopped. The man climbed out of the grave. He barged through his friends and collected some cut branches. He jumped back in and lined the base with them; more slowly now, carefully, so he covered the floor with the fronds as best he could. And then he reached for the body, pulled it towards him and laid it gently in the ground.

Opdycke moved to one of the watchers. 'His friend?'

'His younger brother, sir. Died not an hour ago. Sam says he doesn't know what he'll tell his ma, says it might be better to die here too.'

Opdycke led Barney on, but something shook loose in him. A

wellspring of sadness and longing rose up through his chest and he couldn't control it. He stopped trying to, and found another reason to be grateful for the dark.

*

Ahead of Shire there was a yellow light, a low line of fire that slowly ate its way over the forest floor. It was probably started by spent cartridge papers. He'd seen any number smoking at his feet during the day. Without a breeze the fire was no threat to them. It barely moved.

The night began to offer up sounds every bit as terrible as the guns and shells had been. From all around came the pitiful moans and cries of men who lay injured and dying. Most asked for water or for their mothers. A few invited death to come and take them. After a while, it got so Shire could recognize each individual cry. He tried to shut them out, to whisper with Tom, but it was impossible. Lyman's quick death began to seem a blessing. At times, Shire would miss a voice that had become familiar and guess that another soul had found its peace. The fire crept across in front of them, from twig to leaf. Like a candle clock, it marked the passage of the night.

'Dear God, help me.' A new voice, closer to them. 'I can't move.'

Tom started forward. Shire put an arm out to stop him. 'We can't. That fire will light us up if the Reb's are out there.'

'Please. Dear God!' the voice cried again, then a low sob.

'I can't leave him,' said Tom. 'Not to burn.'

Shire relented. He found the courage to creep forward with Tom until they reached the trickle of fire. Only a pace ahead of the low flames a soldier lay on his back. He wasn't moving at all. His eyes sought them out. 'Are you my boys...? No, you ain't. You's Union boys.'

Shire tried to look beyond the fire, but could see nothing.

311

'We'll have to drag you,' he said. 'I'll do it.' He gave Tom his rifle.

'I'd as soon have you shoot me. I can't move a thing. No good to anyone. I just didn't wanna burn.'

Shire had to stand. He put his hands under the man's shoulders and pulled him away. The Rebel didn't cry at all. Shire propped him against a tree. His hand came away from the man's back, sticky with blood. He tried to smear it off on the ground, but the pine straw stuck to his fingers. Tom unslung his canteen and gave the man a drink.

'We can't stay with you,' said Shire, wiping his hands on his jacket instead.

The man struggled to get his breath back after his drink. He angled his eyes to look at Shire. 'What are you? English?'

Shire nodded.

'Huh. Saved by an Englishman and a Yankee. God bless you anyway.'

Something sharp pricked into the back of Shire's neck. He stopped breathing and fought down the impulse to run.

'Up real easy, Yank.'

He raised his hands. A Rebel snatched away Tom's canteen.

'I'm sorry, Sh…Shire.'

'Shut up. Unsling those packs.'

Shire was turned around. He thought he could make out at least four Rebels in the dark. One pressed a bayonet to his stomach. The man was close enough for Shire to smell the stink of his breath. He could sense the eager weight behind the blade.

'Can't we kill them, Corporal? Seems like a chore to take them back to the regiment.'

Tom was pushed to his knees.

'I wouldn't see them killed for a kindness,' called the injured man. 'Please. They could have left me to burn.'

A second man stepped closer to Shire. 'Is that right? Well, it might have to be their last kindness. What regiment you from?'

'125th.'

312

'Uhuh.' A smile in the darkness. 'I think this boy might be a touch nervous. You forgotten where your home is?'

The bayonet pressed harder. Shire's stomach muscles knotted. 'Ohio. 125th Ohio.'

'Truly?' The man sounded surprised. 'Then it's your lucky day. We got orders for that regiment. Our colonel's gonna wanna to see you two boys.'

*

Opdycke sat on the porch step of the Union Headquarters for what felt like a long time. He needed to get back to the regiment where he could feel more in control. Finally, the door opened and a stream of generals flowed out along with the cigar smoke. Wood wore a face that didn't invite any form of conversation. They rode off down the hill at a canter despite the night. They were halfway back to the line before Opdycke risked a question. 'What will happen, General? What are Rosecrans' plans?'

Wood reined in his horse, and they slowed to a walk. He blew out a breath. 'That man can run an army on the march, but he goes to pieces in a battle. I know I've had my run-ins with him, but he looked spent to me.'

Opdycke said nothing.

Wood eventually went on. 'We held well enough today, but we're on the defensive. Rosecrans should throw a punch. He won't though, prefers to wait and see where Bragg lands his. Best as I can figure we're lined up like a question mark, running north to south. Thomas's Corps holds the curve and seems well set-in. We're in the line that runs straight down below him. Bragg attacked our left most of the day and Rosecrans is still of a mind to send more troops up there. He expects Bragg to carry on trying to get between us and Chattanooga. But Longstreet is out there somewhere. He could aim left or right. We have four corps,' he said, exasperated, 'Why not use one to attack and make Bragg worry?'

Opdycke didn't agree. Attacking armies hadn't often fared well in this war. Let the Rebels spend themselves; they could ill afford it. He kept his own counsel. 'And what of us, General? Where will we go?'

'We're to pull back into reserve, north of headquarters. I wouldn't get too comfortable, though. We'll be needed early enough.'

The formal order to withdraw came soon after Opdycke returned to his regiment. He directed the pickets to be pulled in. Two were missing. One was that English boy, but there was nothing to be done, and he marched the regiment away.

Chickamauga – September 20th, 1863

Shire edged away from sleep as if it were a cliff in the dark. The cold was his ally. When it was quiet his time was measured in fearful thoughts that crowded in one after another. He was easier of mind when he could hear the men quietly talking. It could have been his own regiment but for the southern drawl. They went over the day: who'd lived, who'd died, who'd run. They longed for food, coffee and a fire. Just once he jolted awake to remember where he was: sat against a tree with Tom in a Rebel camp, waiting on a colonel.

They hadn't been taken far. The 125th would be only a short run through the woods if he could get the jump on the guard. But he knew he wouldn't risk it, and he wouldn't leave Tom.

He heard a new guard drag his feet through the pine straw. 'Why in the hell ain't we jus' takin' them back of the line?'

'125th Ohio. Colonel wants to see them, 'cept he's been up with the generals since the brigade commander got hit. He's got the whole brigade now, so I guess he won't be by so much. Probably sleeping somewhere warmer than here.'

'He was a sight today, weren't he? Didn't know when to stop. Like a fox at hens he was. I'm not right sure he should be given a brigade.'

'Might only be for the battle. I need some sleep. Their packs is there, but we ain't allowed to take nothin'.'

The old guard slipped away and the new one sat facing Shire, nothing but a shape in the darkness. 'You boys sit still now. And if my eyes close it's 'cos I'm contemplatin' is all. Colonel Ridgmont will be along in his own time.'

After the sudden clench in his empty stomach, Shire thought to confirm the name, but he knew he'd heard it right. Emotions that had stewed all year rushed in to stir his fear. He pictured

Taylor holding the gun to Old Tom's head. He remembered Clara coming to the school and their awkward, polite goodbye. He saw Father standing in the snow as he left. Deep down he'd hoped to find Taylor dead and Clara free of him.

He should run. He looked over to Tom but it was too dark to see him. He realized that beneath the sharper emotions there was also a stony anticipation: that his burden of all these months would now be made real. There was no reason to be surprised that Taylor would be on the lookout for him. Matlock would have seen to that. The license was wrapped in his pocket. He thought he could slip it out in the dark, tuck it under the leaves. He felt behind his back amongst the twigs and cones. He moved his hand slowly and slipped it into his jacket. The tied roll of Clara's letters, the map and the license were there. At least he'd be doing something if he hid it. The guard shifted and Shire jerked his hand away. It was a stupid thought. He'd never find it again. He might as well hand it over as lose it.

Somewhere in the night, sleep claimed him. The next time he woke the first light of dawn was unveiling a brown forest cloaked in mist.

'Private.' The voice surfaced from Shire's past.

'Colonel, sir.' The guard stood.

'I hear you have a gift for me?'

'They's right here, Colonel.'

Shire squinted up. A tall man bent over him, long hair hanging forward of his face. A gloved hand pulled up his chin. Taylor smelt of week old sweat.

'Dear Lord in Heaven, what have we here?' Then a laugh. 'It's the boy his self, delivered up to me by the Union Army. Well, let's see now. On your feet, Master Shire, and your friend too. Let's take a walk.'

Taylor pulled out his pistol. It looked familiar. It was pushed firmly into the small of Shire's back as he was steered through the woods, away from the sleeping army. Tom and the guard followed but after a short while Taylor stopped them. 'Wait here. This Englishman and I have some business.'

The thought to run flashed through his mind again, but the feel of the gun dismissed it. They went on alone, but not far. There was a flat-topped, sawn-off tree-trunk. Taylor took a seat and pushed up his hat brim with his pistol.

'You might find me somewhat distracted. I apologize. It's been a long night. Once this light comes on I've got a whole brigade to get moving. So I don't have a lot of time. But as you've come so far it would be impolite to rush. And frankly, I admire your tenacity. Where's the license?'

'I don't have a license.' Shire sought to look convincing. 'I didn't know there was one.'

'Really?' Taylor leant forward and took off his hat. He dropped it to the ground, scratched his lank hair. 'Tell me what in the hell you thought you were going to get out of this? I mean, it's a big trip just to tell a tale, ain't it?'

Shire dug for some courage. 'Are you married? Or should I ask if you've had another wedding?'

'Why? Was you hoping she was still fillin' in her dance card? We're married alright. She ain't no debutant English Lady no more. You know, she weren't so different from your friend Grace. Face all screwed up. Don't do this, don't do that. But when it comes right down to it, things slide home just fine.'

Shire closed his eyes.

'Oh, I'm sorry. That too much for your English sensibilities? Or is it that you have no idea?'

'When did you marry? What was the date?'

Taylor pursed his lips. 'After sweet, little Grace died. Clara's Mrs Spencer-Ridgmont, all nice and legal. Where's the license? Matlock knows you took it.'

'How do you know it's legal?' Shire didn't believe him. 'I hope you're not relying on Matlock? He's hardly one to trust with facts and figures. My father knew that well enough.'

'Didn't seem to help him none, did it? No. He's quite a boy, that Matlock. I've long since made up my mind he's not a man to cross. The Devil himself seems to watch over him. Grace dead, your father dead. And he and I have some commonality in our interests. So I'll trust to that. Now, I'm gonna have to press you this time. Where's the license?'

Shire's mind raced as quickly as his heart. Surely Clara would believe him whether he had a license or not. But he'd carried it so long, given up so much to get it this far.

'Private,' Taylor called. 'Bring that Yank in here.'

When they arrived Taylor stood up, took hold of Tom's arm and waved the pistol near his head.

'Now, don't this scene seem familiar to you? Same pistol too. It sent a few souls back above the Mason-Dixon yesterday.'

Shire knew the script, but he wasn't about to test it on Tom.

'No one's gonna miss one Yank more in this mess.'

Shire held a hand out. 'Wait!'

Tom started to breathe in a rush through his teeth, his eyes tightly closed.

Taylor pressed the gun to Tom's ear. 'It'll just be the first shot of the day.'

'I have it! I have it!' cried Shire. He patted the outside of his jacket.

'Well now, why couldn't you have told me that straight up?' said Taylor. And pulled the trigger.

The gunshot cracked but fell flat in the woods. A red mist burst from Tom's head and dissolved into the air. Taylor pushed him away and Tom dropped lifeless to the ground. Taylor turned to the private. 'Go make sure we're not disturbed. Go on.'

The man, his eyes on Tom, started to back away.

'I said I had it!' Shire's hand was across his mouth. He had to catch himself as his knees buckled.

'So you did, so you did.' Taylor advanced towards him. 'Only it's just as easy for me to get it out of your pocket as for you.'

No more than a pace away, Taylor raised the gun to point at Shire's face. 'Should have stayed at home. Wasn't ever your business.'

Shire's lungs were frozen. He thought of Father. There was a crash of leaves behind Taylor as the Rebel private stumbled. When Taylor turned his head, Shire struck the pistol upwards and threw his shoulder into Taylor's chest. Taylor fell backwards over a tangle of dead branches. Shire scrambled on by him to clearer ground. Three quick strides then a cut to his left put a tree between himself and the gun. He kept running, kept switching direction. A bullet twitched his jacket. More shots, one grazed a tree so close that the splinters hit his face. He heard a scream of frustration. He had no idea which direction to take but he dared not stop. He looked back only once but could see nothing but the forest. He tore on and on through the woods, fearful that if he stopped, either Taylor or despair would overtake him. When utterly exhausted, he stood with his hands on his knees and fought for breath. Taylor was always going to kill Tom, kill both of them. It wouldn't have mattered if he'd admitted sooner that he had the license. But he knew that if he lived through this day and this war, he would never be able to stop doubting that. He collapsed to the forest floor and wept.

Fear of pursuit stole back into him. He looked about. The trees were thinner here. It had allowed the bushes and undergrowth to take hold. The slope ahead fell away to a small creek with a high stand of rhododendron on the other side. He stepped through the water and crawled in under the long leaves.

Inside there was a space, a hiding place that as a child he would have been excited to find. Sleep was his only possible escape. He curled up on the cool earth but when he closed his eyes found only the circling memory of Tom's death. He came to see that ahead of him was a choice. He could try to find his way back to the Union lines, or he could go east. In a few days he could get to Polk County and to Clara. He was in Union uniform, but he could find a dead Rebel and change – he could do that – though it brought its own risks. He sat up and drew out the roll of papers from his jacket to look again at the map. The license was rolled with it and he could hardly bear to touch it. He thought of Tom and he thought of Lyman. There was a fight here and it wasn't over. But he'd come to America to keep a promise to Clara; to save her from a bigamist and now a murderer. The chance to go to her might not come again. He could hurt Taylor more by reaching Clara than he could by re-joining the battle. He stared at the map for a long time, as if the answer was written there somewhere amongst the names of the counties, or the towns, or the rivers. But the answer was in him, not in the map.

He'd go east and keep his promise.

*

Barney walked along behind the breastworks that the men had scrambled together. Opdycke surveyed the torn-down branches in front of the scraped ditch where most of the men knelt. Nothing much to stop a shell with. He saw two men, pressed shoulder to shoulder, sharing a thin tree. They watched the woods on the other side of the field. Opdycke knew the Rebels were in there. Plenty of them. A foray forward by the 100th Illinois had proved it beyond any doubt. It was just a matter of when Bragg wanted to throw them forward.

The rattle and boom of battle had started again soon after first light. It had spread steadily southwards towards where Opdycke had been ordered. They were somewhere west of the LaFayette Road, but a half a mile north of their position at the schoolhouse yesterday evening. He knew that they would not escape so lightly today.

Maybe, Opdycke thought, Bragg was waiting until the Union right was bled dry. Rosecrans, apparently because Thomas's Corps was hard pressed on the left, was doing as he had yesterday: sending brigade after brigade up the road to support him. Opdycke looked over his shoulder. There was no second line if they were pushed from this one.

Harker rode up in a hurry. 'Come with me, Emerson. We need to be quick.'

Opdycke wheeled Barney and cantered alongside the young-faced Harker, who shouted across to him as they rode.

'I'm informed we might pull out to close up on Reynolds on our left. Thought we'd better see the general.'

'I thought Brennan was to our left, sir?'

'He is. That's why it doesn't seem right.'

Two minutes later they found Wood on foot with Colonel Buell behind the First Brigade. They dismounted. A staff officer was pleading with Wood. 'At least let me go back to General Rosecrans to confirm the order. Clearly things on the ground are not as he understood them to be. Brennan is still in line.'

Wood held up a dispatch, hit it with the back of his other hand. 'I'll read it again, shall I? So everyone's heard it.'

He read it like a prosecuting attorney. '*The general commanding directs that you close up on Reynolds as fast as possible, and support him.* He's also made it plain to me weeks ago, and to anyone who knows someone in the telegraph office, which is to say the whole Union army, that I should not delay in carrying out his orders. He upbraided me again this morning, in person, for not moving sharply enough. So we shall pull out, and move behind Brennan to support Reynolds.'

Opdycke felt a horror pass through him. As if a shell had detonated nearby.

Harker addressed Wood with a calm that Opdycke could never have mustered, 'Sir, we know there's a mass of Reb's in the woods to our front, probably a whole division. Maybe a whole corps. If we pull out, there's nothing to stop them. The whole right wing will be driven in. With respect, General, we can't pull out.'

'We think it's Longstreet, General,' said Opdycke in a rush, 'arrived from Virginia. We have prisoners who've confirmed it.'

'I don't care who it is,' said Wood. 'My honor won't stand another reprimand from that man. He made it clear last night that we support the left. And this is a move to the left.'

There was a crackle of fire from the front.

'My skirmishers,' said Buell. 'They're engaged, General. It'll be hard to pull out.'

'Then hard it will be.' Wood was bitter as he turned back to the staff officer. 'Tell Major General Rosecrans that I am complying with his order. Go to it, gentleman.'

The whole calamitous meeting was over in no more than a minute. Opdycke remounted to follow Harker back to the brigade. 'This is madness,' he shouted. 'Wood is putting his honor before all else. We should stay where we are. We need more troops here, not less. Longstreet will roll us up.'

'There's nothing I can do, Emerson.' Harker sounded resigned. 'He's had one too many run-ins with Rosecrans. Let's do it smartly so we have time to find another position.'

Opdycke arrived at his regiment and through clenched teeth gave the order to move out. The men sullenly abandoned the dubious safety of their breastworks.

*

In his shallow dream Shire let the guns lull him, as if the rumble was nothing more than thunder rolling through the English hills. But they became louder and more insistent until he awoke and found himself hidden within the bush. The air was warm. He must have slept for some time. He was thirsty and had no canteen but didn't want to leave his refuge. He would have to soon if he was going to start east towards Clara. The decision he'd made before he slept sat uneasily in his gut, like he'd eaten some bad meat.

He heard movement close outside and held himself still.

The bush shook and a dirty hand reached in and clawed at the soil in his sanctuary. The hand pulled in a boy who sat up next to him, dressed in dirty grey and with powder stains on his frightened face. Shire felt his warm, fast breath. This boy couldn't be more than fifteen.

Shire recovered first. 'Morning, Reb.' He put out his hand.

The boy took off his cap and smiled. 'Mornin', Yank.' They shook. 'You want I should get my own bush? You bein' here first an' all.'

'No. No, it's fine. I'm leaving.'

'You run away like me?'

'Kind of.'

Shire saw the boy's canteen.

'You want some? I got plenty. There's a creek just outside. You shouldn't have run away without your canteen.' He passed it to Shire. 'Have it all. I can fill it again in a while. Who you fighting with?'

'Ohio.'

'I'm with Georgia. Fannin County. Figured I could make it home.'

'Which way is that?'

'East, I guess. We were all from there, me and my friends. We did well all day. Yesterday, that is. Drove you boys some. Got driven ourselves. It got to late afternoon and not one of us hurt. I thought we were through it.'

'Do you know Polk County in Tennessee?'

'Sure I know it. It's next up from Fannin, over the state line. We been huntin' there, the three of us. Up the Ocoee River... So late yesterday we come to a field. Big one, full of corn. Two weeks more an' it'd be ready for harvest, 'cept it'd been trampled over so there were only patches left standin'. Other side were a heap of your boys and we were told to charge. We went in, yellin' and runnin' after the flag. "Don't stop to fire," lieutenant said. "Just make the line. Fight 'em there." We almost made it, but there was a cannon. They'd loaded it with canister.' The boy gripped his own arms and rocked back and fore. 'It was pointing right at me, so when it fired I thought I'd gone

323

straight to hell. Felt the heat of it tear by me. When I opened my eyes I was still standing, though it had ripped away my friends.'

Shire passed back the canteen. 'Here.'

The boy shook his head. 'It don't figure, Yank. All those little bits of metal fired right at us and they take my friends. I'm right between them and I don't get a mark. I couldn't sleep none. And all the talk was the battle would start up again today, but all the spirit's gone from me. I was only fightin' for my friends. So I lit out. I don't care 'bout nothin' else. Not Georgia, not the Confederacy, nothin'. I wouldn't have left my friends, though. Who would?'

'No one,' said Shire, quietly. 'No one should leave their friends.' An image came to him of Tuck and Mason, in line, loading and firing. 'I want to give you something... for your kindness.'

'Water's just outside. It ain't no kindness.'

'It was. You've helped me. And I'm grateful.' Shire reached into his jacket and pulled out a dollar, the Union dollar coin that he'd kept since Dan had given it to him in Liverpool so long ago.

'A Yankee dollar. You sure?'

'I'm sure.'

'You know, you Yanks don't talk like I was expectin'.'

'We're a mixed bunch.'

They shook hands again and Shire crawled out from the bush and looked around like he'd discovered a new world: one where for the first time in almost a year, he realized there were people other than Clara that had a call on his fidelity. He guessed it was mid-morning and judged which way was west from the bright sun that angled through the trees. That would make the guns to the north. It seemed about right. He clambered back over the creek and went to find his friends.

*

Emerson Opdycke hurried his men north up the road. It was as he had feared. Behind them, through the trees and over the hills, a rolling detonation of guns spread west. That could mean only one thing: that Longstreet had poured through the gap left by Wood's ludicrous withdrawal. The regiment started to take fire from the woods to their right. He hurried the men along past a field on their left and twisted in the saddle so he could look back. A thick Rebel line appeared across the field's southern edge, but he lost sight of it once Barney gained the trees.

Wood was suddenly there – animated. He ordered Opdycke directly, Harker being somewhere up ahead. 'Colonel, we have to check those men behind you. If not, they will gain the rear of Thomas's Corps, the only one that's holding firm. The day will be utterly lost. I want you to file off the road and out past the 64th, then face about in line of battle.'

If Wood had listened to Harker earlier, rather than his own pumped-up pride, this danger wouldn't exist. But it was too late for that. Opdycke saluted and channeled his anger into action. They would fight here, and he must make it count. He directed the men off the road by the double-quick and into an oak brake. They moved behind the 64th and lined up in the trees on their right. The rest of the brigade was similarly coming behind the 125th, aiming to extend the line further.

Wood was there again. 'We can't wait for the whole brigade. Take your men forward.'

'Fix bayonets!' Opdycke's cry was relayed down the line by his captains and lieutenants. The trees were thin but he couldn't see enough from here, not from behind the men. 'Open a way. Let me pass.' He pushed Barney through until he was in front. He waved his hat. 'March!'

The men stepped out smartly behind him. For a brief moment he recalled them trooping to the river at Cincinnati with the band playing. Now he was marching the same men into battle. They reached a worm fence. It marked the northern end of the field which the Rebels were now well into. He lined his companies up behind the fence and next to the 64th. Together they delivered a thunderous massed volley that knocked the first enemy rank down and checked the rest. But to Opdycke's right he could see that Rebels had gained the higher ground where the field sloped up at its western edge. It was the commanding position. He was exposed.

Again, Wood was there and Opdycke was glad of it. Wood was fighting now. 'Ignore that rise, Colonel. I'll bring Harker up to clear it. Your fight is straight ahead.' Wood pointed, controlling his horse's movement with his other hand. 'Advance firing and push those damned men out of the field. Drive them before they rally. Drive them!'

Opdycke did as he was told. He would have to trust Wood and the rest of the brigade. 'Forward! Companies will advance thirty paces and fire.'

The regiment obeyed as an extension of his will. They strode forward, a solid line of blue, bristling with long, shinning steel. He held out his saber for them to stop and they stopped. He raised it and they raised their guns. He dropped it and the regiment roared the wrath of God and the right. He saw Yeomans go down, a man he'd known before the war. No time to think on that. Barney flinched at a ball that cracked past his ears. Opdycke controlled him, watched as twenty, thirty Rebels fell and the rest retreated. He felt a sudden, angry rush of retribution. This was God's work. He would do it well and without fear.

'Advance firing!'

The men moved past each other, fired as they were ready and gave the Rebels no respite, no chance to stand as the blue tide washed them from the field. Wood recalled them, persuaded Opdycke it was enough, and pulled them all back to the dominant high ground which Harker had taken.

Wood came and shook Opdycke's hand. 'By God that was finely done. Your men fight like tigers.'

Up here on the rise the 64th waved its Union flag, defied the enemy to come on. Opdycke looked down over the field where

he'd fought. He'd done his duty. The Rebels had been checked, in
this place at least.

*

Shire looked out from behind a wide oak tree. There was a small
clearing; not a field, just a ragged patch where the woods had
declined to take hold. In the middle lay a Rebel corpse with a
canteen strapped over his shoulder. There were no other bodies
and no sign there'd been a fight here. The man had likely carried
his injury away from the battle.

Shire jumped as nothing more than a blackbird darted in
across in front of him. In the hour or so since he'd left the bush,
he'd seen two deserters, both Rebels. Each kept their distance and
moved away. He could last a while longer without a drink, but he'd
need a canteen before the day was out. This was as good a place as
any to get one. In a moment, he made up his mind and ran out into
the open. Once he reached the body he lay down in the reedy grass.

The man lay on his front. Shire would have to roll him. He
reached across and gripped the jacket, pulled the man over so
he flopped onto his back. A stiff arm arced to slap Shire for his
intrusion. He recoiled and despite himself let out a cry. The man
had a thick beard flecked with grey and a dark wound low on his
stomach. A single fly crawled between worn, brown teeth.

He recalled the body illuminated last night before he'd gone on
picket, how he couldn't take the canteen. But today he needed to
get to his friends, to find Tuck and Mason. He lifted the heavy head
and pulled the strap over. The clearing afforded a thin view to the
west so he risked a moment longer in the open. He could see a high
ridge, a mountain really, the one he'd climbed with the army to get
here a week ago. If he could get over there, he should be back within
Union lines. And if he took a wide arc to the south, it would keep
him further from the battle and the Rebels. He headed out of the
clearing and tried to judge the right line through the trees.

After a mile or so he found what he took to be Chickamauga Creek. He was hungry but had nothing. He filled the canteen and remembered how he'd filled ten others somewhere upstream two evenings and a lifetime ago; how Lyman had been right. How was he going to explain about Tom? Maybe Tuck and Mason were dead now too, and he should have gone east instead. He stuck to the trees and shunned open ground, even when it meant going out of his way. The guns sounded a long way off but, as his perverse destination, they underlay each step, every doubt and fear.

A stench grew, one similar to when a badger or a fox lay dead overlong under a hedge. Here it was all the more repulsive as he knew it rose from bodies unburied from yesterday's fight. Soon he reached them, stripped of boots, jackets and weapons; some lay in clusters, some alone. All were bloated in the heat. He pulled his jacket across his nose. He first heard and then saw a pig, no doubt escaped from one of the small homesteads. Snout red with gore, it rooted in a ribcage. Shire wretched and heaved on nothing but water.

Just once, across a field from his cover in the trees, he saw Rebel cavalry. They didn't see him or, if they did, he wasn't worth their diversion. He crossed the empty LaFayette Road that had been so busy when he marched north only yesterday. The land began to rise as he neared the base of the mountain he'd been aiming for. There was another road and, mercifully, wagons accompanied by blue uniforms. Shire could have wept, but when he intercepted them he found no welcome. The column drove north in a hurry to carry the wounded away towards Chattanooga. He recalled there'd been a field hospital back near to Lee and Gordon's Mill. It must have been given up. He began to work his way up the dusty column as the midday sun beat down.

More soldiers emerged from the trees on the right; at first one or two, but then more and more, many without weapons, many running. The road became so overcrowded that it was easier to step back into the woods. Shire climbed higher to get his bearings. The trees ended as he crested a rise, and he stopped. His arms hung by his sides and he gazed across a scene of utter defeat.

Immediately below was a wide orchard, and beyond that a line of fields that ran a mile away from him along the side of a ridge. To his left, along the high edge of the open ground, were battery after battery of Union cannon, as many as thirty. They stood quietly, their teams motionless beside them. For up the slope towards them raced a mass of men in full rout, men in blue. They poured out of the forest on the right by the hundreds, by the thousands, and made for the safety of the guns. Shire could see officers amongst them, some fought uselessly against the tide, tried to beat the men back with the flat of their swords. But as many officers ran with the men or rode ahead of them. There was hardly any gunfire, only a strange collective cry of effort and desperation.

A team of men strained to drag a cannon up the slope for want of horses. When two or three abandoned the rope, the weight was too much for the others. The cannon rolled down the slope before flipping and tumbling into men below, leaving a wake of broken soldiers before the panicked mass washed up and over them.

His army had been so strong. How had it come to this? He would never reach his friends through this mess. He'd made the wrong decision.

As Shire watched, the blue wave that flowed from the woods ended, followed a minute later by a surge of men in grey and brown. They ran too, but in joyful, rabid pursuit, and screamed as if they'd been released from hell itself. Some Rebels were in ragged lines, others dispersed like hounds on the hunt. Here and there on the slope a cluster of blue soldiers would stop and turn, pull more men to them to make a stand. But the Rebels were unstoppable: wherever they found an island of resistance, they would form and fire. The island would dissolve and the men join the desperate flight up towards the line of cannon. Shire picked out a terrified, riderless horse that galloped obliquely through the men; one life for him to hope for in the complete chaos. But something, a bullet maybe, buckled its foreleg, and the horse crashed end over end. For a few seconds it struggled, pumping its head to try and rise, but then gave up and lay still.

His army was wholly undone.

At last, the Union cannon answered and threw their shells over the retreating blue and into the chasing men. The detonations pounded through Shire and he screamed in support. The Rebels were checked, and the Union men had a chance to climb. All was bursting earth and smoke and cries. He should leave. He should get back to the road and run to Chattanooga. But that would mean deserting both Clara and his friends.

The smoke showed dirty brown above the horizon. Though it was only noon, the day wore a mantle of dusk. There was a single Union flag being waved right on the edge of his vision, beyond the rout. Around it was a solid wall of men in blue that faced the enemy. An officer calmly waited there on his horse. Shire felt a fragile birth of hope. The officer was too far away for him to be sure, and part of him suspected he was seeing what he wanted to see, but he imagined, he prayed, that it could be Colonel Opdycke on Barney.

He looked back to the line of cannon at the top of the field. The men had started to rally there. Surely that line would hold, at least for a while. There were so many cannon. If he could get behind them he would be safer. Maybe then he could make his way across, see if that was his regiment and his flag. He started to run through the trees. He needed to find a rifle.

*

Taylor could sense the power of the brigade like a small boy holding his first gun. He was on his third horse of the day. To the west, across a long field, he had just seen the Union routed and chased up a hill to the impermanent harbor of their guns.

He was discovering that being a brigade commander had its shortcomings. He now had under him not only Tennesseans, but also Texans and boys from Mississippi, all keen for the fight, all wanting to get away and chase blue tails over Georgia. That's what he wanted to do, if he could only find the goddamned 125th Ohio. General Johnson had told him not to overextend, but it was like trying to ride five horses at once. You had to imagine the regiments that were out of sight, hold a picture in your mind of where they were: over that rise or through that wood. Besides, Johnson was over somewhere helping that rout along. Taylor's brigade was on its own. He'd left Major Jasper in charge of the Hiwassee Volunteers, but wished he had him closer to hand. And under all this confusion and chaos was the seething regret that he hadn't shot Shire when he'd had the chance.

His brigade had been at the pivot when Longstreet broke through, so that from behind him and to his left it was like a wide gate had swung open, with his brigade the post. It was all he could do to stop his colonels taking off west without him. He'd had to pull his pistol on a Texan major to stop him ordering a charge. He would throw his brigade in when he was good and ready.

It was as well he'd kept them together, for while the Yankee right had collapsed, he learned that to the north there was still a whole corps or more that was well dug in. And here were some a deal closer, just up the rise, waving their big Union flag like it was going to save them. He wouldn't even have to fire on them to take that position. They had no support. He'd just move up the road on their flank. He gave the orders and a regiment started forward while his battery of artillery, six good guns, pulled into the field and started to unlimber. He was right, and whatever Yankee brigade that was fell back into the trees to the north. He started to bring the rest of his troops over the field. There were wounded men lying out there. He rode out ahead of his line, a staff lieutenant with him, and found a man in blue unable to rise, a bullet through his thigh.

'What regiment you from?' Taylor called from his saddle.

'Go to hell.'

Taylor jumped down. He didn't have time for this. He placed the heel of his boot square in the wound and twisted his weight through it. The boy screamed.

'Colonel Spencer!' said the lieutenant. 'The man is taken.'

Taylor's eyes didn't leave the soldier. 'My new lieutenant ain't quite used to me yet. I asked which regiment are you from?' He eased up when it looked as if the man might pass out.

'64th Ohio,' he cried.

'Brigade?'

'Harker's.'

That held the 125th. He'd found them. 'That them we just drove out?'

'Yes.' The man clawed at the ground.

'Yes, Colonel.' He gave the wound a last stab and then climbed back onto his horse. 'C'mon, Lieutenant, I do believe I have some work for my brigade.'

He raced back and gave orders to form in line of battle and start north astride the road and into the woods. It was quickly done. There was no resistance, only a few more blue wounded to collect.

'Keep those prisoners close,' he barked.

When they emerged from the other side of the trees, the road split left and right. Major Jasper, on foot as usual, caught up to him. He was too breathless to report. Ahead was open ground. Taylor could see the blue brigade forming on a spur that pushed out from the left. 'There you are, Ohio,' he said to himself, then shouted. 'Bring up the battery. Here, on my right. I want you to fire on those troops.'

'Colonel,' said Jasper, 'what about these Yankees to our left?'

Taylor looked. He'd been so focused on Harker's Brigade he'd missed the long line of blue in the scrub trees. They were nearer to him.

'We must target them first, Colonel.'

He ignored Jasper and rode back to where five prisoners stood. 'Which of you are from the 125th?'

'We're all 64th,' said a corporal, eyeing a bayonet prodded in his direction.

Taylor pointed to the spur. 'See there. Can you see the 125th? Show me.'

'On the right as you look. Furthest into the field. That's their Colonel Opdycke behind them on the bay horse.'

'Much obliged.' He tipped his hat and rode over to the artillery. Jasper followed.

Taylor jumped down and pulled the battery commander in front of the cannon. He pointed at the 125th. 'Direct your fire at the men on the end of that spur. That horse is a good target.'

'Colonel,' insisted Jasper, 'our fight's to the left. Our artillery should support us there.'

'I believe this is my brigade, Major. The line's crumbling behind them. They won't bother us. Send a company or two to cover us if you want.' He mounted up. The moment had come to make his reputation and to finish that runt of an Englishman. He had over a thousand men at his command. 'I'm going straight ahead.'

*

It would have been easier for Shire to make ground against the tide of men than across it. It was a flow of misery, pain and fear that had no time for any man not heading back to Chattanooga. Privates, officers, sergeants, artillery men, loose horses, all made for the rear through the scrub forest. Shire was knocked down several times. He struggled over the uneven ground, through gullies and thickets that conspired with terrified men to block him. He found a rifle, 'US Springfield' on the plate, the same as his old one. They were being tossed aside along with anything else that might slow a man's flight. He collected a sheathed bayonet and looped it onto his belt, a box of cartridges, percussion caps; all standard issue, all familiar to his hand.

The battle raged atop the ridge he'd seen from his viewpoint. He was behind it now. There was some sort of line holding. And then fresh men, ordered men, marching up from the left. They pushed the rout aside. Too few, but some at least.

He caught sight of the hill where he'd imagined he'd seen Opdycke, but it had been cleared of Union troops and belonged to the enemy. His hope waned. He angled his course towards where he hoped Tuck and Mason might be.

Without warning, a snarling lieutenant stepped into his path. He waved a saber in one hand and slapped Shire's face hard with the back of the other.

'Turn and fight! Turn and fight!'

Shire tasted blood on his lip. Rage bloomed inside him. He had an almost unstoppable urge to reverse his rifle and club the man. The lieutenant took hold of the back of Shire's neck and tried to thrust him towards the front.

'No!' shouted Shire, digging his heels in. He wanted to fight but with his friends. He twisted and struck the man's arm away, took a step forward so he was up in the officer's face. 'I'm not running. Can't you see that? I'm going to find my regiment.'

'The fight's here,' the lieutenant shouted back.

'The fight's bloody everywhere.' Shire turned his back, shocked at his own temerity. He hurried off into the scrub bushes, ignoring the swearing that chased after him.

He bent through a fence and stumbled into the corner of a large field. There was a farmhouse with Union artillery beside it; four resting guns. And beyond the farm, more than one regiment drawn up on a spur, which fell away into the field. As he rounded the farmhouse, mercy of mercies, there was Barney, carrying Opdycke atop the spur and behind the ranks. That blessed horse had drawn Shire back to the only home he had left. He ran towards them, behind the 64th Ohio and on to his own regiment. As he raced in, Opdycke called, 'Private Shire. I heard we'd lost you.'

Shire stopped, rifle across his chest. 'Captured, Colonel. Last night. I escaped. Saw Barney, sir.' He realized he was grinning.

'Through this mess? You're a miracle, Private Shire.'

There was a descending wail and a blast. More shells followed and hit the open land behind the lines, overshooting, but not far from Shire and Opdycke. Shire came up out of his flinch. Opdycke was controlling Barney and trying to see south through the smoke. Shire looked with him, over the heads of the men and down the slope, to where a long, thick Rebel line was drawn up in front of the forest. He saw a battery reloading. Sat nearby on a black horse was an officer. He waved his hat at the gunners to speed their work, his long blond hair about his shoulders.

'Lie down, men. Lie down!' screamed Opdycke, though he stayed on his horse. 'Why the hell is he firing at us when he's got a bank of blue on his left flank? The man's a fool.'

Shire was suddenly the only soldier left standing. The Rebel gunners had depressed their barrels, and this time the shells fell amongst the prone men and threw up gouts of red alongside brown earth. There was a single cry. Shire felt sick. He'd come all this way, nearly full circle, only for Taylor to find him and his regiment.

'It's me, sir,' he said to Opdycke.

'What?'

'They're firing at me. It's my fault.'

Opdycke frowned down at him. For a moment Shire thought that the colonel might believe him.

'Don't be a fool. Barney and I have drawn their fire. Find your company and lie down... Lieutenant,' he shouted. 'Get over to our gunners and see why they're not silencing those Rebel cannon.'

Even as the lieutenant left, the four cannon by the farmhouse boomed. Shire watched as one enemy gun was blown apart. White smoke, from their own battery, drifted over him with the familiar smell of burnt hair. He could distinguish it now from the sulfur of the muskets. He was learning the landscape of war. When it cleared, Taylor was still there on his horse.

Shire crouched and went forward down the slope amongst his regiment. He found his company and then, with a wash of relief, saw Tuck and Mason, unhurt, lying next to each other. Ocks, open mouthed, saw him first. Shire ignored him and pulled himself forward on his elbows to get between his friends.

Tuck's face froze, then swept into a smile. 'Where the hell have you been?'

More shells tore in.

Mason patted his back then looked behind. 'Where's Tom?'

'Dead,' said Shire. 'Murdered.' It was the simplest thing to tell them.

'There's a lot of that about today,' said Tuck, with no humor. 'Poor boy.'

'In cold blood,' said Shire, and nodded at the Rebels. 'By that yellow-haired bastard of a colonel.'

'On your feet!' shouted Ocks.

The Union battery, from their better position, had chased off the remaining Rebel gunners.

'You missed one hell of a fight,' Tuck said, getting up. 'The army's whipped, but this brigade sure ain't.'

'Looks like they plan to press your point,' said Mason.

The Rebels were dressing the line, getting ready to charge across the field.

'They're crazy,' said Tuck. 'They ain't takin' this spot.'

But on they came. Three long, spaced lines. Shire counted five flags, all coming towards him.

'Load!' screamed Ocks.

Shire found it easier to work his new gun. The Union artillery opened up again, this time on the Rebel infantry, but failed to check them. There were too many. They came on at a run, breaking formation, running out of the smoke, the Rebel yell rising.

'Aim!'

Shire brought the gun up to his shoulder. He searched for his stubborn spot; that bloody-minded obstinacy he'd inherited from his mother. It had brought him all this way, so it had better help him now. But he found more. He found guilt, and he found spite,

336

and he found Taylor in the middle of the charge. He lined up on him and swore under his breath for Ocks to give the order. The yell grew louder, unearthly. It filled the air. The Rebels, their bayonets lowered, sprinted towards him.

'Fire!'

Two blue regiments, almost as one, fired down into the charge. They ripped apart the air and tore away the Rebel scream.

'Load!'

Shire worked his gun unconsciously. He looked out into the field the whole time. It was a seething mess that staggered and swayed, until the press of men behind came on and the yell rose again.

'Aim!'

Taylor was still there, closer, waving the men on with his sword. Shire drew a bead on him once more.

'Fire!'

The smoke obliterated everything. He concentrated on loading. His rifle was up and ready before Tuck or Mason. He could see movement out in the smoke, shadows of men and flags. As the air began to clear he saw they were only a few yards away. The next Union volley would be at impossibly close range. No one could miss. And the Rebels knew it. Shire could see it in their eyes, in the way some turned their shoulders as if into a driving gale, hear it in their last cry of rage. They'd risked everything on the charge and never fired a shot. The brigade replied to the Rebel yell with a guttural roar of defiance. Shire roared with them. Almost lost in the scream, came the order to fire.

He felt his rifle kick but seemed to feel the volley hammer into the enemy at the same time. From the flanks Union cannon swept canister low into the Rebels and they fell like scythed wheat. The few left standing staggered back, leaving a tidemark of dead and dying and Taylor's black horse. Stranded on its back, its legs kicked into the smoky air. Shire took a step forward, his eyes hunting for Taylor's yellow hair amongst the dead and dying. It was almost impossible to pick one bloodied man from another. He looked to the retreating men, began to load again in the hope that he'd sight him, prepared to ignore the shouted order to hold fire. But he couldn't find him. *He must be dead.* The horse, eyes desperately wide, rolled and finally struggled to its feet and raced away back towards the woods with an empty saddle. *He must be dead.*

He lost count of how many more times they were assaulted. After each respite, he would see men moving again in the dark of the woods. It was as if the trees below hid the whole Rebel army. He was thankful that he couldn't see them all. Each time, a few regiments would show themselves proud of the trees, form under the cannon fire and come on. He couldn't understand how men could live in this noise; how in the Lord's name anyone could charge these guns. These weren't Taylor's men, he was sure of that; that first charge had cost them too much. Whoever they were, Shire, the 125th and Harker's Brigade held them.

Late in the afternoon a second Union battery drew up on the end of the spur. Other lost regiments joined them in support. Shire never believed the 125th would be forced from its position, but nonetheless, it was steadily bled. He came to know the wet slap of a ball striking flesh. He shut his mind to men who crumpled forward from the line, until between attacks he could help carry – or drag – them away.

'Look back there,' said Mason, in one lull. 'That's old pap Thomas himself.'

Shire saw mounted next to Opdycke and Wood was a stony-faced man, a flecked grey beard beneath dark hair. The men cheered him. He wasn't their own corps commander; Shire had no idea where Crittenden might be, or Rosecrans, come to that. But Thomas was the leader here. He sat unmoving on the spur; like a rock, watching the battle, a constant rush of staff officers surrounding his calm. Shire heard he'd set up his headquarters behind the farm.

'Nice to know the old man has faith in us,' said Mason.

'Or maybe we're just the last, ugly girl left at the dance,' said Tuck.

It was near evening and the latest charge dissolved back into the trees. Shire rested on his rifle. Heavy musket smoke gripped the ground below him, pooled amid the grass and the dead. Touched by the lightest of breezes, patches would rise up and twist slowly in the air, like so many new wraiths searching for a different world.

He was weary beyond measure. There was a flash of bright blue and he watched as a bird darted low over the heads of the men and came to rest on a cannon wheel. A bluebird amongst the blue men. The gun team were watching it as he was, as a thing of misplaced beauty, a visitor from paradise. The bird hopped from the wheel to the muzzle, then flew off in alarm when its feet touched the hot metal.

The sun went down and Shire loaded his last round. The orders came to pull out. It was chaotic, and they were harried, but the Rebels must have been spent too. As he marched away, Shire could see only the silhouette of his flag against a dark northern sky. When they reached Rockville, on the road to Chattanooga, Tuck and Mason saw what Shire had seen earlier in the day: a mass of dejected men, disorganized and defeated. His heart sank. All Bragg would need to do was push them, and they would be driven back across Tennessee to who knew where. Clara was as far away as ever.

When the regiment stopped and collapsed exhausted off the road, Shire used his last energy to muster a small fire. He looked over at his two friends, their faces and uniforms dirty with powder and blood. He recalled all of them, the whole squad, clean and scrubbed as they came out of the Tennessee River; Lyman complaining, Tom Muncie's constant smile.

Tuck's weary eye caught his, and with an old man's effort he came to sit with Shire. Shire handed him his Rebel canteen.

'I need to tell you about Tom.'

'Let it be,' said Tuck. 'I've seen so much death today my heart wouldn't find the space for him. Tell me tomorrow when I've made room, or the next day.'

Tuck was so close that Shire could see the sheen in his eyes.

When Tuck spoke, the smoke from the day caught in his throat. 'Shire, I can figure what it cost you to come back. I'm right glad you did.'

Comrie – September 1863

Clara sat beside the high bed, its yellow drapes drawn back and tied to their posts, her book unopened beside the blue-rimmed washbowl. The remainder of the spacious room, like the book, she ignored; its elegant chairs and table superfluous, like lesser relatives not allowed closer to the patient.

Emmeline lay restless beneath a light sheet, her head pressed back into the pillow, her tired green eyes the only pallid color in a grey face. They never opened for long. It was the hottest part of the day and Clara worked a damp cloth across Emmeline's forehead, her cheeks, her thin neck. Where her fingers brushed skin the heat was still there, burning away the cloth's work. She wished the afternoon would hurry on so the cool of evening could find its way in through the open window.

There was a low rumble to the west, on the edge of hearing. It had started yesterday and she'd taken it at first to be thunder, but it didn't have the rhythm of a storm and there was no weight to the air. Moses had been the one to tell her that it was most likely guns.

She'd stayed too long – almost a full month since she'd met with Trenholm in Chattanooga; ample time to be away. At first Emmeline had agreed that they should go, but begged Clara to keep it from the slaves. Yet that ruled out any meaningful preparation. When, days later, Clara tried to move things along, Emmeline had changed her mind, saying she would stay; the Yankees wouldn't hurt an old lady. Evening after evening she'd sat out by the grave until the last light, as if Comrie was above the war, and what transpired away from the hills was of no consequence.

There was never a question of leaving without Emmeline, but she was suspicious of her own motives. If she had any duty remaining in the world it was here. Again and again she'd go out to the graveside, lay the shawl over Emmeline's shoulders and take her out of the evening chill and into the house, there to try again to persuade her to leave Comrie. Emmeline would smile. 'You go. I'm too old to run away.'

But it was all a charade. Clara knew she was complicit in the decision to stay, held here by more than Emmeline's stubbornness. She wondered what it might be like to be in the Union, on the other side of the guns from Taylor.

She wrung out the cloth, pulled away the sheet, and washed Emmeline's arms, her legs, her feet. Maybe leaving here would be good for her mother-in-law. If she could get her away from Comrie, from its memories and its lingering grief, perhaps Emmeline might yet feel renewed. She wasn't so old, but her limbs were thin and frail, as pale as the bed-sheet. The doctor had come but once, soon after the fever started. Though Clara had sent for him since, he'd not attended again. It was a long trip out to Comrie, the Copper Road less used. She feared to send Moses out to find him. People round about knew that Emmeline was sick, down in the mills and the nearby farms. They would pass the word. The doctor would come if he could.

Mitilde came in, and with her help Clara sat Emmeline up and tried to get her to drink. She opened her eyes and for a moment recognition surfaced.

'All liars,' she said. 'Father and son, both. Don't marry him. Go on home. Better blood there.'

'Huh,' said Mitilde, 'she's a little late on the advice, ain't she?'

'You're a good girl,' mumbled Emmeline. 'Wasted in this pen where not a friend comes by. Go on home. Only lies here.'

'I'll get rid of this water,' Mitilde said, leaving them alone once more.

The distant guns sounded again. As she had so often since the war started, Clara imagined a rider climbing the drive to deliver the news that her husband was killed. There was a time when the thought was terrifying, and later when it stirred a certain tragic

342

romance in her. Now, all it touched was shallow guilt.

She leant close to Emmeline's ear and whispered, 'What lies?'

Emmeline turned her head and her eyes wandered over Clara's face. 'I saw it... that look... after the accident. I saw it. Same look as his father. Their lips set tight and their eyes shutter up. They're liars, but they're not good ones. His father deceived me to this place.'

'How so?'

Mitilde returned with fresh water.

'The Africans. I'd have stayed in Virginia if I'd known. We look after our own people. They were given to our care. I wouldn't have come.' Emmeline closed her eyes.

'You go, miss,' said Mitilde. 'I'll tend to her.'

Clara didn't move. 'What does she mean?'

'Who knows? Minute ago she thought you ain't married.'

'She talked about Africans. Does she mean you? Moses?'

'Well I sure ain't from Africa. If you's stayin' then I've got things I can do.'

'Tell me. Please.'

Mitilde sat down heavily on the end of the bed. 'We ain't supposed to talk on it.' She wouldn't meet Clara's eyes.

Clara waited.

'Is she asleep?'

'Yes.'

'There was a day,' said Mitilde, 'a day when we still had the two boys. Their father, old Master Robert, he and the white hands, suddenly they was runnin' for their horses, hollerin' like injuns. Master took the dogs with him. We didn't know what it was, but they spent the rest of the day out in the woods hunting for somethin'. At dark they came back for torches, then stayed out all the night. Next day, before I was out of bed, I heard a ruckus, and when I went to the door the dogs were at some poor man under one of the huts. Blacker than any of us he was, screaming somethin'. After they got the dogs off and put chains on his arms and legs and a collar on his neck, he looked right at me. I couldn't tell one word he was sayin' from another. They took him away. Never saw him again. But that weren't the end of it. Master Robert, he wanted to know who it was as helped him. Seemed plain to us that the man had crawled under there of his own mind, but that weren't enough. No one 'mitted to it, so he whipped Moses. Right there in front of the boys and Miss Emmeline. Wouldn't let them go inside. It put ten years on him. He weren't never the same after that.'

Clara came and sat next to Mitilde. 'You mean this was a fresh slave? From Africa?'

Mitilde looked at her plainly then, as she might regard a disappointing child. 'I call food fresh, miss, or flowers. Not gen'rally people. But yes, from Africa.'

'I'm sorry. It's just that it's illegal to bring them from Africa, it has been for half a century.'

'Huh. That's a Yankee law, made for a Yankee conscience. It weren't kept here. It went on. In secret, but it went on. And what kinda law is it that says Africans must be free, but it's fine to keep us already here as slaves? We can still be sold, or bred, or rutted on. That's only half a law.' Mitilde turned to look at Emmeline, who was more peaceful. 'I care for her, sure I do. But to hear her goin' on over some African she never knew, when she's seen us whipped, seen the old master sell our children away... Makes my insides turn over.'

Clara wanted to ask more, but Mitilde looked empty.

'You know what I am to her?' she said.

'What do you mean?'

'I was raised way down in Georgia. Had plans to marry. My master came and took me away while my man was in the fields. Never once saw him again. I was carted up here, scrubbed up and put in the best clothes I'd ever had. Maid's clothes, mind, but fine ones. Then there was a weddin' but it weren't mine. I was led into the house by Master Robert his self in front of all his guests and made a weddin' present to Miss Emmeline. Her china tea set was the next gift after me... Sometimes I gets to wondering, what's more precious to her, me or the china?'

Clara tried to take her hand but Mitilde stood and walked to the window. The guns growled from far away. 'Seems like the Yankee law is comin' closer though, miss, don't it. Maybe this place'll give up all its secrets then.'

Chattanooga – October 1863

Shire stood in line with his diminished company at the regimental wagon to draw his rations for the day. The mules that had pulled it there were unhitched and returned to where they were borrowed from; the regiment had none of their own since the battle two weeks ago. He was cold. He was always cold now.

There was grumbling up front and it seemed each man had prepared a complaint – some witty, some abusive – for the commissary sergeant. When his turn came, Shire received his half-ration in silence. A fatty strip of sowbelly and a cracker for breakfast; beans and a cracker for dinner; crackers and coffee for a supper with no meat. No pepper, no salt, no soap or candles.

Along with Tuck and Mason, he trudged off through the mud to the row of small fires made up for those that wanted to eat right away. That meant everybody. No cannon fired today from the hills. The only rumble was internal. He took his skillet and put the pork in it, tried to cook it slowly so the fat wouldn't sizzle away to nothing. He ate the cracker, unable to wait on the meat.

'I've a mind to cook the beans as well,' said Tuck, 'or they'll torment me all mornin'.'

'Won't the lack of them torment you more?' asked Shire. 'At least they're something to look forward to.'

It was Mason who replied, 'It's a sad state of affairs when all we have to look forward to is some hard beans that wouldn't fill a chipmunk's pocket. We were better off marching. At least we could forage and the scenery changed. Hell, I'd rather be fightin' than inside of this siege or whatever you wanna call it.'

'Old Rosy should never have given up Lookout,' said Tuck. 'If he'd kept it we'd control the river and this piece of pork might be bigger and, what's more, have some pork in it.'

Shire looked to where the great promontory of Lookout Mountain stood under the grey clouds. It dominated the approach from the west and the Tennessee River. While the Rebels held it, all the Union food had to come in via a tour of the mountains to the north. Rebel cavalry stole or burnt most of it.

He knew there were some big cannon up on Lookout, as there were along most of the long ridge across the plain to the south. Some days they lobbed shells the couple of miles into town. But at that range they weren't accurate and the boys mostly ignored them. After the storm of Chickamauga, it was like a little light rain.

After they'd retreated, first to Rossville and then down into Chattanooga, Shire thought the Rebels would only need to knock on the door to take the city; but they had come on slowly and the Union artillery discouraged them. The remains of the army had set to fortifying the town, using the old Rebel works and improving them. First an outer line of forts and now they worked daily on an inner line. Though they all complained for the want of good food, he hardly ever heard a complaint about the work. Any sort of defense was better than standing in line, out in the open, waiting on musket balls or shells. They had all seen it; seen their friends killed for lack of a breastwork or a ditch. The time they had spent building Fort Granger at Franklin, back in the spring, was put to good use.

'I heard Captain Yeoman's going home,' said Tuck. 'They don't think he'll heal a while.'

'Where'd he get hit?' asked Shire.

'In the thigh.'

'No. Where in the battle?' Shire felt the need to piece together the events before he'd re-joined the regiment on the second day.

'I don't know. Some little end of a big field. Only advance we made that day but it was a pretty one,' smiled Tuck, but then saddened. 'Williams died up at the hospital. Surprised he lasted this long. Seems like half the wounded we helped off the field have died since.'

Shire had counted the men as best he could at their regimental parade yesterday. They were down around four hundred, a third of the regiment lost at Chickamauga. How many of those were down to him? He knew Tom was. How many more had died because of Taylor's crazy charge? Strangely, it was Lyman's death that visited him the most; perhaps because it was the first. He saw, again and again, Lyman take Mason's hand from his neck and the blood drain away into the pine straw, as if it was nothing more than horse-piss in a stable.

They worked the morning on the fortifications. He was glad of the activity to get warm. In the afternoon they had the picket, so went forward to the line of rifle pits out on the plain. They were relaxed and marched in full view and easy range of the Rebels in their own pits. There was no sniping. It had begun as a tacit understanding between the men; a life or two snuffed out here wouldn't change much. When they heard that Rosy had endorsed it in a communication with Bragg, Tuck had said, 'Shame they don't think on it a bit more and let us all go home for the winter?'

Cleves acknowledged Shire with a nod and walked up with them. He was friendlier since the battle, or at least not so unfriendly. 'Pay's arrived,' he said.

'Now what in the hell use is that?' said Mason. 'There ain't a thing to buy. Why not keep the money safe and use the pay wagon for salt beef?'

'Be some card games later or some dice. I got some dice. You in, Tuck?'

'Maybe.'

They lounged in the pit, not caring to keep guard. The afternoon dragged. A few hundred yards back of them a Union column marched purposefully, some men with ladders, others with picks or shovels.

'That's the 64th,' said Tuck. 'What they at?'

The regiment arrived at a lone house, distant from the edge of town. As Shire watched, a good number of men disappeared inside, while a few scaled ladders to the roof. Hammers banged away, and what little furniture the house contained they carried outside.

'It's in the field of fire from the new works,' said Mason. 'They don't want it standing in case the Reb's come at us. Shame. It's a handsome house.'

Slate was worked from the roof and carefully lowered, window frames were prised out, planks from the upper story handed down to the men below and the porch ripped up. It was a curious sight, how quickly two hundred men could take down a house that took perhaps six men a season to build. It was orderly, no man allowed to take anything away until there was nothing left standing but a chimney stack, which was roped and pulled down. The whole exercise took less than an hour.

'That'll improve a few shanties tonight,' said Shire wistfully, watching as each man carried off some spoils. He'd gained two planks himself a few days back and pegged them upright to keep the wind from getting into his shelter tent. That was the full extent of his 'shanty'. He'd like to improve it before the winter came on. He shivered at the thought and turned away.

'I'm bored,' he said, then shouted. 'Hey, Reb?'

The heads in the rifle pit across the way turned to him. 'What is it, Yank?'

'You got any papers?'

'Some.'

'What you tradin' for, Shire, you ain't got no paper?' said Mason.

'No. But you have.'

'I was gonna trade that in the Union... Especially now the pay's in.'

'You'll get more for a Reb' paper. Come on. We're coming out!' He stood up.

It wasn't the first time they'd done this. Tuck went with them and three Reb's came out to match. No one took their rifles. They all shook hands.

'What have you got?' asked Shire of a corporal who was standing forward of the other two.

'Paper from Atlanta. Week old. Has a battle report in it sayin' how we whipped you. What you got?'

'Harper's Weekly,' said Mason. 'From before the battle, sayin' how we was gonna whip you.'

'That's a fair trade I guess, but more laughs for us.' They swapped. 'Got any coffee?'

'No,' said Shire. 'We can get you some if you'll lend us the use of the river?'

'Huh. If it would get me some coffee, I'd oblige. You English?'

'Yes. Would your paper list officers killed or wounded?'

'Some. Only the ones not listed before. Got someone in mind?'

'Colonel Taylor Spencer-Ridgmont. Tennessee.'

'I know him,' said one of the other boys. 'All yella hair longer 'an a horsey tail. I know him.'

'He's alive?'

'He was a couple of days ago. His regiment's not so good though. Heard he drove them in at a hard spot.'

'That was us,' said Tuck. 'We were the hard spot.'

Lookout Mountain – October 1863

The two letters had arrived at the same time and Taylor had opened them out of order. So he'd discovered his mother was dead before he came to know she'd been ill. He thought that climbing Lookout Mountain might help him to get a grip on it, away from the officers and men. Not that he'd felt unmanned by the news; more angry than anything else, but then he was pretty much made up of different shades of anger. He knew that about himself. It wasn't always the most useful characteristic in a war, but he couldn't help it if he so easily perceived the fault in others. For want of anyone else, he fixed on Clara. He blamed her for not telling him sooner, though the letter was dated four weeks ago. He blamed her for not preserving his mother, and blamed her for being at Comrie at all when she was supposed to have left.

He'd come here with his family once, all of them. Even back then people would climb to this spot for the view. He'd been what, six or seven? He remembered he'd got short of breath, but his father pushed on anyway, so he'd come up with his mother. When they'd reached the top, Will and Father were sat well out on the rock, close to the edge, closer than he'd wanted to go. He had gone and hid his fear as best he could. Why couldn't Will have fallen that day? When everyone was there to see, and it wasn't left for only him to bear witness. He couldn't think of one time after Will's death that the three of them had done anything together – not one. Now they were all gone. No one to see how fine a soldier he'd become, how he'd led the charge at Chickamauga; no one to be proud of him but himself.

A few soldiers were out on the precipitous rocks, sightseeing and larking about. They were forward of the cannon that were lined up like they'd declared war on creation. So high here. If anything it encouraged a detachment from earthly worries, as if you were half way to heaven. His fellow officers had needed to learn from their maps all the landmarks that were laid out before him, but he knew them well. Right below, the Tennessee River made an almost complete loop, several miles long, with just a small neck of stubborn ground holding out at its northern end. The contained land was Moccasin Point. Rising beyond were Signal and Raccoon Mountain, these two the front row of an audience of wooded ridges that sat neatly one behind the other, sliced at precisely the same level by some ancient scythe. To his right, as the river turned east again was Chattanooga, tucked in tight to the south bank. Before it, a wide flood plain pushed out as far as the long, raised vein of Missionary Ridge where his Hiwassee Regiment was posted. He hadn't brought his field glasses, but the day was clear for once, and he could see the Union Army's outer and inner defenses close to town. Men were working on them down there and ringing blows, metal on metal, carried up on the breeze.

A black vulture, its wings flat, drifted across his eye line. He couldn't recall ever having seen one from above.

He knew his army would never take those works, not by assault anyway. For a start they'd need a commander with the guts to do it. That wasn't Bragg. He was more interested in arguing with Longstreet and any other general he could find to antagonize. Hell, there were even rumors that the generals had got up a petition for his removal. President Davies had tucked them all back in. What would they gain by taking that little town down there anyway? Then it would be the Federal cannon on the mountains north of the river, looking down on them. Better to send out the cavalry, cut their supplies, make them scuttle off back to Nashville from where they'd started in the spring. He laughed inside, realizing he was no longer thinking of his mother but was back on the war again.

Comrie was his now; only himself and Clara. At last he could get Will's grave moved. In fact he'd write and tell Clara to get it done, so he'd never have to ride past it again. Then she could leave. The Yankees were penned up below, but if Shire had escaped death at Chickamauga and was down there, it was better to get her away. He might have no family left but he still had a reputation and a marriage to protect. He knew he had at least one battle ahead of him: to win Clara back. Maybe it would be easier after the war, after the fighting; easier for her to help him cultivate a gentler self. Once winter arrived, he'd see if he could get home, see what state the place was in and raise some more recruits. There'd be some hiding up in the hills around Ducktown, but he knew where to look.

His old commander had recovered to resume his duties, so Taylor's temporary command of the brigade had proved to be just that. He'd been told he was too reckless and needed to 'exercise more judgement' before he could expect promotion. Fools. They could have finished off that army down there if anyone had been prepared to push the men on to Chattanooga. He'd get a brigade soon enough. They needed him, needed men who would fight. But for now he was back with his sorry little regiment, down to a hundred and fifty men. If he didn't get some more, they'd be rolled up into some other outfit and then where would he be?

The war again. You couldn't escape it. He left the soldiers to their view and started back down the mountain. It held no novelty for him, and it seemed that no solace was required.

Chattanooga – October 1863

'C'mon, Shire. Who else is gonna know? Horse ain't gonna tell no one.'

Shire looked down on Cleves, who was doing his best to construct a friendly smile with the few brown teeth he had left.

'I'll make up the mush on the quiet an' bring you half. No one'll see.'

The rain beat noisily on the corrugated metal roof that was close above Barney's ears. Cleves had just stepped inside the lean-to and was soaked through. As wet as an otter's pockets, as Aaron used to say.

'It's not going to happen,' said Shire. How had he ever been scared of this man?

'Please. I'm gonna fail long before that horse does. Why, he looks fine. I ain't even got my half-ration today as I was away visitin' at the hospital.'

That didn't seem likely. More probably he'd gone there to scrounge for food. Shire couldn't entirely blame him, he was hungry himself. Hungry as soon as he'd eaten. The heavy October rain and the Rebel cavalry were conspiring against them. Rosecrans was gone, fired by Grant and replaced by Thomas, but it had made no difference.

'Let me make it plain,' said Shire, eager to put an end to this. 'If I had a bucket full of thick porridge, rich with cream and sugar and honey, I'd feed it all to Barney before you saw a thimbleful.' He pushed a blaspheming Cleves out into the rain.

Cleves was right about one thing though: Barney looked in the peak of health. Especially when compared to the other animals penned up in Chattanooga. Many mules and horses had already succumbed, collapsing into the mud before they were dragged away. The colonel wasn't usually one to make exceptions, but it appeared he had in Barney's case. Kept on his own, he'd enough corn that he could take his time chewing. And cover too. This lean-to was better than most soldiers had. Shire was glad to be in here. Tired as he was, he didn't sit. He preferred to lean on Barney and enjoy his warmth and the sweet, familiar smell.

Opdycke had been the only colonel in the brigade who'd stayed mounted during the fight at Chickamauga. And both he and Barney had remained unharmed both days, from shells and bullets alike. The regiment had come to see the horse as their lucky charm. So much so that Shire knew, Cleves aside, few of them would think to steal his feed, despite their own privation. To Shire he meant even more. He'd ridden him for a short way on the road to Chattanooga. He'd sighted him across the chaos of the battle when he'd begun to think he'd never find his friends again. And here, alone in this shelter barely big enough for the two of them, he could wish he was back home in a stable with his favorite, Old Tom, on a wet autumn day. He rested his head on Barney's warm shoulder and closed his eyes.

He didn't like melancholy and fought against it when he recognized it in himself, but what was his life now if not melancholic? Certainly it was easier to reside in what was lost rather than what might lie ahead. The marching used to help, had given him the sense of moving on, of getting somewhere; in Chattanooga there was nothing – only waiting – working over the past on each slow, new day.

The heavy canvas that served as a door was pulled aside and Shire opened his eyes.

Ocks sneered at the scene. 'Isn't that a pretty picture.'

Shire felt a jolt of anger and straightened up.

'I thought I'd check on Barney. I saw Cleves coming out.'

'He got nothing from me. Not that he didn't try.'

'He didn't look best pleased, although he never does.'

'I was wondering when you'd turn up. What is it this time?

Have you been promoted again? Or found another night picket for me?'

'We each have to take our turn. Nothing special about you, boy.' Ocks took off his hat and looked for somewhere to sit. There being no room he moved the colonel's saddle and made himself a space on the floor, grunted as he sat down. 'Now, I'm here, you won't mind if I stay a while. Those boys never stop talking. We could have a bit of English peace and quiet.'

Shire resented the intrusion, but was silent for a while; there was just the noise of the rain and Barney's chewing. For want of a grooming brush, he tore at some sacking and started to rub Barney down.

It was Ocks who broke the silence he'd asked for. 'From what I hear you were all over that battlefield, once you'd escaped.'

Shire said nothing. After the fight he'd intended to keep quiet, but everyone had a tale to tell and his was better than most. So he'd told it more than once over the long evenings; an edited version that didn't involve Taylor, and had Tom Muncie killed on the picket line. Obviously the story had reached Ocks. Only Tuck knew the truth.

'Many boys would have made for the hills once they got clear. And you've more reason than most. Why didn't you – what's their word for it – skedaddle?'

Shire rubbed Barney all the harder. 'Wasn't quite that simple.'

'You'll not get a better chance. Not now we're all cooped up.'

'Maybe not.' Then more provocatively, 'You don't seem to be stopping me.'

Ocks leant back, put his hands behind his head. 'Whole Rebel army's doing that for me. Why should I worry? If you try it, I'll be after you quick enough. When we lost you, I thought you'd be either dead or shipped off to prison. What was it then? Too scared to take your chance?'

Shire had reflected many times on his decision in the month since the battle. He looked down at Ocks. 'Maybe I want to be on the right side of things,' he said. 'But then you wouldn't know about that. I could have gone, was all set to. Don't you feel anything for this army? This regiment? They do have a cause, you know.'

Ocks smiled. 'I've seen enough wars. There's always a cause fed to the ranks, to the likes of you and me; Queen and country, homes and sweethearts, God. Not usually the way of it when you look at the interests a little higher up.'

'This isn't some British expedition to secure the Empire,' said Shire. 'It's their own countrymen they're fighting. And for an idea.'

'Who's idea?' said Ocks. 'I'll warrant there's plenty of poor boys up in those hills dressed in butternut, who'd make a different speech, every bit as convinced of the right of it. The North invading, forcing their ways on 'em, trying to turn 'em Yankee.'

'Taylor shot Tom.' It was out before Shire could debate it. He saw the surprise on Ocks' face.

'You saw him?'

'In cold blood. With less care than for a dying dog. For no other reason than to scare me.'

'Why didn't he kill you?'

'That's the side you're on. That's the man whose interests you're protecting.'

'I'm here on my own account.'

'Matlock's payroll more likely.' Shire was enjoying having the upper hand. 'And he's packed you off with half the truth, hasn't he?'

Ocks stood up, his face close to Shire. 'Why don't you tell me the truth then?'

'He married her. Taylor – married – Grace. Her father insisted on it after Taylor got her pregnant. And Matlock was party to it. And then Taylor's married Clara. I'm not here to stop a marriage. I'm here to annul one.'

Ocks looked thoughtful. 'They couldn't let that pass.'

Shire had just one bullet left and he spent it.

'And he raped Grace.'

'How could you know?'

'*Against her will*, is what she said to me. And Taylor bragged about it. So you see it doesn't matter if Clara's married legally. I still have to tell her. For Grace as well as Clara – whether you try to stop me or not.'

Ocks' face hardened. Shire tried to hold on to his courage.

'It doesn't change anything,' Ocks said. He put on his hat. 'We're still the small men being fed a line. I've got myself to look out for.' He leant so close that Shire felt the warmth of his breath. It was Ocks' turn to sound out the words one at a time. 'So – watch – your – back.'

Polk County – November 1863

The field slave sat behind Clara in the corner of the wagon, only the sacking to soften the bumps and ruts for him. The air was damp and the clouds low as the mules pulled the wagon from the hills. Only Hany had supported her idea for the trip into town. Moses and Mitilde were against it: it wasn't safe. Clara had insisted, and used her new authority as the lady of the house. If it wasn't for this necessity, there would soon come another.

George, back at Comrie, was lame, an abscess deep in a hind hoof that he refused to ground. It was too deep to drain, and they had no flax seed to mix with bran to make a poultice. There were other household items needed too: lamp oil, soap, perhaps some sugar. Heaven only knew how much would be asked for them. In the end Mitilde had got up quite a list but insisted they took the field slave along as protection. She gave Moses a long earful of what not to do.

Clara was up front with Moses and Hany, as it had been so often before. Yet even Hany was quiet, perhaps as wary as Clara was. They'd seen no one else on the road. Today was Clara's wedding anniversary but she didn't mention it. The autumn colors that had adorned that day were limp in the trees and cold on the muddy ground. It was some weeks since the funeral but the feeling of loss hadn't eased. She'd not realized quite how much she had come to depend on Emmeline.

She'd decided it best to bury her at the church, thinking that Comrie should be a home and not a graveyard. But when she had gone to make arrangements, she saw how the graves on the slope had multiplied since the battle south of Chattanooga. The soldiers made their own long row, the headstones fashioned all alike. It hadn't seemed the place for Emmeline anymore, so she'd picked out a spot in the woods at Comrie. She'd tried to get the slaves to move Will to be with Emmeline, but they flat refused to dig up the dead. She'd have him moved in the spring, when she could hire someone in to do the work.

They began to pass fields with the wheat bent heavy by the rain. When they came into the village of Ocoee, the shutters were closed and one young woman, sweeping leaves from her porch, wore black as Clara did. She looked up as they passed and rested on her broom. Clara nodded her head in quiet acknowledgement of their shared grief, but received nothing in return.

As they were leaving the village, a man of middle years waved them down. He came and stood beside Clara when Moses pulled up the mules.

'Mr Tanner,' Clara said, looking down.

'Ma'am,' he said, taking off his hat. 'You're headin' for town, plainly.'

'We are. Can we do something for you there?'

'Well, that's kind, ma'am, but it weren't that. I feel awkward to say it, but well, I don't think it's wise to go.'

Clara hid her annoyance: she'd won this argument once. 'We've need of flax seed. I've a lame horse in my stables. It can't be put off. We had no trouble in the hills and there are four of us. Why should town be any different?'

Tanner looked over her companions. 'Beggin' your pardon, ma'am, but are you carrying a gun?'

'No.'

'Then how you figure that a white lady and three niggers is safe at all? Truth is, that feelin's are up in town just now. Lots of boys lost there. Many of 'em fightin' in a war they wanted no part of. Here, too. I could point to three houses from this spot, every room full of nothin' but grief.'

He scratched the back of his head as he went on. 'To put it more plain, ma'am, the talk is your husband threw them in careless, where it weren't called for.' He held up his hands to forestall a reply. 'Now I's no way of knowin' if it's true or not, but folks need somewhere to put their anger. And I couldn't see you head on into town without layin' it out. I lost a nephew myself, but I know none of it ain't down to you. I've got some flax seed you can have.'

'Miss,' said Hany. 'What about Cele? I ain't seen her in three months. We're close. I'd like to see her. I can walk in from here if you don't want to go?'

'Hush it, child,' said Moses, not unkindly. 'It's gonna have to wait on another day.'

Clara nodded and Hany began to weep.

'I'll get the flax seed,' said Tanner.

Moses turned the wagon.

The journey back was more miserable than the aborted one out. They had the flax seed for George, but nothing else. And Hany's crying went on and on, so it was all Clara could do not to snap at her. With that sad accompaniment, her own thoughts became darker. Why was she still here? Trenholm had asked her to go; Taylor had told her to go. Emmeline was dead, and now the very people she lived amongst blamed her for their own bereavements.

Why was she here? She could have made plans after the funeral and already be in Charleston. She looked at Hany. Though it was November, she wore her best summer dress under her shawl. She was weeping inside her faded yellow bonnet. Moses held her hand where they thought Clara couldn't see.

She liked to think she was being noble, taking responsibility for 'her people', who couldn't manage without her. Where would they go if she left? The truth was they were the ones running the place. She was just the new queen bee they buzzed around. She gave them a focal point; that was all. They weren't why she'd stayed.

Her mind edged around another reason, like a deep, truthful pool she was hesitant to step into. She'd rather the battle had been lost. Lost so the Union would come on, and maybe Shire, and then she could find out why he was here. With each and every decline she had suffered in her new life, he took on greater importance. He was a connection to a world she'd happily left but wanted to touch again. What if he was in the army and at that battle, even now lying in a crowded grave? The thought hurt and she chastised herself. She had no idea where he was. He might never come. The truth settled into her as they climbed into the low clouds that lay like a shroud on the hills.

After they reached the top of the switch-back drive and passed the lonely headstone, she took Hany with her into the house.

'You want dressin'?' Hany asked when they'd reached Clara's room. Her eyes were red. ''Cos there ain't no one to dress for.'

'No. You're right. There's no one here now. Not for me.'

Hany looked hurt.

'Oh, don't take on again, Hany. I don't mean you. I want to take you with me. Only you.'

'Take me where? We just got home.'

'Away. You heard what Tanner said. People have turned against us. What reason is there to stay? We'll go to Charleston. I need you to help me pack and you need to do the same yourself.' She was thinking out loud. 'I'll tell Mitilde tonight, or tomorrow. We'll have to risk the town to get to the train.'

'I don't wanna go.'

'Maybe Moses can take us in before sunrise.'

'Miss, I don't wanna go. This is my home.'

Hany's strident tone finally reached Clara. 'I need you to come. It'll be better for you.'

'What about my mammy and Cele?'

'They'll be safer in town. And we can see them before we go to the station. To say goodbye.'

Hany was louder still, almost shouting. 'I ain't gonna say goodbye. Don't make me, miss? Please don't make me.'

Clara's own cares overwhelmed her and she broke. She shouted back, 'I will make you. I will. I can tell you what to do for your own good. You will come with me and we will say goodbye to your mother and sister.'

Hany bent forward and screamed at Clara, 'She ain't my sister!' Then fell back to sit on the bed, weeping. 'She's my baby – she's my child.'

Clara stood for a long moment before she sat down next to Hany. It was as if the full knowledge had been lying there all along, formed and waiting. She knew it with complete certainty even as she half-whispered the question. 'She's Taylor's, isn't she?'

Hany didn't answer or nod, but lifted her hands to hide her face and her tears. They sat there for what seemed an age before Clara's shock grudgingly gave an inch to compassion. 'How old were you?'

'Thirteen. Nearly fourteen when I had her. I'm sorry. He'd have hurt me again if I'd told you. He sold her away when he knew you was comin'. Her and my mammy. Said I could visit only if I kept it quiet.'

There were footsteps outside. The door opened without a knock and a breathless Mitilde burst in. Clara saw her wonder at the scene and Hany's tears, saw her dismiss it for something else. 'Soldiers, miss. Didn' you hear them come up the drive? Lots of them.'

A surfeit of horses crowded the yard. At first Clara thought there must be more than a dozen Confederate soldiers, though only one was mounted. But as she edged between the steaming animals, she saw that many weren't saddled, but tied instead to a trooper's horse. She ducked under or stepped over the ropes. Out of the stables came two soldiers, one leading her best ploughing mare. And the mules that had just brought her back from Ocoee were already commandeered and roped. Moses was standing to one side, watching helplessly as his charges were gathered up.

The trooper on the horse slouched over his pommel, ignoring Clara. 'Hey, Elliot. Get out to the pastures, see if they have any out there.' He spat a gob of tobacco juice into the mud.

Clara came to stand below him. He wasn't much to look at, not compared to cavalry officers she'd known in England. If he was an officer? There was no badge of rank on his damp, grey coat. He wore a slouch hat that looked anything but military, and no gloves.

He cast her a glance, but didn't touch his hat brim or sit up. 'Howdy, ma'am.'

'Is that all you have to say?' The man was sat on his horse and stealing hers, and he couldn't even muster an ounce of contrition. 'Is this country now so wild that horse thieves can simply ride in and take whatever they want from my stables?'

'I have orders, ma'am. I'm right sorry.' He didn't sound it. 'I can leave but one on each farm. If you got one that ploughs and rides, I can leave you that one.'

'This isn't a common farm,' Clara waved an arm at the mansion. 'We've got steep fields to plough and we need those mules to get us into town.'

'Hey, Lieutenant,' called a trooper. He was standing next to Moses and had a rope on George. 'You want I should take this old fella? The horse I'm meanin', not the nigger.'

'That horse is lame,' shouted Clara. 'We're about to bind a poultice on him.'

'No,' shouted back the lieutenant. 'Leave him be,' and then more quietly to Clara, 'I guess that's the one you'll be keeping, ma'am.'

It was too much. She was a duke's daughter and she wouldn't suffer this. She reached up, grabbed the front of his coat, and pulled with all her anger. 'You will get down from your horse when you talk to me,' she yelled.

Taken unawares, the lieutenant had no time to move his weight. Clara artfully knocked his mount's front leg with her bottom, so it moved away a step, helping him to fall towards her. He landed heavily in the mud. His men laughed.

'My husband is Colonel Spencer-Ridgmont and will hear of this,' she barked into his face as he struggled up. 'General Cheatham will hear of it!'

The lieutenant rounded on his men. 'Get about your business.' The laughter died away. He started to put his hat back on, but thought better of it.

'My apologies, ma'am,' he said. 'My manners escaped me. We've been in the saddle some days. My orders come from General Wheeler. We have to take... we have to requisition the horses. The army's in sore need of mounts since the battle. So we can get round the back of the Yankees and cut their supplies. I'll of course give you a docket. The government will pay.'

Pay in Confederate dollars, she thought; of no use if the Union came. And she realized that was what she wanted now: for the blue army to push Taylor away. The fight went out of her, and she felt nothing but a wash of sadness.

The lieutenant was reaching into his saddlebag for some paper. 'But seein' as how you have a lame horse and it's a big place an' all, I reckon I can leave one other.'

'Bring your papers inside,' she said weakly. 'I won't have it said the colonel's house is not courteous. I'll have some food brought out for your men.'

It was only later when she watched from the portico, as they rode away down the drive with all but two of her horses, that it occurred to her she could have asked to go with them. They might have escorted her to town. Hany waited quietly a few steps behind her. She couldn't blame her – of course she couldn't – but she couldn't bear to be near her either. Without turning, she said, 'I'll tend to myself. Ask Mitilde to find you something to do.'

Chattanooga – November 1863

Colonel Emerson Opdycke was the Corps Officer of the Day. He ate a strip of dried beef as Barney picked his way through the cold streets of Chattanooga. Late in the afternoon, the November sun, down behind Lookout Mountain, had barely taken the edge off last night's hard frost. The ground was slippery where it had been trampled by hoof and boot. The sky was a deep winter blue. He had a moment for himself.

The beef was tough and over-salted, but superior to crackers and pork fat. He took some water to ease it down into his aching stomach, let Barney amble to give him time to eat. It wasn't far between Thomas's Army Headquarters and Grant's Departmental Headquarters. Today's unusual duties had already taken him to the former, as well as to the generals commanding each of the three divisions in Granger's Fourth Corps; his corps now, after the re-organization some weeks ago.

A newly arrived company, its freshness given away by the consistency of its uniforms, drilled in front of a church to the shouts of a fat sergeant. He must be new too.

Opdycke considered the irony that today's temporary assignment was itself based upon his temporary command. He was only in charge of the brigade because of Harker's continued absence: Harker had been away in Nashville for two weeks. Like the rest of the army, the brigade had been re-organized. Instead of the five regiments that had fought at Chickamauga, it now had no fewer than nine, though they were so depleted from deaths, wounds and sickness, that it totaled about the same number of men as before. By dint of commanding the brigade, he'd qualified for this 'special' duty: a lowly colonel, rubbing shoulders with major generals. You'd have thought someone would notice the disparity and ask why this man hadn't been promoted. He'd left his own regiment for Captain Bates to tend to. No problem there. Bates knew his business.

He didn't resent being busy, far from it. He coped with the exigencies of this war better than most, and enjoyed the higher contact that these temporary responsibilities opened up for him. What he resented was that they *were* temporary, despite his delivery to the Union of a fine Ohio regiment, and despite its solid performance at Chickamauga. Were he a West Pointer, from the regular army, he'd have a brigade by now. Was that such an unworthy thought? Though he was here to serve the Union in whatever way God saw fit, he could serve them both better with a higher command.

He saluted an officer holding a horse while a young lieutenant picked at its hoof. He looked about him at the ordered activity. It compared favorably with last month: where before the streets and camps had been populated by skeletal horses and sullen men, now the army was at least fit to fight. And the ambulances and burial parties had been supplanted by supply wagons or artillery caissons. It was the difference between decay and preparation. Even the cold weather imposed a certain cleanliness. The frost tightened the mud so the wagons rolled faster and the men's step quickened. It was a fair trade for a few less degrees.

He rounded a colored work gang spreading river sand on a thicker patch of ice. He had to admit that Grant was doing a good job. Given command of the newly created Military District of the Mississippi, he had promptly fired Rosecrans and re-organized the armies beneath himself. Thomas, quite rightly, had inherited the Army of the Cumberland, semi-besieged here and awaiting re-enforcements coming from the west. Burnside kept the Army of the Ohio around Knoxville, and to Grant's friend Sherman was given the Army of the Tennessee, which was rumored to be close by. After Grant's arrival, the supply issue was quickly resolved. He'd aggressively taken the south bank of the river below Lookout

372

Mountain. So now supplies arrived safely by steamer as far as Moccasin Point and were brought the last few miles by wagon. Half-rations had become two-thirds and then full. The situation had so improved that last evening Mr Gartner had presented Opdycke with a fat turkey. Dr Hart had joined them and there had been butter, peach sauce and potatoes. The richness had been a surprise for his famished stomach and it was still sore, but he smiled at the memory. Two weeks ago he would have felt obliged to share it with the men, but as they were faring better too, he'd indulged himself.

A fresh breeze, off the river but hinting of the mountains, pushed away the mixed must of men and horses. He arrived at the Departmental Headquarters; a large house, two columns holding a modest veranda forward of the upper story. There was a high picket-fence in front of a garden that hosted tall, naked trees. He tied Barney to a post rail, between horses a hand or two taller. Horse size correlated to rank, it appeared. After making way for staff officers hurrying out, he stepped inside. Rawlins would be the chief of staff, but Opdycke would find some lesser light to make his report to. He found his way to a commandeered dining room. It was much as the last headquarters: order and activity, haste but no panic. A pair of telegraphers clicked away like arrhythmic woodpeckers. A smiling staff officer received him, but stayed seated.

'Colonel Emerson Opdycke, sir. Fourth Corps Officer of the Day.'

The smile had set. 'Your full designation please, Colonel Opdycke.'

'Colonel of the 125th Ohio, Third Brigade, Second Division, Fourth Corps, Army of the Cumberland – sir.'

'A colonel? As Corps Officer of the Day?'

'That's right.'

The man listened politely enough to his report, but clearly with more important things to return to. Once done, Opdycke made to leave, but instead his arm was appropriated by none other than Charles Dana. He was pulled into the hall and out of the way. They'd met once or twice since they were introduced by Wood after the first day of Chickamauga, when all outcomes had still seemed possible. He was flattered that a representative of the War Department valued his views. All the same, he couldn't bring himself to actually like the man. Dana wasn't in the army after all, and he usually left Opdycke feeling he'd been interviewed rather than consulted. The niceties were barely observed.

'How does Sheridan suit you as your new division commander?'

Opdycke had no need to be guarded; he had nothing negative to say. 'I think he suits me well. He's tight on discipline, but the men respect him. He has a fighting reputation and we are a fighting brigade.'

'Yes. I think we can rest easy with Sheridan. And Wood? Do you miss Wood?'

This was more contentious, and Opdycke had covered this ground with Dana before the re-organization. It was Rosecrans who had gone. Wood still had his division. There was nothing to be gained by criticizing him. Wood had done his best to sponsor Opdycke's advancement.

'On reflection, I see that Rosecrans was more at fault than Wood at Chickamauga. It's hard to disobey an order, no matter what the circumstances.'

'Yes, I understand. He speaks well of you. No doubt reward will come your way, once we push out of here.'

'You think that will be soon?' Opdycke forgot his own ambitions for the moment.

Dana pulled him closer than was comfortable. 'Sherman is no more than a day away. Grant has designs to bring him round to our left. And with Hooker in place to the west, we can stretch the enemy and perhaps force Bragg away.'

'I've been with Thomas today. He said nothing?'

Dana lowered his voice further, 'They are not often of the same mind, Thomas and Grant. Though a scant half a mile apart, they prefer to communicate through staff officers rather than in

374

person. *Too sluggish to leave its trenches,* is what Grant's said of the Army of the Cumberland. I don't know if he really thinks that or if it's a goad. Certainly he'll look to Sherman to do the heavy work when the fighting starts.'

'Does he not know he'd have no Army of the Cumberland but for Thomas?' Opdycke bristled.

'Please, take no offence, Colonel. Understanding your broader mind on these matters, I only wish to be open with you. Perhaps it's because Thomas is a Virginian.'

'All the more reason to trust him, when he's stood by the Union to his personal cost.'

'Quite so. I'm sure your orders will come. In a day or two, when Sherman is fully up.'

'I'd best look to my brigade then.' Opdycke fitted his hat. He wanted to be away from the man. But Dana walked with him down the hall and stopped him with a hand on his shoulder as they passed an open doorway.

'Here he is.'

Opdycke looked into the room. It was quieter than elsewhere. There was a desk by the window and a man slouched in a chair, sat obliquely so he was in profile. His dress didn't imply a major general, more a slightly scruffy army clerk, his beard trimmed for expediency rather than for any affectation. He clamped an almost finished cigar between his teeth as he read. Opdycke had seen him before, in the spring of '62 at Shiloh. Grant had somehow recovered from near-disaster to claim the field. Luck, many said. If so, then the luck had stuck to him since. After taking Vicksburg in July, this was his reward: to have the whole department and be fated to come to their rescue in Chattanooga. Would his luck hold, wondered Opdycke? Or would Bragg pen him up, until his reputation dimmed sufficiently for Dana to whisper in the ear of the War Department, and have him shelved like Rosecrans before him? He moved on for fear he'd be caught staring.

*

On into the evening, Opdycke conducted his duties with a changed perspective. Dana, civilian though he was, would be privy to Grant's plans. It wasn't idle gossip he'd passed on. There would be a push soon, a full engagement. He sensed the men were ready for it, though it was barely two months since Chickamauga. With their rations restored, they were prepared in body at least. And the change in leader had been a necessity. Rosecrans, though well respected, had lost the fight and been culpable to boot. The troops needed someone new, someone with a history of success.

There was something more. He'd sensed it building in the weeks past, and he felt it again as he rode Barney tiredly back to his billet, listening to the low buzz around the fires and in the shanties. The men played their harmonicas and fiddles, covered their cards or dice as he passed by. He sensed a brooding resentment. Not insubordinate. Not really aimed at the colonels and generals; more at fate, perhaps. That they had lost a battle where they knew they'd been holding their own. That the country and their families should think the less of them. That so many friends lay dead after a lost day. Having endured in Chattanooga and held onto it, they were eager to get away, but not away home. They wanted to go south and prove that they were as good as the armies sent to rescue them. Perhaps he was fooling himself. Maybe that was just how he wanted it to be.

It was past midnight when he stiffly dismounted outside the house. This had been his home since they were moved under Sheridan. The guard took Barney to the lean-to and Opdycke went into his own room. It was snug, courtesy of the unmet Mrs Kelly whose house it once was. He felt he'd earned this spot. And it had allowed him to give wholly to the officers the only partitioned tent the regiment now owned. That in turn had helped free up the lean-to for Barney. He had no compunction in putting him before the men as regards to shelter. An officer could lead more effectively when mounted. He'd demonstrated that beyond question at Chickamauga. While Barney might be putting a few extra soldiers out in the cold, ultimately he would pay them back in battle. Some of them had the shelter of the rest of the house. There was a selection of snoring from the other rooms. What would Mrs Kelly have thought?

He sat down at the bureau, the only piece of furniture in an otherwise empty room. He took off his hat and ran both hands through his hair. Though tired, he wasn't quite ready for sleep. There was a letter from Ohio – from Major Moore. He thought to open it but considered the day's duties had been more than done. He needed to take his mind away from obligation before he could rest. He would write to Lucy. Yes. It would be good to get a letter away if battle was close. It would ease his mind. He found some clean paper and moved the lamp closer.

He told her of this day, proud of his duties if not his rank. He told her that mercifully Colonel Harker had returned from Nashville during the evening and could resume command of the brigade; though he'd himself keep command of a demi-brigade – five depleted regiments. He told her the army might soon be strong enough to push on again, but not to worry.

Kiss Tine and tell him to be good always,
Emerson.

On reading the letter back he saw that he had hardly got away from military matters. He blew the ink dry.

Major Moore's letter was right there. Tired as he was, curiosity got the better of him. He expected it would be more news on how slowly the recruitment of the final company, Company K, proceeded. He'd gratefully received the eighty men of Company I only last week.

But it was instead about the matter of the English soldiers, which Opdycke had asked him to look into. Moore had visited the Governor's Office in Columbus. Governor Tod told him that Ocks had presented letters of introduction from no less than the Duke of Ridgmont, with whom Tod had some business relations. Though it was odd that Ocks had requested a specific regiment, it had appeared to be a gift horse, so the governor had simply forwarded him on to the 125th. Moore had discovered that the Duke of Ridgmont was a noted supporter of the Confederacy in the English Parliament. In relation to the boy called Shire, he'd checked the regimental records which gave an address in Medina County to which Moore had gone. The lady he'd met there said the English boy had befriended her son, one Daniel Canton. The boy had fallen on hard times so signed up.

Opdycke found his eyes were closed. He rubbed them and searched for his place in the letter. Moore said that the lady was obviously fond of the boy and he'd left a package of clothes with her, so evidently he planned to return. With the clothes had been a single opened letter. As Moore could see it had been written in Tennessee, he thought it might have a bearing. He had made a copy, which he enclosed.

So Ocks might be sponsored by a foreign Confederate supporter. Opdycke needed to be awake to make sense of this. His eyes were closing again. He'd read the other letter when he woke. And he'd get them both in here as soon as time allowed. Armed with the information he had, he thought he could then get to the root of things. But not now, now he needed to sleep.

Chattanooga – November 24th, 1863

It appeared to Shire that most of the Division stood looking to the west as he did, though for much of the morning there was little to see. Except for its lower slopes, Lookout Mountain was masked by clouds. But every short while, the cold wind would strip them away to reveal the flash of guns and the arc of shells through the wet air. The defending Rebel cannon, high up on Lookout, were like an organ placed inside an entrance of a church. Each detonation rebounded from the mountains over the river. He wished he had something to do other than watch. When the veil returned, the noise endured, the echoes never entirely dying away.

In the afternoon, he had fatigue duty with Tuck and Mason, but the usual banter was lacking. When they finished, they climbed into one of the smaller forts on the outskirts of town that afforded them a better view. By now there was gunfire to the northeast as well, where they knew Sherman's Army of the Tennessee to be.

'Seems everyone's in the fight but us,' said Tuck, downcast. 'Why did they keep us here all this time if they weren't never gonna let us fight?'

'We had our fight yesterday,' said Shire.

'Huh,' said Tuck. 'That weren't no fight. Just a little push was all. Our brigade wasn't even in it.'

It had seemed like the whole army had paraded out the previous afternoon. But only a fraction of it had been used to push the Rebels from a small knoll sat in the middle of the plain that stretched south and east to Missionary Ridge.

'That was Grant reminding Bragg there's a whole other army in here,' continued Tuck. He slapped his arms against his side, trying to warm up. 'That way he'll keep his troops on the ridge, instead of sending them off to help defend that mountain from

Hooker, or the other way to see off Sherman.'

'Bragg ain't that dumb,' said Mason. He pulled his collar up to keep out the drizzle. 'No one's gonna attack that ridge. We might as well shoot ourselves and save him the bother.'

'Well, they should use us for somethin',' said Tuck, with a heat that surprised Shire. It wasn't like Tuck to get riled. 'Too sluggish to leave our trenches, are we?' They'd all heard Grant's rumored comments. 'Well, I'm game. I've had enough of this town and I don't need no cocksure Sherman boys telling me they know how to march and fight. Nor those easterners under Hooker neither, all in their nice fresh uniforms. Bullet passes through new cloth just as easy.'

'Have you forgotten how easy?' asked Mason. 'You should know when you're lucky.'

'If he's got three armies, he should use three armies,' said Tuck. 'What's the point of having something and not getting the use of it? Why, you wouldn't keep three horses and only ever use the two?'

Strictly speaking, Hooker's force was only a detachment from the Army of the Cumberland, but Shire couldn't be bothered to quibble. The guns boomed on, mocking them and their static army from both directions.

'Maybe we should just be glad that we're not up on that mountain,' said Shire. 'It's cold enough down here. Let's go and find somewhere to get warm. Or at least less cold.'

At that moment the clouds lifted to allow them a view of the northern end of Lookout Mountain. It was a good two miles away, but they could see flags there, climbing the lower slopes.

'Sir? What flags are those?' Shire asked a lieutenant nearby who was using field glasses.

'They're ours,' he said. 'But they're a long way from the top of that mountain.'

*

380

Shire wanted to be alone in the evening, but Company B had its turn in the Kelly House so he was loath to give up the warmth. Instead he took himself away from Tuck and Mason, who appeared in no better a mood than he was. Two months in a muddy town with poor fare and nothing but winter to look forward to had dampened their humor. The cannonade from outside was hardly soothing. He felt as taut as a fiddle string. He found a corner, borrowed a paper and withdrew into himself.

The same sentence presented itself over and over again, and eventually he curled up, put his head on his pack and tried to sleep. The floorboards vibrated in gentle sympathy with the guns. The best he could manage was to drift in and out amidst the subdued chatter in the room. He lost track of time, but hunger roused him and he went outside in the dark to search for a fire. The cannon had stopped. As he left the house, Tuck grabbed him. 'Come and see,' he said.

'I'm going to eat.'

'Come and see!'

Tuck led him away from the house, turned him to the west and Shire forgot his hunger. The clouds had all gone, the air was clear and there was nothing but eternity and a full moon. On any other night the stars would have been show enough, but not on this one. There, on the side of Lookout Mountain, was a belt of campfires touching the edge of the vast, cold sky. Amongst and above them were a thousand fireflies, each a distant twinkle, sparking a sudden streak across the slope, left or right, up or down. Set against the deeper shadow of the mountain it was as if a great, enchanted dragon, from ages past, was rising from the earth. He could hear a dim crackle, like a far off brush fire, eating across the slope.

He was transfixed. 'What is it?'

'What d'you think it is, sleepyhead? Skirmishers out trading shots on the mountain. The boys are well up if you get your bearings.'

Shire became conscious that the dark around him was crowded

with soldiers all seduced by the scene. 'I guess war's pretty from a distance.'

He watched for some time for fear of never seeing such a sight again, until hunger won out. They pooled their rations and boiled up a salty bean soup with such shreds of meat as they had. But they ate in silence. Tuck left to go and sleep. The other soldiers finished their own meals and departed. In the end, Shire was left alone to nurse what remained of the fire. There would be a hard frost again tonight. He used to love the hoar frosts at home: on the lane down to Eversholt when the hedgerows turned white and the grass, thickened by a coat of ice, would whisper and squeak under your boots. Good view from there too: Hill's End Field with Alder Spinney and Berry Brook, the coppice wood. Everything in its place. Not trampled and defaced by an army, with the trees cut for breastworks or to clear lines of fire. He'd trade the sight he'd just seen, Lookout Mountain all lit up, for a single breath of home.

How far away it all seemed. He'd arrived in New York by this time last year. His new life, his army life, had interposed itself between him and his past by much more than its due. The weight of experience, he supposed: the places he'd seen, the people he'd met, the suffering and death. It all stacked up above his former, gentler existence and compressed it, pushed it away as if it belonged to someone else.

What if he was there now, back home, summoned in an instant by some miracle? What would he have left? No father, no Clara or Grace. Grief and guilt welled up together – inseparable. For all its gentleness and its communion with the more peaceful byways of his memory, Ridgmont no longer contained the people he had loved. He'd left them all when he'd stepped out into the snow a year ago, with no idea of the power of the world beyond. It had taken hold of him and steered him ever since.

Clara felt most distant of all. It was over three years since he'd spoken a word to her. She felt more like someone he'd heard tell of, an idea or a sentiment. She'd broken the connection –

asked him not to write. Why had he come? Could he remember anymore? Did his stomach still tighten at the thought of her? Could he remember the taste of her kiss, or feel the touch of her breast beneath their joined hands?

Perhaps – sometimes, when the weight of the present was less heavy. When the cold and the hunger and the weariness were at bay – then he could remember her: a child in a tree, in dappled light, asking him to make a promise; a girl in a bonnet, turning in the lamplight to look up at the stars; a woman he'd helped up after a fall, her warmth and fragrance pressed into him.

He fed the fire a few scrawny twigs and it crackled in thanks. Father stayed closest – settled in his heart. It was as if he was nearby. Not a day would pass without a thought of him or even a quiet word that Shire might send his way. He would hear his admonishments, echoes from Shire's youth that kept him honest.

Ocks was a more tangible connection to the past. Other than orders, not a word had passed between them since he'd told Ocks the truth. Instead, Shire felt he was watched more closely, more sullenly. But then Ocks was his sergeant and everyone was sullen, stuck in this muddy town.

He sat there for hour upon hour. The stars and the full moon circled slowly around him. When finally he stirred, thinking he should sleep, he found the frost had crept in outside the light of the fire. He stood, his legs stiff and his eyes tired. It seemed darker. He looked up, perplexed. There were no clouds. He turned and saw the moon had lost its shape. A hard shadow had stolen almost all its light. He'd never seen an eclipse before. Tuck would want to see. But his heart darkened with the moon. He considered himself an educated man, but this night had already held unearthly sights. A soldier's dread took hold and he hurried towards the Kelly House. He wouldn't wake Tuck. Once he'd made a place amongst the press of bodies, sleep eluded him, chased away by a preternatural foreboding. It wasn't until close to dawn that he slept.

*

He woke suddenly. He was afraid but didn't know why. There'd been a dream but he couldn't grip it. Shouting from outside distracted him. He rose and followed soldiers hurrying out into a purple, frosty dawn. Cheers rolled up towards them from the regiments to the west, a breaking wave of euphoria and celebration. Hats were thrown in the air, backs were slapped. Shire found Tuck, who gripped his shoulder and hugged him.

'They did it!' Tuck pointed to where the first sun touched the stone bastion of Lookout Mountain. Shire could see three large flags being waved up there as if summoning the Almighty to witness their victory.

'We're not out yet,' said Tuck, 'but that'll give old Bragg somethin' to think about... What's the matter with you? You look like your world's ended.'

'I had a dream,' said Shire, recalling it with a cold fear and suddenly oblivious to the celebrations around him. 'I was shot. In my chest.' He thought of Lyman. 'I was shot. Up on that ridge. Today.'

Chattanooga – November 25th, 1863

Colonel Opdycke chafed at the absence of orders. It was early afternoon and he was on Barney, forward of his demi-brigade. He'd been sat there since well before noon. He'd had the men stack arms and rest on the ground. All the other brigades, north and south of him, were waiting too. Even with the men seated or lying it was an imposing sight. He imagined what it must look like to the enemy. Four divisions, perhaps twenty-five thousand men, of the Fourth Corps had advanced out of Chattanooga to the east, onto the great plain that separated the town from Missionary Ridge.

All five miles of the ridge could be seen from where he sat on this cold, dry day. Its nearest point was less than two miles from him over the flat. To the south, his right, it stretched down to the gap at Rossville, where the Army of the Cumberland had spilled defeated from the field of Chickamauga two months ago. From there it had just the short end of Chattanooga Valley to separate it from Lookout Mountain, back in Union hands courtesy of General Hooker. To his left the ridge ran north, towards the Tennessee. Before it reached the river, it started to fragment, lost its straight crest and decayed into a collection of hills and slopes with aspects this way and that. From there came the grumble of Sherman's guns. He was trying to win the left as Hooker had won the right. It was galling, thought Opdycke: that they should be so inactive, while Sherman and Hooker fought for the honor that the Army of the Cumberland so desperately wanted to win back.

A thin dog trotted in front of him, giving Barney a wide berth. There were a few about. Opdycke didn't approve and there were none in his regiment, but others kept them as unofficial mascots. They served a purpose of sorts. He hadn't banned them from his whole demi-brigade yet, the five regiments he commanded under

Harker. All solid regiments, especially the 64th, which he'd placed in front of the 125th.

His soldiers had been given one hundred rounds a piece as a precaution, but he knew none would get used. They were only here to make a demonstration, to keep Bragg mindful that he couldn't deplete his center to support his flanks. But Bragg would need to leave precious few soldiers on that ridge to defend it. It was five hundred feet high and he had counted over forty cannon just from his vantage; there would be more back of the crest. He could see troops on the move up there, certainly, heading north to fight Sherman. Yet he saw no troops pulled from the defense of the crest itself, or from the rifle pits forward of its base. If he were a Rebel today, he'd be hoping the Army of the Cumberland would be foolish enough to charge. That wouldn't happen. Sherman had more than enough troops to take the Rebel right. And that lost, Bragg would defend his flanks and pull back in the night. Opdycke could see it all clearly enough.

So would Grant, he thought, and glanced forward and left to Orchard Knob, the small hill taken two days ago that now served as Grant's observation post. They were all in there: Grant, Thomas and the Fourth Corps Commander, Granger. No doubt all waiting for news from Sherman that he was astride the north end of the ridge. The generals would have seen what he'd seen, what the whole snubbed Army of the Cumberland had seen: Sherman's boys climb up the slopes over there before noon. There'd been nothing but noise since. So they all waited together.

There was movement amongst the men, some stood and looked to the north. Opdycke's field glasses were in his saddle, but he was slow to reach for them. Even without their aid he could see that Sherman's blue troops were falling back across the slopes they'd climbed earlier.

'What is it, Colonel? What can you see?' asked a corporal in the 64th. He put the glasses to his eyes. Those troops weren't just falling back, they were running, only a handful turned to fire and slow the pursuit.

'Sherman is having a hard time,' was all he said. How would this play out on Orchard Knob? Grant would have to make another move.

'Why don't they let us fight, Colonel? We'll show Sherman's boys how to fight.'

He waited a long, anxious hour. Were they going to move to the left and support Sherman? That's what he would do. Or was the day going to end with them having been no more than spectators? He considered ordering an inspection of arms; it would sharpen the men up. But then a battery of artillery raced through the brigade and unlimbered to their front. Over to their left, Wood's Division stirred. A staff officer rode to Harker, who summoned Opdycke with a wave.

'Emerson,' he said, when Opdycke reached him, 'have your men fall in and advance to that line of trees and there form line of battle. We are to take the rifle pits in front of the ridge. There will be a signal of six guns firing from Orchard Knob to start the advance once we're in line. And Colonel, stay well back in your demi-brigade. I need you directing troops today, not leading them.'

'Once we take the pits, sir, what then?'

'The order is to stop there.'

Dear God! 'We might as well stop at the gates of hell. We'll be right under the guns from the crest.'

'I'm aware, Emerson. So is Sheridan. He's having the order verified. Looks like they're improvising now Sherman's been checked. Grant has to at least make Bragg think that we might storm the ridge. Sitting here isn't going to fool him. I'll get word to you. Just get to those trees.'

Opdycke turned Barney from Harker and raced back to his troops. He yelled at his regimental commanders to have the men fall in. Around him the sergeants began to bark, the men shouldered their packs and rushed to collect their muskets from the stacks. Color-bearers untied their flags and shook out the folds to catch the breeze. The army came alive. To his left, Wood's Division was moving out, and to his right, beyond the rest of Harker's brigade, he saw Johnson's Division rousing as well. He felt the scale of it. It would be a charge beyond any he'd ever seen.

The 64th marched off briskly and the other columns followed on. They advanced several hundred paces out into the plain until they reached a line of open timber that paralleled the ridge – still over a mile away. The order was given to 'left-half wheel' and the 64th came into line of battle. He had the 3rd Kentucky and 79th Illinois come in left and right of them, all faced squarely at Missionary Ridge. The 125th and the 65th Ohio he held in a second line behind. In that formation they advanced into the bare, well-spaced trees. When the Rebels started to fire, at least they would afford some protection. Even at his thought, the first cannon boomed from atop Missionary Ridge and their shells came screaming home. They were ranging shots and poor ones at that. They did no damage and barely made Barney twitch. But the dogs jumped in alarm and raced back towards Chattanooga, tails between their legs. So much for mascots. The familiar smell of acrid smoke drifted on the breeze, his blood raced and a wave of adrenalin soaked through him. There was a snatched thought of Lucy that he tucked away.

'Have the men lie down,' he shouted, and waved above the din to make his point. His order was taken up with alacrity and all around the men lay prone, packs on their backs, hands over their heads. Opdycke stayed on Barney. He wanted Harker to be able to find him. A few lieutenants and captains stood amongst the men. Surely new orders would come. It didn't make sense to only take the pits. He rode to each regimental commander to tell them what he knew, ending with Captain Bates and the 125th.

A shell exploded behind the regiment. 'If we stay here long enough,' said Bates, 'those gunners will find their range.'

'There'll be a signal soon. Watch me. Keep the regiment behind the 64th, but give them a couple of hundred yards start. We're ordered to take the rifle pits only.' He tried not to show his misgivings. 'We'll look at the ground when we get there.'

'Boys are keen, Colonel. Someone just needs to let them off the leash.'

Six cannon barked from Orchard Knob in neat succession, the first Union guns to answer those atop the ridge.

'Someone just did,' said Opdycke. He blew out his cheeks, drew his sword, and cantered off to the 64th Ohio to order them forward.

*

Shire lay on the forest floor, his hands over his ears, willing himself into the earth. He'd not been lucky enough to be next to one of the trees when ordered to lie down. Tuck was on his right and Mason beyond Tuck. Shells were flying high over them to fall harmlessly behind the regiment, but they screamed a murderous descending note as they passed.

Mason's head turned towards him. 'Well, this ain't a whole heap of fun,' he shouted. 'I preferred it where we were.'

A shell, better sighted, landed not ten paces from them. Shire felt the jarring concussion through the very soil before a shower of earth rained down on him. He heard a Union cannon fire, at last answering the Rebels, then another and another at even intervals. Bugles ordered him to his feet and he settled his rifle to his shoulder. Ocks chivvied those slow to rise. There was a sickness in Shire's stomach, he blew out breath after breath and felt the blood pumping in his ears. Through the thin trees, he saw the backs of the 64th move off in front. To either side their solid line reached towards other regiments with flags waving red, white and blue. Polished rifles flashed in the sunlight. Another shell rent the air and the earth. It was torture to stand here.

The colonel rode back from the 64th and mercifully let Captain Bates order them forward. His first step on the dry twigs was both a terror and a relief. The shellfire was in full flow.

'We're lucky they don't have anyone as can shoot up there,' shouted Tuck.

Presumably aiming for the first wave, the Rebels still overshot, so that the shells now landed in the trees ahead of Shire. He stole a look to his left. The blue line stretched for as far as he could see through the bare trees. Officers walked forward of the men with swords pointed to the front.

'Well,' he shouted back to Tuck, 'at least we have a few friends on our side.'

'Let's hope they don't have too many friends up there,' said Tuck, nodding towards the ridge.

A shell landed to their left in front of the 65th and men went down screaming. The line marched on. In a few minutes they emerged from the trees and Shire had the full terrifying scene set out before him. Missionary Ridge was still a distance away, and along its abrupt crest cannon, dozens and dozens of cannon spewed shells down from the heights. Not a second would pass without a burst of white smoke from somewhere along the ridge. Shells arced out over the plain to fall steeply and finish vertically. The detonations became closer and more constant. Union cannon replied. A battery at a time they limbered up and moved out in front of the infantry. Mile upon mile of blue lines stretched out across the plain. The division away to Shire's left was ahead, approaching the ridge. The one to his right lagged behind. On they went. Without an order, the regiment started to increase its pace. There was the ripple of musket fire from ahead. The familiar terror of Chickamauga returned; only this time Shire was advancing, not defending.

Colonel Opdycke cantered back. 'You're too close on the 64th,' Shire heard him scream at Bates. 'Hold here a minute. Lie down!'

Ocks echoed the order. 'Lie down! Lie Down!'

It was harder to do that than go forward. Shire heard Tuck curse as they both lay flat on the cold grass. He prayed that the next shell wouldn't murder them both. The colonel raced away across the open ground, back to the 64th. There was an explosion,

Barney's head shot up and he reared, throwing the colonel to the ground. He was quick to rise but Barney was away from him, blood pouring from his mouth. The horse ran left and right in distress, shied from a shell burst and came cantering towards the 125th. Shire was on his feet without thinking.

'Lie down!' screamed Ocks, but Shire ignored him. He ran towards the horse, but slowed to a walk as he got closer. He extended his arm until Barney saw him and slowed – then stood, shaking in fear. A bullet or a shell fragment had passed through his mouth and severed one side of the bridle.

'Okay, boy. It's me. You know me.'

Barney's eyes were wide and white, but he suffered Shire to come closer and take gentle hold of the damaged bridle.

Colonel Opdycke walked up, putting his hat back on. 'Thank you, soldier, but your life is worth more than a horse.'

Shire thought the colonel didn't sound entirely convinced in the matter. 'I don't like to see them suffer, sir.'

The colonel turned on hearing the accent. 'Private Shire.' It was as if he had something more to say, but thought better of it as another shell detonated between the lines. 'Barney needs to be taken back. Will you get him somewhere safe for me?'

'On your feet!' shouted Captain Bates. The regiment rose again behind them.

Shire thought of his dream, of what might be waiting for him up on that ridge.

'Fix bayonets!' There was the scrape of steel and the regiment started towards them.

'Thank you, sir,' he said, 'but I mean to stay with the regiment. I'll find someone.'

Opdycke nodded. 'As you wish.' He took his field glasses out of the saddle, stroked Barney once and strode away.

The regiment came level with Shire.

'Won yourself a ticket to the rear, have you?' said Ocks.

Shire ignored him. 'Cleves,' he called, spying him in the last rank. 'Here, take the colonel's horse back and find someone to fix him up. If he's not well cared for I'll brain you.'

Cleves didn't need to be asked twice and led Barney away.

Ocks shook his head and Shire made his way back to his place beside Tuck.

Mason shouted over. 'I don't suppose you thought to offer us that opportunity?'

'No,' answered Shire. 'I knew you'd be insulted.'

As they went on, the pace quickened. The ridge began to loom above them. He could see the soldiers on its crest depressing their guns. It was a forlorn hope, he thought, that any army, no matter how many thousands strong, could wrestle that place from a determined enemy. Ahead of them the musket fire intensified, an octave above the thunder of the cannon. The flags of the 64th raced forward. The 125th moved to the double-quick.

'Sweet Jesus Lord Almighty!' Tuck was looking to the left. Shire's frightened gaze followed.

There, climbing the lower slopes of the ridge, was a patchy stripe of grey and brown. Not an ordered rank, but a clawing, uneven line, their backs to the Union flags that started up the hill behind them.

'They're running!' screamed Mason, and started to run faster himself.

Shire felt the elation sweep through him and the whole regiment. A guttural roar poured out as they raced over the ground after the 64th. He passed injured men, dead men, but no one stopped. On he raced until they crested a low breastwork and jumped down into a crowded pit beyond. There was no target for their rage. The pits had already been taken by the 64th. Without orders to go further they'd stayed there. There were Rebel soldiers too, most unhurt, some with their hands in the air, some not so lucky. A man clutched at his ripped and spilling stomach as if trying to hold too many apples to himself. Captains and lieutenants tried to reform their companies, or to start the prisoners back to

Chattanooga. There was no rear breastwork to the pit so it afforded no protection from the ridge. Shire could see it didn't start to rise here, but a further two hundred yards away. He climbed out to follow Tuck and Mason. No sooner was he up than a round shot tore down the length of the pit behind him with a muddy slap. The men in there were reduced to a wet, red tangle of blood and limbs. Shire couldn't move. He closed his eyes to the horror.

Tuck yanked him away by his jacket. 'C'mon,' he yelled at him. 'This is a death trap. We've got to get to the slope.'

He knocked Tuck's hand away but went with him. Others also made for the ridge to escape the cannon and musket fire from above. The regiment had lost all shape and was completely mixed in with the 64th. They raced on towards the start of the slope. There were a few huts there. Beyond them Shire could see that here too, the Rebels were running, or rather climbing, up the hill. At the huts, the Union men crowded for shelter. A shell exploded a flimsy shack and the men scattered. Shire ran with them. Minie balls smacked into the ground around him. He was almost at the slope. It wasn't smooth, but scratched with rills and hollows. He made for the spot that afforded the best cover from above, threw himself hard against the slope. He fought to catch his breath, then lifted his head and looked into the smiling face of Ocks.

'What are we doing here, boy, eh? Why's your bayonet not fixed? Too busy playing with the colonel's horse? Two minutes and then we'll get up there to look at the view.'

Shire pulled his bayonet from its sheath, fixed it.

'You loaded?' asked Ocks.

Shire nodded. He'd been loaded all day.

'Have a pop then. They're all pretty slow on that hill.'

Shire looked out from the cover of the slope. There were many easy targets, but he wasn't about to shoot someone in the back. Instead he picked out a man half way up who stood out against the skyline, standing to fire down into the pits. He took aim, surprised at how steady he was, let out a breath and squeezed the trigger. The silhouetted form twisted sideways, before slumping forwards and out of sight.

'Any luck?' called Ocks.

'Yes, Sergeant,' said Shire, starting to reload. Whenever he'd fired before, it had always been as part of a volley, where you were never sure if it was your bullet that hit home. Here, he knew he'd just killed a man. Was he going to muse on this now? Moralize, rationalize on how he had no choice. He couldn't think his way out of this fix. He rammed the ball home and looked about him, saw Tuck and Mason lying not far away. Next to them Private Oliver Brown was sat frantically tamping tobacco into his pipe. More men came until there must have been thirty or forty gathered together. The colors were here, held by young Lieutenant Mellish who swept his gaze across them. 'We want our colors to be the first on top of this Union hill, don't we?'

The boys replied with a snarling growl.

'Then follow me!'

*

Colonel Taylor Spencer-Ridgmont had never seen so many soldiers in a single view. Not at flat Stones River, and not at Chickamauga with its trees and hills. Today, below him on the plain before Chattanooga, they were beyond counting. Regiment after regiment stretched out north to south. They moved only half-hidden through the leafless trees, like some crawling swarm of blue beetles.

The guns on the ridge began to fire from either side of him, the shells falling away and down onto the plain. They were overshooting. He was able to follow a shell in flight, to watch it arc out, for a moment higher than the ridge, before it began to plummet, ever more steeply, to explode behind the blue lines. He set his own will to pull the shells from the air, drag them down earlier and into the blue ranks. No one was correcting the elevation. At last he saw one shell find its mark, and steadily the detonations crept nearer, as if they were herding the Union Army on towards him. The first regiments emerged proud on the tree line and onto the grass, beautifully aligned, stars and stripes mixed with regimental flags, buttons and barrels glinting in the sun. It was almost enough to make you miss the old Union.

Some of his men stood beside him on the edge of the crest and guessed at the numbers. He could see they were nervous. It was understandable that this sight might take their courage, courage that had before now been sapped by the cold and short rations. But they would fight; they always did. Though they were the besiegers, his army had its own supply problems: his regiment had been on half-rations for weeks, stuck up on this ridge with little or no cover from the deepening cold. Not that Taylor had suffered with them; the table was plentiful enough amongst the officers. He'd had Major Jasper send messages to the commissary to see what could be done for the men but had heard nothing in reply. So now they looked lean and cold. Along the front he'd been given to cover, the men were spaced out to seven or eight feet, in part because half were down in the rifle pits a couple of hundred paces out from the bottom of the ridge. Major Jasper was down there with them. A curious order, he thought, as he walked along the line. The boys below were to wait until they had the Yankees close, fire one volley and then retire back up the ridge; it was hardly worth it. Perhaps it was designed to tempt the Yankees to come on. He'd rather have his men up here. That way he could afford to thicken his line and create a small reserve.

It wouldn't matter. The Yankees might demonstrate out there on the plain, but nobody was fool enough to charge this ridge. He could defend his patch with half his men if he had to. The Yankees started to become misaligned; the formation in front of him was ahead of the rest, coming on at the double-quick towards the rifle pits. The cannon barked again and again and began to take their toll. Flags raced out ahead of the regiments.

'What will we do, Colonel?' said one man, wide-eyed. 'There's so many of 'em. We can't shoot 'em all.'

'If they come up this hill I'll shoot 'em all for you. They ain't that stupid. I wish they were.'

Looking again he saw his men get off their volley from the pits and start running back to the slope. A few men in blue had fallen, but it hadn't checked their charge. His own men were lost to sight under the ridge. The Yankees made the pits and then stopped. There was a commotion at the nearest battery – it had been his battery until he lost the brigade. They'd stopped firing. Taylor hurried over.

'What is it?' he demanded from the artillery lieutenant. 'Why have you stopped?'

'They're too close. We can't depress the cannon any more. They're inside our range.'

'Then fire along their line where the range is greater. You don't have to hit the ones right in front of us. They've stopped anyway.'

'Should I fire north or south?'

'It don't matter. They're all Yankees.' He went back to his regiment. The battery was realigned to point obliquely to the south. When they fired they found a good range on the rifle pits straight away and started doing some real damage. That was better. Other batteries were doing the same up and down the line, so the enemy in front of him was being hurt as well. They'd have no choice but to retreat. But as Taylor watched, unable to credit what he was seeing, they came on; a few at first, but then more and more. They were coming to the ridge. *Good.*

*

Colonel Opdycke had commandeered a horse from his nominal aide, Abner Carter, the Regimental Quartermaster for the 125th. So he was mounted again on the plain in front of the rifle pits. It allowed him to see all the better that he was losing control of his demi-brigade. Half of them had stayed at the pits, exposed to heavy fire, while the rest had run for the slope. Some were even beginning to climb. His regiments had become hopelessly intermingled.

He looked around for Harker but couldn't see him. Instead a mounted staff officer, not one he recognized, rode up to him through the crash and thunder.

'Who ordered the men up that ridge?'

The man's uniform was fit for a dinner dance, thought Opdycke. 'No one. It's a safer place than the pits. Who are you, sir?'

'I'm on Granger's staff. You must order those men back off the hill. The instructions were only to take the pits.'

'Are you going to order Wood's Division back as well?' Opdycke shouted and pointed to the left where hundreds were halfway up the ridge. Each cluster of men formed a wedge with a flag at its apex, as if a row of sharp teeth was biting up the slope.

'I can only deliver what orders I have,' said the staff officer, angrily. 'I've already told Harker.'

Opdycke looked back to his troops on the hill. Some were coming back down. The order must have reached them by some other route. They were safer where they were. It was madness. Couldn't they get through one battle without this incompetence from the generals?

'Does Sheridan know?' He controlled his new horse as a shell detonated not twenty paces away.

'Not from me.'

'Well, let's go and find him. I'm no use here until I have better orders.'

He scanned behind the lines. Sheridan wasn't hard to find. He was conspicuous on his great black charger over to the right, a small man for a big horse. He was drawing enemy fire even as Opdycke arrived, staff officer in tow. Sheridan took out a hip flask and raised it in an act of willful bravado to the cannon that fired from the crest.

'Here's to you, General Bragg,' he said.

'General,' Opdycke could barely hear himself. 'This officer is telling me to pull my troops off the ridge. Are those your orders?'

'It would be a great pity after they've suffered so much to get as far as they have.'

That was hardly a clear directive, but before Opdycke could press the point, a second staff officer cantered in, slewed to a halt and saluted Sheridan. 'I have an amendment to your orders, General,' he shouted. 'If you think you can carry the ridge, you are to take it.'

'Thank God,' said Sheridan. He called to his aides and sent them off through the tumult to his brigade commanders. Opdycke considered that it was the men running this battle not the generals. Sheridan turned his charger to the front. 'Colonel Opdycke!' he shouted, dark eyes ablaze. 'Kindly help me get these boys up that hill?'

*

Shire's foot slipped on the loose earth and he fell flat on the slope. He clutched with his free hand for a hold and gripped some old, dried bush root, enough to stop him from sliding down. Around him everyone was finding their own frantic way up the slope. Lieutenant Mellish, somehow able to climb as well as hold onto the thick staff of the colors, had picked them a steep section. They couldn't be more than fifty feet up. Shire made another effort. He climbed a body length higher, then rested and reached for his canteen. Around him the men were blowing hard, having been cooped up in Chattanooga for two months. Yet the steepness itself protected them. They were in their own bubble of safety while the battle raged above and below them.

An order was passed up from man to man.

'We're to fall back to the pits,' shouted up a boy Shire didn't know, perhaps from the 64th.

'What?' The lieutenant beat his head against the flagstaff.

'Mother of God.' He began to step and slide back down the slope and ordered the men to do the same.

Shire was about to follow when a big paw grabbed the back of his jacket and held him to the slope.

'You bloody stay where you are,' snarled Ocks.

'We're ordered off the hill.'

'All of you!' bellowed Ocks. 'Don't move. You too, Lieutenant, unless you want me to throw you down. Dumbest damn Yankee order I ever heard. Look over there. Half your bloody army is climbing this hill. Sure as my arse is hairy, we'll be ordered back up as soon as the generals pull their fingers out of theirs. Now stay here!'

No one moved.

'We'll wait a while,' said the lieutenant.

Elsewhere, clumps of men descended and started towards the crowded pits. Many were hit. Some chose to stumble backwards, not wanting to be shot in the back. About Shire the men waited uneasily. Some took their chance to reload, though it was awkward on the slope. There were long fearful minutes, wondering if he'd be sent up or down; each was as perilous as the other. He felt about as safe as he might shut in a coffin. But sure enough, he saw the officers turn the men once more, form them as best they could and send them through the hellish fire back to the hill.

'Now, Lieutenant,' smiled Ocks. 'I think we have a little lead.'

Shire started to climb again. It was slow going. He could only stay on his feet by going left and right up the slope. There was nothing to trouble them other than the climb itself, until amongst the din of cannon and muskets a swish, like a sudden passing flock of geese, rushed through the air to pepper the slope to Shire's left.

'Canister,' panted Mason from above Shire.

Looking away to his right, Shire could see a battery of cannon atop the ridge. Unable to fire directly down the slope at the troops that climbed beneath them, they'd instead turned their barrels to fire across at Harker's Brigade. As Shire's group had climbed the highest, they were attracting attention.

There was a rill that ate into the slope thirty feet higher. It would give them cover and Lieutenant Mellish led them towards it. Before they could get there a second volley tore in above Shire. The lieutenant and the two men with him were plucked from the slope and hurled to the left. They rolled away below, trailing loose stones, their lifeless limbs flailing. The flag, dropped on the slope, slid down the hill to Shire. As it reached him it stopped like a death sentence. The staff was bloodied and the cloth torn.

'Looks like it's your turn,' said Ocks, still climbing.

'I'll take it,' said Mason. 'This ain't your war.'

Shire handed Mason his rifle instead.

'Maybe not,' he said, picking up the thick, bloodied staff, 'but it's my army.'

*

A shell detonated well behind Colonel Taylor and he spun around to look. The Union batteries, unable to fire at the rifle pits anymore, had started to aim for the crest. Taylor looked to his horse, pegged out on the other side of the ridge. It was getting harder to replace these animals. He was doing nothing here for the moment. It would take but a minute. He gave the regiment over to a captain and marched off, mounted the horse and took her back a way further where he tied her to a scrub bush. He hurried back but made sure he walked; it wouldn't do for the men to see an officer run.

The air transformed into a solid blast of sound which drove right through him, through his gut and through his mind. He was slammed to the earth. A second detonation and he was bounced from the soil to land again. He struggled to recover his sense and his vision. He could only think that a shell must have struck close by. But as he sat himself up he was showered with a storm of splinters that pelted the ground like wooden hail. There was a tower of smoke behind the gunners, who'd been wiped away. The caissons had been hit; all of the ammunition had gone up. He groggily looked to his own line. Half of his men were down.

He got up and staggered to the crest. Some of his men were reaching down the hill to pull comrades up the last of the slope. A man in front of him was on his back and gasping for breath.

'Up. Get into line!' ordered Taylor.

But the boy was too spent and couldn't be used. There were only a dozen more, some just making the summit. All exhausted.

Major Jasper was on one knee.

'Where are the rest?'

'Ain't no more,' said Jasper between sobs and gasps. 'There was half the Union shootin' at us as we climbed. They're comin'. And they got a face on 'em like they won't stop for nothin' nor nobody.'

Taylor felt a gnawing dread crawl into his gut. He found one of his lieutenants and spun him around. 'You get over there to the brigade commander,' he shouted into the boy's face. 'Tell him I need more troops if I'm to hold. Go on!'

He leant out from the crest and looked down. He couldn't see anyone, but he knew the Union was coming.

*

Shire used the flagstaff to steady himself as he climbed. Men let him pass to the front with the colors. A spattering of musket fire twitched the flag as it caught more of the breeze the higher up they got. What was he doing? Was he choosing to die today? Every moment he expected to be hit. There was no shouting; the men used all their breath to climb. They were past halfway up now, taking it in turns to kneel and pick off Rebels foolish enough to show themselves on the skyline.

A bullet sparked off a rock right by his head and the dust stung his cheek. He closed his eyes tight and cursed. It tipped the balance between fear and anger. He *was* angry. He'd been storing it up for so long, since he got to America. He was angry at getting burned, getting beaten up, getting laughed at. He remembered poor Tom. That bastard Taylor was likely up there somewhere.

'Look!' someone below shouted and Shire followed the man's arm to the left, along the ridge. It was such a sight. They were the highest of any band in their brigade, maybe their division. But to the north, Wood's Division had reached the crest and swept up and over as each group of men gained the top. He couldn't see above the crest, but the men weren't thrown back. More and more followed and disappeared. They must have gained a foothold. He snatched a look the other way. Johnson's Division was climbing too. The whole Army of the Cumberland was angry, rampant; feeding on its two months of frustration and shame since Chickamauga. Despite their fatigue, Shire and the men cheered and rededicated themselves to their own climb. Around him the men's faces set hard. There were only two outcomes: either they would take this ridge or die in the attempt. It was as simple as that.

He climbed on. What he took to be a small rock tumbled down from above. As it passed he saw it was a shell, the burning fuse turning end over end. There were more. One bounced off his leg before it fizzed away down the slope to explode well below. More shots snapped past him. One hit the man below him in the shoulder. Shire looked up as the men with him replied in kind. There were more cannon up there, on the right. Soldiers swabbed the barrels as they prepared to fire.

'Tuck!' Shire shouted. 'Shoot the gunners!'

Ocks drew his long pistol and picked off one man, while Tuck directed more fire until the gunners fell back.

He was nearing the crest. At any moment he thought to see a figure lean out above him and fire. They couldn't miss. He paused to allow a few more to catch up: Tuck, Mason, Ocks. They all gathered their breath. Everyone except Shire took time to load. There was a huge explosion followed closely by another. They all hugged the slope. Over to their left, a high column of smoke fed on itself as it climbed high into the sky. Debris rained down on the troops climbing over there.

'Caissons,' said Ocks, answering the unasked question. 'One of our shells must have hit. First explosion will've set off the second. There'll be panic over there. Shame it wasn't in front of us.' He looked at Shire. 'Time to go.'

Shire understood. 'Ready?' he said, his heart pounding in his chest. He could hear barked Rebel orders just above him.

Everyone set themselves. Shire screamed and scrambled the last few yards over the edge, lifting the flag. He had a dozen men around him. Bayonets levelled, they roared forward. He thought to see a full regiment of Rebels ready to kill them for their audacity. Instead there were only a few dozen. Even then it would have been enough to throw them back over the edge, had not most of the enemy been running. Guns fired beside him and he saw two Rebels fall. A cannon battery to his right was limbering up to escape. More men came over the crest. Shire raced out ahead of them. He saw the battery horses fall in their traces, shot by Union bullets to prevent the cannon's escape. It made him angrier still. A Rebel came at him, for the colors, his bayonet pointed at Shire's stomach. He tried to parry with the staff but it was too heavy and he was too slow. Tuck yelled and stepped past him, ran his own bayonet deep into the man's side. The man twisted but Tuck kept his weight on him, pushed and levered him to the ground. There were soldiers with their hands up, pulled roughly into the blue ranks. Shire veered towards the cannon. There was a line of defenders there. Not more than six with an officer. All had their rifles pointing at Shire. He ran at them, screaming 'Tom... Tom!'

The officer pulled down his hand sharply. Shire couldn't hear him over the noise but saw his mouth shape... 'Fire.'

The bullet struck his chest so hard that he felt as if he was knocked backwards. There was a moment of utter emptiness, no weight, no thought. The colors flew from his grasp and he landed hard, sitting upright like a drunkard. Blue coats ran past him. One picked up the flag and raced on to the guns. He watched, knowing it would be the last thing he would ever see, as his army swarmed over the cannon. There was a big Rebel there, sweeping about with a ramrod. Bayonets surrounded him and he gave it up and wept. Shire thought he'd like to weep too. If only he could breathe. And there was gunpowder grit on his teeth. How many cartridges had he bitten open today? He tried to spit but his mouth was too dry. He should lie down. You weren't supposed to die sitting up. Tuck was there and supported him, held him and looked at his chest. 'Shire!'

He eased in a quarter breath and it hurt like hell.

'There's no blood,' said Tuck, and started to unbutton Shire's jacket close to a neat hole in the cloth.

He risked another breath. It hurt the same as the one before.

Tuck gently lifted Shire's shirt and smiled. 'Why you're just a little dented.' He carefully pulled out the roll of letters and the map from Shire's jacket pocket.

'All saints to glory,' said Tuck, holding them up in front of Shire's face. A hole went in through the thickest part of the roll. Out the other side protruded the flattened end of a minie ball.

Shire pulled his own jacket wider. There was a small but angry red circle above his heart. The skin was barely punctured. He started to breathe a touch more deeply. There was a sharp point past which he couldn't go, but he was alive.

More and more troops came over the crest. Tuck helped him to his feet and they walked slowly to the captured battery – four cannon. He held onto Tuck. There was jubilation all around: hats thrown into a purple sky bruised with smoke, soldiers dancing in celebration and chanting after the fleeing enemy.

'Chickamauga! Chickamauga! Chickamauga!'

The Army of the Cumberland – his Army of the Cumberland – had been redeemed.

Missionary Ridge – November 25th, 1863

Shire lent on the tall cannon wheel and pulled the stopper from his canteen. The water was warm on his dry lips but tasted good; a drink the other side of death. He swilled away the dry, salty gunpowder.

Mason brought back his rifle with a smile. 'I thought we'd lost you.'

Shire could only put a hand on Mason's shoulder. He could barely breathe, let alone talk. Troops were up all along the ridge. Woods' Division had swept south to meet with Sheridan's. And to the right Johnson's Division were up too. Missionary Ridge was back in the Union to stay. The noise was abating. What cannon fire there was belonged to the captured batteries, turned to fire after the retreating Rebels. Shire saw Harker come up, come and pat a cannon then pull his hand from the hot barrel. Opdycke wasn't far behind, trying to piece his regiments back together.

Shire didn't know what to do next with this new and surprising life. He took his hand from Mason's shoulder and looked at it. It was dirty and there was blood on his palm. But mostly it looked as if it belonged to someone else.

Ocks shouted over to him and Tuck, and Shire wearily walked to where Ocks was arguing with a young Confederate captain. A half dozen rebel soldiers sat dejectedly on the ground.

'Only food we got is in these packs,' said the captain. 'These men will need to eat, damn it.'

'Packs are to be confiscated,' snarled Ocks. 'Orders. If you wanted to hang on to them perhaps you should have put up a fight.'

The captain looked like he might start a new one.

'Shire, Tuck, collect up these packs. Guard these men until we can start them to the rear. And watch this captain.'

They did as they were asked. The packs were so light, Shire suspected they were empty. The captain glared at him. The man looked around his own age and anything but defeated. Why should Shire care how this man felt? The Union army had won the day this time. He stuck out a hand and the captain grudgingly handed over his pack. It was heavier than the others. Tuck moved away a few steps and started to go through them. 'Their hardtack is worse than ours,' he said, and spat out a mouthful. 'No wonder they got beat.'

Shire pulled open the captain's pack. Inside were tied up rolls of paper, and pencils worn down to no more than a thumb's length. He untied the paper and leafed through what appeared to be a diary, or at least an account, of this man's experiences and that of his army. Each piece was signed as Mint Julep. There was also an envelope addressed to none other than Fountain Carter in Franklin, the very man he had waited table on back in March. The captain was watching him with a sour face. Shire recalled the smart house out on the Columbia Pike, the well-tended back garden and, strangely, the apple cream pie he'd served.

Back over by the cannon a small man on a black charger came up onto the ridge, his eyes bright with victory and purpose. Shire recognized him as General Sheridan, and watched him begin to organize the men to get after the Rebels. 'C'mon, boys. We've bagged Tennessee. Time to get started on Georgia.'

Perhaps the day's fighting wasn't done. Shire turned his head in the direction that Sheridan waved his sword, and sure enough, there was Georgia, its ridges rippling away from them for mile upon mile until they faded into the dusk. This was just the first.

Men were slow to get into line and he realized how tired he was. His legs ached from the climb and the sweat was cold and wet under his clothes in the late November chill.

'Let me have those,' he said to Tuck, and collected up the packs.

'We'd best get in line.'

'I'll catch up.'

He waited until Tuck was gone before he stepped back to the Rebels. He set the packs down amongst them and handed the captain his. 'Nothing much we need in here.'

'I'm obliged to you.' The captain looked relieved.

'Is this the 20th Tennessee?'

'Some of it.'

'Are you Tod Carter?'

'Captain Tod Carter.'

'I met your father in the spring. Your brother Moscow, too. We helped them gin some cotton. You have a fine home. I hope you get back there.'

Shire offered his hand. Slightly reluctantly, Captain Tod Carter shook it.

Surely they'd done enough? But Sheridan evidently didn't think so and had them move out. Though, as they started down the farther side of the ridge, and into the early evening gloom, Shire couldn't see any corresponding movement north or south. It appeared only Sheridan was taking up the chase.

They stumbled on, the regiment advancing along a poor road. The occasional rifle shot came at them from down the slope. As the darkness began to settle they lost sight of the enemy.

Shire was lightheaded. He'd got barely any sleep last night and the climb had drained him; that and the shock of taking a bullet, even if his letters had caught it for him. He fell out of the column and took a knee. Tuck stopped with him while the regiment marched by. Officers followed behind to collect up the stragglers and chase them on. It was just Shire's luck that it was Opdycke himself, on foot again, that found them.

His words were kind, the men having done so much. 'C'mon, boys, you need to keep up with the regiment.'

Shire managed to stand, saw the recognition on the colonel's face by what frugal light there was left.

'He's winded, Colonel,' said Tuck. 'He'll be alright, but he got hit as we came over the crest. He was carrying our flag.'

The colonel's eyes widened. 'That was you, Private Shire?'

'Yes, sir. I got Barney away though. Before we came up.'

'I saw.' Opdycke nodded. 'I got another mount but it got shot halfway up, so now I'm making do. I watched the flag go over from below.'

Shire thought he heard a catch in the colonel's voice.

'And I'll never forget it.' He offered Shire his hand. 'Perhaps I'll be inclined to think better of the British after today.'

Shire wiped his hand on his jacket and they shook.

'I'm going to order you to the rear this time, since you declined my earlier offer. If you can't keep up, you're better off back on the ridge. Your friend can take you. I'll let Captain Bates know, but be quick. This isn't a night to be out alone on these slopes.' He strode away down the hill and left them in the dark.

Tuck took Shire by the arm and turned him back towards the ridge, now dotted with a line of fires below the early stars. Shire held his ground.

'What is it?' asked Tuck. A shot rang out somewhere below them.

'What the colonel said. About being alone on these slopes.'

'What of it?'

'I've earned it this time,' he said. 'The colonel knows I have.' He was half speaking to Tuck, half to himself.

'Whatever it is you're trying to say, you can tell me while we walk back up this hill. C'mon.'

'I'm not going that way. I'm heading out. Now's my chance, Tuck, don't you see? The Rebels will be falling away south. I could make it to Clara, do what I came to do. Once the dust settles and we're stuck back in the regiment, it'll be too late.'

'Have you lost your mind?' said Tuck in a harsh whisper. 'These hills are crawlin' with both sides. If the Rebels don't get you, you'll be taken for a deserter.'

'No I won't,' said Shire, choosing to only address the latter danger. 'If I come into Union lines it'll just be taken as the usual confusion after the fight. You know that. I've already found my way back during one battle. No one came off that ridge with Sheridan, not that I could see. If I go north and east, I could make it through before the gap closes. Come daylight I could be clear of both armies.'

'You're hurt. We don't know but that ball might have cracked a rib or somethin'.'

'I'll be fine. You go back – or catch up.'

'And what'll I tell the colonel now he's so fond of your English hide?' Tuck sounded angry. 'That I done lost you out here?' Then more quietly. 'How far d'you reckon it is? To where you need to get.'

Shire had looked at the map so many times he could see it in his head. 'Less than forty miles in a straight line. I know roughly where to go.' He'd asked among the few civilians left in Chattanooga. 'Four days, perhaps five if I move at night.'

'Well, alright then.' Tuck pushed out a loud breath. 'I'm coming with you.'

Shire felt a wave of love. That's what it was, pure love. 'I can't ask that of you. This is your army, your cause. You can't desert it.'

'Seems to me you've been takin' on my cause,' Tuck said gently. 'I'd like to take a hand in yours. Besides,' he went on, 'we won't be desertin'. Just takin' furloughs as is owed us. Once we're done, we'll come back, make our case to the colonel, or say we was captured or some such. It'll be alright.'

'Maybe. The army's in the habit of shooting deserters.'

'Now I'm only gonna come if you stop callin' us that,' Tuck admonished him. 'We'll be fine, as long as we're there and back quick enough. He saw you take that flag over, he knows you ain't no coward. That's gotta be worth somethin'.'

'I've no idea if Clara will be there anymore,' admitted Shire.

'Well then, let's set out and see,' said Tuck. 'That full moon'll be up later so we should use the dark while we can.'

'Thank you, Tuck,' said Shire. It was a hopelessly inadequate thing to say. They picked a direction as best they could, and headed away from the regiment.

PART IV

Chickamauga Station – November 1863

The inky black smoke from the departing train was lit from below by a host of lanterns and torches. It billowed upwards and disappeared into the cold, dark sky. The train station at Chickamauga was only a hundred yards away, but there was no point in Taylor trying to reach it with what was left of his regiment. There was a thick mass of soldiers in between, none of whom were showing any respect to their officers.

The scene of chaos that swam around him matched his own confused mind. Major Jasper, also mounted, sat next to him. Together they were a small island in a sea of lost men, all pushing in different directions, waves of panic rolling through them so that they pressed against Taylor's horse. He kicked and struck out but it made no difference.

'We can't go no further, Colonel,' shouted the major above the crowd. 'We'll lose what men we got.'

Taylor looked over his shoulder at his miserable collection of men; somewhere around thirty and a couple of captains – not even a company. What would the army do with him now?

When the Yankees had come over Missionary Ridge his command had simply dissolved. He'd seen some of his men lay down their rifles and put their hands up, some beaten to the floor, and others turn and run. Barely anyone had fought. He'd emptied his pistol, but there was no one to make a stand with. He'd no choice but to run too, lucky to find his horse where he'd tied it. Once mounted, he'd tried to rally his troops but it was useless. They'd raced past him and down the other side of the ridge, while the Yankees whooped and hollered and tossed their hats, too surprised at their own success to put together much of a chase.

There were squads waiting, ready to burn the bridges over

the streams once they crossed them after sunset. And now here they were, wondering, along with the rest of the army, what the hell to do next. He had no idea where his general was. It was all just a leaderless rabble looking to get away before the Yankees got themselves organized and came on.

'Let's lead them out this way, sir, towards the warehouses.'

Taylor nodded and let Jasper take the lead as they battled to turn their horses in the crowd. As they moved away from the station there was more room. He looked down on happy faces and realized the mood wasn't all despair. The soldiers, free of command, were helping themselves to whatever they could find in the storehouses. One sauntered by with a ham swinging from his bayonet, a sack of crackers under his arm. Another took a pull from a jug of molasses so that it dribbled thickly from his beard.

His own men looked on. 'Where the hell did all this food come from?' he heard one say. 'Why, we ain't been but three miles away for the last two months. There's more victuals here than at a county fair!'

He was right. Through open warehouse doors Taylor could see men slitting sacks and breaking open boxes. 'Shouldn't we stop them?' he half-heartedly asked a nearby officer. The man had no hat; Taylor couldn't make out his rank.

'Who with? I don't think they're of a mind to listen just now. Besides, orders are to burn it. We've not got the wagons or the room on the trains. Might as well let the men carry off what they can.'

Two men wrestled over a bag of flour which exploded to ghost them both as well as their neighbors. There was a flurry of curses.

'Were you on the ridge?' Taylor asked the officer.

'Towards the left. Close to Bragg's headquarters. They swept us off there like we was dried wheat. Maybe if this food had made it up there these last few weeks, the boys might've had some fight in 'em.'

Taylor sat quietly. Whatever damage had been done to his reputation was likely to be shared by most of the army; they'd all suffered the same fate. He watched a detail, which had kept some

414

discipline, set dry wood against one of the warehouses. A team of six artillery horses, in harness but with no cannon to pull, were led past by two bewildered gunners.

'Colonel?' It was one of Taylor's captains. 'Can the boys get some of the stores? Seems everyone else is... Sir?'

What was he supposed to do? There was one soldier stood laughing on a barrel. He held a stack of army kepi hats and was skimming them out over the crowd, one at a time. Taylor started to laugh too. It was all gone to hell.

Jasper answered the captain for him. 'Alright. But only half the men. Second half can go when they return.'

The captain split the men into two groups and hurried one set off to the stores. The rest looked on anxiously.

'Do you know what the plan is?' Jasper asked the officer.

'I've seen Bragg and Breckenridge about, but I ain't got no orders yet. I heard Cleburne held the right most of the day, so perhaps there's some sort of rear guard. That might allow us to get away south, maybe to Ringgold, or halfway to Atlanta, I don't know. I'm hoping more of my men will come in. I lost more in the skedaddle than on the ridge.'

Taylor's mind found its way to Comrie. If the army retreated south – which it must – the counties to the east of Chattanooga, including Bradley and Polk would fall to the Union. The Yankees would want to secure the rail line through Cleveland and there was no one to stop them. They'd be almost certain to pay a Confederate colonel's home a visit. Comrie would be no more than a smoky ruin in a matter of days. His name would be too, if Clara was still there and Shire contrived to get to her; though how the boy could get away from his own army was hard to see. Perhaps there was still time? There was nothing he could do here: the army would take weeks to right itself.

A train whistled loudly behind them as it pulled in to replace the one that had left. His men returned from the warehouse, laden with food, smiles bright in the torchlight. The second batch raced past them. Taylor wished the officer good luck and nudged Jasper's horse a few steps away.

'Major, I'm going to give you command of the regiment.'

'Are you going to find some orders, sir?'

'No. You can do that.'

The major's face contracted.

'Here's what I figure,' said Taylor. 'We got but thirty men. If we're lucky, maybe you can collect another twenty out of this fix, but any which way you look at it, there's no regiment. The army is gonna have to re-organize, and the Hiwassee will be rolled up into some other unit for sure. If I can get over to Polk, I reckon I can bring some more boys in before the Union gets to 'em. There are a few farms in the hills where they think they can ride out the war untouched, but I know where they are. Mules there too, I'll bet. I'll take four men with me and Captain Gibbs.'

'But, sir, we oughta check with the general. Otherwise it's... well it's desertion, sir. I mean that's how it might be seen.'

'Look around you, Major. It's a goddam mess. What you call desertion, I call initiative. The general will be happy if I bring in twenty men to replace some of the ones lost. That way we might have the numbers so some other regiment can roll into us. Then we can keep our positions.'

'You'll be close to Comrie, sir.' The major wasn't leaving much unsaid.

'Happen I will,' said Taylor. 'Won't hurt to make sure my wife is safe and sound. Once we've got the recruits we'll go due south in the hills and find the army wherever it pitches up. Two weeks. You keep the boys together until then.'

'What will I tell the general?' The major slumped wearily in his saddle.

'Captain Gibbs,' called Taylor, ignoring him, 'I want you and your four fittest men.' He led them over to where the two gunners were pondering what to do with their team of horses – and relieved them of the problem.

Hamilton County – November 1863

Shire woke slowly to the pleasant aroma of smoked meat, but when he opened his eyes the hooks on the wooden beams held no hams, only their salty memory. He'd slept deeply. There were the slippery edges of a dream. He'd been a schoolboy and his father was the teacher. He'd been asked to shake the start of day hand bell but it wouldn't ring.

It was unusual to wake in his own time. He was used to the insistence of a bugle or a shouting sergeant. He stared up at the beam and recalled finding the empty farm in the night. Tuck had chosen the smokehouse over the home. Light came in through a wide open door. Not fresh morning light, but the heavy, worn light of late in the day. Where was Tuck?

The weight of desertion fell on him. Not desertion. They'd go back; say that they'd been captured but had escaped. It would be alright. After Opdycke left them, they'd returned up the ridge and into the Union lines. Tuck had reasoned that it was safer than being in front of them, and that the rear of the army would have fewer pickets. It was good to have Tuck along. The rest of the night was a jumbled memory of hillside fires, injured men and ambulances. They'd moved north along the west side of Missionary Ridge until they reached its scrag-end, where it decayed into small hills and knolls. Sherman's dead littered the ground. They had no light but hurried through the horror as best they could. When there were others nearby, they pretended that they were searching for fallen comrades. Then, quite suddenly, they were beyond the army. They'd struck west and marched as long as they could through the night.

From somewhere nearby came the rhythm of a saw; a small one from its pitch. He stood up and tried to stretch, but instantly his bruised chest complained. He should look at it. Only he wanted to see what Tuck was up to. He put his head outside. The noise came from another small building across the yard that might have been the springhouse. Shire's wariness returned. Their capture story wouldn't play so well if a Union cavalry patrol found them. He went back for his rifle then hurried across the yard. The door was wide open.

'Afternoon,' said Tuck.

The sawing stopped but Tuck wasn't holding anything. Next to him was an old, grey-haired, white man who blew sawdust from a small piece of wood, then closed one eye and looked down its length. There was an assortment of pieces laid out neatly on a bench, some connected to what looked like small windmill sails. Longer slats were laid on the floor in a circle, like an open flower, perhaps to be assembled into a barrel.

'This here's my English friend I told you about,' said Tuck.

The old man glanced at Shire. 'Looks much the same as yourself, only a mite lower. You English usually sleep all day?'

'The army gets you out of the habit of regular sleep.' He looked over the wooden components and tried to fathom what was being fashioned.

'There's fresh water.' The old man nodded to a pail and a wooden ladle. 'I can warm you up some rabbit in a while. Not much though.'

Tuck smiled at Shire's puzzlement. 'You won't guess.'

'Some sort of pump?'

'A pump,' said the old man. 'Now I could make a pump. Some purpose to a pump.' He picked up a file and started to smooth the sawn end of the wood. 'But that's not my line. I prefer to think of myself as an artist rather than a practical man.'

'It's a whirligig,' said Tuck, smiling. 'I've seen one or two in my time, at fairs in Kentucky. Never seen one being built though.'

'I used to wander Kentucky, too,' said the old man. 'In the south mostly. Allen County, and Monroe.'

'Too far south for me,' said Tuck.

To assuage Shire's puzzlement, the old man showed him a sketch in charcoal. It was a windmill of sorts.

'What do you plan to do with it?'

'What to do with it. People always ask what to do with it. What does it do? What's it for?'

Shire took a long drink from the ladle and felt the better for it. 'I'm sorry.'

'It's alright, son. I guess you have to see the whole article to 'preciate it.' He laid the finished piece on the bench. 'But you boys can help me. You've been across the state and the country so your friend tells me. I've been holed up a while, ever since I found this place empty and decided it was time to start over.'

Tuck came and stood closer, so they were either side of him and could look at all the pieces. The old man picked up a wooden cog. 'Trouble is, I'm not so sure how best to put it back together. There's lots of ways I can do it. Some cogs here, some sails there. I've some bells from the old one to attach an' make it sing. Should I build it just the same as last time, or do you think folks might expect something different? Something new.'

'Did people not like the old one?' asked Shire.

'Most did. Some didn't... I'd make two smaller ones if I thought it would help.'

'I think one's best,' said Tuck. 'One big one.'

'And what about color. I don't want to paint it to offend no one.'

'It's hard to go through life and not upset anyone,' said Shire. 'I used to try... Now I'm told to shoot at people. Seems to me your whirligig can't hurt anyone.'

'It's all still red, white and blue out there,' said Tuck. 'Keep it plain, is my advice. Once you start putting stars or stripes on there, people start countin' them and get all riled if you don't have the right number in the right place. Keep it plain.'

'Huh... Plain. Don't sound right to someone in the entertainment business.'

'Well,' said Shire. 'You have all these fine pieces, so you'll have to build something.'

The old man nodded and picked up his saw.

'Let me see your map,' said Tuck. Shire tried to reach into his jacket but winced at the pain. 'Give me a hand here.'

With Tuck's help, Shire eased off his jacket then lifted his shirt. There was a purple bruise bigger than his hand surrounding an even darker center. It was all sore to the touch but the skin wasn't broken.

'You could do with bathing that,' said Tuck.

'It's all on the outside, I think.' Shire pulled the roll from his jacket. 'The map's not much use this close.' He carefully untied the leather cord from the roll, trying not to make the damage worse from the bullet as he separated the map from the letters and the license. A flattened lead minie ball dropped to the floor.

'Hah,' laughed Tuck, picking it up. 'That's a keeper.' He handed it to Shire.

Shire held it suspiciously, like it might still kill him, and passed the map to Tuck.

'We can follow the rail line towards Cleveland,' said Shire. 'We crossed to the north side of it last night where it runs through a tunnel under Missionary Ridge. Cleveland is Bradley County. After that we're in Polk. I have a vague idea where Clara is, but we'll have to ask.'

'Ask!' said Tuck, unfolding the map. 'That'll be interestin'. Whichever side they support they're liable to rat on us. And we need to keep a distance from any rail line. It'll be patrolled for... Well if that don't beat all... Looky here. That bullet went clean through Chattanooga. Right where you was hit. I wish we were in camp. I could sell this map as a genuine, first-class miracle. Makes you consider that providence might have an eye on you.' He held up the map.

But Shire hadn't heard any of it. He was staring down at the marriage license, where the bullet had passed cleanly through his father's signature.

*

420

Before they left, Shire showed the map to the Whirligig Man and asked if he knew Comrie. He said he knew of it but not precisely where it was. He told them to avoid Cleveland; it was usually full of soldiers and he had no time for the place. Instead he gave them directions to a farmhouse round to the southeast of the town. The Widow Spriggs lived there alone, he said. She would be able to tell them the way. They could trust her. 'Say the Whirligig Man sent you.'

In return for the rabbit stew, and while Tuck kept watch, Shire helped to file smooth some more of the pieces. They weren't going to move on until after dark anyway. It felt good, for once, to help with something that had nothing to do with the war.

When the last of the light was almost gone, they had no excuse to stay any longer. Two shots snapped far away out in the night with long, tailing echoes in the cold air. The old man produced a wooden soldier and handed it to Shire. 'He got broken. I fixed him, but I'm thinking maybe the new whirligig don't need a gun on top.'

Shire held it up. He could feel the join where the torso had been glued back together. 'I'll look after it.' He put it in his pack and shouldered his rifle. Tuck swung open the yard gate and they marched on into the darkness.

Comrie – November 1863

The chandelier hung low and lonely in the cold parlor, unused since the wedding a year before. Had Clara determined, for some strange reason, to waste her dwindling oil to light it, there would be little to illuminate. The large mirrors that used to gather and re-use the light had gone on ahead; as had the family portraits they'd helped to brighten. Only paler squares and rectangles on the blue, floral wallpaper showed where they had once hung. No wall clock, no vase, no chaise longue. The square grand piano, squat and defiant, remained, kept company by a small table and two chairs left out of necessity.

She walked to the window. The floor was loud without the carpets. Down below the portico, on the circle of shingle, Raht had four more wagons loading. They would be the last. One had the Comrie name on the side, but the others he had ordered in to get this done quickly. He'd called in last week and suggested it was time to hide the valuables; that if the dam was going to burst, it might be soon. The last room was almost attended to. What was left would have to take its chances with the house itself.

Clara pulled a chair to the piano, thinking to play, but the first notes sent a melancholy echo about the house. She stopped and consulted her mood. Why did she feel an obligation to save any of this? The possessions were Taylor's and she owed him little care. He'd not even returned in the last months, when the army was static and barely two days' ride away. Not that she'd wished him to come. She'd dreaded it.

Earlier, the nursery had been emptied of sentiment and hope, neither of them really hers. She'd watched painlessly as the rocking bench – half-crib, half-seat – was carried down the stairs. This house, like her marriage, had seen little of love. Would it be so sad for her if it were burnt away to a memory? But here she still was. It couldn't be long until the Yankees came, not after today's news.

This morning the ringing had invaded her dream and steered it to the church in Ridgmont. When she'd come fully awake a distant bell persisted. It was somehow insistent – wrong. It was Thursday and besides, too early for a church summons. The rhythm was different. The church had only one bell, but normally it chimed a pair of notes close together. Today there was a pause, as if the second note struggled to keep pace. Mitilde had arrived. 'It's the warning bell,' she'd said. 'Someone's gotta ride to church.'

Clara had gone herself, taking George now he was better, but she didn't push him. Others hurried there too, some walking arm in arm, fearful of the news. Rumor had seeped out of the church and people were talking of another great battle at Chattanooga, but this time the South had been defeated and was in disarray. Inside, the reverend told all he knew: that a rider had come up from Cleveland in the night, that the Union Army had broken out, that the Confederate Army had been pushed south and Tennessee was lost.

She closed the lid over the piano keys and felt a tug of fear, not just for herself and the people here, but for the place. She needed it to survive. Otherwise truly everything would have been lost. Was that her answer? That Comrie was the only thing that she had left.

There was a tap, tap, on the open drawing room door. It was Raht, sweating despite the month. 'I'm sorry, Clara, if you are ready we can take the piano.'

'Of course. And it's me that should be sorry, doing nothing to help.'

'It's almost done. It will be dark before we get to the Halfway, especially with so many wagons coming the other way.' He looked downcast. 'So many have left Ducktown. I'm afraid it won't stay a secret where your possessions are going. There are too many drivers and that McGhee at the ferry, he has a big mouth.'

424

'It can't be helped. Are there any mines working?'

'Only one. I have so few miners. Most are in the army or have fled. There is one captain left running a single team. He guards the mines when I'm not there. We've been supplying the new copper rolling mill in town, but no doubt that will cease now. It appears we have built it for the Union... You should come with us. I must insist. Mr Trenholm will never forgive me if I leave you here. Our home is your home. It will be safer for you.'

It appeared the sensible thing to do, to run and hide in the hills. But it felt as though it would defer something already overdue; and there would have to come another day, when she crept back out into the world. If Comrie's story was to end soon, she wanted to witness it, not to have been some imposter who arrived well after the beginning and left before the end.

'Why is your mine captain on guard if it's so safe?'

'We have a lot of smelted copper hidden in the mines, waiting out the war. Your piano and other treasures will be down there too. You are right, the hills are not the safest place, but they are safer than here. Anywhere is safer than here. Union sympathizers will be quick to point to a Confederate colonel's house.'

'You've stayed. You had a choice to go and you stayed.'

'What choice? To walk away from the mines and everything I have worked for? This was not a choice. And if I hadn't hired a substitute I'd likely be dead like he is, poor soul.' Raht dropped his voice. 'But when the Union is here again, then I might go, at least to get my family away. You could come with us. Or I can take you through the hills to Charleston and to George?'

Clara put her hand on his arm. 'Come, Julius, let's get the piano loaded. Or you'll never get to the Halfway.'

She would stay, and wait for news of the two men she'd lost.

Once the convoy of wagons had wound its way down the drive and into the woods, she found Mitilde and took her out to the portico. Clara had the brown paper parcel given to her by Trenholm. She took out the flag. It was a good size.

425

'Here,' she said, 'help me wrap this around a pillar.'

'You sure, miss? Yankees ain't here yet.'

'It'll be too late if they find us without it.' She recalled the Union flag she'd watched lowered in Cleveland when the war started. 'I expect there are a few old flags being looked out about now.'

Hamilton County – November 1863

Colonel Opdycke waited in the flickering camp light for his tent to be erected. Normally he'd be happy to share the men's hardship – their own tents were yet to catch up – but he was bone tired, having chased Rebels for two full days after the battle with scant time for sleep. And there was more work to do. New orders had arrived. They were to be ready to start for Knoxville by seven in the morning. He would need to consider the order of march, consult with Harker, gather his regimental commanders. Yet he wanted nothing more than to lie down and sleep.

Mallets struck the pegs with practiced ease and the detail tightened the guy ropes. From out of the dark his cot appeared and was carried inside. A chair and a desk followed. A blooming lamp silhouetted insects on the canvas. Around him campfires were nursed into life, larger logs pulled in to surround the fires. Tripods went up, pots were filled and hung up to boil. There was the familiar wedded aroma of coffee and wood smoke. Opdycke spared a smile and admitted this was a part of army life he enjoyed.

There was no threat tonight; they had pulled back towards Chattanooga. Other divisions had finally taken the lead. Despite their losses, the boys were in good spirits: they'd whipped the Rebels and the shame of Chickamauga was wiped away. It had never been down to them in the first place.

More could have been achieved. In the darkness after the battle, Opdycke had seen at first-hand a furious Sheridan beat away one of Granger's incompetent staff officers. Only his division had got after the enemy that night. Unsupported, they'd lost more men in the chase than in the charge itself. The Rebels had escaped away south, to recover and fight another day. Now Sheridan was to take the division northeast instead, to save

General Burnside and trap Longstreet. Missionary Ridge had been just one victory; the war went on.

Once the tent was ready, he carried in his own saddle, brushing off the soldier that tried to help him. Harker had gifted him a staff lieutenant, Kinsman, to help him run the demi-brigade. He followed Opdycke in and began to lay out papers on the desk. Opdycke had seen the butcher's bill from Missionary Ridge yesterday when the regimental commanders had sent in their numbers. It had been lighter than he'd expected. Kinsman presented him with a revised list. He looked at the names of officers killed or wounded, but only for the 125th did he scan names from the ranks. Private Stanton – Shire – was still listed as missing. He'd reminded Captain Bates this morning that he'd sent the lightly wounded Englishman and his friend to the rear.

'I'll check again,' Bates had said, 'but there's no word of them back at Chattanooga. Not in camp and not on the hospital lists. They may yet turn up. More likely they were taken or killed getting back to the ridge.'

Opdycke thought that unlikely: any organized Confederates had been ahead of them that night. And he didn't want to believe he'd unwittingly caused their loss.

'Would you like some coffee, Colonel?'

'Thank you, yes.'

Kinsman stepped outside and Opdycke sat on his cot. He fought the urge to lie down. He recalled the private letter from Colonel Moore that he'd declined to read in Chattanooga. That seemed an age ago. If Shire was lost then it might hold a name. It was at least reasonable to read it. He retrieved it from one of his saddlebags and opened it.

It was addressed from a place called Comrie, Polk County, as long ago as June '61. It was in the major's hand, being a copy, but the tone was that of a young lady. It was signed simply *Clara*, but the notepaper had a crest and the name Ridgmont. The content was both warm and sad at the same time.

While your letters are a comfort to me I feel it can no longer be right for us to write. Taylor would not understand, and I will have no secrets from him.

Despite the implied intimacy, Opdycke read on.

Our friendship was that of children, and I must look to my new life and future marriage here. I therefore ask you, in sadness, to no longer write, but hold me only in your memory as I will you.

A duke's daughter come to Tennessee to marry, but with some earlier unlikely attachment to a young schoolmaster. He determined to learn all there was to know, annoyed that he'd put it off before. His coffee arrived, and he was about to ask Lieutenant Kinsman to send for Sergeant Ocks when he found he'd no need to.

'There's Sergeant Ocks asking to see you, Colonel. From the 125th. Should I send him away?'

'No,' said Opdycke. 'I'll see him. Let the regimental commanders know to attend me at nine o'clock.'

Kinsman opened the tent flap and waved Ocks inside before leaving himself. Ocks stood stiffly to attention, his gaze aimed somewhere above the colonel's head. The British certainly knew how to stand up straight. He'd seen flagpoles more at ease. He stayed comfortably on his cot with his coffee and put the letter to one side.

'Sergeant Ocks. This is a little out of channels, isn't it? Does Captain Bates know you're here?'

'No, Colonel. It's an unusual matter, sir.'

Opdycke sipped his coffee and wondered how to play this. 'Well, I've a lot to do, so you'd better get straight to it. And please, stand easy. We're not on parade.'

Ocks' shoulders dropped a quarter inch. 'It's about Private Shire, sir. And Private Tuck. They've absconded.'

Opdycke kept his face neutral. 'Absconded? I don't think that's the military term. Do you mean deserted?'

'Yes, sir. Deserted, sir.'

'Captain Bates has them listed as missing. Why would you know better?'

429

'I know their business, sir. Shire's at least. He had an errand to complete, not far away. Someone he knew back in England. I know where they've gone.'

'And you're suggesting I send a squad to find them? Bring them back and shoot them?'

'Up to you if you want to shoot them, sir. But I'd like to go and fetch them myself.'

It was a presumption that he would even consider it. 'It's not a good time for furloughs, Sergeant. And you've not yet told me what this concerns. Are you connected to this errand?'

'I just thought you'd want them brought back in. We've not so many men we can spare them.'

'Assuming I would spare them.' Something about Ocks' attitude irked him. He was so sure of himself. 'I know these boys. Good soldiers, both of them. Why would they desert after a victory? You'll have to do better.'

'There's a lady's honor involved, sir. That's as much as I know.'

Opdycke stood up and moved to his desk. 'The lady being a Lady, in fact. The Lady Clara Ridgmont.'

Ocks lost his rigidity and looked at the colonel.

'Perhaps your British secrets aren't quite as well kept as you think. Her father is a Confederate supporter in the House of Lords.' He moved closer to Ocks. 'Did you know that? Of course you did. And she had come here to marry. No doubt someone of standing. Who?'

Ocks said nothing.

'Come, Sergeant. Don't waste my time,' Opdycke's tiredness was getting the better of him. 'I know this Lady lives in Polk County. Somewhere called Comrie. I could find out easily enough. Please spare me the effort.'

'She's married already. To Colonel Taylor Spencer-Ridgmont, a cousin of hers. You've met him, sir, in a manner of speaking.' A hint of a smile infected Ocks' face. 'If I'm not mistaken, his brigade charged us when we were by the farmhouse at Chickamauga.'

It was Opdycke's turn to be surprised. Shire's words came back to him, *They're firing at me. It's my fault.* 'That madman? Why?'

'He'd rather Shire was dead, that's why. The boy has something he wants to tell his wife.'

'What could be so important that he'd waste so many men?'

Ocks offered a modest shrug. 'His reputation. Perhaps his standing with the duke. If you let me go, I can find out.'

Ocks wasn't sharing everything. That much was obvious. 'And who do you serve in this tangle, Sergeant Ocks? The boy joined us without you and he's run off without you. It doesn't appear that you are close?'

'I'm loyal to myself mostly. But I'm a soldier before anything else, and I'm in your bloody army and your bloody regiment. So that's my loyalty. Otherwise I could have left already.'

Ocks' insubordinate tone tightened Opdycke's mouth. He was loath to let the man have his way. A wagon groaned and squeaked by outside the tent, so near that Opdycke could hear the mules breathing. What if he denied the request? He might never come to understand all this. He didn't trust Ocks, but the boy, Shire, had carried the regiment's flag over the ridge; hardly the action of someone who planned to desert.

'Very well, Sergeant,' he said. 'I'll let you go and trust you to bring them back. Then I'll decide what's to be done with them. I imagine you want some papers from me?'

'That would help, sir.'

'But mark me, Sergeant. If you're playing me, or if you "abscond" as well, it'll be you in front of a firing squad.'

'Very good, sir,' said Ocks. 'Thank you.' He made to leave, but then turned. 'One more thing, sir. I'll be needing a horse.'

The Copper Road – November 1863

Before they left Chickamauga Station, Taylor changed the four men Captain Gibbs had chosen: they were all from Polk County and they wouldn't do for the work he had in mind. Captain Gibbs wasn't from Polk or McMinn, but from Monroe. The replacements he picked were from middle or western Tennessee and had arrived in the regiment by happenstance. Thin and bedraggled, they could barely muster a full set of teeth between them, but they were hard men, having seen all a war brought on. They looked surprised and pleased to find themselves mounted, albeit on artillery horses, and with what tack they'd been able to find amongst the rout. The last man pulled the one spare horse.

Taylor led them in a shallow curve to the east, staying inside Georgia. So when, after a day and a half of hard riding, they came to Polk County, they were already into the hills close to Conasauga. From there he headed north, took his band by little-used paths and coves. It was unlikely the Union Army would venture far into this country, but there was no sense in taking chances.

He heard the racing Ocoee well before he saw it and emerged just where he'd planned to, down from the Halfway House an hour before sunset. He knew a good crossing where the water sped over shallows above a set of rapids. It was easy enough in the summer, but he was lucky to find it passable this late in the year. The horses stumbled and slipped on the stones, unsteadied by the fast water that reached for the soldiers' boots.

Taylor scrambled out the other side and up onto the Copper Road in the gloom. Half the trees were bare, lending the familiar valley an untidy look. They swayed in a brisk wind that chased down the river. He didn't expect to meet anyone this late in the day, but they went west with rifles loaded all the same. They were unlikely to hear anyone coming above the noise of the river. They would have missed the boy altogether had he not got up atop his boulder in the river and waved his arms above his head. Taylor called a halt as the boy jumped barefoot from rock to rock, rod in hand, until he pitched up on the road in front of them, hatless and smiling.

'Howdy,' he said.

Taylor smiled back. 'A little late in the day for fishing, ain't it?' He dismounted and the men followed suit.

'Oh, I bin here all day. Well, most of it leastways. Daddy said fishin' was all I was fit fer and he was too tired to beat me. He had me fixin' up the raft, him being at the whiskey last night, and I dang near broke my thumb knockin' in a tack... See.' The boy thrust a slightly bloodied thumb close to Taylor's face.

'So you did,' said Taylor, pushing the hand away.

'How old you, boy?' asked Gibbs.

'Fourteen, I think. Daddy says he don't know for sure.'

'Anyone else on the road?' Taylor tipped back his hat.

'Naw. You the first I seen all day. Ain't seen a copper wagon in more 'an a week and most folks have left Ducktown. Daddy says they's shuttin' up the mines on account of the war. So we ain't gettin' reg'lar tolls no more.'

Taylor put a hand on the boy's shoulder. 'You're the McGhee boy, ain't you? Your Daddy runs the ferry?'

The boy's smile widened further. 'How d'you know that? I don't know you.'

'Oh... I know your Daddy. I bet business is hard on him?'

'Sure is. *Road's not what is was*, he always says. *But it's all I got*. It's gonna be my ferry when he's dead. My Ma's dead long back.'

'Colonel,' said Gibbs, 'he's a mite young and on the simple side for us, don't you think?'

'Don't worry. We ain't started on the recruitin' yet. Did you catch anything today, boy?'

'Only what I ate.' He nodded at the remains of a small fire off the road. 'Nothin' worth takin' home. Daddy said I need a big fish before I show my face ag'in. I'm cold though.' His smile wavered. 'But I got me a good rod. See.' He stood to attention, coat open, holding his long stick as if it was a musket. The soldiers laughed and his smile returned, bigger than ever.

Inside the coat Taylor saw a dirty shirt, badly tucked into trousers designed for an older and better-fed man, a belt the only defense against gravity.

'What's that say on your belt-buckle?'

The boy twisted the buckle and looked at it. 'It says, U... S... Daddy says that stands for the United States.'

'Don't you think that's a little disloyal, this being a Confederate State we're in?' Taylor took a rifle from one of the soldiers. 'Give me a percussion cap,' he said, extending his hand.

'What's disloyal mean? It's the only one I got. Traded it for a crossin' when Daddy was asleep. You won't tell on me, will you?'

'I won't tell,' said Taylor. 'Could you jump up on that rock there for me. The big one backing onto the river.'

'Sure.' The boy scrambled up with his rod. 'You can't fish much from here, though. Better out in the river.'

'Now turn and face me. And stand to attention again, like you did before. That's good.' Taylor raised the gun and took a slow bead on the boy's chest.

'Colonel?' said Gibbs

'Just a moment, Captain,' said Taylor with one eye closed.

The boy was still smiling. 'Sir, can I ask you somethin', sir?'

'Quiet now, boy.'

'Yes, sir.'

The bullet caught him square on the sternum, so he didn't spin either way. He simply fell back off the rock and out of sight into the river. The crack of the rifle chased off down the valley with the wind to die under the sound of the water.

'Sir,' said Gibbs, taking off his hat and hanging his head. 'Have you done much recruiting?'

'I've got some business before we start on that. His daddy lives a quarter-mile down this road. He may have heard that shot, and he's a mean old bird. So be ready.'

He led them at a canter until the ferry house came in sight this side of Greasy Creek. A leashed dog, tied to a post in front of the house, started to bark. McGhee stumbled outside, a bottle in one hand. He quietened the dog with a swipe of his hat. Evidently, he'd not heard the shot.

He may just have heard the next one sent right at him. He doubled up as it tore through his gut. 'Your boy's dead in the river, McGhee,' said Taylor. 'And I'm requisitioning this here ferry.'

November – Comrie 1863

It was only a few steps, but Clara hurried through the cold and breezy air to the kitchen. Waiting in the empty house for the Union to arrive had her on edge. She needed something to do.

She let herself into the warm. Mitilde and Hany were sat at the table. All was ordered and clean: black spoons, ladles and knives hung on the wall; skillets, pots and pans were suspended above her head. Though not yet mid-morning there was the sweet smell of a pie. This was a work space, its purpose and duties mostly set within the day. Not like the house, which was tuned to longer arcs of time: to business, to marriage, to war.

'What are you doing?' asked Clara.

'Just some prep'ration,' said Mitilde.

They were making garlands, tying sprigs of fir and cuts of holly onto weaved stems of ivy. She thought it unlikely there would be a Christmas at Comrie, but at least they were keeping busy.

'May I help?'

Hany made some room and slid some greenery Clara's way. There were two children in the corner, quiet since Clara came in. She smiled at them.

'You want the children someplace else, miss?' asked Hany.

As a rule, they were not allowed in the kitchen unless working. 'No, let them stay. It's cold out.' She wondered if she should stay herself. She sensed that she'd altered the mood. It had been the same whenever she spoke with them these last two days. There was no animosity, no disrespect; but it was as if they were all waiting on the end of this world, with hardly any view of the one that would replace it. Surely the house would burn, but she had no idea what would become of the slaves, whether they'd be taken away or left here.

She'd resolved to leave them and return to her own brooding, when there was the clatter of horses in the yard. Hany looked out the window and took a step backwards. 'It's Master Taylor,' she said, and reached for Mitilde.

Clara looked out herself and saw Taylor dismount. He had five soldiers with him. 'Stay in here.' Her voice sounded shrill. 'Get some food ready.'

Outside, the wind blew her hair across her face. She pulled it away to see Taylor hand his reins to Moses.

He turned to her. 'Why's that grave still out front?'

He looked ten years older. 'Come into the house. We'll get you and your men something to eat.' She started to lead the way.

Taylor gripped her shoulder and spun her around. His blond hair was tangled, his beard untidily climbing his jaw. 'I asked you a question.'

Clara searched his face for a hint of the man she'd once imagined; there was so much hate there. 'The slaves wouldn't do it. They were afraid. It didn't feel like the most important thing.'

'It was the *only* thing I asked you to do. That and to leave.'

'Come inside.'

'Where's my mother?'

'What?'

'Her grave. Where's she buried?'

'At the top of Long Bank,' she said gently. 'In under the trees. I thought we'd move Will there in the spring, perhaps build a low wall.'

'We'll move him now. How many slaves are here?'

'Come inside. You're tired. The ground's half-frozen and the Union Army might arrive any time.'

'Captain! Find what slaves you can. In their cabins most likely as there don't seem any work going on. Bring the strongest four round front with some spades and a rope.' He squeezed her arm. 'How many?'

She tried to pull away. 'Thirty-four, and the children. You're hurting me. Your army took the rest. I haven't lost any if that's what you mean.'

'You want us to take down the flag out front, Colonel?'

'No,' said Taylor. 'It don't matter much. Might give us an edge if any Yankees show up.' He let her go and marched into the house.

She rubbed her arm and, despite herself, followed him through the echoing house to the hunting room. Unlike other rooms, she'd left it mostly as it was: a bison and a mountain lion watching from the walls; the decanters untouched since Taylor's last visit, one filled a pale yellow, one a ruby brown; a cigar box open on the table. Taylor tossed aside his hat, poured himself a whiskey and sat down in the leather chair. He drank as if it was water.

He was in the same uniform he'd worn for their wedding, less the sash. But the frockcoat was a darker, stained grey. The braid was worn at the cuffs and had lost its gold sheen; buttons were missing from their ranks. She could have forgiven all that. It was the man that was tarnished beyond repair.

'What's the matter? Don't I look good enough for you? Only I couldn't get to the haberdashers lately, what with the battles an' all. At least I got all my parts.' He held up his arms in display. 'Am I not the man you married?'

'I've found out a few things about the man I married,' Clara tried to keep her voice even, but some bitterness slipped out.

Taylor poured more whiskey. 'Where've you hidden everything?'

'The mines. Julius helped move it all.'

'You sure he didn't head north with it? Still, not the worst place. Though I doubt it'll ever come back here. Do you think we should burn the old place ourselves or leave it for the Yankees to play with? You know, it's funny, you'd think I'd be more attached to it.' He looked as if he was wondering on it. 'Trenholm's got my money in enough places that we'll be just fine whenever the war ends.' He stared at Clara. 'We could build somewhere new, bigger and better, my way instead of Father's. What do you think?'

'What are you doing here?'

Taylor stood and collected a fiddle that lay on a high shelf. 'This was Will's,' he said. 'I tried to play it once, a few months after he died. That was the only time my mother ever struck me. Should we bury it with him, d'you think?'

'I know about the child.' Clara watched him carefully, but his face was flat, unreadable.

He put the fiddle back, then lifted the lid on an old travelling trunk. 'And what child would that be?'

'There's no use denying it.'

'I don't think I denied anything.' He was digging through the trunk.

'I dragged it out of Hany. She had to tell me.'

'Did she now?'

Clara stayed silent. What more could she say?

Taylor lifted out something wrapped in an old brown cloth. 'You're not hoping for an apology are you? Was I to let a little pickaninny stand in the way of true love? Why, Daddy used to say how some of his friends could have filled a church pew with their black babies. Profitable too. At least I didn't sell her across the state. I wanted to keep our Hany sweet, in case I wanted some more.'

Clara had to put a hand to her mouth. 'When the Union Army comes, she'll be free of you, and so will I.'

'You appear to be mistakin' this for a social visit.'

There were two graves to dig: one to give up a casket, and one to receive it. Captain Gibbs had gathered most of the slaves into the yard, but Clara saw a few were missing, including Hany. Taylor sent one soldier to oversee the two digging the new grave next to his mother, and Gibbs to watch over the four digging up William. He climbed up onto the cold porch to join Clara, still carrying whatever it was he'd taken from the trunk. She kept her distance, wondering if this was all he'd come for: to make sure the grave was moved before Comrie was lost. Having fretted at the arrival of the Union Army, now she prayed they would come soon.

The slaves removed William's headstone first and struck the top of the casket after only a short while. But as it had been set slanted and facing west, it took most of the morning to get right under it. Clara followed Taylor down the steps when they were nearly ready to lift it out. The slaves found it hard to get the ropes underneath. In the end Gibbs had to kick one to climb down and help lift it up. There was an audible settling inside as the casket came level. The polished wood was barely faded once it was wiped down; but they wouldn't risk the brass handles, so the slaves lifted the box to their shoulders to carry Will away.

'Colonel,' said Gibbs. He pointed to the northwest. It was still windy and cold and the clouds raced over. Below them, more than a dozen trails of smoke angled up out of the Tennessee Valley. 'I guess that's the Yankees about their business. Coming this way.'

'We'll be done in under an hour. Get everyone into the yard.'

'You want us to fill in this hole?'

'No. Maybe the Yankees'll find a use for it.'

The new grave was ready for Will, though not so deep as his old one on account of some roots that there wasn't enough time to break up. Clara crossed her shawl and watched them lower him in. The slaves stood back, hands held before them, and the soldier took off his hat.

'What you waitin' on?' barked Taylor. 'He's had all the prayers he's gonna get. Fill it in and set that stone.'

With more hands it was quickly done. Taylor sent everyone but Clara back up the hill. The wind washed through the trees. She searched for some tenderness or understanding for him, tried to pretend it was someone she'd just met staring down at the two headstones side by side.

'Well,' he said, 'as Mother used to say, that's a good job done. I always hated that grave where it was. Would have played on my mind to leave it there.'

All Clara could find to say was, 'She'd be glad to be next to him.'

'He was her favorite, d'you mean?'

'How could I know?' She'd watched Emmeline sit by the old grave for three summers.

'Only you left to love me now, Clara.' He took the object from the cloth. It was a fine white china plate with a pink rose in the center. Stepping to the side of Will's new grave, he leant the plate against the headstone.

Clara tried to think of a way to ask what this meant, but Taylor started to walk away. She was about to follow when he drew his pistol and turned back to face her. She couldn't move, and had no voice. The plate seemed to shatter as the gun fired. The broken pieces collapsed over the grave.

'I always was the better shot,' said Taylor.

'What are you doing?' she cried when they reached the yard.

'No sense leaving any valuables behind,' said Taylor.

All the slaves, Mitilde too, had been bound by the hands and a long rope passed between their arms. They sat or knelt on the cold dirt floor, keening softly, the children huddled close to their mothers. Only Moses was unbound and stood looking on, his unchecked tears running into his grey beard.

Clara stepped in front of Taylor. 'There's nowhere to take them? The army will be here soon.'

Taylor ignored her and instead spoke to Moses. 'You wouldn't make it. You know you wouldn't. I know you're a loyal old boy. You stop those niggers in the woods from telling any tales now. And if between you and that Union flag you can keep them from burning the place, I might send Mitilde back to keep your bed warm. You didn't think that was a secret did you? You know, when I was a boy I used to get all worked up at nights thinking about visiting her. But I knew Mother wouldn't stand for it, and then Father gave me a few younger ones to play with. Kinda regret it though. Maybe it's not too late. Now if you put the Union onto us, it'll be her I kill first.'

Clara ran to Mitilde, but Taylor caught her by her wrist.

'You might want to get a warmer coat yourself,' he said. 'Gets cold up in the hills.'

'No!'

Taylor smiled. 'Only way out now. Should've left sooner. There's plenty of old Indian trails we can take. Father would have seen the funny side of it, going south instead of coming north. Some of them should make it, long as it doesn't snow. And I've got somewhere pleasant you and me can spend the night – get reacquainted.'

'I'll be dead before I come with you, Taylor Spencer.' She broke free of his grip.

'You forgot the Ridgmont, cousin.'

Clara only saw the movement from the corner of her eye as he brought his fist to the side of her head like a club. She fell hard to the floor, heard a scream from Mitilde, and knew nothing more.

Polk County – November 1863

It was hard for Shire to sleep through the danger, though the swaying wagon did its best to soothe it away. Next to him, Tuck didn't seem to have the same inner conflict; he'd sleepily stolen the only blanket – which smelled of dog – and was gently snoring. Shire turned on his side, tried to find some point of comfort on the wood.

Following the Whirligig Man's directions, it had taken two nights to get to the Widow Spriggs' farm. They'd found it this morning at dawn. She'd interrogated them from the safer end of a shotgun before she'd let them in and given them a heaven-sent breakfast. Shire reflected on the fact that so far he'd been better fed as a deserter than he had been in the army. After a few hours' rest, the Widow had put them in her wagon, pulled the canvas over and drove them east. Moving and resting at the same time was a luxury, but was granted only by the increased risk that they might meet outriders from either army. In the end, a full breakfast and the well-sprung wagon won out, and he dozed again. When he woke it was darker somehow. He looked out past the Widow, sat driving the mules, and could see the sky had turned a heavy grey. This road had taken more than a year to follow. What were the chances of Clara being at its end? If she was, what came after? Perhaps he'd be back on this road tomorrow, headed the other way. He slept again.

The wagon stopped and his eyes shot open. He sat up. The Widow reached back and shook Tuck awake. 'Sorry, boys. This is as far as I can go.'

They both crept forward either side of her and looked out. To their left were three plumes of smoke knocked diagonal by the wind.

'When there was only the one smoke stack I was happy to keep on,' said the Widow. 'The latest one is the closest. If that's your army's work, I don't want to be on the road and neither do you.'

They gave her their thanks, jumped down and shouldered packs. She handed Tuck some bread and chicken wrapped up in a muslin cloth. 'Got more than I need for just me. That's Ocoee up ahead. Best to skirt round to the south. This is the Copper Road. Stay off it where you can, but use it as a guide. You'll know when you get to the mountains, they start up sharp. There's one like an upside-down funnel, Sugarloaf it's called. The road goes on by it into the hills beside the river, but before then you'll hit a branch that goes north. Take that. 'Bout a mile up you'll see another cut steeply upwards. That'll take you to Comrie. Good luck to you.'

They got past the village alright, but kept in sight of the road. The land was up and down, like a tablecloth all rucked up. The dark mountains ahead were brushed by clouds blown out of the east. If the wind had been from the west, maybe they'd have heard the cavalry coming up behind them sooner. As it was, they found good cover only just in time. A squad of Union troopers raced by. Once they'd gone, Tuck hurried Shire deeper into the woods before they circled back towards the road and up a rise. When they crested it, they found themselves looking down on a grist mill.

Shire lay down flat on the forest floor, his breathing rapid after the climb. The sharp scent of the pine straw cleared his head. Tuck lay down next to him in the shadow of the trees. They had a clear view of the mill a couple of hundred paces down and across an open field. There were around twenty Union troopers dismounted down there. Two men and a woman were herded away by lowered rifles. The woman had her hands to her face; one of the men was waving and shouting as a soldier pushed him in the chest and backed him up a step at a time. Whatever the man was saying was drowned out by the steady rush of the weir below the mill pond. Shire doubted it mattered.

The soldiers were practiced at their work. While some laid a charge against the thick wood of the weir, others smashed flat boards from the porch to stack against the mill walls. Then they all backed off to where the civilians stood while the weir was blown. The air turned solid with sound. Stone and wood was thrown high into the air to fall back into the sudden wave sent chasing past the mill. The troopers whooped. The man stopped his protestations and his arms fell to his sides. The soldiers returned to their work and in only a few minutes, helped by the wind, the whole tall building was alight, sending another column of smoke into the air. Finally, the great water-wheel tore itself from the blaze and fell into the river.

'C'mon,' said Tuck. 'They'll be moving on soon. We should too.'

The undulations across their line-of-march got higher and steeper, but as the Widow said, you couldn't miss where the mountains truly started. The Ocoee raced out of them like a jail-break. When they found the road up to Comrie they chose to risk staying on it, the forest being steep and rough. Even then it was a hard climb, with no respite in the grade. They stopped often, not knowing how far it was. So it was a relief when the road broke into the open.

A wide and steep meadow rose above them, the grass untidy at the start of winter. The road switched back and fore to climb to what looked like an ancient temple, until they perceived the house held behind the white columns. Around one of those columns was wrapped a Union flag. Shire wasn't sure what he'd expected, but Comrie looked incongruous as well as threatening placed so high in the hills, the grey clouds racing above its red tiled roof. It was as if they had climbed all this way to find a tomb.

Tuck, usually to the front, waited on Shire to take the lead. Shire supposed it was his show. 'Let's stay in the trees, get round to the left,' he said. It allowed them to climb slightly closer to the house before they would have to leave the forest. Across from them was a sleeping flower garden. There was a wooden seat hung from a beech tree, its rusty chains squeaking in the breeze. There was no one about; no livestock, no dogs. Shire could see some grand stables behind the house, its sliding doors open;

beyond that was washing, straining on a line.

'Nothing else for it,' he said, and started towards the house. They went slowly, guns held across their chests. Edging back around to the front he could see the door open up there in the portico.

Tuck stopped him with a touch to his arm. 'Look.'

They walked to a pile of fresh earth next to a hole.

'A grave?' asked Shire.

'I guess. Though it ain't dug level. Looks like there might have been a headstone this end. It's been emptied. Maybe today, maybe yesterday.'

Shire had seen enough graves dug this last year, but this one unnerved him. It had no business being in this spot. There was a young tree planted close by that hadn't taken well. This whole place felt empty. If it hadn't been his long-sought destination, he'd have gladly turned and headed back down the hill.

'There ain't nobody here,' said Tuck.

Shire moved past him. 'Let's look in the house.'

He climbed the steps to the portico. The sun shone briefly on the pale stone before the next cloud-shadow chased it away. One of the pair of heavy doors was held open by a hook on the wall. Shire followed his gun inside. It took a few moments to adjust to the gloom. Daylight filtered down the staircase the other side of a large hall and it was no warmer in here than outside. Their boots, no matter how softly placed, echoed off the stone floor. Unbidden, Shire recalled entering the church at Ridgmont so long ago. Comrie felt every bit as empty.

'If'n you is tryin' to sneak in, I had an ol' horse that could do a better job.' The voice came from an open door on their right. 'Only me here. You don't need your guns.'

They moved in to find an old man, grey woolly hair and beard, sat in the only chair left in a large room. He was looking fixedly out of the window and held a crystal glass half full of whiskey.

'I seen you in the trees. Why didn't you come up the drive? Only me here.'

'We weren't sure of a welcome,' said Shire.

The old man turned his head to them. 'You sure ain't much of an army to look at. Thought you'd be bigger. Hah!'

Shire put his gun aside. 'Is there really only you?'

'Yeah. Might be one or two more niggers out in the woods, but I'm the only one in here. Don't usually get to come in the big house much; not since the old master died. Thought I might as well get the use of it. It ain't much to look at, not with all its fancy orn'ments gone. Not worth the burnin'. Nothin' in it to burn.'

'We're not here to burn it, sir.'

'Sir? You blue boys gonna call me sir? Hah. I been a boy all my life, though I's been the oldest soul here for a dozen years... Sir. You can call me Moses. Led his people out of bondage, he did.'

'I'm here to see Clara. Lady Clara Ridgmont.'

The old man looked more closely at Shire. 'She ain't here. Only me here. You really ain't gonna burn it?'

'We ain't,' said Tuck. 'Can't speak for the whole Union Army though. I wouldn't hide inside when they arrive. How long's everyone been gone?'

'Oh, a couple of weeks. Just me since then. I guess I's the caretaker, you might say.'

'You put up that flag?' said Tuck.

'I did.'

'And I suppose you hung out the washing and dug out that grave by yourself too. You must be a fit old boy.'

'I'm a boy again, am I? No matter.'

'When did they go?'

'I told you. A while back. Gone through the hills, no sense chasin' them. They's long gone.'

Tuck looked at Shire and shrugged. Shire came closer to the old man, squatted down so he looked up at him. 'Sir,' he said, 'Moses. I've come a long way to find Lady Clara – a long way. I've fought my way with my friend half across the country to get here. I have something important to tell her. I need to know where she is.'

Moses' eyes were shining. His voice hinted at breaking, 'I'm right sorry, but she's gone.'

Shire stood. A great weariness and emptiness overtook him. All this way. All this way just to be lied to by an old man.

'That cavalry will be along soon enough,' said Tuck. 'We can't stay.'

'I know,' said Shire. Leaving Moses by the window they walked back outside to where a windswept Tennessee was laid out before them.

'Maybe we're best hiding out in the woods ourselves,' said Tuck, ''til the cavalry's done its worst.'

'Maybe,' said Shire, not yet able to take the first step backwards.

'I know where they is.' From behind the pillar with the flag came a young, black girl. 'Least, I think I do.'

'Hany, no!' shouted Moses from inside.

Her hair was loose and she wiped spent tears from her cheeks with the back of her hand. 'They only left a couple of hours ago, all of 'em. Miss Clara, too.'

'Where? Where did they go?' Shire asked.

Moses appeared at the door. 'Hany, no! He'll kill Mitilde. Miss Clara too.'

'I saw him.' Hany turned on Moses, shouting, 'I was watchin' from the woods. He hit her out cold, slung her over his horse's saddle like she was a sack o' grain.'

Moses leant on the door frame and said no more.

'Who?' said Shire. 'Who the hell took her?'

'Why, Master Taylor, of course,' said Hany, as if it was obvious. 'Him and his soldiers. Took them all on up the hill.' She stepped up close to Shire. 'You boys got to go save her.'

Comrie – November 1863

As Clara woke, the moan of the wind and the pain on the side of her head were one and the same thing. When she sat up they parted. Outside, the wind was keening; a lament, buzzing through the trees, rising and falling as if it was the source of all wretchedness in the world. Inside, her ear was hot and sore. When she moved her jaw the whole side of her face shot through with pain.

There was daylight, let grudgingly in by four small, barred windows onto a plank floor. She was alone, but the room was prepared for many. Around its edge, run through large, metal eyes screwed into the wood, was a dark chain with manacles attached at even intervals. On the walls hung what she took to be neck braces, some plain hoops, others spiked for she knew not what purpose. She fought down the urge to scream.

The room smelt of clean wood. There were two stacks of metal pails against the wall across from her, and two chairs by a small table in one corner. Above it was a shelf, populated with a set of ledgers, bright lettering on their spines.

She stood up and found her balance. Her shoes had been removed, her ribs ached and she was thirsty. The only door was locked. She went to a window. The glass was clear and she looked between the bars. There was a second hut twenty yards away across open ground. Beyond it were trees, their empty boughs tugged and released by the wind. And above the trees rose a high grey cliff. It was so loud. This was the Cherokee wind that she had heard with Moses in the summer. She must be high on the ridge above Comrie. Where were Mitilde and the others? In that other hut? Where was Taylor?

She looked for water but there was none. She moved to a chair and put her hands to her face and wept, wept for the loss of everything she'd ever had or wanted. Wept for herself and for her only friends, roped back into a bondage they'd so nearly escaped. When the tears eased she tried to put her mind to escape. A chance might come if she was contrite with Taylor. She could steal one of the horses, but even then she was unlikely to get far. Slowly she accepted that the one thing left to her was to try to protect Mitilde and the others. She couldn't abandon them.

With nothing to do but wait, she took a ledger from the shelf. They were identical to the Comrie annual ledgers, a year embossed on each spine. It wasn't a continuous sequence: several years were missing and the last book was for 1856. She opened one marked 1845. She recognized Robert Spencer's block capitals. Only a dozen or so of the pages were used, but on each was a column of names, all biblical, but only one name per letter. They started with Abraham for the men and Abigail for the women. On each new page the names began again, the same names in the same sequence, but not always extending so far down the page. A cost, value and a destination was set against each, along with a note of payment received and profit made, which was totaled. The final page summed all the others to a yearly total, next to which it read – *Adjustment*.

Emmeline had been just as good a liar as her husband.

Bolts shot back on the other side of the door. It opened and let the howl momentarily inside. Taylor stepped in, holding his hat. 'You're awake. Good.'

Clara's hand went involuntarily to the side of her head.

'I'm sorry, of course,' he said unconvincingly, 'but we needed to get away. I see you've found something to read.' He came over and put his hat on the table.

'Another of your secrets?'

'Hardly mine. I was barely seventeen when the last shipment came through. No – my father's secret. He kept it from Mother too, until he got her safely married and moved out here from Virginia. I don't think she ever forgave him for that. Not that she had such high ideals. She didn't mind the use of the slaves, just didn't want to trade in them. And Father never had much to do with Africa, far as I know. He'd buy them after they were smuggled in, down on the Georgia coast. A long march up from there, at night mostly, until we got into the hills.'

The pain slowed Clara's thinking.

'Oh yes,' said Taylor, helping her along, 'he took me a few times. Part of my education, he'd say. After we reached here, they'd go every which way, depending on what sales Father had lined up. Some through the mountains to the Carolinas, some to the plantations out west. We got a better price for them than home-grown niggers. They were stronger too – the ones that made it.' He leafed through the ledger on the desk. 'But the numbers were small. A hobby – or a statement, that he'd do as he pleased, regardless of any Yankee law.'

Clara felt sick.

'Upsets you, does it? Just like Mother. I don't recall you ever asking me to set them free?'

'You haven't been here to ask. Besides, your war will take care of that. I'm glad of it. I wish I'd never come... But why is it all still here? The huts, the chains. Your father's dead. You can never use them again, thank God.'

'I'm using them right now, ain't I? And God's doing nothin' but howlin' outside. And if the war takes a different tack, who knows? Maybe,' he said, thoughtfully, 'maybe it's out of sentiment. Why I've kept them, I mean. We're a sentimental people. Moses tends to the place. Not much to do. Fix a window that's blown out, make sure no raccoons have moved in. He's kept it smart, don't you think? It was only him we let up here. Father thought he helped one to try and escape once, so we had to whip him half to death. We told him if he did it again, we'd let him die in these chains on his own.

'You know, this was the place my father brought me most, to show me the ropes, if you'll pardon the expression; our time together. When I was fourteen, he cleared all the Africans out to the other hut but one, left her chained in here for me, a whip by her side. Told me if she struggled any I was to use it. She was strong too, but the whip settled her.'

'Why are you telling me this?'

'You want to know all about me, don't you? Everyone else seems to want you to. Little Hany, for instance. I brought her up here. She thought it was so fine, too, being up on the Master's horse. When she came inside and saw the chains she couldn't stop from shaking. Didn't need the whip though.'

Clara couldn't look at him. She turned away.

'Don't you want to know the complete man? How I came to be me? Did Mother not share how she thought I shot my own brother?' Taylor's face hardened and he fingered a whip coiled and hanging on the wall. 'Has your precious Shire not found you to tell tales?'

It was a shock to hear Shire's name from Taylor's lips. 'Why is he coming?'

'Oh yes,' Taylor turned to her. 'I know he's been planning to visit. Only he got on the wrong boat so there was a war in the way. Why, he and I even had a friendly chat at Chickamauga. What are you thinking? What could he have to tell you? What could be worse than what you already know? Perhaps I should tell you? It won't matter soon. Let's get comfy first. I'd like to whisper it when we're real close. Come over here... C'mon now.' He took the whip from the wall. 'I don't want to have to persuade you.'

She took two steps towards him. 'Your men...'

'They ain't gonna bother a husband and his wife.'

He forced Clara to the floor and then took one hand almost gently, like he had on their wedding day, before locking it into a manacle. He did the same with the other hand. 'Now what about something for that pretty neck?' He stroked under her chin, then stretched his thumb around and pushed up, so her head was bent back.

'Please? Don't do this. You don't have to do this.'

'Oh, I think I do. Just one more time.' He reached for a metal collar, looped it about the chain behind Clara's back, pushed her down and closed it around her neck. She was held to the floor, her wrists up beside her head. The links of the chain pressed into her scalp. She screamed and the wind screamed with her. Taylor placed his hand over her mouth. 'They ain't going to hear you. Not with God blowin' away out there.'

Yet as he said this, the wind stalled – the howl died away and there was a moment's peace. From outside, Clara heard two clear gunshots.

Comrie – November 1863

Shire turned another sharp corner behind Hany. If the climb to Comrie had been hard work, this was steeper still. If he slipped, he'd tumble all the way to where the path switched back below him, and have to hope he could hang on.

Hany had led them out the back of the house, between some slave huts and on through a small cemetery – wooden crosses, no names. Beyond it a narrow path started sharply upwards. There was scant undergrowth between the trees, and the path was only wide enough for one man or one careful horse.

He could see Hany was frightened. She stopped to look up. 'I ain't been up here for some years. I ain't allowed.'

'But this is the way they came?'

'Yes, sir. I was watchin'. Miss Clara, she was out cold in front of the saddle. And the others were all roped together like I ain't never seen.' She began to cry.

'We need to hurry,' said Shire.

'How many soldiers?' asked Tuck.

'Four, I think. Though I was lookin' at Mitilde and Miss Clara mostly. But yes, Master and four soldiers.'

They started to climb again, sheltered from the easterly wind that threw the clouds off the hills above them. Up and up, until Shire imagined they could see almost all the way back to where they'd left the army three days ago. At last the grade began to soften, enough for Comrie to disappear from sight below.

Suddenly, from above came an unearthly wail, like nothing Shire had ever heard on this earth, as if the mountain itself was proclaiming some age old distress. He ducked down instinctively, and Hany lay on the path and curled up in a ball, arms to the side of her head. Only when the wail subsided could they begin to reason with her.

'I can't go no further. I can't.'

Shire sat down next to her. 'How far is it? We need to know what's up there?'

'Ghosts. That's what Moses tells us. Cherokee ghosts that'll eat your soul.'

'It was only the wind,' said Shire, as much to himself as Hany. 'What else is there?'

She started to edge back down the path. 'There's two huts. Huts for slaves,' she cried. 'The path leads right to 'em. You can find it.'

The howling picked up again and Hany hurried away. They didn't try to stop her, but turned and started upwards again.

As the slope eased further they came off the path. The wind carried the faint smell of tobacco. Staying low, they crept on, aware that the light was behind them. Shire spotted the first guard, smoking a pipe and stamping his boots against the cold, his musket beside him. There was a second, ten paces further left. He was sat with his back to a tree and huddled beneath a blanket, head down and seemingly asleep. Shire lay down with Tuck, their faces close. The wailing wind made it safe to whisper.

'They ain't too attentive if they ain't seen us first,' said Tuck. 'We could charge them from here before he could level that gun at us. But I reckon we should get round behind them in this forest light, wait on that wind to howl good and they'll never know we're comin'.'

'Kill them, you mean?'

'Well, what the hell else do you think I mean? Invite them over for coffee? We need to even the odds.' He reached his arm down to his boot and drew out his short knife.

Shire had no knife. Instead he took his bayonet from its sheath at his belt. It had no handle, only a metal ring to fit over the barrel. He took a rag from his pack and wrapped it round the ring and the lower blade so he'd have some purchase.

'I'll take the one stood up,' said Tuck. 'If they spot us, go in fast.'

They left their packs and rifles and, watchful of the standing soldier, picked their moments to move from tree to tree. It seemed to take an age, and all the while Shire was thinking of the sleeping man he was about to kill. It was for Clara. There was still a war and this was the enemy. Once past the soldiers they could move a little faster and circle back towards them. Shire held the blade tightly through the cloth and came up behind the tree with the sleeping man on the other side. He could see wood shavings. The man had been whittling some shape, just like Tom Muncie used to. He looked over to Tuck, barely five strides from his own quarry, crouched, his face tight. They shared a nod.

Tuck sprang forward, but Shire froze. He saw Tuck loop a hand over his man's mouth, bring his knife up hard into his back. Despite the hand a dying scream escaped. The scream triggered Shire and he rushed forward. His own target threw off his blanket, tried to rise but was off balance. Shire pushed him back with his left hand, held the man pinned against the trunk. Arms clawed at him. He brought his bayonet up in a swing from behind, so it went in under the ribs. The face contorted. The Rebel stiffened and Shire felt the end of his blade come up hard against the tree. There was no scream, not so much as another breath before the eyes died. Shire held him there, his hand tight on the bayonet until Tuck reached him. They were both breathing hard.

'Pull it out,' said Tuck.

Shire pulled, the rag and his hand wet with blood. The blade was held tight by the flesh. He remembered Ocks' advice and twisted it free. The sudden release made him take a step back and the man fell.

'Alright?' asked Tuck. He looked every bit as terrified as Shire. 'Four rifles for us now. And just three of them.'

They checked the Rebels' muskets and found them loaded. Recovering their own, they stole further uphill until Shire could see a break in the trees and two long huts between pale cliffs, which rose sheer, as much as a hundred feet, on either side.

Through the pass was only grey sky; there was no higher ground beyond. And the wind whipped from the gap like it was escaping through hell's gates, all the trees within bent towards the west like cowered slaves. It sang as if the devil himself had placed some giant reed amongst the cliffs, so he could blow out a tune to suit his mood.

Huddled together in the lee of the left hut were a cluster of unhappy horses. As it was still daylight there was no light from either hut, no other sign of life. Shire and Tuck stayed hidden, rifles laid out beside them.

Shire tried to wipe the blood off his hands. 'What next?'

'They gotta come out sometime,' said Tuck, 'to swap the guard. It's cold so they'll swap often. We should wait on that.'

'I don't want to wait. The wind's so strong. It'll make it a hard shot.'

'We're close enough. Ain't but thirty paces and we're firing straight into it.'

'From what Hany said, Clara could be in danger right now. What if we frighten the horses? That'd bring them out.'

Tuck ducked his head down and pulled Shire's down too. 'Don't look like you'll need to.'

Two men came out of the left hut, moved towards the horses and set about feeding them.

'We'd better take our chance,' said Tuck, reaching for a rifle.

Shire did the same. 'Neither of those two is Taylor. He must be inside. Once we fire he'll know we're here.'

A scream, intertwined with the wind, but a scream. The two Rebels stopped what they were doing and looked to the right hand hut.

'He's got her in there!' It was Clara, he was sure of it.

'Alright, I've got a bead on the tall fella. Tell me when you're set and we'll fire together.'

Shire lined up on the second man, urgency killing any trace of pity. The wind unsteadied his rifle, so he couldn't fix his aim.

'C'mon, I can't hold this all day.' But just as Tuck said this, the wind died.

'Now!' he said. He didn't hear Tuck's gun over the firing of his own.

The smoke cleared and Shire saw both men fall down amongst the horses. Grabbing their second rifles they both stood and raced over the open ground. One man looked dead, the other held his gut and screamed. They were no danger. Shire raced for the door of the right hand hut. He reached for the handle, but heard a shot from behind and spun. A soldier had stepped from the other hut and fired, missing them both. It wasn't Taylor. Tuck recovered before Shire and raised his stolen rifle, but it was too late and the man was on him. Using his rifle like a staff, the Rebel cracked the butt hard on Tuck's head. He went down. The Rebel stepped over him and lifted his rifle, ready to drive it down into Tuck's skull. Shire fired from the hip, and the recoil ripped his gun from his hands. But it had done its work and the man fell, a bullet through his shoulder. Shire looked at Tuck. There was blood there. He started towards him until he felt a barrel pushed firmly into the small of his back.

'Stand still. Otherwise it ends now.'

He did as he was told. Taylor edged around him. The man Shire had shot was down on one knee, his hand failing to staunch the blood that poured from his shoulder, eyes tight and teeth clenched against the pain.

'That looks bad, Captain,' said Taylor.

The captain was unable to reply.

'Well now,' said Taylor, addressing Shire. 'Looks like you've partly solved a problem for me.' He swung his pistol from Shire to Captain Gibbs' chest, fired, and swung it back again before Gibbs hit the floor.

'Any others alive out there?'

'One by the horses,' said Shire. Anything to distract Taylor from Tuck, who wasn't moving.

'Let's take a look,' said Taylor, and gestured Shire along with his pistol.

They walked over and the soldier was still holding his stomach. Shire had seen enough wounds to know it was mortal. Taylor shot the man despite his pleading. Shire flinched.

'A kindness really,' said Taylor. 'At least they'll have no tales to tell. Assuming anyone ever finds them. And if they do it'll just look like you and your friend there took care of them. And he don't look like he'll be bothering us anymore. But let's not get ahead of ourselves. I believe there's someone you're anxious to meet.'

He pushed Shire through the door. It was darker inside. Shire stumbled. It took him a moment to adjust to the light. Across from him a woman half-sat, half-lay against the wall, chained to it at the wrist and neck, her hands held beside her dark loose hair. She'd been crying. The side of her face was bruised. She wore a creased, checked dress but no shoes. The dress was dirty from the hut floor. For all of that, Clara was beautiful. He saw the recognition dawn in her face, a flicker of hope, which died as Taylor pushed in behind him.

'You got nothing to say to the lady? After comin' all this way? No? Well let's get you set too, so I can relax.' He motioned Shire to sit down, just out of reach from Clara, manacled his hands behind his back, the chain passing between Shire's arms.

Taylor spoke as he worked. 'Let me help you out? How about, *sorry*? Sorry I came all this way. Sorry I stuck my English nose into your husband's business. 'Cos if I hadn't, you might be safe. Your husband wouldn't have needed to come back and make sure I wasn't whispering tales in your ear. Your husband could've trusted to the Yankees to burn the place and not you. Your husband could have let you live.'

Taylor pulled out a chair and sat wearily in front of them. He ran a hand through his long, greasy hair.

The word husband goaded Shire. He should at least say what he came to say. But they'd both soon be dead, so what was the point?

To give her one sad glimpse of understanding before she died? Taylor was right. If he'd never set out then none of this would have come to pass. He looked at Clara and she gave him a weary smile. Despite everything he returned it; it had been a long journey for just one smile.

'What to do? What to do?' said Taylor. 'Well I guess I can't take those slaves anymore. Only me to drive them and I ain't got time to tend to them all. Plenty of money elsewhere. I can't burn the huts or I'll attract the Yankees. So they'll have to stay locked up over there. No point wasting good bullets. But I'll need to go back down the hill and see to Moses and Hany. It's a lot of trouble you're putting me to.' He sprang up and kicked Shire high in the stomach.

Shire would have doubled over but the chain held him. He tried to ride out the pain, tried to draw breath. Clara looked almost spent. Perhaps she saw Taylor was beyond mercy or pity; Shire knew he was. He'd killed Tom Muncie in cold blood, killed his own men.

'I'm sorry for you,' said Clara.

'You're sorry for me?' said Taylor.

'Sorry that you had such a father who brought you here, let you see these things. Sorry that your parents couldn't believe it wasn't your fault that your brother died... I believe you. I think your mother wanted to. Only she'd already had the trust wrung out of her. There wasn't any left for you. Let Shire go. Whatever secret he has for me he can keep.'

Taylor sat back in the chair, laughed and wiped his sleeve across his nose. 'Very touching,' he said, 'that you should think to know my family history so well. Only, even if I had it in my heart, I don't think young Shire here could let it be. No. I'll be the gallant colonel, the only one to make it back to my army. My boys all lost to the Union. My wife and home lost too. No one other than Moses and Hany know about this place. And I'll take care of them. Then I can spin whatever tale I want.

'As to Shire's little secret...' He came and crouched next to Shire, patted his jacket and reached inside for the papers. 'Kept it close to your heart. You must really be sweet on her.'

'I made a promise is all,' said Shire. 'And I keep my promises.'

'Very noble.' Taylor tossed aside the map and the letters. He unfolded the damaged license. 'What a lot of grief over a single sheet of paper.' For a moment he looked remorseful. He stroked Clara's bemused face. 'For me,' he held up the license, 'this was the false marriage.'

'Now,' he shook his head, 'my dear wife, you and I have some unfinished business, and I don't think you'd want this boy watching on.' He opened the chamber to his pistol, reached into his pocket and started to load.

Shire felt only certainty. Certainty that he'd failed Clara, certainty that he was going to die. He thought of his father. The chamber clicked closed. Footsteps. The room went a shade darker.

'Tuck?' said Shire.

Taylor made to rise and turn but Clara threw out her legs, kicked Taylor's feet from under him. He went down on his knees, lifted his pistol too late to the figure looming over him. It was knocked away.

'For Grace,' said Ocks. He placed his own pistol against Taylor's shoulder and fired down, so the bullet tore through bone, heart and bowels before halting somewhere within. Taylor slumped sideways to the floor, an arm reaching, clutching at nothing, before it fell still.

Comrie – November 1863

Shire considered that the thunder was the only sound that wasn't water. Heavy, thick rain smacked onto Comrie's front steps like a continuous roll of muskets. It was joined by the run-off from the roof which, unable to otherwise cope with the deluge, had given birth to several temporary waterfalls. The flood tumbled down the steps and onto the river shingle of the drive, which was reverting to its natural state, that is to say, underwater. The transient pond was peppered so hard by the rain that a low mist lifted from it like smoke.

Shire looked out from the portico and thought there were worse places to be. The storm stopped them from leaving; they would sit easy in their rockers until it was over. It had receded once already, and they'd shouldered their packs and blankets, collected their rifles; but before they could say their final goodbyes, the lightning had struck close and the rain had come on again, heavy as nails.

'If you ask me, this storm seems kinda personal,' said Tuck. He put the fiddle he'd found inside to his chin, bowed a long note on each string and then adjusted the pegs. 'I think I could find blue sky behind us if I was inclined to get out of this chair. God must want us to stay. I imagine you don't object?'

Shire didn't. The journey in prospect was bad at both ends: leaving Clara at this one and finding Opdycke at the other. Despite reassurances from Ocks, Shire was nervous of their return. He smiled at Tuck, who sat there with an angled bandage wrapped around his forehead. 'It'd be a shame for us to drown in a storm after all we've been through,' Shire said. 'I like to look out on the rain, though.'

Tuck plucked at the strings, worked in a little speed, started a foot tapping and set the bow into a fast jig, not a note out of place. Shire was amazed.

When Tuck finished, Shire said, 'There were always fiddles in camp. I never saw you play.'

'Lost mine with my parents in the fire. Didn't have the heart until now.'

Clara came out to check on her Kentucky patient before he left. She gave him a glass of buttermilk and fussed around his dressing.

'This here's a fine fiddle. I hope you don't mind me playing it.'

'Keep it.'

'Truly?'

'That fiddle hasn't been played for a long time. It was only kept as a memory. I'd like you to have it.' Her eyes strayed to Shire only the once before she returned inside.

Tuck smiled and turned the fiddle over in his hands. The thunder rolled again and the rain beat on. 'You know,' said Tuck, 'I ain't looking forward to you mooning over this girl in the months to come saying, *I wish I'd said this, I wish I'd said that.* This storm might be God's way of telling you to go and talk to her. Chance might never come round again.'

When the critical moment had come, she'd had more presence of mind than he did. He'd come all this way, but in the end Clara was the one to kick Taylor's legs away and help save herself. Where did that leave him? He'd been thinking on the right things to say ever since they came down off the ridge two evenings ago. Clara had been in distress of course, so that wasn't the time; not with Taylor's blood still busy staining into the hut floor. Ocks had unchained them and they'd gone outside, but the scene was hardly much better: a litter of dead men and a chorus of wails from the other hut. Finding Tuck alive, they'd taken him in out of the cold, while Clara, despite everything, went to calm the captives and release them. Shire and Ocks had prepared to stay there the night, they didn't want to move Tuck further, but to Shire's joy he'd come round. He was sick more than once and couldn't quite get his sight. They'd put him on a horse and started back down the path in the dusk, led by Moses.

It was Moses who'd brought Ocks up the hill when he'd arrived. With the die cast, Moses said, he thought the boys might need all the help they could get. Or perhaps Ocks hadn't been as gentle with him as they had.

That evening, back in the house, Clara had busied herself helping Mitilde with Tuck, rather than talk with Shire, perhaps not asking questions she didn't want the answer to. He'd left her to it, found Ocks in the hunting room instead. In the end, Ocks seemed to have kept his secrets better than most.

'You deserted too,' Shire had said. 'We're not making the colonel think well of the English.'

'Oh, you might be surprised. Unlike you, I got his permission to leave. You'll not be getting any promotions soon, but I think he'll let you back into the fold if you tell him the truth. He's an honorable man.'

'Why didn't you tell me about Grace? I've spent all this time thinking you were going to kill me.'

'I didn't know who to trust,' said Ocks. 'Certainly not Matlock. And what with you leaving the night before poor Grace was found. There'd been talk before, over the two of you and her child. I thought the truth would show itself if I waited.'

'I should have gone to see her. The night I left. I might have made a difference.'

'Perhaps. I doubt it. I couldn't. I walked her home that night. She'd been to see Matlock. She'd been drinking, was unsteady but wouldn't take an arm, wouldn't talk to me. I saw her inside. I thought she was safe. When they found her, I was told she had a mark above her eye. Gossip was that it was me or you. I suppose I thought it could have been you. At least then I wouldn't have to blame myself. But she must have set out to the church after I'd gone, fallen on the way.'

'It wasn't your fault. You did what you could. She never told me about you?'

'Wasn't nothing to tell. And now I know why. I think she liked me right enough, but she was married, wasn't she.'

'Will you go back?'

'To England? I don't think so. Seems like a step backwards. Besides, I'm signed up same as you. And it's not a bad army. Might see if I can make captain? I had a deal with Matlock, to stop you getting to Clara. Somehow I don't think he'll pay out.'

'He doesn't have to know I made it.'

Ocks toyed with the cigar box. 'There's something else.'

'What?'

'Matlock was the last person to see your father alive. At your home. Doctor said it was a seizure, but Matlock must have gone round to keep him quiet. I think that's how he knew you were coming here. He's been reading your letters.'

Lightning stuttered to the west and interrupted Tuck's fiddling. 'I'd swear that was below us,' he said.

Shire felt his face sour and his gut tighten at the thought of Matlock. It wasn't quite all wrapped up, but Matlock was an ocean away and there was no proof.

Yesterday morning he'd got his chance to talk to Clara. He couldn't wait any longer. Ocks had taken a party back up to the ridge to bury the bodies. They'd decided to wait until spring to burn the huts as they didn't want to attract attention. Tuck was resting in bed so Shire went to find Clara, who was with the horses in the stables.

'Hello, Shire,' she'd said. 'Come and see my new horses. The army's taken enough, so I plan to keep these.'

She wore a simple dress, fit for work, her hair tied back to that end. She looked older, certainly – it had been three years after all – weary too. She was as beautiful as he remembered: her hair as dark, her skin browner. But her smiles were shallower.

'They look like they need a rest,' said Shire, 'time to recover.'

'There was a time here when I was bored. Now I'd be happy to have a little boredom.'

'That won't last,' said Shire. 'I know you too well.'

'You do... You're the only person who truly knows me anymore, who's seen me at home and here. I'm sorry about your father. Tuck told me.' She started to brush out a mane.

'Do you want to know more? About Grace I mean.' Shire had seen her pick up the license at the hut. He didn't know if he should leave it with her. He had no more use for it.

'Do I need to?'

'She's dead. There was a baby, but he died.'

'Poor Grace... I remember that there was a child. It was a scandal. Father let the vicar stay on... Matlock talked him round. Then Grace came to work at the house.'

'The vicar died before Grace. Matlock knew all about the marriage. He was there.'

'I saw his signature. The other was torn out.'

'Shot out.'

'What?'

'It doesn't matter. The other witness was Father. He regretted it. He wanted me to tell you that. Matlock had a hand in much of this.'

'When?' Clara asked. 'When did she die?'

'Early November last year. I've asked Ocks, but he says he can't be sure of the exact day. Matlock had sent him away. I know it was close to your wedding day. I asked Moses.'

'So you came to tell me I might not be married, and instead you're telling me I might not be a widow.'

Shire didn't think it was meant to be said unkindly. Clara might have been talking to herself. It was a lot for her to take in. But somewhere in those words she seemed to ask what he thought had given him the right to come at all; to play in the affairs of his betters.

'I came to keep a promise,' he said. Yet he'd long known the promise was merely a wrapping for something else.

Clara stepped under the horse's neck and began to brush the other side. 'We were children, Shire. If I'd known it was going to cause so much trouble I would have freed you from that promise long ago.'

Shire didn't know what more to say. That's how she viewed his coming then: as 'trouble'. He'd given up his whole world just to be put in his place; come all this way and got no closer to her at all.

Tuck had finished his milk. The rain hadn't eased one bit. 'Maybe we should stay. Ocks can tell the colonel we're dead.'

'We've not been invited,' said Shire.

'You ever feel you have much choice at all?'

'I chose to come to America, to come here.'

'I guess I chose to join the army. But sometimes, I get to feelin' we're just like the sails in that old boy's Whirligig, set to running when the wind starts to blow. All we can do is give ourselves up to it, hope we're in one piece when the storm plays out.'

Shire thought of the patched-up soldier in his rucksack. 'As on this Whirligig of time, we circle with the seasons.'

'What?'

'It's from a poem. I was a scholar once.'

'I know. Where you goin'?' Tuck asked as Shire stood and walked past him.

There was something he'd forgotten to ask.

*

Clara was in the kitchen. The rain drummed on the roof. She felt safer with Mitilde and Hany. Others came and went. Not that she was scared of Shire and his friends, not physically, far from it; but of what more she might learn, or was it what more she might feel? Here was warmth and work and chatter.

470

Shire had changed. For one thing there were two or three men dead up the hill down to him. He wasn't the boy she'd left at home, certainly not on the outside. He looked leaner but stronger at the same time. And he carried a scar like a tear on his right cheek. She realized she had no idea what he must have suffered to get here. How had she ever deserved that?

Those last moments, when Ocks arrived and she'd kicked away Taylor's legs, kept returning to her mind. She'd had no choice, but despite everything Taylor had done, it still felt like some last betrayal.

The Union Cavalry had finally turned up the previous afternoon. Thirty or more of them trotted up the drive, left and right, until they passed by the men filling in the old grave and came on up to the house. Some had gone to the side, gathered wood to pile against the walls, with no regard to the Union flag bandaged to the column out front.

Clara ran out to argue with the captain, but Ocks gently moved her to one side.

'Good afternoon, Captain,' he'd said, giving a stiff salute.

'Sergeant,' said the Captain, perplexed. 'What are you doing here?'

'Orders, Captain. From my colonel. 125th Ohio Infantry. We're to protect the place. It's not to be burnt, sir.' He produced a folded order.

'We?' said the captain. He read the paper. 'How many men do you have?'

'Three of us, sir.' As he said this, Shire and Tuck came out to the top of the steps, rifles at their shoulders. Clara suppressed the urge to send Tuck back to bed.

'A very small detachment. These orders allow you to come here. There's nothing about protecting it.'

'The colonel was occupied, sir, getting the brigade ready to march to Knoxville. But those were his orders.'

The troopers were busy around the place. There were some

shouts out back and Mitilde appeared to the side of the house, chasing a trooper with a broom as if he were a dog caught in the kitchen.

'This house belongs to a Confederate colonel, Sergeant. It has to burn. I'll take it up with your colonel later.'

'Begging your pardon, sir, but it'll be pointless taking it up after you've burnt the place. And it doesn't belong to that colonel anymore. He's dead, sir. Buried him this morning, but we can unearth him if you want to take a look. This lady was his wife, sir.'

Clara wasn't sure what expression to use, so used none.

'Then we'll burn a Southern lady's house, rather than a Southern gentleman's.'

'She's English, not Southern. Just her and the blacks, sir. Not much point setting them free and burning down the only place they know.'

'Damn it, Sergeant, have you got an answer for everything? English like you is she? Are your men American at least?'

'Partly, sir. But you take it up with Colonel Opdycke and General Sheridan if you want to.'

'General Sheridan. What's he got to do with this?'

'I don't rightly know, sir. They were all there. Sheridan, the colonel, that Dana fellow from the War Department. Has some fine friends our colonel does, sir.'

Clara had no idea who these people were. And if she was any judge, Ocks was making this up. But it did the trick. The captain barked an order and the soldiers returned to their horses and mounted up. Shire and Tuck broke into laughter as soon as the troopers had ridden away.

'Miss? Miss Clara!' It was Hany, almost shouting. The rain plunged down outside the kitchen. 'Maybe you should go and lie down? You's not heard a word I said.'

'Hany!' admonished Mitilde 'You ain't got no cause to speak to Miss Clara like that? Besides, there ain't a thing you say that you won't say again a minute later.'

'I'm sorry,' said Clara.

'I was askin' if we is free? Now the army's been here an' all.'

'Yes,' said Clara. 'Yes you are.'

'But what does that mean? What am I free to do?'

'Huh,' laughed Mitilde. 'You're free to ask Miss Clara if you can stay, that's what.'

Hany turned on Mitilde. 'I don't need to ask that. Not after I saved you and everyone else by takin' those soldiers up the hill.'

Clara didn't really know what it meant either. Things shouldn't just stay as they were. But for now, they all just had to keep safe. 'What it means, Hany, is that if you choose to stay, you won't have to live apart from Cele anymore.'

And then there were lots of tears.

If only her own decisions were so simple. She was free too, of course, freer than she'd ever been. Hadn't that been what she'd wanted to start with? Free of her family, free of England and its strictures, free of Comrie if she chose – and free of Taylor. No. Not of Taylor. Not yet. At least not free of the man she'd once thought he was. The one she sailed across the ocean for. He'd take a while longer to die.

*

Shire knocked on the door, heard Mitilde's deep voice inside.

'This ain't a knockin' door. You just comes in. I 'spect it's that young Englishman you's so fond of.'

The door opened.

'Well c'mon in. You English like standin' in the rain?'

He stepped inside and took off his dripping cap. All three women stared at him, two with broad smiles. Perhaps he would prefer it out in the rain.

Mitilde knocked Hany's arm. 'C'mon, girl. We got chores in the house.'

'We do? Oh, sure, we do.'

They both stepped out. Hany started to run and squeal through the rain as Shire closed the kitchen door behind her.

'We'll be on our way when the rain stops,' said Shire.

'I know,' said Clara, too quickly.

'I thought I'd come and say goodbye and ask if I can start writing again.'

Clara laughed. Not a half-hearted laugh but a long, deep, delicious laugh that Shire found both wonderful and disconcerting at the same time.

'What did I say?' he asked, smiling himself.

Clara put her hand under her nose to help her stop. 'I've missed you so much. Only you could leave your life at home, fight a year in a war to get here, kill several men on my account and then ask for permission to write.' She started to laugh again, until her eyes watered. She wrapped her arms around him and put her head on his shoulder. He held her awkwardly. She edged her head into his neck. Her hair smelt of home.

'But it's always been that way with us,' he said. 'You telling me what to do. Always.'

Eventually she stood back from him, straightened his jacket. 'What happens for you now? How long are you committed to the army?'

'Another two years,' said Shire, feeling the weight of them; he'd barely survived this one. 'Or to the end of the war. Ocks tells me we're heading up to Knoxville. I might get a furlough sometime. Assuming they don't shoot me for desertion.'

'Deserting to kill a Rebel colonel.'

'It wasn't me that killed him,' said Shire. 'I'm still trying to work out who saved who. Did I do the right thing by coming? If it just brought more trouble on you.'

'Oh, there was always going to be trouble. I meant what I said to Taylor. I felt sorry for him. With a father like his, he never had a chance. I didn't love him at the end. I hadn't for some time. Thank

474

you, Shire. Thank you for keeping our promise.' She looked down at her hands. 'In your letter, the one you sent as my cousin, why did you use the caroling to let me know it was you? Your handwriting would have been enough.'

'I don't know. It was something that came to mind.' It had come to mind quite a lot. 'As to the promise, well, we both know it meant more to me. I'm not sure how I'm going to feel when I leave. Now I'm not trying to get here anymore...' *Get to you.*

'We're both all at sea.'

'You don't know what you'll do?'

'Stay for now. There'll be a will. But it'll have to wait on the war like everything else. I don't even know if I was married. I can't go back until I know. And then only as a widow, otherwise how could I? And these people, they need someone, until they decide on their own way.'

They were quiet for a while, and Shire realized that the rain was too. There was even a touch of sunshine outside.

'Stay safe, Shire. Please. Do that for me. Then there's someone not too far away.'

What could he say? She was still Clara Ridgmont, youngest daughter of the Duke of Ridgmont – and he was still a schoolmaster's son. 'Ocks'll be looking for me now the rain's stopped, but I've got something for you.' He reached into his jacket and took out the wooden soldier and passed it to her. 'It's just something I collected along the way. I'll only break it again if I keep it in my pack. You'll look after it better.'

She looked at it curiously. He supposed it was an odd gift.

They walked through the house and out onto the portico. The sky was clearing and Tennessee looked fresh and washed. Clara had had two extra horses led around to go with the one Ocks had brought. One of them was Taylor's mare.

'Are you sure?' asked Shire.

'I can't let my patient walk and it seems unfair to let you do so alone. Perhaps the army will buy them from you.'

Shire had never owned his own horse before. He went to kiss Clara on the cheek, for once not asking permission. She turned her head and their lips half met. He pulled away, embarrassed, then hurried down the steps and mounted. It was a fine horse. It was fine tack.

'She's been harshly handled,' Clara called down from above. 'She might need a little patience.'

'I know how to look after her,' he called back, 'if she'll let me.' Then he turned and followed Ocks and Tuck down the drive.

Epilogue – Charleston – January 1864

George Trenholm stepped down from the cold terrace of Ashley Hall and into the Italian garden. The paths were precisely cut between the miniature hedges that framed the sleeping flowerbeds, or surrounded bare, thorny rosebushes. For once he was away from Richmond and could attend to his own affairs rather than those of the Confederate Government. The latter increasingly consumed him. It was winter, and though the war didn't stop for the season, it at least abated. Fewer soldiers marched, fewer ships sailed. The Confederacy should pray for a long winter.

But there were, as ever, decisions to make. Proileau's letter, safely in Trenholm's jacket, was apologetic: the Liverpool office had been busy, there were pressing matters with the British Government, ships to be commissioned, goods to trade; he'd not been able to spare anyone until the autumn to send to Ridgmont. Yet the delayed results were conclusive enough.

The gravestone showed Grace Harland to have died on November 7th, the day before Clara's wedding, as Matlock had said. There had been no vicar in residence at the time, her own father having only recently died. Proileau's man had determined that the verger had made the original entry in the parish records as the 8th. But this had been 'corrected' to the 7th and initialed by the subsequent vicar after the event. When asked, he claimed this correction originated from the head of the Ridgmont estate, Isaiah Matlock, after the poor girl's original gravestone had been struck by lightning. How very convenient of God to lend Matlock a hand.

But Proileau's man was thorough enough to visit the registrar. There the date of death was still held to be the 8th; the very same day that Trenholm had sat with a lonely girl in the hall at Comrie, comforted her, and later walked her up the aisle. He knew something of law; enough to guess that the fact that the girl was probably dead a few hours before the wedding would have no bearing – it was the same day. The marriage was void.

He completed a lap of the outer circle, swiveled on one foot to take the right-angled turn that aimed him towards the fountain in the center. It was too cold to have the fountain running. He'd get it turned off. His Italian garden reflected an earlier version of himself, when he was obsessed with building railroads and founding banks: it was all order and precision. Any diameter drawn across it would find a mirrored design on either side. Somehow, it felt false to him now.

A letter from Clara had reached him just last week. It had come up through Ducktown and across the mountains of North Carolina. Clever girl. The Union may have taken Tennessee, but the Appalachians remained a law unto themselves.

He'd already heard that Taylor had absconded during the Rebel retreat from Missionary Ridge, but had expected him to surface sometime. Instead, Clara's letter had confirmed his death and been candid in its detail, telling him everything; of the slave huts, that Taylor murdered his own men, that he would have killed her but for her friend from England, how Comrie had been saved. Her trust in Trenholm was touching, he supposed she had no one else; he'd hate to take advantage of that. She'd even asked him to maintain the deceit with her father that Taylor was lost defending Comrie. She couldn't bare her parents to know the truth.

He should have gone there after seeing her in Chattanooga, insisted that she and Emmeline came away. All of this could have been avoided. But to what end? Taylor was beyond redemption.

He'd known about the African slaves, of course; Robert's hobby was the joke amongst their mutual friends. It made no serious money, and Trenholm would have no part of it. He'd trade slaves under the law but would not import them and break it. And he'd tried to dissuade Robert. Whatever slavery was to become, it had to move forward, become more benign. That didn't include

Africa and slave ships. And it would pass away more abruptly soon, unless the war changed course.

This friend from England that Clara referred to must be the elusive Shire. Quite an effort. Good for him.

Crows settled noisily away in the oaks, the only sound to compete with the tumble of water. He reached the fountain, the middle of this shaped little empire. It had been important to him to know he was at the center of things in the past. Not so anymore. What mattered now was to keep moving, keep afloat, survive until a new center took shape.

What should he do? The marriage was illegal, though Clara couldn't know that. If it were revealed, she'd have no claim on Comrie even if Taylor had named her in a will. But at least then he could expose Matlock; there'd be no place for him to hide.

Where should he look for guidance? To the law? To his conscience? He was the bondsman for Taylor – he was implicated, legally and morally. And who's law? Comrie was in the Union now.

And what of the duke? No, that no longer mattered. Whether he spoke for the Confederacy in Parliament or not, the British were staying out of this war. That much was clear. And what business he had with the duke was small scale.

There was much to consider, but he didn't like to ponder overlong. Whenever some employee or partner placed in front of him a long list of pros and cons, he would push it away.

'What's the telling point?' he would always ask. 'Act on that.'

He'd get this garden redesigned, make it less formal, blur the edges, allow the paths to wander.

He was Taylor's bondsman – sworn to pay the price if Taylor could not lawfully marry and defaulted on the bond himself. He had a duty to Clara. That was the telling point. Let bravery and honor get its reward – for once. He pulled Proileau's letter from his jacket, tore it through twice, and threw it into the fountain.

Historical Note

My particular joy in writing *Whirligig* was finding a way to weave the fictional narrative between actual events and alongside real people. I could be reading the history, at a battle site or in a period home, or perhaps feeling my way forward through the writing itself when I'd experience a deeply satisfying collision between my story and the history. It was as if I'd just recovered some long lost memory.

The collision might only help a particular scene: the stealing of the bee-hives in Franklin is based on contemporary accounts. At other times it redirected the whole book. When I visited the Liverpool Maritime Museum, I was looking for the right ship to take Shire to New York. Instead, in their archives, I found George Trenholm, one of the wealthiest men in the South, a blockade runner with offices in Liverpool through which he helped manage the Confederacy's critical trade in Europe. He gave me access to a layer of politics, big business and wealthy self-interest. His dealings redirected me to sit in the Strangers Gallery in the House of Lords, to search in Hansard for debates on British neutrality. He steered me to the boom times in Nassau. All this flowed from that day in Liverpool.

The spine of my narrative is provided by the 125th Ohio Infantry. My story goes where they go, we fight where they fight. In battle I keep their movements and actions tight to the history. Not only were they a wonderful regiment that fought at most of the western theatre's major battles from 1863 onward, but also there are a number of books written first hand by soldiers from the 125th. Colonel Opdycke's letters home to his wife were the most useful of all. He is my eyes and ears in the Union Army, gloriously opinionated and a doughty warrior. Barney, although his name feels a little anachronistic, was also real horseflesh and bone.

Comrie itself is fictional. I didn't want a stereotypical plantation house, and so when I found the Copper Road, George Barnes, and the mines at Ducktown, I placed Clara and her new home high in the Appalachian hills. Taylor is entirely fictional, as are the Hiwassee Volunteers. How could I impose such a man on a real Confederate unit?

The shipping of slaves from Africa was made illegal in federal law from 1808 but continued in varying degrees of secrecy for another fifty years. In the last documented case the Federal Government prosecuted the owner and crew of the *Wanderer*, which landed slaves in Georgia in 1858. The prosecution failed.

There were times when the narrative and the history didn't fall quite as perfectly as I needed it to. Therefore, on occasion, I have used the notional license of a fiction writer to bend it to my narrative. The biggest liberty I have taken is with Opdycke. After the first day of battle at Chickamauga, his ride with General Wood to the Union headquarters at the Widow Glenn's house is fictional. And although he would not have been far away, I have no evidence to suggest that Opdycke was present when General Wood made his fateful and dubious decision to follow Rosecrans' order and pull out of the line, bringing on the Union defeat.

The riot in New York is also fictional. The major draft riots, which lasted days and took regiments of Union soldiers to suppress them, took place after Gettysburg in 1863. However, large areas of New York were under the sway of the gangs and there were frequent battles between them and the police before and throughout the war. The Union was already experimenting with the draft in late 1862, certainly in Ohio (hence Dan's call-up) so the riot is totally plausible. The horrific sight of a hanged black man would not have been uncommon during these sorts of disturbances.

I have no such excuse for Shire and Dan observing the collection of the telegrams that were thrown from the steamers off the southern Irish coast. This practice started in November 1863, a year after Shire sailed.

Shire himself is utterly fictional. During WWII my father worked as a boy on the Duke of Bedford's estate at Woburn, helping to tend the great horses that they kept working right up until then. Shire's birth, if ever he had one, was in my father's notes from that time. The names of the horses, Shire's friends, were the horses my father tended.

Acknowledgements

There were so many books read and consulted in support of *Whirligig* that it would take several pages to list them. Amongst those that I could not have done without was the wonderfully written *This Terrible Sound* by Peter Cozens, which guided me through the complex battle of Chickamauga. Also indispensable was his history of the battles for Chattanooga, *The Shipwreck of Their Hopes,* and Wiley Sword's *Mountains Touched with Fire.* These two were my companions when Shire was under siege in Chattanooga and fighting his way up Missionary Ridge.

I am in debt to all the soldiers of the 125th Ohio who wrote letters during the war and to those survivors who wrote their recollections. In particular the letters of Emerson Opdycke collected together by Glenn V. Longacre and John E. Haas in *The Battle for God and the Right.* Also the war time memoirs of Company B's Ralsa C. Rice in *Yankee Tigers* and the collected letters in *Opdycke's Tigers* by Charles T. Clark. *George A. Trenholm – Financial Genius of the Confederacy* by Ethel T. S. Nepveux was a wonderful (if quite expensive) find.

I'd also like to thank the Civil War Trust for their incredibly useful and detailed battle maps and for all they do in helping to preserve civil war sites. Thanks go as well to the national park rangers at Fort Donelson, Stones River and Chickamauga who were endlessly patient with my more obscure questions. I'd like especially to thank Ken Rush, Director of the Ducktown Basin Museum, whose kind help unwittingly attached me to the bottom right hand corner of Tennessee.

Nearer to home I wish to thank I wish to thank everyone who has helped or encouraged me: friends, writing colleagues, favorite aunts, my editor Karl French. Also my M.A. colleagues

Glen Brown, Tracy Fells and Jacqui Pack for their collective help in reading drafts of the book, Bea Mitchell Turner and Zoe Mitchel for their ongoing support, and my tutor at Chichester University, Stephanie Norgate, who made writing at once richer and simpler for me. Even closer to home I'd like to thank Anita Hobbs for her help with proofing, Juliet Croydon for the Whirligig illustration, and my neighbor Julia Brown for producing the battle maps.

And finally, *at home*, my biggest thanks and love to my wife Sally, for encouraging me to begin, giving me the time and the space, and lending me her confidence when mine was lacking.

Made in the USA
San Bernardino, CA
19 July 2017